MEN OF THE NORTH #7
THE DANCER

Copyright © 2018
By Elin Peer
All rights reserved.
No part of this book may be reproduced in any form without written permission from the author, excepting brief quotations embodied in articles and reviews.
ISBN: 9781719985574
The Dancer – Men of the North #7
First Edition
The characters and events portrayed in this book are fictitious. Any similarity to real persons or organizations is coincidental and not intended by the author. Recommended for mature readers due to adult content.
Cover Art by Kellie Dennis:
bookcoverbydesign.co.uk
Editing: martinohearn.com

Books in this series

For the best reading experience and to avoid spoilers, this is the recommended order to read the books in.

Forbidden Letters – Men of the North # 0.5
The Protector – Men of the North #1
The Ruler – Men of the North #2
The Mentor – Men of the North #3
The Seducer – Men of the North #4
The Warrior – Men of the North #5
The Genius – Men of the North #6
The Dancer – Men of the North #7
The Athlete – Men of the North # 8
The Fighter – Men of the North # 9
The Pacifist – Men of the North #10

To be alerted for new book releases, sign up to my list and receive a free e-book as a welcome gift.
elinpeer.com

PLEASE NOTE

This book is intended for mature readers only, as it contains a few graphic scenes and some inappropriate language.

All characters are fictional and any likeness to a living person or organization is coincidental.

DEDICATION

To Angie

My badass truth teller friend.
Thank you for always having a cold drink and a warm smile when I stop by your house.

Elin

CHAPTER 1
Zero Tolerance

Solomon

You can't kill a person without giving up a part of your humanity.

As a soldier I've executed seven men and I remember each of their names, faces, and final moments. Not because I want to. It's just a fact that taking another man's life somehow leaves a mark on you. Like their last breath creeps inside of you and stays there as a burden to bear.

"You wanna do this one?" Zasquash asked me while chewing on the last part of his apple. "I did the last two."

"Maybe Khan will pardon him," I muttered in a low voice while leaning against the wall.

Zasquash raised an eyebrow and gave me a "yeah, right" look. We returned to watch our ruler, Khan Aurelius, and his brother Magni interrogate Ray, who had made the mistake of his life yesterday when he killed his wife.

"I already told your men this many times. I never intended to hurt her, it was an accident." Ray's voice, which had been pleading when Zasquash and I tracked him down in the woodlands five hours ago, had now turned hoarse from arguing his case.

Sitting astride a turned-around chair in front of Ray, Khan leaned his chest against the backrest with his arms resting on top of it. I wondered if he unconsciously wanted the back of the chair as a shield between himself and the Nman who had committed the most gruesome crime in our country. Khan's eyes were fixed on Ray with a hard glare. "You want us to believe it was an accident that your wife fell down the stairs?"

"Yeeessss," he pleaded, his movements stressed as he turned from side to side.

Magni had been pacing the room but turned and hissed, "We should fucking kill you on the spot for insulting our intelligence. Women don't get handprints around their necks from falling down a staircase."

"I... I... I tried to wake her up. I might have grabbed her a bit harder than I intended."

Unlike Magni, Khan kept his voice calm but stern. "You thought strangling Josephine would wake her up?" Khan's face scrunched up in revulsion. "If that were true, then why did you run?"

Ray was sweating; he pulled at his shirt, which was damp and clung to his body. His eyes were darting around. "It looked bad and I panicked."

Magni towered over Ray, who shrunk in his seat. "Bullshit, you ran because you're a pathetic coward."

For five hours Ray had insisted on his innocence. Now with Magni screaming at him, he leaned forward covering his head with his arms, hiding from the inevitable.

Magni kicked at his chair and roared in fury. "Be a man and take some fucking responsibility."

Zasquash and I exchanged a glance when Ray's shoulders bobbed up and down with the muffled sounds of his sobbing.

"Look at me, Ray," Khan ordered and when Ray lifted his head, his voice trembled with defeat.

"I'm going to die, ain't I?"

It had been a call from neighbors that alerted the police and when they arrived to find Josephine in a pool of blood on the floor, Ray had already made a run for it.

After Zasquash and I were called in as members of the Domestic Violence Unit, it had taken us four hours to track him down. Under normal circumstances we would have dealt with Ray without involving others, but this wasn't a normal domestic violence case. Ray had been married to Josephine, a Motlander bride who had picked him in the Matching Program only seven months ago. She was not the first Motlander to experience domestic violence, but she was the first to lose her life. Informing our Commander, Magni Aurelius, had been a no-brainer. He had arrived within the hour and the fact that he'd brought his brother and our ruler, Lord Khan, was a testament to how severe this situation was.

The Council of the Motherlands would be horrified to hear that one of their own had died a violent death. It was to be expected that they would shut down the Matching Program that had served as one of the biggest integration projects between our countries.

Khan leaned back on the chair and stretched his legs in front of him. "You knew when you married Josephine that we have a zero tolerance of violence against women."

Ray had his head down again. "But I loved her."

Khan's voice was patient. "No one said that you didn't, but something went wro…"

Magni interrupted Khan, fisting a hand into Ray's hair and pushing down on his neck while hissing at him. "You're fucking wasting our time. Just man up and tell us the truth. What were you two fighting about? We keep asking you the same questions and you give us vague answers. What led to the argument and how did she die?" With a growl he let go of Ray, whose hair was ruffled where Magni's large hand had been.

Ray turned his head away and kept crying.

"Magni is right, you can die a liar or spit out what really happened," Khan added in a matter-of-fact tone.

"I'm telling you the truth. I loved her." His voice broke. "I would die for Josephine. She means *everything* to me."

"She's dead, Ray, and you're going to tell us how she died."

Ray used the back of his hand to dry his right eye. "She fell down the staircase." He pointed up and moved in his chair, which stood right next to the place where Josephine's body had been when we arrived.

Magni looked tempted to kill Ray on the spot. "You pushed her, didn't you?"

Khan's hand silenced Magni. "Our men spoke to your neighbors and we've been told that it wasn't the first time you and Josephine were heard fighting. You have a fiery temper, don't you, Ray?"

His shoulders were still bobbing up and down when he lifted his arm and used his sleeve to dry away his snot and tears. "I swear I didn't mean to kill her."

"But you did!" Magni pressured and with contempt oozing from him, he pulled Ray's hands down.

"No." Ray squirmed in his chair and moved back to create distance between him and Magni. "Josephine was going back to the Motherlands."

"On vacation?" Khan asked.

"That's what she said." Ray's voice cracked again. "But she packed all her clothes and that's when I knew she wasn't planning on coming back."

"And you snapped," Magni shouted. "Didn't you?"

Ray used his shirt to dry his nose and eyes. "You don't understand. She was going to leave me."

Rising up to his full height, Magni scoffed. "Oh, I understand alright. The whole fucking country was laughing at me when my wife left for the Motherlands. It tore me apart, but I didn't fucking kill Laura for it." Magni took a step back, shaking his head at the broken-down Nman in front of him.

"I'm sorry. I'm so sorry," Ray kept repeating. "I loved her so much. I never meant to kill Josephine."

A sound of metal legs scraping over the floor came from Khan's chair when he stood up. "We're done here."

Pushing out from the wall, I squared my shoulders and waited for orders.

Khan and Magni were both still facing Ray. With his head held high and his legs spread in a strong stance, Khan spoke in deep rumble. "You are a disgrace to our nation and your violent actions will cost all of us. Rumors have flourished in the Motherlands for hundreds of years that we Nmen are violent monsters who murder our wives. By killing Josephine you proved them right. What you did was abhorrent and cannot be excused, tolerated, or forgiven. All the Motlanders who oppose the integration between our nations will demand that the Matchmaking Program be shut down."

Ray's shoulders hung low and his face was stricken with grief. "I'm so sorry. I'm so sorry."

Khan turned his back on Ray, walking toward me and Zasquash. "Make sure everything is filmed and done according to protocol."

"Yes, Lord."

"Any questions?"

"An eye for an eye?" Zasquash asked.

Lord Khan crossed his arms and took a second to look up the stairs from where Josephine had landed before he spoke. "There's no need. An eye for an eye only serves as rehabilitation to teach a valuable lesson. Ray won't get a second chance, and we need to send a strong signal to the world that we stand firm on our zero-tolerance policy."

"Understood."

"Let Ray pick his preferred way of dying and get it over with."

Zasquash and I nodded and moved forward, pulling Ray up from the chair. Even with his sunken shoulders and head hanging low, Ray was no small man, and there was a sadness in me for having to take the life of someone as young, strong, and vibrant as him.

Magni and Khan looked on as Zasquash and I led Ray outside where a few police officers were still waiting.

"Leo," Magni shouted behind me and waved the police inspector over. "Did you talk to all the witnesses?"

"Yes, Commander, all neighbors were interviewed and they tell the same story." Leo stopped in front of Magni. His long dark hair was in a messy bun on top of his head and his dark beard trimmed in the new fashion with a square look and a single bead braided into it. I'd worked with Leo many times and we'd shared beers in pubs over the years. He was someone I respected and considered a close friend.

"Good." Magni patted Leo's shoulder and turned to give me a nod. It was my cue to do my job.

"Ray Dermuth, you have broken the most sacred of our laws and admitted your guilt. Today, August 11th, 2447, will be your final day. Do you have any last words?"

Ray raised his head up and looked at me with eyes red from crying. "Can I make a last request?"

"What is it?"

"Josephine had family and I know they will have questions. Can I write them a letter explaining how much I loved her?" He gave a deep sigh. "I don't want them to think I was a monster."

"No." Magni stepped closer. "There will be no letter. You can record a message for them. Whether her family chooses to watch it is up to them."

Ray dipped his head with a low "Thank you."

Using my wristband, I recorded Ray's message as he spoke in a hoarse shaky voice.

"The day Josephine picked me was the happiest day in my life. I loved her from the moment we met, and we had so much fun together." Ray wet his dry lips, his hand scratching his neck. "Sometimes we got into arguments and yesterday morning things got out of hand. I would never hurt Josephine. I mean I never planned to hurt her.

It just happened when I found out she was leaving me. I guess, I panicked and..." Ray used the heel of his hand to dry away more tears and shook his head like he couldn't believe it had really happened. "I'm so sorry." He sniffled. "I held on to her when she wanted to leave. Josephine, she..." Ray swallowed hard and his voice broke again. "She insulted me, calling me names, and when she pushed to get away from me, I finally let go. We were close to the stairs and she lost her balance, falling down and landing at an odd angle."

A memory from my past was pressing as I remembered how close I'd come to Ray's destiny seven years ago. Willow hadn't died from her fall, but her broken arm and bruises could have cost me my life.

"I'm hoping this video message can clarify what happened between me and Josephine and show that I didn't kill her in cold blood. I loved her more than anything and I'm deeply sorry."

I ended the video and Zasquash placed his hand on Ray's shoulder. "Any wishes as to where you want us to bury you?"

He let the heels of his hands run over his eyebrows down to his mouth where he exhaled deeply. "Could you spread my ashes in the forest? I've always loved the woods behind my house."

I exchanged a glance with Khan, who gave a small nod.
"We can do that."

"What about Josephine?" Ray asked. "What will happen to her?"

"She's going back to her family in the Motherlands," Magni answered.

I had once been in the Motherlands and seen a graveyard so I added. "They use bio-urns and she'll grow into a tree of her family's choice."

"They do?" Ray's head lifted. "Can it be a magnolia tree? Those were her favorites."

"Her family will decide what happens to Josephine." I frowned. "The only thing you get to pick is how you want to die. The easiest way to go is a bullet, but if you prefer we can break your neck or slit your throat."

"Can I do it myself?" Ray's eyes fell to the gun on my hip.

"No." Magni stepped closer. "You could easily turn the gun on one of us."

"Can I at least look out over the mountains?" Ray lifted his chin to the beautiful view with millions of fir trees in the distance and the lake that was so still that it reflected the clouds in the sky.

Without a word, I walked Ray in the direction he had pointed and let him stand with his back to us. The sky was beautiful with the evening red from the sunset.

"I love this view," Ray mumbled. "I wish it was a clear day and there were no clouds."

Raising my gun, I pointed it at the back of his head, not saying a word as he continued.

"Fluffy, white clouds were always my favorites. As a kid I used to lie on my back and watch them drift by. My friends and I would disagree on what shape they had. I would see a dragon and they would see something different." His voice was trembling with emotions.

I let Ray talk and disappear into a different time.

"Josephine loved the thunderclouds. It excited her when there was lightning and thunder in the air. One time she curled up to me and we sat out here watching the show from afar counting between the thunder and the lightn..."

Bang.

Ray never ended his sentence. His body fell heavily to the ground, his life gone and his last moment branded in my memory like another scar on my troubled soul. Another weight on my subconscious.

Men of the North #7 – THE DANCER

As if he wanted us to never forget him, thunder rolled in less than three hours after he was dead.

Magni, Khan, Zasquash, and I were in a small pub in the local village where the bar-bots had seen better days and the five local patrons kept looking over and whispering about the unexpected presence of their ruler and his brother.

Khan had declared that he and Magni would just have a single beer before they went back home, but by now we were on the fourth pint; he seemed to prefer the wooden bench in this small pub to the golden palace he called home.

"Did you tell Pearl?" I asked.

"Yes. She has informed the Council in the Motherlands." His eyes were fixed on his index finger that tapped the side of his glass. "They want a meeting."

"Do you think they're going to shut down the Matchmaking Program?"

"They might," Khan muttered with his face stern. "Unless we can talk them out of it somehow."

"I told Boulder and Finn about Josephine's death. They're at the school reunion and wondered what was taking us so long." Magni pushed his empty glass away and called for the bar-bot. "Another round over here."

Zasquash had never met Finn and Boulder, who were Khan's and Magni's best friends, but I knew I had told him about them.

"You're right, Magni, we should get going." Khan's head turned to me. "What about you?"

A fist-sized knot formed in my stomach. "Me?"

"Yes. Everyone is already at the reunion. We're the only ones missing."

Magni groaned. "Why the fuck would you ask him that? Solo can't go and you know it. Besides, it's past midnight; they'll all be sleeping now."

The thought of Willow sleeping made me look down. I missed her so fucking much. What I wouldn't give to see her one more time.

Khan leaned back and crossed his arms. "I say it's time we lifted Solo's restraining order. He's not going to hurt Willow."

Magni stiffened. "But..."

Khan's raised hand silenced Magni. "What happened was unfortunate but I think we can trust Solo now. He should go to the reunion."

"But he's not invited," Magni objected.

"Not true." I spoke up with hope in my chest. "Mila invited me. I told her I had too much work."

"Yeah, well, Mila and the others don't know about your restraining order."

Khan leaned his head back and looked up at the ceiling. "It's been long enough." He refocused on his brother. "Magni, we've all made mistakes and Solo paid for his. It's been seven years and he's a grown man now. I say he can go."

Magni's deep inhalation made his chest rise up. "And what do you think Hunter is going to say about that?"

Khan's only reply was a shrug.

"You sure you want to face him again?" Magni challenged me.

Pushing out my chest a little, I snorted. "Don't insult me. I'm not scared of Hunter."

"Why would you be afraid of seeing this Hunter?" Zasquash asked with his eyebrows drawn close.

"I'm not," I insisted. "He might be a great soccer player, but I've always been the better fighter."

"Hang on," Zasquash slammed his glass down on the table. "You're not talking about Hunter Hercules, are you?"

"Yes. The soccer player." Khan leaned to the side when the bar-bot reached in with four new beers.

Men of the North #7 – THE DANCER

"I fucking love Hunter. That man is brilliant with a ball." My friend lit up like a little kid. "I'm his biggest fan."

"Maybe in height," I muttered, since Zasquash was seven feet tall like me.

"Hunter is Willow's twin and he's very protective of her." Magni squinted his eyes as if the beer was blurring his sight.

My jaw hardened. "It's been seven years."

"So? You think a man ever forgives you for stealing his sister away?"

"I didn't steal her."

"If you go to the reunion there will be drama. It's guaranteed." Magni dried his mouth with the back of his hand. "I hate drama."

"This isn't about you, Magni." Khan leaned toward his brother. "Solo wants to see Willow again, but at the same time he's scared that she won't talk to him."

Magni scoffed. "Since when did you become a fucking expert on his feelings? All he should worry about is not getting killed by Hunter."

"What the hell, Solo." Zasquash gave me a blameful look. "Why did you have to get on Hunter's bad side? He seems like the nicest guy in every interview I've ever seen."

My body tensed and I pulled back in my seat. "I don't want to talk about it."

Zasquash turned to look at Magni and Khan. "I know about the restraining order. I've been given instructions to report it if Solo ever goes missing, but all Solo tells me is that it was a misunderstanding. Would one of you tell me what the fuck really happened?"

Magni wiped his beard of beer foam and leaned his elbow on the table. "Did Solo ever tell you how he got to be part of my Huntsmen unit?"

"Sure. He was the best, brightest, and strongest of his generation. He tells me every fucking day." Zasquash grinned in his usual casual manner, his dark eyes full of mischief.

"There's some truth to that, but it was how he used his skills that made the difference. You two are partners and it's only fair that you know."

Zasquash agreed with Magni while I sank back in my seat with a displeased grunt. If it hadn't been Magni and Khan in front of me, I would have asked them to shut their mouths. My past was *my* past and even though Zasquash was my best friend, I hadn't told him everything.

"When Solo was fourteen years old, he was handpicked to be one of the ten Nboys to take part in the first experimental school where we mixed children from the Motherlands and the Northlands. At the school, there was a girl called Willow whom Solo fell in love with," Khan began, and just the mention of her name gave me heart palpitations. Looking down in my beer, I said nothing as I listened to Khan and Magni tell my story while my mind took me back ten years.

CHAPTER 2
Meeting Willow

Year 2437 – Ten years earlier

Solomon

We had walked through the forest to meet the Motlanders. All ten of us boys were tense with excitement and still in a bit of a shock after being told that we would get to meet real females in person. Nathan was the only one of us who had a mother and sisters. For me and the other eight boys this would be our first meeting with the mysterious "other" gender that we had only seen in movies.

As the oldest, I led the way forward and stopped when four kids suddenly showed up between the trees.

"I found them," a girl shouted and stared at us with curiosity.

I stared back, taking in her short height, brown skin, and puffy hair with tiny black curls before letting my eyes move to the three other children beside her. One was a boy but he looked young and wouldn't challenge my position as the alpha among the boys. Of the other two females, the one to the right stood out to me right away. The girl was the tallest of the four. With her long legs and curvy figure, I guessed her to be my age or older. It was like a chemical explosion in my brain and my spine straightened. Why did this girl give me the same tingling sensation in my stomach as when I dove from cliffs with my friends? My palms were tingling and my heart was pumping fast as we stared at each other.

She was beautiful with the way the soft light from the sunbeams shining through the tree crowns reflected on her gorgeous brown hair, which fell down to her navel and looked thick and impossibly straight. Like all boys in the Northlands, I had long hair too but mine was often tangled, and it wasn't uncommon to find pine needles in it from fight training, where we rolled around on the ground. Hers looked soft and perfect.

More women and girls were showing up behind the four children but I only scanned them before my eyes went back to the stunning girl. She was looking at the other boys behind me, but when her eyes found mine again, I forgot to breathe. Even while we all played some initial games to get to know each other, I couldn't stop looking at her every five seconds. Often, she looked back at me; sometimes with a small smile.

Willow. Her name was Willow. I heard one of the other kids say it and tasted it on my tongue, wishing I could say it aloud.

Kya, the female mentor, instructed us, "We're going to learn each other's names while we walk back to the school. You only have one minute with the person next to you before we switch. There will be a quiz when we get back to the school and whoever can remember the most names wins, so pay attention."

I pushed Storm back when he tried to get in front of me to pair up with Willow. He shoved back at me with a side glance at the pretty girl, but there was no way I'd let him win the right to be the first to walk next to her.

"I'm Willow." Her smile was blinding as we began walking side by side in front of the long line of children.

"I'm Solo. I'm fourteen. The oldest of the boys. Strongest too."

"I'm twelve but I'll be thirteen in a few days."

That surprised me. I had guessed her to be older. "When?"

She blushed a little. "In October."

We were in August so it was more than a few days away, but I understood her need to grow older fast. I couldn't wait to be an adult either. No more mentors telling me what to do or punishing me for having an opinion.

"Have you ever met a girl before?" I loved the sound of her pleasant soft voice.

"No. Only you."

She laughed. "We are eight girls. Nine if you count Shelly, but she's fifteen and an assistant teacher."

I had seen Shelly and although she was closer to me in age, she was in no way as intriguing as Willow.

"They say Shelly is a genius."

I gave Willow a smile but her words didn't really register. It was like I couldn't think straight around her.

"Switch," Kya called out and I had to walk to the back of the line while Hunter moved up to talk to Willow.

"Hi, I'm Sky." The girl was pretty too, but my eyes wouldn't stop searching to see if Willow was smiling or laughing with first Hunter, then Storm, Plato, and every other of the Nboys that she was introduced to.

Before the day was over, I had appointed myself the protector of Willow. That's why when Nero made a comment about her that night in the boys' room, I made an example of him. Using my size and strength, I pressed his face down on his pillow long enough that he couldn't breathe and got scared. "Don't ever make comments about Willow's looks again." I sneered and went back to my own bed.

A few other boys were slow to get the message. Two weeks into the school year, I caught Storm using his hands behind Willow's back to imitate her curvy shape while grinning. It didn't surprise me that he showed an interest in Willow. He was almost fourteen like me and she had that effect on pretty much all us boys.

Storm wasn't grinning when I pulled him behind the school and pressed him against the wall while twisting his arm back. "Don't make gestures like that behind Willow's back, or I'll fucking break your hands, do you understand?"

Finally, he and the others understood that when it came to Willow, I wasn't amused.

She made me feel out of control and emotionally unstable. A smile from her could make my day and release a swarm of butterflies. But seeing her partner up with someone else for morning massage gave me a headache and a burning sensation in my throat.

I couldn't touch her and I never knew what to say to her. From the first time I saw her, Willow had been the first thing I thought about in the morning and the last before I fell asleep. It was like a sickness with no cure.

And then one Wednesday morning it was my turn to partner up with Willow for morning massage.

"Feet, hands, shoulder, neck, or scalp?" she asked me with a shy smile.

"Shoulders." I had known since the first time Raven gave me a massage that I wanted nothing more than for Willow to do it. Raven had asked me to lie down flat on my stomach and then she had simply planted herself on the small of my back and begun massaging my neck and shoulders.

I figured that it might be the only way I'd ever have Willow sit astride me and even though there was nothing sexual in our morning massages, I fantasized about feeling the weight of her body on top of mine.

"Do you want me to take off my shirt?" I asked her.

"If you want to."

I stripped out of the shirt. Feeling proud of my already muscular body, I lay down on my belly looking around at all the other students who were being massaged while listening to calming music.

Willow kneeled down close to my head. "Solo, can you turn on your back?"

It was a different way of doing massage and I knew she wanted me to place my head in her lap. When I turned and positioned myself against her, she began applying soft strokes down over my shoulders and neck. I was a teenager full of raging hormones, and her hands on my naked skin had an immediate unwanted effect that quickly resulted in a visible problem when I felt a tent rise in my pants.

I sat up to hide my predicament. "Ehm, Willow, would you mind doing it the other way?"

"You wanna be on your stomach?"

"Yeah, if you don't mind." I was already turning around and although it was uncomfortable, at least I was hiding the boner in my pants.

I didn't breathe when Willow crawled onto my back, her legs on either side of my body, her hands rubbing my shoulders with more force than before.

"Does it hurt?"

"What, the massage?"

"This one." She pressed her finger down on a spot.

My ears reddened.

"It's white. Can I pop it?"

I was mortified that Willow, whom I wanted to impress, was staring at a white pimple on my back that I hadn't known about. Of all the days, why did I have to have one today?

"Solo, can I? It's fun to pop them."

"No." I reached for my t-shirt and pulled it over my head with Willow still on my back.

"What's wrong? All teenagers have some. Everyone knows that. I'll have them too soon."

"What are you doing?" Kya approached when I rolled on my side, making Willow fall down.

Embarrassed I got up and didn't look back when I walked out the room. "I have to take a piss."

It took me five long minutes to swallow my pride and go back. By then the kids had swapped and it was now my time to massage Willow.

"What do you want?" My voice sounded much too serious.

Willow wasn't smiling either. Her eyes were fixed on the mat on the floor and, chewing on her lower lip, she gave a low answer, "I don't know. You choose."

A tingling in my hands began as I kneeled down and signaled for her to get down too. "I'll massage your scalp then." It was supposed to sound like it wasn't a big deal, but my tone revealed the eagerness that I felt when she lay down and brushed her long brown hair behind her. At least she couldn't see how my hands trembled when I touched her hair for the first time. It was as soft as I had imagined and when she closed her eyes, I bent down to soak up the fragrance of her long strands.

Women and girls were still a mystery to me, and to sit here and touch Willow's hair was among the top three things that had ever happened to me. Only the time I hunted down and killed a wild boar came close to giving me the rush I felt at that moment. My fingers played with her silky hair before massaging her scalp.

Her hands were folded on her belly, a small smile on her face.

"Ten minutes left," Kya said and I looked up at the clock with confusion. Had it really been twenty minutes since we began the morning massage? How could I have wasted so much time pouting in the bathroom when there was so much I wanted to experience with Willow?

Her hands. I had to hold her hands.

"Do you mind if I massage your hands?"

Willow opened her eyes and gave me a small smile. "That would be nice."

Men of the North #7 – THE DANCER

Moving to sit beside her I reached for her right hand and swallowed a gasp when she didn't lift it from her belly but let me touch her blouse. We weren't allowed to touch a girl's belly. Not even during massage. It was always limited to hands, shoulders, neck, scalp, and feet. My fingers had briefly touched a forbidden part of her and it made me almost dizzy.

Willow turned her head a little and watched me as I massaged her hand. In the beginning I was too shy to look at her face, but when I interlaced our fingers and she squeezed my hand, I stopped breathing for a second and locked eyes with her. I had massaged other kids, but the others had been passive and never squeezed my hand back.

Time stood still when I looked into Willow's green eyes. They had the same bright color as the moss that covered the trees around our school this time of year. Like those trees, I felt covered in a blanket of beauty and softness. And when a smile grew on her face, my heart grew with it.

"What's so funny? Solo, why do you have that goofy smile on your face?"

"Nero, mind your own business," Kya reprimanded. "No talking while massaging. We still have six minutes left."

For those six minutes, I massaged Willow's hands and exchanged long smiles with her. She was gorgeous, and I studied everything about her from the symmetrical arch of her brows, her long black lashes, the silver and brown specks in her eyes, to the freckles across the bridge of her nose.

"Thank you," she said in a soft voice when our minutes were up.

I inclined my head, unable to speak with my throat bursting to scream out with joy. I had held the hand of the most beautiful female in the world and she had smiled at me. Not just a small polite smile like I'd seen others do. Willow's smile had been genuine and lit up both of her eyes, making small crinkles appear around the edges.

We moved on to reading time and for the first time ever, Willow chose to sit next to me on the floor, leaning against the wall with her feet stretched out in front of her.

I kept my head in my book but didn't read a thing. My full attention was on how close Willow was. Shifting the book to my other hand, I put my hand down next to my body, desperate to feel closer to her. I held my breath for seconds, hoping she wouldn't move away.

After a few minutes, she put her hand down next to mine. We weren't touching but every single nerve ending in my body was on full alert.

With hope in my pounding chest and the slowest of movements as to not scare her away, I moved my pinky finger closer to hers. When our fingers brushed against each other I looked down to make sure it was really happening.

She didn't move. Instead she kept reading with a tiny smile on her face.

For as long as I could remember, I'd been told females were off limits. Magni, the biggest and most lethal warrior in our country, had promised us Nboys a violent death if we touched the girls. But a force stronger than anything I'd ever felt made me move my pinky finger closer. Inch by nerve-wracking inch, my pinky hung in the air until I placed it on top of hers.

When she still didn't move it away, a surge of excitement filled me from head to toe, and, holding my breath I risked it all by linking our pinky fingers together and smiling at her.

Willow smiled back and that's when everything in the world fell into place.

"I like you," I whispered low.

Men of the North #7 – THE DANCER

She looked around making sure no one was watching and then she mouthed in silence, "I like you too."

It was like a secret bubble belonging only to her and me. Empowered by her words, I took her entire hand in mine for a few happy seconds, envisioning a future with me and Willow being mated for life.

CHAPTER 3
Morning Swim
Year 2447

Willow

"Careful of the swans," I shouted out in warning as Raven ran toward the lake and jumped in with a big scream and an even bigger splash.

When her head resurfaced, I was picking up her sandals and the towel that she'd left scattered on the brink of the water. She laughed. "Are you coming in or not?"

It was early and the sun was still low in the sky, hiding behind the trees in the forest.

"I'm cold."

"Then come swim. It'll warm you up." Raven took a few strokes to underscore her words.

Stepping out of my sandals, I touched the water with my right foot and quickly pulled it back. "Mother of all Gods, it's freezing."

Raven swam closer and stood up, the water reaching the top of her bathing suit. "Aren't you dancers supposed to be tough?"

I narrowed my eyes at her. "Being a great dancer and liking cold water are two different things."

"Yeah, but don't you have to push yourself to do things your body doesn't want to do? Like when you're tired or your body hurts but you keep dancing. You've done that, right?"

"Of course."

"Then you can do this. Just set your mind to it. Ignore the discomfort and get in here already."

Taking a deep breath, I ignored the pain from the cold water and walked out to the sound of Raven cheering me on.

"Cold, cold, cold." I began swimming with fast movements. Raven was right there next to me and shooed the swans when they came closer.

"Why did I say yes to a morning swim?" My legs were kicking to get me warm. "I never liked it as a child either."

"Morning swims are the best."

"Solo used to convince me to swim here, but at least he..." I didn't finish the sentence because there was a sharp pain to my heart as if an invisible hand was squeezing it.

"He what?"

I turned and moved back toward the edge of the lake.

"Willow, where are you going?"

My voice was weak. "I think the cold is giving me a heart attack."

"A what?" Raven laughed. "Don't be silly. It's not *that* cold."

"I just felt a pinch in my chest."

"It's nothing. I promise. What were you saying about Solo?"

"Oh." I stayed close to the edge and used my hands and feet to tread water. "Nothing. It was just that he used to help me not freeze."

"Really? And how did he do that?" Raven rolled onto her back and did a few lazy backstrokes in the water.

"I'm not sure. I guess being close to him was enough to keep me warm. Anyway, I don't want to talk about him."

"Right." Raven moved into an upright position too and looked at me with her hands doing the same downward circular motions as mine. "Or maybe you do want to talk about him."

"I hate him!"

"You hate him?"

"Yes."

"Hate is a strong word, Willow. You're a Motlander. You should know not to carry such heavy emotions in your heart. It's not good for you."

"He hurt me, Raven. I could have died." Raven was one of the few who knew what had happened before I left the school, since we'd talked about it.

Raven's expression turned serious. "How come you never ask me questions about him? Aren't you curious to know what Solo is doing today?"

"No," I lied.

"What if I told you that he still hurts people?"

I narrowed my eyes, trying to get a better read on her. Was she serious?

"My dad told me."

"Boulder told you about Solo?"

"Yes." It was like an invitation floating on the water between us. An invisible envelope with information that I could pick up and study if I chose to do so.

Weakened by the cold water, I took the bait. "What did your father tell you?"

"Some of the Huntsmen who helped track you two down when you ran off were impressed with Solo's abilities. Think about it; he managed to stay out of their reach for eight days leaving false tracks and covering the real ones. It shouldn't be possible to fool a whole unit of elite soldiers like he did. It proved how intelligent and skilled he is.

I snorted. "Yeah, well, I'm not a fan."

Raven ignored my comment and kept talking. "Obviously, they wanted to kill him for what he'd done to you, but you took that option away from them when you threatened to kill yourself if they did." Raven made a splash in the water.

"They discussed what to do with him and Pearl suggested that they put his skills to good use while keeping a close eye on him. You know, to make sure he wouldn't go after you again." Raven moved closer to me in the water. "It shouldn't surprise you that Solo became a soldier and a Huntsman."

I swam forward a little and spoke in a flat tone. "No, it doesn't surprise me. That's what he always wanted."

"Three years ago, a special unit was formed with the largest of the Huntsmen. Solomon qualified."

I scrunched up my face. "What, because of his height?"

"My dad says that he's taller than Magni."

I looked away – too curious to ask her to stop talking about Solo, but at the same time not liking the subject one bit.

"Willow, he's on the unit that deals with domestic violence. They are known to hurt and kill people. That's why some call them the Doom Squad."

I paled. "Solo wouldn't kill anyone."

"It's his job." Raven swam to get up to me. "You know how uncompromising Nmen are when it comes to women."

"Yes."

"The Doom Squad takes care of any man who can't keep his hands to himself. They deal with situations where a female has felt violated."

I didn't know what to say.

"Isn't it ironic, Willow?"

"What is?"

"That a man who came close to being killed for improper contact with you, twice, ends up as a soldier on the Doom Squad?"

I kept swimming. "It doesn't change how I feel about him. I still hate him."

"I didn't think it would change how you felt about him. I just thought that maybe you'd like to know what he's doing."

What I mostly wanted to know were personal things like whether or not he'd moved on and forgotten about me, but since Solo hadn't come to our reunion, I had no way of asking him.

"I'm just glad he didn't come this weekend." I turned my face away. "If he had shown up, I would have been forced to tell him how much I hate him."

"Yeah, it's probably for the best that he stayed away," Raven agreed.

We swam a little more, my head full of painful memories until Raven initiated a welcome change of topic.

"I still can't believe Shelly and Marco got married last night!"

It was a safe topic that would take my mind off my own tragic love story, so I jumped at it. "Shelly looked so beautiful."

"Yeah, but for someone as smart as her, I don't get why she would marry." Raven pushed her curly dark hair back and splashed a floating leaf away. "I mean Marco is definitely a nice man compared to most of the Nmen, but it's disturbing how marriage is coming back into fashion."

"I plan to marry."

Raven gaped at me. "You're joking?"

"No, I'm not."

"Why would you want to marry?"

I looked over at the two swans who were patrolling the other part of the small lake. "There's something beautiful about being a couple. Like those two." I turned my head and looked at her. "You know they poop in this water, right?"

"Who does?"

"The swans."

"Don't change the subject. Who are you marrying?"

"I'll know when I meet him."

"Oh, so hang on, I thought you were still on about the marriage pact you made with Solo."

I raised both eyebrows and made a sound of disgust. "I can tell you with one thousand percent certainty that I'd rather eat all the poop in this pond than marry *him*. What part of my hating him didn't you get?"

"No, I got it, that's what had me confused."

"Willow…" The sound of my brother shouting for me had us both looking up.

"Hey, Hunter." Raven grinned up at him and shouted back. "Are you going to swim with us?"

"No." When he got close to the water, he stopped with his face twisted in a murderous expression.

"What's wrong?" Both Raven and I swam over to him. "What happened?"

"It's time to go!"

"Now?"

"Yes."

Raven looked from Hunter to me and back. "Why?"

He lowered his brow and spoke the three words as a low warning. "Solo is here."

My heart was already racing from Hunter's strange behavior, but his words made me feel nauseated. The water that had been so cold before now felt too hot. "Solo is here at the school?"

Hunter held up my towel as I got out of the water. "Yes, I just saw him. He wants to talk to you, but I told him to fuck off."

Wrapping my towel around my bikini-clad body, I picked up my shoes and began walking.

"Hey, wait up," Raven shouted and flung her towel over her shoulder. "Are you going to leave right away?"

I looked straight ahead, a bubble forming around me full of all the things that I had wanted to tell Solomon for the past seven years. This was my chance.

Raven ran up behind me, but I kept walking fast. "Honestly, Willow, if anyone should have to leave, it should be Solo. You were here first."

Hunter groaned beside me. "Willow, you're not talking with him. Just go get your things and we'll get out of here."

"No, Hunter. I'm not running away from him. If Solo wants to talk, we'll talk. I have *plenty* that I want to say to him." Every syllable came out through gritted teeth.

Hunter and Raven walked beside me in silence as I marched through the forest in long strides.

"Where is he?" I asked when I didn't see Solo outside the school.

"He must have gone inside. I think Archer offered him breakfast."

I'd known coming to this reunion involved a risk of meeting Solomon again. To be honest, I'd hoped he would show up and I'd fantasized about the ultimate revenge. I wanted him to suffer when he saw how healthy and happy I looked. He was supposed to see my beautiful brown hair that he'd loved so much and feel the need to touch it. I wanted him to see what he could never have.

It was so typical of Solo to show up when I was wearing a stupid old and ugly mint-green towel instead of one of the cute outfits I'd picked out to look stunning.

To hell with it. I was mad at him for everything he'd done to me when I was fifteen and for screwing up my sweet revenge fantasy. I was supposed to see him with my hair soft and curly like he loved it, but I wasn't going to hide from him even though I looked a mess and probably had algae stuck in my hair. For a second, I considered getting rid of the towel and waltzing in to confront Solo in my red bikini. That would take him by surprise for sure and show him exactly what he was missing out on, but Hunter wouldn't understand, and chances were that he would try to cover me up while I was spewing my anger at Solo, which would take things to a whole other level of awkward.

The entrance door to the school slammed against the wall when I opened it with too much force. I didn't care. I was fueled up with seven years of rage. Taking the five steps to the kitchen I opened the next door and stared at Solo.

Geez!

I blinked my eyes. The last time I'd seen him, he'd been seventeen and tall for his age. Now he was a giant, making the other two large men in the room seem small. Archer and Marco were watching me, but I focused on the man I'd been foolish enough to give my young heart to ten years ago. I had expected him to have a long beard, but his was short and styled. Solomon stared back at me, with his neck muscles tensed up, his stance rigid. Oh, Mother Nature, he was an older version of the young man I'd fallen so hard for when he made me feel important and loved. Those blue eyes that looked gray in the right light, his dark blond hair, and the shoulders that I had sat on when we snuck off to bathe in the lake and he threw me through the air in playful fun. This enormous man had once been my best friend and fiercest protector. He had known how to make me laugh and he'd convinced me that we'd have a future together.

Stop it, stop it.

My tone was hard when I spoke. "I'm taking a shower and then we'll talk."

Solomon blinked his eyes and parted his lips with a look of surprise.

"You should both eat first," Archer suggested but I wasn't interested in food. All I could take in was Solomon and the way he looked at me like he wasn't sure what to do. Finally, he cleared his throat. "I'm ready to talk when you are."

Hoping he didn't see how much my legs were shaking, I used an assertive tone. "Meet me by the lake in twenty minutes."

My arm was pulled back by Hunter, who demanded my attention. "You're not going anywhere alone with *him*."

I ignored Hunter's attempt to control the situation and gave Solomon another hard stare before I walked to the shower room, throwing a last order over my shoulder: "Be there."

Once I was in the shower and the hot water ran down my body, I held up my hands to see them tremble. This was the effect Solomon had on me, and I would need to dig deep and find the strong woman inside me who wouldn't be intimidated or charmed. Solomon had once come close to destroying me and I would never give him or anyone that sort of power again.

CHAPTER 4
Reunion

Solomon

My body felt restless as I waited for Willow down by the lake. I paced the grass, sat down, stood up, threw rocks in the water, and ruminated about what to say to Willow when she got here.

It shouldn't be hard. After all, I'd thought about her every day for seven years, and yet, now that I was minutes away from speaking with Willow again, I wasn't sure what to say. Twenty minutes ago, she had stormed into the kitchen where I stood with Archer and Marco, my previous mentors. Even in her state of anger, Willow had taken my breath away. She had been beautiful as a teenager, but in these last seven years, she had grown into a force of nature. She was lean and toned from her dancing, her hair darker than it used to be, or maybe that had been the wetness of it.

I heard her footsteps before I saw her, my trained hunter's instincts picking up on the sounds coming from the forest trail. My eyes zoomed in and two seconds later she came out from the trees walking toward me. I sucked in a breath, her beauty messing with my head. Her long hair was still wet from her shower, and her incredible body dressed in a blue dress with flowers in white and teal colors that went to her mid-thighs. Her hard steps and determined expression stood in contrast to the soft femininity of her swaying hips and long tanned legs, which were mouth-watering.

Keep calm.

My palms were clammy, but I squinted against the sun and stood ready to receive her fury.

"Why did you come?" It was the first thing she said to me when she stopped at a seven-foot distance.

"I was invited like the rest of you."

"You knew I'd be here." It sounded accusatory.

"I hoped you'd be here."

She lifted her index finger and stabbed it at me. "Don't even try to charm me. I'm too angry with you to fall for that. What you did was unforgivable."

Her words made my heart sink. My biggest motivation for coming here was the hope that maybe she could forgive me. Disappointed, I looked away.

Willow took a small step closer, her expression and tone stern. "Don't you have anything to say for yourself?"

I took a second before I answered, "Would you listen?"

She stared at me as if unsure whether to go or stay. "I have questions."

"You can ask me anything."

Walking past me, Willow went to sit on the grass close to the lake. I followed and sat down an arm's length away, my body feeling heavy and disheartened. The last time I saw Willow there had been love in her eyes. Now, there was only resentment, and the way she had moved away when I sat down hurt.

"What do you want to know?" My legs were bent in front of me. Leaning my arms on my knees, I kept my gaze on the vegetation down by the edge of the lake.

"I have so many questions that I don't even know where to start."

"How about I start then?" I sighed and turned my head to look at her. "Willow, I owe you an apology."

She narrowed her eyes but kept looking straight ahead.

"Asking you to run away with me was wrong. I don't know what I was thinking and the fact that you got hurt… it kills me to think what could have happened."

She didn't answer.

"Willow, will you turn and look at me for a second, please?" The situation was awkward and alien to me. I wasn't the kind of man to use such words as please and sorry, but this had to be done.

Willow still refused to look at me, but the way her jaw tensed told me I had her full attention.

"I'm sorry, Willow." The words hung in the air for a long time. "I'm really sorry."

"You should be." In a slow movement, Willow got up and walked to stand by the water, her arms hugging her waist. I gave her time and didn't force the conversation.

"I trusted you." Her words were low, but I heard them.

"I know."

"You told me you'd protect me."

I groaned and looked down. Every fucking night before going to bed, I blamed myself for what happened that day she got hurt.

"I could have died, you know that, right?"

"Yes."

Willow turned her face and gave me another accusatory stare. "We had no business being alone in a huge forest. We were children."

"That's not true. I was seventeen and stronger than most adult men."

"But I was only fifteen."

"So what? You were a woman. You told me so when you started bleeding, remember?"

Willow turned to face me. "Because you would never stop talking about our future."

"But you said that you were a woman. It was your exact words."

She threw her hands up in the air. "Getting your period and being capable of reproducing isn't the same as being a grown-up."

I counter-argued, "You can't put an age on when you're ready for love. Everyone is different. I was ready to be with you when I was fourteen. You were fifteen when we ran away, and you always said that girls mature faster than boys."

With an outburst of frustration, Willow walked closer to me. "Don't talk about love. What you felt for me wasn't love, it was an obsession."

I jerked my head back and swallowed hard. "An obsession?"

"Yes. You were jealous of any other boy who spoke with me and you wanted me to commit to marrying you when we were only kids. Who proposes to a child? That's just sick."

All the blood left my face and I fisted my hands. I understood anger, but to call me sick was unfair and unexpected. When I didn't respond to her accusation, Willow turned back to the brink of the water, letting me sit to think about the time we were younger and I proposed to her.

"We shouldn't be here. What if someone sees us?" Willow whispered and giggled low with her face turned up to meet mine.

I peeked out from the wall we were hiding behind. "They're all watching the movie."

It had become a tradition to have movie night every Thursday and because of the warm weather, we were watching it outside with us kids sprawled out with pillows and blankets on the grass.

When Willow had gone to the rest room, I had taken the chance to have a few stolen seconds alone with her. For weeks now, we'd been holding hands in secret, but I was dying for something more.

"Willow, I really like you." My eyes were glowing with intensity as I took her hands.

"I really like you too, Solo."

My body stiffened at first when she reached up on her toes and hugged me. I had never been hugged by her and I knew it was forbidden. Still, my arms wrapped around her and I hugged her back. Her hair smelled amazing; her body was a perfect fit to mine. And then she kissed me – a soft kiss to my cheek that had me lifting my hand to feel the spot while looking at her with awe.

"You kissed me."

"Is that okay?" Her sweet smile was worthy of an angel.

My brain reacted by instinct and made me lean in, stopping only when I was nose to nose with her. It was enough time for Willow to move back or stop me if she wanted to, but instead she slid her arms around my neck.

That's when I kissed her.

It was like I could touch the tips of the trees in the forest that surrounded us. I was flying high with euphoria that Willow had let me kiss her on her lips.

"I love you," I whispered and kissed her again.

She smiled up at me with those green eyes that changed color depending on her mood and the light. "I love you too."

No one had ever spoken those words to me and in that moment, it made complete sense to me that Nmen had fought and given their lives for hundreds of years to be with a woman. The rush of Willow's soft smile and sweet words overwhelmed me with emotions and hopes for the future. I sank to my knees and hugged her waist while pressing my face against her belly. "Do you mean that?"

Willow caressed my hair and giggled again. "Why wouldn't I?"

I looked up at her. "Do you mean it? You really love me?"

She cupped my face. "I love you, Solo."

Still looking up at her, I felt my heart hammering in my chest. "Will you be mine?"

"Yours? Do you mean your friend?"

"My wife. Will you be my wife?"

Willow frowned. "I'm not old enough."

I got up and squeezed her hand. "Will you marry me when we're grown up?"

"Oh."

"I'll fight for you in a tournament if you want me to, but you're a Motlander; you can choose to marry who you want."

"I can?"

"Yes. Pearl married Khan."

She widened her eyes. "You want us to be like them?"

"Yes, Willow. I want to spend the rest of my life with you. I love you."

"Oh, okay." *She smiled.* "I guess we can do that."

I lit up. "So, you'll marry me?"

"Yes."

"Let's make a pact then. Let's be together for the rest of our lives. Like wolves. They mate for life too."

Willow bit her lip. "But what if you change your mind? I think some of the other girls like you too."

"I don't care. I only want you."

"Okay." *She hugged me with excitement.* "And I only want you."

We nuzzled our noses against each other and kept smiling, my chest exploding with happiness as I let out a deep breath. "I want to fast-forward and marry you right now."

"Me too. Can I tell Hunter and my friends?"

"You can tell everyone that we have a pact and that when you're eighteen we'll marry." *I held her hand.* "We're mates now. I belong to you, Willow. I always will."

"I was in love. Not sick." My tone was harder than intended and it made Willow turn around to face me again.

"Oh, so we're talking again?"

"What do you mean?"

"You've been quiet for ten minutes."

"I was just thinking about the time I asked you to marry me."

She snorted. "You mean pressured."

It was like getting stabbed with a knife. "You think I pressured you to agree?"

"Yes. You've always been domineering and pushy."

Unable to sit still, I got up and shoved my hands into my pockets. "I'm not going to deny that I know what I want and that I go for it. It's the quality stamp of an Nman."

"Hunter isn't like that and he's a fine Nman."

I scoffed. "How did you think your brother became one of the biggest soccer stars in our country?"

"Talent."

"And determination. He wanted it and worked hard to get there. You can't blame a man for that."

"I can when he pressures a child into marrying him. Good thing that I was lucky enough to see in time what a colossal mistake marrying you would have been."

Needing a bit of time to calm myself from the insults to my person, I walked to the water.

"Solo." Willow was standing behind me, closer than she had been before.

"Yes." I kept my back to her.

"Why did you do it?"

"Do what?"

"Ask me to run away with you."

My shoulders lifted in a deep intake of air and I spoke on the exhale: "You know why."

"Most of what happened, I don't remember."

"Yeah, well, I remember everything like it was yesterday."

Willow moved to stand by my side, her arms wrapped around her waist again. "Over the years I've suppressed a lot. That's why I have questions."

I turned my head to give her a quizzical look. "You really don't remember?"

"No."

"Nothing?"

She broke the eye contact and squatted down to pick up a stone that she threw into the water. It was a soft throw and the stone landed with a plop.

I squatted down too and picked out a stone that was small and flat, throwing it in a perfect skip that made it jump over the water five times before going in.

"You were always good at that."

"Ah, so you haven't forgotten *everything*?"

"No. Not everything." She turned her face and gave me a cold stare. "I still have memories that haunt me."

CHAPTER 5
Questions

Willow

"I remember pain. Lots of pain."

Solomon frowned at my words, picked up another stone, and threw it in the lake. "Pain because of your broken arm?"

This time the stone didn't skip across the water but made a splash and disappeared. Part of me wished I could do the same and escape this confrontation with the man I had once had childish notions of spending my life with.

"My broken arm was only one of the things that hurt." I sat back on the grass, crossing my legs in front of me. "Being on the run was painful. The endless hours of walking and running, the sleeping in the wild and getting eaten by mosquitos, the bathing in ice-cold water, and the fall where I broke my arm and got a concussion. "All I remember from those eight days is *pain*."

Solomon, who had been squatting, sat down too when I continued, "I wasn't in the same physical shape as you were. You painted a picture of lazy days swimming in rivers, roasting food over a fire pit, and snuggling at night. But that's not what happened."

"I told you we'd have to get away from them first."

My eyebrows rose up. "As if the grown-ups would have ever stopped searching for us."

"If you hadn't gotten hurt, Willow, we could have hidden for as long as we wanted to. The woods here are endless and with time everyone would have assumed us dead."

My answer was a low sneer, "Which is exactly what we would have been."

"You don't know that."

"Come on, Solo. You're no longer a naïve child. We would have been miserable and starving as soon as the winter set in. We would have missed our friends and family."

Solomon looked down. "I didn't have a family to miss."

I frowned, refusing to be sucked down by the love I'd once felt for this man. I wouldn't allow myself to care. If I did, I'd be doomed again. "Well, I did have a family, and you took me away from them."

"We said that we'd start our own family. Don't you remember?"

I widened my eyes at him and made a "pst" sound. "Do you even hear how crazy that sounds? Giving birth in the forest with no doctors around. How is that protecting me… or our child for that matter?"

Solomon was tearing at his hair and had his elbows on his knees looking down. "I already apologized. What I did was wrong."

"So why did you do it?"

"Because I panicked. You were going back to the Motherlands and I thought I'd never see you again. Maybe if Lord Khan hadn't changed the rules, but with the new bridal law we couldn't marry until you were twenty-one. You were fifteen and I knew if we had to spend another six years apart, the chance of you changing your mind and not wanting to marry me was huge. Motlanders don't like Northlanders and once you lived there long enough, I'd lose you. The thought of never seeing you again, Willow… it…" Solomon sighed and trailed off. "It made me fucking desperate."

I'd known this part and yet hearing him say it mattered to me. For a long while we didn't speak. I lay down flat on my back, closing my eyes and soaking up the morning sun.

I should get up and walk away. I hate Solo and nothing he can say will change that, my mind argued, but my body didn't want to leave. Despite the long silence between us, being close to this giant of a man brought me a sense of peace that I hadn't felt in a long time. It puzzled me that after all these years he didn't feel like a stranger. The only explanation I could come up with was that I had idolized him for three years while I was at an impressionable age.

A warning sounded in my head. *Be careful, Willow. Don't get comfortable.*

"I should thank you."

Solomon's mutter made me squint one eye open. "For what?"

"You saved my life." He rolled onto his stomach and plucked at the grass. "If you hadn't pleaded for the soldiers not to kill me when they found us, I would be dead now."

"That's right. You can add that to my long list of painful and traumatic moments with you. I was terrified."

"You were brave, Willow. Remember how you stepped in front of one of their guns?"

"I remember you pulling me away and not understanding that I was trying to save you."

Solomon smiled at me and it made me look away. I couldn't afford to let my front down around him. His smile had once had the power to make me turn my back on everyone else in my life. My anger was my shield and I held on to it for dear life.

"It wasn't that I didn't understand what you were doing. I just couldn't allow you to put yourself in danger because of me."

"What happened after I was sent back to the Motherlands? Did you get punished?"

"Of course." His voice remained flat, but his face hardened and his fingers curled into his palms. It was clear that my question had brought back memories he preferred to forget, but this wasn't some cozy talk and I didn't care if my questions made him uncomfortable.

I gave him a sideways glance. "How bad?"

Solomon intertwined his fingers, bending them backward with cracking sounds. "First, Hunter attacked me when I tried to apologize to him. I assume you know about that. Later, Magni wanted me to promise that I wouldn't seek you out again. When I refused, he beat me half to death."

I lowered my brow. "What's wrong with you Nmen? When did violence ever solve anything?"

Some new light entered Solomon's gaze. "Magni's partially deaf in one ear because of that fight we had. Did you know that?"

"No."

"He says he wasn't trying to kill me, but it sure felt that way."

I tilted my head. "That's why I never heard from you. He beat you into submission."

Solomon turned to look at me with his brow lowered. "I was seventeen, and I stood my ground like a pigheaded fool. It cost me a week in the hospital. After that they placed me under a restraining order."

"What does that mean?" I pushed up on my elbows, giving him another sideways glance, but seeing Solomon's bulging triceps stretching the sleeve of his t-shirt made my heart beat faster, so I averted my eyes again.

"I was banned from entering the Motherlands or contacting you in any way. Even if you had come to the Northlands I couldn't have gone near you. The restraining order was basically their way of honoring your wish not to kill me, but only as long as I kept away from you."

"Then how come you can talk to me now?"

"Khan lifted the restraining order."

"When?"

"Yesterday."

I was quiet for a long time, thinking about all the times I'd wondered why he never reached out to me.

"You said you had questions."

I nodded. "It's all a blur to me. Maybe it was my way of processing it, you know, to block it from my memory. But over the years I've had nightmares and I'm not sure what's real or fantasy anymore."

He waited for me to ask a question.

"Solomon, did we..." I paused, not sure how to phrase it. "Did we have sex?"

His face stiffened. "You don't remember?"

"No. I have memories, but they're unclear and foggy. I know we slept together for a week under the stars and there was a lot of kissing, but did we go all the way?"

As if I had offended him, Solomon pushed up from the grass and walked away from me.

"You said you'd answer any question I had," I called after him and he stopped and turned.

"Let me get this straight. You don't remember if we slept together but you have nightmares about it. Is that it?"

"Yes."

"The thought of being with me wakes you up feeling scared?" His voice was strained, with gravel in his timbre as if it hurt to talk. "Or is it disgusted?"

"Just answer my question. Did we sleep together?"

"What do you think?"

"I think we did."

Solo rubbed his forehead, his jaw tense.

"Hey there."

We both turned around to see Mila coming toward us.

"I brought you some lunch."

"I'm not hungry," Solomon muttered.

"Suit yourself, but you've been down here for a while and it's hot. At least drink something. Archer says people get grumpy when they are hungry or dehydrated."

"Thank you, Mila." I got up to take the basket.

"Willow, are you okay?" Mila whispered.

I gave her a reassuring smile. "We'll be done soon."

"Okay." She brushed a hand over my shoulder and gave me a concerned smile before she left.

Solo and I didn't talk until Mila was gone again and by then I'd opened the basket and was popping water balls into my mouth.

"You want some?" I asked. "There's some fruit and cake too."

Solo came over and picked up an apple. "So, tell me, what else do you have nightmares about me doing to you?"

"Taking me away from my family."

He took a noisy bite of the apple.

"Why won't you tell me if we had sex?"

"You know as much as I do, Willow. You're just suppressing it."

"So, help me remember."

"Why would I when you've done such a good job at blocking what happened between us?" Solomon took another big bite and threw the apple into the lake.

"Okay, then tell me about the fall. I remember us being chased by a bear for days; is that why I fell?"

He scrunched up his face. "No, we weren't chased by a bear for days. Geez, you've really got it all mixed up, don't you?"

"There was a bear. I'm certain of it."

"Yes, there was a bear and a whole fucking army of Huntsmen chasing us. That's why we jumped."

"I didn't fall?"

"No. We jumped."

"I remember almost drowning in water and falling down a waterfall."

"It wasn't that big."

I lifted my arm. "Big enough for me to break two bones and get a severe concussion. Do you see this scar?" I pulled my hair away from my neck. "That's from that day too. Most people remove their scars but I kept mine so I would never forget how close I came to dying because of you. But maybe you suppressed that part."

"I fucking stopped the bleeding and gave you CPR. Trust me, I'll never forget seeing you hurt."

I hadn't known that he'd performed CPR on me and it rattled me. If Solomon had saved my life, everything I'd been telling myself for seven years could be a lie. Picking up a piece of cake, I unwrapped it and nibbled at it with my fingers shaking a little. No, he had to be mistaken and I wouldn't be fooled to let down my guard around him.

"I have pictures from my stay in the hospital. The scratches, cuts, and bruises. I looked like a castaway."

Solomon's answer came fast and with a tone of frustration. "Which is why I insisted we give up running. You wanted us to keep hiding, or have you forgotten about that too?"

Shaking my head, I felt annoyed with him. "I had a concussion. I wasn't in a position to make rational decisions."

"Willow, I was trying to save you. That's why I built a fire to lead them to us. You were so worried the soldiers would kill me."

The cake was crumbling between my fingers much like the shield of anger around my heart. I clung to it with desperation. "Yeah, well, there've been days when I wished they would have."

Solomon dropped his chin and it took him seconds to respond. "You wish that I'd died that day?"

It was an awful thing to say and my hands were shaking more now. I should apologize, but seven years of built up grief and my deep-rooted fear that he could hurt me again had me spewing more awful things at him. "Because of you my brother has trust issues. Because of you I never got to say goodbye to everyone at the school. Did you know that I was whisked away in the middle of the night? Because of you I have nightmares. Because of you I have a heart that I never want to follow again. You took something pure and destroyed it with your reckless impatience." My voice broke from all the emotions in my chest.

Solomon's ears grew redder by the second. "Is that why you're with Tristan?"

I stared at him. "Who told you that?"

"Hunter did."

It was impossible not to see the pain in Solomon's eyes, so why wasn't I feeling the satisfaction my revenge fantasy had promised me?

"Are you with him because he feels safe and I don't?"

"Tristan isn't..." I was going to tell the truth. Tristan was a friend and nothing more. Hunter would have mentioned that I was with Tristan to make sure Solomon didn't make any kind of move on me.

"Tristan isn't what?" Solomon tucked his hands under his armpits and looked down, his body positioned to shield him from my words.

"Tristan isn't reckless. He's kind and funny."

"And you're happy with him?"

I looked away feeling uncomfortable with lying. Sudden memories of being in a hospital bed connected to feeding tubes worked like gasoline thrown on my inner fire of anger. This man was dangerous to me. The minute I saw him in the kitchen I'd known that part of my heart would always want to run to him. But I was smarter than I'd been at fifteen and I would use every mental weapon I had to keep him from destroying my life again. I straightened up to my full height. "Yes, I'm very happy with Tristan. What about you? Are you married?"

Solomon lifted his face and looked at me like he didn't understand the question.

"Are you married?" I repeated.

"Willow, you and I... we..."

First, I stared at him in disbelief. Then I erupted in a hollow laugh. "You're not serious?"

"A hundred percent. I still love you."

Damn it. I had been so prepared to spew all my anger at him, but hearing Solo say that he still loved me softened me, and I couldn't afford to be soft around him. In a desperate act of self-defense, I poured all my energy into my armor of anger. "I don't care. I feel nothing for you except *hate*. Whatever dreams you had about us marrying, forget it. We were children when we made that pact and I guarantee that it will *never* happen in this lifetime."

Solomon's face tensed up and the veins on his neck popped out.

I squared my shoulders and looked him straight in the eye. "There is no pact and no marriage! All there is left between us are painful memories and a deep feeling of hate. I will *never* forgive you for what you did to me."

Solomon's face was as red as if I'd slapped his cheeks. The warm apologetic man turned icy. "They say all it takes to move on is closure. I think this qualifies." He took a step back. "You can tell the three men watching us from the trees that I'm no threat to you. The Willow I loved is obviously gone."

I wanted to shout at him to get the last word, but I could think of nothing to say. He was right. I was no longer the naïve, adoring girl who had loved him without conditions. I was the cynic with the broken heart who stood without moving, watching Solo disappear out of my life for the second time.

It's better this way. He only brings pain with him.

As soon as Solo was out of sight, Hunter came running from the trees followed by Magni and Archer.

"Why were you spying on us?" I asked with annoyance.

"We were making sure you were safe."

"I didn't know you were watching us."

"That was the point." Hunter looked over his shoulder to where Solo had left. "What happened?"

"The last thing he said was that I should tell the three men watching us that he's not a threat to me."

"He saw us?" Hunter wrinkled his brow. "That's impossible."

Magni snorted. "I trained him. Of course, he knew someone was watching. Solo is clever and his instincts are fine tuned."

"I told you not to throw away that bad nectarine. I bet he heard it," Archer scolded Hunter.

"I'm taking a swim." Magni pulled off his shirt and walked to the water. "I need to cool down."

"Me too." Archer stepped out of his shoes and when he began pulling his clothes off, I walked away.

"You're not going after Solo, are you?" Hunter called behind me.

"No. I'm going back to the school."

My brother fell into step next to me. Loud splashing sounds behind us revealed that Magni and Archer had gone into the water. "What did you and Solo talk about?"

"I can't remember."

"But you talked for a long time."

"Not really. There were a lot of silences too."

"Did you tell Solo that you never want to see him again."

"Pretty much."

Hunter groaned. "You sure he got the message?"

"Yes."

"Good."

The rest of the way we walked in silence and when we got to the school Solomon was already taking off in his drone.

I watched him when his drone rose into the sky, his eyes on me before he turned his head away, leaving me with some of his last words resounding in my head. *They say that all it takes to move on is closure. I think this qualifies.*

Hunter leaned his head back and followed Solomon's military drone as it took off. "Are you happier now?"

"Yes." It was what he wanted to hear and what I wanted to believe. "I'm much happier."

CHAPTER 6
New Assignment

Solomon

Zasquash was waiting for me when I returned from the reunion.

"How did it go?"

"She hates me."

He walked next to me. "Sorry about that. What about Hunter? Did you at least make up with him?"

"No."

Zasquash gave a deep groan and opened the door to the small headquarters of the Domestic Violence Unit where we worked. "Why not? Did you put on your charm like I told you to?"

"Yeah, I did the tap-dance routine, the stand-up comedy act, and still nothing helped." I rolled my eyes.

"Ahh, that explains it. I'll bet you blew the comedy act. You never had much humor to begin with." Zasquash followed me into the kitchen.

"I'm only here to pick up some stuff. I'm off duty for two days so I'm heading up to my cabin." I opened the fridge to get something to drink.

"Sorry, but your cabin will have to wait. Leo called us with a new assignment. We have to go."

"Can't some of the others go?" Sounds of voices from the gym further down the hall told me at least a few of our colleagues were here.

"Nope, Magni gave an order and he wants you and me to go."

I slammed the fridge closed and pushed both my hands through my hair. "Shit."

"What is it?"

"Magni used to give me the shittiest of assignments to remind me that I should be grateful that I wasn't executed. I'll bet this new assignment has to do with my talk with Willow today. Magni is just making sure I remember my place. I'm sorry that you're being dragged into this mess."

Zasquash frowned. "I don't know, man, Leo sounded pretty excited about it."

"All right." I held up my hands. "I'm just warning you. Don't get your hopes up. We might be asked to visit all the Motlander brides and do trivial interviews about their level of happiness or some shit."

Zasquash pushed me aside and opened the fridge. "Nah, man, Magni wants us because we're the fiercest of his warriors. He wouldn't waste our time like that."

"Trust me, he would."

"I know there's some weird shit going on between you two, but Magni is smart. He knows that we're the best team at tracking down people and handing out lessons to the fuckers who need to know what it feels like to be the smaller one in the relationship." While talking, Zasquash pulled out a container. "We just got these new ones. You've got to try them."

He pulled out the balls of water that I'd seen as a child visiting the Motherlands. It was the same sort Mila had brought Willow and me by the lake today.

"Isn't this the coolest thing ever?" He peeled one and popped it in his mouth. "You can get them with beer now too."

I grabbed a handful and headed out the door to the drone I had flown in to the reunion. "Come on, let's find out what the assignment is about."

"Turn around." Zasquash was right behind me. "I wanna see if you can catch a water ball with your mouth."

Coming to a full stop, I held my mouth open. "Try it."

Zasquash threw hard enough for the damn ball of water to hit me right between my eyes and burst. The volume of his laughter told me it was no coincidence.

"Asshole."

"Told you that your sense of humor sucks."

An hour later we walked into Police District Three, where our friend Leo came to meet us.

"What's up?" Zasquash asked and plunked down in a chair. "Who do we need to chase down now?"

"No one." I looked at Leo. "If you had a runner, you wouldn't have asked us to meet you here. We would be at the last place he was seen."

"That's right. This is an assignment completely different from what you've ever done before and to be honest, I'm not sure why Magni insisted that it was given to you two."

"What is it?"

"There's a group of Motlander artists coming to the Northlands to impress us with their culture. They're going on a tour around the country as a part of the overall integration program."

"So?"

"So, there's heavy security around them and the three of us have been selected to personally guard the star of the show."

Zasquash sat up. "What star are we talking about?"

"It's this lady." Leo headed over to a computer and pulled up a hologram of a woman. "Salma Rose – she's twenty-seven, five-foot-four, and one of the greatest singers in the Motherlands." We all looked at the hologram showing a beautiful woman sitting on a beach, looking out over the ocean with her hair blowing in the wind and her sunglasses raised up in her hair.

"She's coming here?" Zasquash got up and moved closer to the image. "When?"

"In ten days. There will be almost thirty artists and technicians but she's the main attraction."

"Why do we have to have three people to protect her? I could do that alone." Zasquash crossed his arms and gave us a challenging stare.

Leo placed a hand on the desk and leaned to the side. "Don't fucking get possessive of her. She's not going to fall for an old scarred warrior like you."

"Hey, I'm only six years older than her. That's nothing, and why wouldn't she fall for me? I'm tall, dark, and handsome. It's what all women want."

Leo gave a rueful twist of his mouth. "You've been reading too many steamy novels from the olden days. Things have changed, my friend."

I sat down on the edge of a table. "The question remains. Why three men to guard one woman? It seems excessive."

"Because if anything happens to this fragile rose, we're screwed. My boss has given his personal guarantee that our police force is capable of keeping the artists safe during their tour."

"Fine, but if the police have it covered, then why are we here?" I asked and used my thumb to point to me and Zasquash. "We're soldiers."

Leo shrugged. "That was Magni's order."

"I know why." Zasquash glanced at the other policemen buzzing around in the large room. "Everyone knows that we Doomsmen are the biggest, badest, and most feared soldiers in our country. It's obvious Magni wants us in visible roles to discourage any fool who might try to get close to the artists."

Leo squared his shoulders, his muscles showing through the thin uniform shirt he had on. "Hmm. Either way, by bringing in the freak show and pushing you two clowns to the front, it will look like the Doomsmen are responsible for the security while in reality we policemen are doing the actual work, as always."

It wasn't the first time Leo called us freaks, and Zasquash was quick to give him shit for it. "Hey, cry-baby, do you need a hug to cheer you up?"

"No thanks, I don't trust your mutant arms," Leo retorted with a straight face and changed the projection. "Here's the tour schedule. We'll meet the artists by the border and escort them from there. It's all noted down."

I studied the list, where names were followed by descriptions like singer, dancer, musician, and technician. "At least I don't see the Butterflies on here."

"Who are they?"

"This popular group of three singers. I went to one of their concerts ten years ago."

Leo scrunched up his face. "How is that possible?"

"Remember that I told you how I was in the first experimental school and we had a field trip to the Motherlands? It lasted a week and we went to see a factory, a concert, and the beach. You know, to experience what the Motherlands are like." I looked at Zasquash. "Don't give me that face. I fucking told you about it plenty of times."

"Yeah, you did. But I don't remember hearing anything about butterflies."

Leo stared at me. "You never told me about it, and now my head is exploding with questions."

"All you need to know is that it's a good thing that the Butterflies aren't on the list, because they were awful."

"But what was it like, seeing so many women at once?"

"Fine." I smiled. "One time we went to a pool at the hotel, and the thing is that in the Motherlands men and women shower together.

"No fucking way." Both men narrowed their eyes in suspicion. "You're messing with us."

"No, it's true. We saw several naked women."

"Holy fuck!" Leo's hands flew to his head. "For real?"

"Yes, for real. It would have been amazing except for the fact that we only saw women who were old and wrinkled."

"Aww, why did you have to tell me that part?" Leo spun around with his hands still in his hair. "Fuck you, Solo, I had such nice pictures in my head."

I laughed. "What I want to know is how come the three of us were teamed up together for this task. That can't be a coincidence."

Leo shrugged. "It's not. None of my colleagues wanted to work with you two."

Zasquash snorted and looked around. "What's their problem? Are they scared of us?"

"Intimidated is maybe a better word. You do have a reputation."

Zasquash and I exchanged a look and he shrugged. "Yeah, we do. Otherwise we couldn't do our job, could we? Your colleagues should be smart enough to know that it's a good thing that most men piss themselves when we show up. It makes life easier for the police as well."

"Uh-huh." Leo lifted his chin. "One last thing. When we meet the performers for the first time, you two will stay in the background. We don't want them to run back home because they're afraid of you. I'll greet Salma Rose when she arrives and introduce her to you."

"Sure, that's fine with me. As long as you let her know that we're the chosen ones." Zasquash winked.

Leo lifted an eyebrow. "I'm sure you'll tell her that yourself."

"Salma Rose," Zasquash pronounced the name slowly. "I like it." He turned and gave us a pointed stare. "I call dibs on the first shift when she gets here."

"Fine, but you understand that your role isn't to entertain her or talk to her, right? You're supposed to be aware of everything around her and keep her safe."

Zasquash squared his shoulders. "I can do both."

Leo clapped his hands together. "Good. In that case, welcome on board."

CHAPTER 7
Touring

Willow

I was star-struck when I first saw Salma Rose. Her songs were giant hits and I knew the lyrics to most of them. The fact that she was going on the Northlands tour had been one of the reasons I'd let Pearl talk me into joining when a spot opened up at the last minute.

Now, I stood in front of my building and stared into the drone that had just landed, seeing one of my biggest idols. The man who had stepped out to greet me moved closer. He was shorter than me but his hair was puffed up in the latest fashionable hairstyle, one that made him appear taller.

"You must be Willow Darlington." He smiled and pulled up the sleeves of his multicolored shirt, revealing that he was fond of jewelry. All his finger rings and wristbands distracted me, and I blinked my eyes and moved my head to look at him. "What?"

"Is your name Willow?"

"Yes."

"May peace surround you. I'm Ben." He moved forward to take my hands in a formal greeting.

"Are you a performer too?" I asked.

He smiled. "No, my job is behind the stage. I'm Salma's manager and friend. We've worked together for years and I take care of a lot of the practical matters to make Salma's life easier."

"Oh, that's nice."

"I promised Pearl Pilotti that I'll be looking out for you on this tour."

My hand flew to my chest. "Me?"

"Yes, don't look so surprised. I was told that you're very special to Pearl and her husband Lord Khan. She said that you are one of the finest dancers in the Motherlands."

"Pearl said that?" I gaped at him.

"Yes, she did. Let me take your bags and you can get in and meet the lovely Rose herself."

My hands felt clammy when I got into the drone and took the seat next to Salma Rose.

She didn't take my hands but smiled. "Peace and all that to you."

"May peace surround you too."

Geez, could I sound more formal?

Don't stare at her. Don't stare at her. My smile was a little stiff and I blamed it on the fact that my heart was racing like crazy and my legs were shaking.

"I like your name. Willow Darlington. It has a nice ring to it. What a perfect stage name."

"Thank you." I beamed at her. "It's my real name, though."

Salma's long hair had a color similar to mine and she possessed a natural beauty with her fine features and golden tan. "Lucky you. My real name is Barbara Clemens, but Salma Rose sounds so much better, don't you think?"

"I like Barbara Clemens." When she frowned, I quickly added. "But Salma Rose is much better as a stage name."

"I came up with it as a child when I used to dream about being a star." Salma was distracted by Ben, who got on board and took his seat.

"All right, ladies, next stop is the border, where we're meeting with the rest of the group. It's a long flight, but don't worry, I brought snacks."

I inclined my head in a polite manner. "Thank you."

"It's funny. You look like me. Same hair color, gray eyes, cute..." Salma tilted her head. "We could be sisters."

I lit up. "Really?" There was no need to tell her that my eyes were green and only looked gray sometimes.

She smiled back at me. "Yes. Obviously, you would be the big sister since you're taller."

"Huh. It's true, you two do have similar features," Ben agreed. "Although Willow would have to be the younger sister since there's five years between you."

"Impossible." Salma's face scrunched up.

"Willow is only twenty-two." Ben used a matter-of-fact tone and turned to me. "I couldn't help notice that you're very tall. I'm surprised because all the dancers I know are on the smaller side. You have to be among the tallest women I've ever seen." He was picking through a bag as the drone took off. "You'll have to help me. The file I got on you made no sense. I thought they'd made a mistake."

"What do you mean?"

He pulled out small containers with fruits, nuts, and biscuits and handed them to us. The drone was for four people and each seat could be rotated a hundred and eighty degrees, making it possible for us to either face each other or look out the windows that ran all around the drone.

"It says that your height is fifty-nine. I figured they forgot the one and meant you were one meter and fifty-nine centimeters but after seeing you, I know you're much taller than that. I mean, you're taller than me and I'm one meter and seventy-two centimeters."

"I'm one meter and eighty centimeters."

Salma widened her eyes. "Oh, wow. I'm only one meter and fifty-four."

I smiled at her. "That would be five feet. The Northlands don't use centimeters like we do."

"Five feet?" She wrinkled her nose up. "That's sounds like *nothing*. I'm more than the length of my foot times five."

"It's not *your* foot. It's a fixed measurement of a little over thirty centimeters."

"Who decided that? I've never heard something that bizarre. To measure people by the length of someone's foot – and who in the world have feet that big anyway?"

My smiled widened. "It's how they've always done it in the Northlands."

"Let me guess, you took the culture-prep-course they sent us?"

I didn't get a chance to answer before Salma continued talking. "It's so brave of you to join the tour last-minute. You must be terrified. Especially after Lily chose not to go for safety reasons. To be honest with you, I was close to canceling myself, but I've been assured that we'll be safe. Right Ben?" Salma looked to Ben, who was chewing on a handful of nuts and held his hand to his mouth before he spoke.

"You have my word, darling. The ruler of the Northlands has guaranteed that his best security staff will be there to protect us. I told Lily the same thing, but her family kept pressuring her to stay home."

"It's a great loss to the Northlands that they won't get to see Lily White." I lowered my brow. "She's probably the best dancer in the world."

"Oh, we all adore Lily. She and I are friends." Salma leaned over and touched my arm. "But now we get to enjoy your dancing. I'm sure the Northlanders are going to love you just as much as Lily. And think of the great adventure it will be to see the Northlands for ourselves."

"I've seen the Northlands."

Both Ben and Salma stared at me. "You have?"

"Yes, that's how I know Pearl. I lived there for two and a half years."

"I was going to ask you about that, but I didn't want to jump you with a question about how you knew the rulers as the first thing."

"It's ruler, not rulers. Pearl isn't a ruler. Only Khan is," I corrected Ben.

He and Salma exchanged a glance before their questions rained down on me.

"Were you married?"

"When did you live there?"

"How long have you been back in the Motherlands?"

I held up a hand. "Let me explain."

Ben leaned forward in his seat with an eager expression.

"When I was twelve I was selected to participate in an experiment. It was the first school with children from the Motherlands and the Northlands. There were ten of us and ten of them. It turned out that I was selected because one of the boys, Hunter, had been a twin when he came from the Motherlands at three. I was his twin and they reunited us."

Salma tilted her head. "Your mother was a peacekeeper, then."

"Yes. It was never her intention to be a mother, only to do her part and give birth to one of the Northmen. I'm not sure what went wrong or why she ended up with twins, but she didn't want to live in a family unit and care for us. My brother and I lived together until he was three and delivered to the Northlands. Back then his name was Jeremy, but all Nboys are given new names when they arrive in the Northlands."

"Yes, I heard they have peculiar names." Ben offered me some of the nuts he was eating and I took a small handful.

"Northmen are named after heroes and gods. It's their belief that it makes the boys strive to be great themselves."

"So, Jeremy became Hunter?"

"Yes, Hunter Hercules, after the Greek god."

Ben giggled. "That's funny."

"I know, but you shouldn't make fun of their names in front of them," I warned. "They are proud men."

Ben shook his head. "No, of course not, I would never be that rude."

"But Willow, if you have a brother who is a Northlander does that mean…" Salma tilted her head with a thoughtful expression.

"It means I'm part Northlander too."

"Oh." Salma sat back.

"That's why I'm so tall. My father was a Northlander."

"Wow." Salma moved in her seat. "All right. Now, with you being such an expert on the Northlands, do you have any advice for us that we should know about?"

I scratched my collarbone. "Just be yourself but don't touch them. It's not that they don't like to be touched. It's just that they have strict rules. Touching a woman can get a man killed."

"You're kidding."

"No." My face was serious. "They are taught from early childhood that the greatest honor a man can achieve is to marry a woman. They hold tournaments and fight to win a bride but there are so few Northlander women that only one man in a hundred thousand can win a woman. With that honor comes huge prestige and a million dollars."

"Darling, they still use a monetary system like in the old days," Ben addressed Salma to explain the concept of dollars.

She looked confused. "That means nothing to me. How much is a million dollars?"

"Enough for them to live in luxury for the rest of their lives."

Salma moved in her seat. "I'm starting to think I should have taken the culture course. Why didn't I, Ben?"

"Because you were busy and sometimes you overthink things, honey. It's better to approach everything with an open mind."

Salma used both her index fingers to circle her temples, her eyebrows drawn close together. "But now I worry that they won't like our performance if they're that different from us. What if they hate it?"

Eager to calm her fears, I smiled at her. "They won't. I was in the Northlands for a reunion party with my old classmates ten days ago, and I can assure you that the Nmen enjoyed our dancing very much. They said we looked like fairies when we danced."

"But what about my music? Will they like my songs?"

I gave her another reassuring smile. "They'll love you, Salma. Just remember not to touch them and no matter how charming or good-looking they are, you can't get too close or they might think you want to be with them."

Salma chewed on her lip again. "But touching is such a natural thing for me."

"I understand. Me too. But you don't want anyone to get in trouble or die because of a misunderstanding, do you?"

"Oh dear, no, of course not. That would be horrible."

Ben leaned back in his seat. "I can't believe they would oppose touching that much."

I gave a small shrug. "Once we get there you'll understand. Imagine what life would be like for the few women who live there if they didn't have strict rules to protect them. We women would be in constant fear of being kidnapped and raped."

"What?" Salma paled. "They don't kidnap women anymore, do they? I was told those stories are just old rumors."

Ben's eyes told me to be careful and I was starting to sense that Salma Rose wasn't as confident and fearless as I'd thought.

"Don't worry, Salma. It's ingrained in all boys from early on that they can't touch a woman. Just use common sense and stay close to the guards. You don't want to go around on your own."

Ben put a calming hand on her arm. "You'll be fine, dear. As long as you don't touch them."

Salma turned her chair to look out the window. "But what happens if I touch them by accident? Will *I* be in trouble too or do these laws only apply to men?"

"The laws are made to protect women. There are no laws against touching males."

"Then what about Ben? What if they all go after him?" Salma looked back from her chair with concern marring her pretty face.

"They won't. Homosexuality isn't paraded in public."

"I'll be fine, darling," Ben assured Salma. "Don't you worry about a thing."

In the four hours we flew to get to the border, Salma, Ben, and I spoke about her career, the current political situation, my brother Hunter, and what we would miss in the Motherlands these four weeks that we would be touring. Salma hadn't slept well the night before and took a nap, while Ben talked about his long list of famous clients and his excitement that romance movies and books were now allowed in the Motherlands again.

"There's an exciting script on my table that I'm hoping to find actors for. Part of the story takes place in the Northlands and I promised the director I'd look for talent while I'm there."

"That's exciting."

"Yes. I'm always open to spotting new clients. How about you, do you have an agent?"

"No."

"Maybe we can work together. I'm good to my clients, you can ask any of them."

"How many do you have?"

"Oh, about twenty. I've got singers, actors, and even a few sports stars."

Men of the North #7 – THE DANCER

When we reached the border, the gate between our countries was closed, with border drones hanging in the air. We could see from the sky how a group of around thirty people were already gathered on the Motlander side with two drones taking off, implying that some of them had only just arrived as well. On the Northlander side, two drones were waiting. One of them was about twice the size of the one we were arriving in. The other was a huge transport.

"They are waiting for us." Ben tapped his finger against the window of our drone, which was slowly descending. My eyes were on the twelve Nmen standing in front of the drones. All of them had serious expressions and police uniforms, except for one tall man who was military. We were too far away for me to tell what part of the military he belonged to but none of the men looked familiar to me.

Ben was the first to exit when the doors to our drone opened.

"It's going to be fine," he told Salma, whose eyes were darting around. "Just stay close to Willow while I go talk to the other organizers."

I didn't mind when Salma hooked her arm under my elbow and kept me close like a safety blanket.

"Just pretend we're going on stage. It's all a performance," I whispered.

She straightened her posture and loosened her tight grip on me.

"We should all be here now, so let's get this tour started," a woman around fifty said in a loud shrill voice and waved her hands for us to step closer. "I'm going to call out your names and you'll gather in the groups you belong to. That way we can all get a quick idea about who's who.

"Let's begin with the organizers. My name is Kerri, and this is Ben and Luba. We're here to make things run smoothly. Then we have the technical crew. If you could stand over there so we can all see you." Three men and two women walked over to stand in a cluster and Kerri read out their names.

"The Floral Chorals, please gather here to my right. There should be ten of you in the choir." The women smiled and moved to stand in two rows as if they were about to perform for us. Each one of them raised a hand when Kerri called out their names.

"Great, now if the Enlightened String Orchestra could gather over there." Kerri pointed to her left and read out fourteen names.

"And last but not least we have our two solo artists – Willow Darlington, who is a dancer, and Salma Rose, who needs no introductions."

Everyone was smiling at Salma, who raised a hand and waved.

"Our first stop will be in a town called Kingston where you'll be performing tomorrow night. You should all have received the program of the twelve towns we'll be visiting over the next four weeks. Our original plan was to make this tour last for four months, but we understand that it was too big a commitment for several of you with your busy calendars. At the end of our tour you'll be performing at the palace and get a chance to meet Lord Khan, the ruler of the Northlands, and his lovely wife Pearl Pilotti."

Excited murmurs broke out among the crowd and Salma leaned against me. "I bet you've already been to the palace, haven't you?"

I confirmed it with a low "Uh-huh."

Luba stepped forward. "All right, it's time to get on board the drone and get going. Ben and Salma, you two will be in a separate drone. Your contact is a man named Leonardo da Vinci."

Men of the North #7 – THE DANCER

"Oh, maybe he can paint your picture," I joked and squeezed Salma's arm. "Told you they're all named after great men."

The gates swung open and we walked across the border. Salma kept her head high but her fingers bored into my arm and almost without moving her lips she whispered, "I'm scared, Willow. Where is Ben?"

"You'll be fine. My brother and several of my friends are Northlanders. They are good people."

"Ben," I called out to him and he came running, which made his puffy hair sway back and forth.

"I'm right here, my jewel." Being slightly out of breath, he hooked his arm under Salma's and led her forward. Like me, he had bags that hovered just above the ground and followed the GPS in his wristband.

"Can Willow stay with us?" Salma asked and kept me close.

Ben looked back to Kerry and Luba, who were walking with the rest of the group. "Yes, that was my plan, but how about I talk with Kerri and Luba about that once we get to the first town? Right now, we're all a bit on edge, and I think it's better if we get going."

"It's fine," I assured Salma, who was reluctant to let go of me when I had to steer to the left and she was going to the right.

Ben kept his arm linked to hers. "See, darling, they look like nice people, don't they?"

I scanned the two men in front of the drone that Salma and Ben were headed toward. I didn't blame Salma for being nervous. Even though the larger of the two was smiling at her, it was a different sight than what she was used to in the Motherlands. The men stood tall and with their chests out in a masculine stance. None of them had bright colors or jewelry to soften up their hard appearances, and the dark uniforms and neck tattoos made them look dangerous.

"Willow dear, did you hear me?" Luba called out behind me.

I turned and made eye contact with her.

"You're going on the big drone."

"That's fine." I nodded to emphasize that I'd understood and moved into the line of people getting onboard. The drone was similar to the one that I'd flown in ten years ago when my class had gone on a weeklong field trip to the Motherlands.

After we were all seated, ten policemen came in. One of them spoke up. "Welcome to the Northlands."

Everyone replied with polite smiles and thanked him.

"My name is Cameron and if you're on this drone, I'm in charge of your security. There are only three main rules that we need you to follow." The large brusque-looking man held up a hand and counted on his fingers. "One: Stay with the group. Two: Tell one of us security personnel immediately if someone is harassing you. And three: Keep an eye on your colleagues. If someone is missing, alert us right away."

We all nodded our heads and Cameron did a last head count and found his seat before the drone took off.

I wrote a quick message to Hunter letting him know that I had arrived in the Northlands by sending him a picture from the large drone. "Going on a field trip again. See you soon."

Hunter sent me back a photo from his locker room showing me his muddy shoes. "Last training for the season. Two hours in drenching rain. I should have become a dancer instead."

I stared at the picture, enlarging the background where one of his teammates was changing. I couldn't see his face, but he was naked and it made me a bit flustered. I looked around to make sure no one had seen it.

Delete it, the Motlander part of me whispered in my head, but the Northlander part of me looked a little longer.

I liked big, muscular men and I wondered for a second if Solomon looked like this now.

Don't think about him, I ordered myself and sat back in my seat. *This is a new start. It's my chance to make new memories in the Northlands.* The promise of a fun adventure ahead had me smiling. This was perfect. For as long as I could remember, I had felt restless. The hours I danced at the local theater and the lessons I gave children on occasion were my highlights.

I had friends that were nice and caring, but few of them understood the sarcasm and irony that I'd picked up while living in the Northlands. Some of them were curious about the years I'd lived at the school, but I could never explain it right and their attention span was short anyway.

The sad truth was that I was twenty-two and carrying around an undefined feeling of being restless and lost.

I moved my head and saw one of the police officers staring at me. He turned his gaze away but my feminine pride was awakened. In the Motherlands, men didn't look at me that way and although he wasn't my type, it dawned on me that this would be my first journey into the Northlands without my brother as my protector. I was a single woman entering a land with ten million men. The thought alone was both frightening and exhilarating.

When the guard looked over again I didn't look at him but my mouth flirted with a small smile.

CHAPTER 8
Kingston

Solomon

I stood outside the hotel, waiting for Leo and Zasquash to arrive with the songbird that we were babysitting for the next four weeks. It was raining and I was already annoyed with the situation. A man crossed to the other side of the street instead of passing me. I was used to others finding me intimidating, and with the deep scowl on my face I probably looked like I was contemplating something evil.

I wasn't.

In my head, thoughts of how miserable I would be following some little Motlander around for a month were running amok. I preferred to stay away from large crowds of people, and now I'd have to suck it up and deal with her performing her concerts before thousands of people. No more sleeping in the wild or running in the forest. I sighed and shifted my weight from one foot to the other. Leo, Zasquash, and I would have to find a way to divide the hours between us. If I didn't get my exercise and some alone time, I'd be cranky as hell.

My wristband beeped and I accepted the message.

"Look up, fucker."

I leaned my head back but didn't see any drone in the sky.

A loud whistle made me take a step forward and turn around to look up. Zasquash was waving his hands at me five stories up. "They have roof parking."

I waved back at him. So much for Leo telling me to meet them in front of the hotel. With a last deep sigh, I made my way inside and waited in the foyer until Leo and Zasquash came out of the lift with a man and a woman between them.

"Hey, you skunk. Glad to see you decided to join us." Zasquash was smiling.

"What did you do?" I frowned at how different he looked.

"Nothing," he whispered as he not at all subtly moved his eyeballs toward the female, whom I recognized from her picture as Salma Rose.

"Ahh." I didn't point out that Zasquash, whose beard had been down to his collarbone yesterday, now had only stubble and that his hair was braided back making my friend seem like a tamed version of the man I knew. At least he was still wearing his dark uniform like me.

"Let me introduce you to Ben and Salma." Leo swung a hand and looked at the two Motlanders. "This is the infamous Solo that we were talking about."

They both leaned their heads back and gaped a little as they looked up at me.

"Nice to meet you both."

Salma Rose collected herself first as she reached out her hands to me, but then reconsidered and pulled them back. "I'm sorry. Willow told me not to touch you."

I was stunned. "What did you say?"

"We flew up here with an expert and she explained about your strict laws. She told me not to touch you."

My heart was hammering. "Willow Darlington?"

"Yes. The dancer."

"Why wasn't she on the list?" Zasquash gave Leo a blameful look.

I focused on Salma, pointing a finger to my chest. "Did Willow tell you to specifically not touch *me*?"

"Do you know Willow?"

"Yes. We were… ehm… classmates."

Ben and Salma broke into large smiles. "How wonderful. She'll be so excited to see you again. She spoke very fondly of her time here in the Northlands."

"So, I take it she wasn't talking about me specifically, but all Nmen?" I asked again because the thought that Willow somehow felt possessive of me made me dizzy.

"Yes, it was a general recommendation. She said if I touched you Nmen it could lead to a misunderstanding and someone getting hurt."

"Oh." My shoulders fell. "I see. Yeah, she's right. Don't touch anyone. It's better that way."

"As I said." Leo smacked my shoulder while looking at the Motlanders. "You're in good hands with Solo, Zasquash, and me."

Salma kept close to Ben but inclined her head with a courteous "Thank you, Leo."

"Of course. Let's get you settled in to your rooms. I was told you'll be on the fifth floor with most of the other performers."

I had to be sure I'd heard them right and took a small step closer. "Did you say that Willow is part of the tour as well?"

Ben confirmed. "Yes, she should be here any minute."

"Then let's get you to your rooms before this place gets busy." Leo gestured with his chin. "Solo, would you mind getting the codes to their rooms?"

I walked over to the small reception desk and was surprised to see a real human.

"What can I help you with?" the man asked.

"Ehm... I need the codes for some rooms."

"Can you give me names, please?"

"Salma Rose and Ben... ehm, I'm not sure about his last name."

"I don't have a Ben on the list, but I do have Salma Rose in our royal suite, where there's three bedrooms." The man spoke with excitement. "We never used to have the need for hotel suites that size, but more and more Nmen have wives and children now."

"Uh-huh." I leaned on the counter. "How come you don't have bots to do this sort of work?"

A sly smile spread on his face. "The police said that only people who had a function could be present, so I figured that I might as well be helpful and give you all a warm welcome."

I shrugged. "As long as you know what you're doing."

His smile stiffened a little. "I'm the owner of this hotel. Personal service is a what sets us apart from other places." The older man kept sending stolen glances in Salma's direction. "She's the singer, isn't she?"

I positioned myself so as to block his view of her. "All you need to know is that she's under *my* protection."

"I was only asking."

My face was stern. "And now you know."

His tone turned a bit sour. "Do you prefer to do face recognition or fingerprints?"

"Can't I just get some codes?"

"No."

"Fine. I guess face recognition will work."

"Great. Then all I need is for each of the guests who'll be using the room to come over here and get set up in the system. It'll only take a second."

I turned around to wave my group over and after setting it up, the owner of the hotel gave Salma a sugarcoated smile.

"If there's anything I can do to make your stay more pleasant, please let me know."

"Yup. You can count on it," Zasquash said while Ben thanked the owner of the hotel.

More people filled the foyer and my eyes were scanning for Willow. Being taller than everyone else in the room, I had a full overview. She wasn't there.

"Solo, are you coming?" I wanted to stay in the foyer to see Willow for myself, but Leo was holding the doors open with an annoyed look on his face. "Hurry up."

The suite on the fifth floor was large enough that there was a small living room and three bedrooms. Salma and Ben each got one, and Leo, Zas, and I would share the last room, since we'd be rotating shifts between us.

"Are you sure you don't mind sharing one room?" Ben wrinkled his nose a little. "You'll be sleeping in another man's dirty bedsheets."

Zasquash and I exchanged a look and he laughed a little. "We've done much worse than that."

"Oh, I get it." Ben made suggestive eye movements. "I take it you two are more than colleagues?"

"Yeah, we're friends." Zasquash gave a shrug.

Having more experience with Motlanders, I cleared my throat. "I think Ben was asking if we're in a sexual relationship."

Zasquash narrowed his eyes and gave Ben a puzzled look. "Is that what you meant?"

"Well, you implied that you've done more than share each other's dirty bedsheets, so…"

"Fuck no!" Zasquash took a step away from me and swung his hands through the air while looking at Salma. "I'm only interested in women. I just want to clear that up."

"It's fine if you…"

"I'm not!" Zasquash interrupted Ben. "What I meant was that Solo and I have gone without sleep for days, slept on floors, and fucking pine cones. Hell, we've even slept in trees on occasions. We're used to rough conditions and sharing bedsheets isn't one of them."

"There's no need to get upset." Ben kept a polite smile. "Willow told me homosexuality isn't spoken about, so I apologize for assuming."

"Don't worry about it." I put my bag in the shared bedroom. "It used to be something no one spoke about but that is changing. I suppose we have you people to thank for it."

"Did you and Solo really sleep in a tree?" Salma, who hadn't been very talkative, finally opened her mouth to speak.

"Sure."

"Why?" She looked completely baffled.

"Because it was raining hard and it was either that or sleeping in mud."

"Don't you have tents in the Northlands?" If it weren't for Ben's looking genuinely clueless, I would have told him to go fuck himself.

"Yes, we have tents, but Zas and I are Huntsmen. We're special forces. Surviving in the wild and tracking people is our specialty. We don't always have time to set up camp."

"Wow. Aren't you scared of being in a dark forest by yourself?" Salma pulled her sleeves down over her hands. "I heard you have wolves and bears up here. I would be terrified."

Leo gave her a patient smile. "We've been trained to survive in the wild since we were children. That part doesn't scare us. Going on stage like you do and singing to people... now that would freak me out."

"Ohh..." she chuckled. "I don't blame you. I freak out too. I suffer from horrible stage fright."

"Didn't you choose the wrong profession, then?"

"Maybe. But I've learned to cope with it and two minutes into the concert, I'm calm and happy."

"At least being a star makes you rich, right?" Zasquash took a seat on the living room sofa.

Ben, who came out from his bedroom, leaned against the door frame. "We're both rich."

"Awesome." Zasquash grinned. "Good for you, Ben."

I rolled my eyes and addressed my friend. "He means that in the Motherlands they don't have income the way we do. No one is rich, and no one is poor."

"Right. I knew that," Zasquash claimed and held his head high.

I doubted it. It was more likely that he didn't want to appear uninformed. "They have a point system and each individual can only have so many. If you contribute in a way that earns you more points than you need then you are rewarded with the joy of deciding who you want to give your excess points to."

"They force you to give away your points?" Zasquash moved to the edge of his seat starring at Ben. "And you let them?"

Ben chuckled. "An individual serves the community so the community can support the individual."

"Say what?"

"It's the motto of the Motherlands," Salma explained to Zasquash, whose whole face was scrunched up as if they were offering him maggots for dinner. "We live by the big five. No killing, no greed, no borders, no pollution, and equality for all."

Zasquash turned his head and gave Leo and me a troubled look. "I thought the brainwashing was just a rumor. That shit sounds like the world's biggest sect."

Ben and Salma laughed. "We're no more brainwashed than you are. It's just a different way of living."

Zasquash leaned back in the sofa again, spread his arms on the back of it, and placed his right ankle on top of his left knee. "I think what you have is some fuckery that you were force-fed since childhood. Makes me even happier that I was lucky enough to be born a free man."

"All this talk about cultural differences is fascinating, but our guests have traveled half a day to get here and must be starving." Leo looked down at his wristband. "According to the program, dinner will be served in twenty-five minutes in the downstairs restaurant." He looked up at Salma. "Do you want to eat with the others or do you prefer to order something that you can eat here?"

Salma sat down on a chair and held on to the armrest. "Staying here is fine with me."

Ben moved over and squatted down in front of her. "Sweetie, everyone will expect you to show up." He lowered his voice. "If you don't some might think you're arrogant."

Salma bit her lip. "It's just that it's a lot of people."

"I know. But you can do it."

Leo and I exchanged a look, confused about why eating dinner with her fellow performers would be a problem for Salma.

She rubbed her face. "Maybe if I take a minute to rest first."

"That's a great idea." Ben got up and offered his hand to pull her up from the chair.

We watched in silence as Salma walked down the small hallway and closed the door to her bedroom before all three of us turned to Ben.

"What was that about?" Leo pointed to her door.

Ben sighed. "Salma suffers from anxiety. It's not something you have to worry about. I'm here to help her handle it."

"Anxiety?" Zasquash shook his head. "You mean she's scared?"

"Yes."

"Who is she scared of? Tell me and I'll beat the fucker up."

Ben tugged his lips. "I'm afraid it's not that easy. Right now Salma is doing fine. She has been for months, but an attack can happen at any given time and we never get a warning."

I shifted my balance. "But what is she afraid of?"

Ben threw his hands in the air. "Of everything. Of dying, of losing her fans, of falling onstage, of people not liking her, of her family forgetting about her because she travels too much. If it's not one thing, she'll find another to obsess about. Anxiety is like the tricky monster hiding in your brain. It feeds on your worst fears."

I scratched my head. "So, hang on, are you her psychologist or something?"

"No, I'm her manager. I just so happen to love her and I've learned how best to support her as the anxiety progressed."

"You love her?" Zasquash narrowed his eyes. "Does that mean you two are in a relationship?"

"She depends on me."

"Yeah, but does she fuck you?"

Ben frowned and folded his hands in front of him. "Oh, Sweet Nature, you Nmen truly are blunt and crude."

"Yeah, you'll get over it. Just answer my question."

Ben squirmed a bit. "Salma and I share an emotional bond."

A smile grew on Zasquash face. "I take that as a no."

"You would be correct to assume that our relationship is platonic in nature." He brushed invisible dust from his chest and avoided looking at us. "Now, if you don't mind, I'll take a short nap too. It was a long flight." Ben got up and stood there like he was waiting for our permission to be dismissed.

"Go ahead." Leo crossed his arms. "We'll stay here and make sure that no one gets past us."

As soon as Ben closed his door, Leo sat down next to Zasquash while I took the chair.

Leo spoke in a low voice. "What do you think?"

"She's beautiful but clearly a little mental," Zasquash concluded. "Other than that, they seem nice enough."

Leo scratched his ear. "I meant, how do we divide the hours between us?"

"Oh, then why didn't you say that?"

"Are any of you tired now? We have to rotate sleeping."

There was no way I wasn't going down to the dinner. I wanted to see if Willow was there; even while sitting here and listening to Leo talking, my knee was bouncing up and down with impatience.

"We only need one man on duty when she's in here. The hotel is secured from the outside, so the threat is low. The other two can float, eat, or sleep. When she walks around the hotel, I want two of us with her at all times. During concerts we'll all be present."

"I don't mind taking the first night shift," I offered.

"Great. I'll replace you at five. The sound tests aren't until eleven a.m. so you can still get five hours before we have to leave the hotel." Leo turned his head to Zasquash. "With us covering the night shift, you can sleep tonight."

"Thanks, but what about my morning run? I can't function if I don't get some exercise."

Leo leaned back. "Then get up at six and run for an hour. I'll bet a princess like Salma isn't an early riser anyway."

I clapped my hands and got up. "Sounds like we have a plan. Only four weeks to go before this circus is over. How about I run down and check out the dining area? Just to make sure it's safe and secure."

"Good idea." Leo got up with me and looked down at Zasquash. "Ping us when the two Momsies wake up from their beauty sleep. We're going to check out the hotel."

"Hey, Solo."

On my way out the door, I looked back at Zasquash. "What?"

"Look for a pool, will ya?"

I didn't tell him that I was only interested in finding Willow.

CHAPTER 9
Unwanted

Willow

I saw a ghost.

Or at least I reacted as if I saw a ghost.

One moment I was smiling and chatting excitedly in the lift with Morten from the orchestra, whom I had gotten to know on the flight here. The next moment the doors slid open and we walked out, taking only a few steps before I saw Solomon. My body came to a full stop and I froze with my left leg in front of the other, my smiling face turning into an "oh-no" grimace.

From there my nervous system took over. Like an animal coming across a much bigger predator I went into flight mode and pivoted around to get back into the lift. Morten, who had been half a step ahead of me, missed the whole thing. With frantic movements I pushed the panel and pressed myself into the corner. It was stupid, as Solomon had seen me just as well as I'd seen him. My heart pounded and I hissed low, "Come on, come on," as the doors finally slid together.

Ten days ago, I'd confronted Solo by the lake at the reunion but it hadn't left me with the vindicated feeling I'd hoped for. I'd said things that were out of character for me. Things I now felt bad about. That day I'd been fueled by seven years of anger, but I wasn't sure my armor of hate was thick enough to go for a round two with him so soon and definitely not without warning.

A small scream escaped me when a hand appeared and the safety mechanism in the doors made them open again.

"Did you forget something?" Morten popped his head in.

"Ehm... yes. In my room. I forgot something in my room." It was hard to speak with my throat feeling dry and swollen.

"Oh, okay, I'll just see you later then." He moved out of the way so the doors could close.

As the lift began going up and my heart rate went a little down, I thought about the possibility that I was going crazy. Maybe I hadn't seen Solomon. Maybe it was just my brain playing a trick on me. There was no way he could be here. Solomon worked with domestic violence cases. It was probably my unconscious fear of running into him while being in the Northlands that had made me imagine it.

Go down and check again, I told myself, but my legs were like jelly; I needed to sit down and gather myself before going anywhere.

What if he's really here? Did he come to talk with me? Is he stalking me?

My head was spinning with all sorts of emotions from anger to curiosity as I plunked down on the bed in my room.

Enough!

Just go downstairs like an adult and you'll see for yourself that it was just your imagination. He's not really here. And if he is... then... I thought about it. *You'll just tell him to go away.*

I pumped myself up in front of the mirror and when I heard voices in the hallway, I walked out of my room thinking that I'd be safer in a group.

"Oh, hey, Willow. Is that your room?" Ben was coming toward me with an entourage of two Nmen and Salma. "I feel like I've neglected you." He stopped and took my hands. "This makes everything so much easier. We're neighbors."

"How lovely." I hoped my smile looked relaxed.

"Were you heading down to dinner?"

"I was." I waved back at Salma, who called out my name.

"Great." Ben tugged my hand under his arm and turned around to reach for Salma. "Look at me arriving with two goddesses."

I inclined my head in a greeting to the two security guards that I'd seen at the border. They filled out the hallway as they walked side by side.

"Hi, I'm Zasquash," the taller of the two introduced himself. He was the same height as Solomon, and from the way his skin was tanned and weathered I suspected he spent a lot of time outside in the sun.

"It's nice to meet you." I returned his warm smile and noticed the laugh lines around his eyes.

The smaller man was serious and had an aura of authority about him. He had on a police uniform with short sleeves that showed off his tattooed arms, and on his chest was his name "Leo da Vinci."

He greeted me with a short "Hello" while I scolded myself for thinking of him as small. Next to Ben the man looked large and he was more than a head taller than me.

Both of the Nmen stared at me like I was a celebrity that they knew.

"Oh, where are my manners?" Ben chuckled. "This is Willow Darlington." He turned to me. "These gentlemen are here to keep us safe. Leonardo da Vinci and Zasquash... ehm... I don't think I know your last name." Ben was leaning his head back to look up at the huge man, who flashed his teeth at me in another smile.

"Zasquash will do just fine."

I tilted my head. "Is that your real name?"

"Yup."

"And whom were you named after?"

"A famous biker who was known for his loyalty and no-bullshit attitude."

I raised an eyebrow. "And his name was Zasquash?"

"Yup. Bikers had funny names, but it suits me." The large man burst into a contagious grin and elbowed his colleague. "Better to be named after a badass biker than some painter."

Leonardo gave him a pointed stare. "Leonardo da Vinci was a genius. I'm proud to be named after him. And for the record he was much more than a painter. He invented things too." He turned to me. "You can just call me Leo."

I bowed my head again. "May peace surround you, Leo. And of course, the same to you, Zasquash."

Zasquash shifted his balance. "Yeah, peace and quiet to you too, Willow. We've heard a lot about you."

"You have?" I was going to ask from where when Ben pulled me along.

"Dinner is waiting."

My head turned back and questions were on my tongue. Had Ben and Salma talked about me? Had Solomon?

"Make sure that I sit with you and Willow," Salma whispered to Ben in the lift.

I smiled at her and noticed that her fingers pressed into Ben's arm as if she was nervous and clinging to him.

Zasquash exited the lift first and stood like a wall of a man on the side while we walked out. Most of the other performers were already gathered in the foyer and many smiled and waved at Salma, who was by far the biggest star among us.

I more sensed than saw her insecurity and stepped quickly to her side. There was no sign of Solomon and I calmed my crazy thoughts, telling myself that Zasquash could have heard about me from one of my many friends here in the Northlands. I was tired after a long flight and it was possible that I had taken some other Nman for Solomon.

"This way." Luba, one of the organizers, waved her hand. "Dinner will be served in here. It's a buffet, so help yourself."

"How about you two find a place to sit and I'll get us something to eat," Ben offered Salma and me before looking over his shoulder. "Leo, would you and Zasquash be so kind as to assist the ladies to a table while I get them some food?"

I didn't appreciate being treated like a fragile flower. "It's okay, I can get my own food."

Ben nudged me with his hand in the small of my back. "I know, but Salma would enjoy your company and it's easier this way."

Salma looked up at me with her beautiful gray eyes. "He's right. I get nervous around strangers."

I conceded and followed Leo, who led the way to a table in the corner of the large dining room. "This should do." He waited until we were sitting down before rocking back on his feet. "Enjoy."

"Won't you and Zasquash eat with us?"

"No. There's no real food on that buffet anyway. It's all vegetarian. We'll eat when you're back in your rooms." He nodded his head and walked to stand by the wall where he could keep an eye on things.

Salma leaned closer to me and held a hand to her mouth before she spoke. "They're different than I expected."

"The Nmen?"

"Uh-huh. Less savage."

I couldn't help a glance in Zasquash's direction. The man might have a warm smile, but he had an aura of danger around him and I wasn't sure Nmen got more savage than him.

"What did you expect?"

"I don't know. They seem more educated and civil than I thought they'd be. I mean except for their crude words and large bodies they're not that different, are they?"

I laughed. "Oh, they're different for sure. You just don't know them that well."

"But we had a nice conversation about cultural differences. It was nice and they weren't aggressive in any way."

"Aggressive? Why would they be aggressive? Their job is to protect you."

A line formed between Salma's eyebrows. "I know. My therapist said the same thing."

"You have a therapist?"

"Yes. It's because I suffer from anxiety. Ana, my therapist, said that this tour would be a great way to prove to myself that I can do anything."

I placed my hand over hers and squeezed it. "I think she's right. We can do much more than we think we can."

Salma's eyebrows flew up. "Do you have anxiety too?"

"No. I mean except from the occasional PMS breakdown, I'm fine."

She smiled. "That's nice. I wouldn't wish what I have on my worst enemy. Anxiety has ruined my life."

I blinked at the harshness of her words and the intensity in her eyes. "But you're so successful."

"Here you go, ladies. I brought you a little bit of everything." Ben arrived with two plates full of salad, and bread, pies, and some tofu. "They have fruit, chocolate cake, and sorbet ice cream for dessert if you're interested."

I reached out for the plate that he handed me and thanked him. "I'm not used to being pampered like this."

"Happy to help." With the plates set in front of Salma and me he dried off his hands. "All right. If you're all set, I'll get myself a plate too."

"Go ahead," Salma encouraged him and looked down when two people from the orchestra approached our table. They swerved away and chose a different table.

"Hmm, that's odd. I thought they were going to join us."

Salma sighed. "It's me. Not you."

"What do you mean?"

She picked up a cherry tomato and looked at it with a sad expression. "Meeting new people is difficult for me. I get insecure and look down or away. People think I'm arrogant, but I'm really just..." She trailed off as her shoulders lifted in a sigh.

"Scared," I finished for her.

"Yeah." She met my eyes and popped the tomato in her mouth. "Did you think I was arrogant today when you met me?"

"No. I thought you were warm and kind."

Salma's whole face lit up. "You did?"

"You were very different from what I expected."

"Because you've heard that I'm a diva?"

I didn't deny it, but just nodded a little and took a bite of my spinach pie.

"Sometimes I get nervous before a concert and I take it out on the people around me." Salma picked up her piece of bread and pulled it apart. "That's why I like to have Ben around. He knows not to take it personally. I don't mean the things I say. It's just my fear speaking."

"I'll remember that if you take it out on me."

We ate in silence for a few minutes, both lost in our thoughts, and then she dropped the bomb.

"Did you meet your classmate yet?"

My fork stalled mid-air. "What classmate?"

Salma looked around. "I don't see him right now, but one of your old classmates works as security on the tour. He was just as huge as Zasquash. Dark blond hair and blue eyes."

Men of the North #7 – THE DANCER

"Solo. Was his name Solo?" I wasn't blinking and my voice was trembling.

"Yeah. I think so. Wait a minute. You don't look happy."

My heart was pumping fast and my eyes were darting around searching for him. "No, I'm not happy. I *hate* him." It sounded immature and dramatic, but I couldn't help myself. When it came to Solomon I had to protect my heart.

Salma pulled back. "You hate him. Why?"

"It's a long story."

"Oh, I'm sorry, Willow. I can tell you're upset."

Craning my neck, I couldn't see him anywhere. "If he's supposed to be security, why isn't he here?"

"They take shifts, I think."

Leaning back in my chair, I folded my arms in front of me, my foot tapping.

"Are you okay, Willow?"

"No!" I was ready to scream in frustration. "Just promise me that if you do have an anxiety attack and Solo is around you take it out on him. He deserves every foul word you can think of."

Salma stared at me with her eyebrows lifted up high. "Wow, Willow, are you sure you don't suffer from anxiety yourself? You sound as angry as me when I'm scared."

"Do I? Huh. Is this really the worst you can get?" To everyone else but Salma, I would look mad to my bone, but of course she was spot on. I was scared.

Solo was my weakness. What if I fell in love again and let Solo come between Hunter and me. I couldn't allow that to happen. My pulse was racing. Why was Solomon here? And why hadn't Pearl warned me?

"They should have told me he'd be here. I would have never agreed to go on this stupid tour if I'd known he would be around."

"Who are *they*?" Salma's whole body was turned toward me now.

"Pearl and Lord Khan. They were the ones asking me to take Lily Rose's spot." My jaw tensed. "They *know* we have history."

"Who does?"

"Me and Solo," I said with a tone of annoyance. "They *know* how much I hate him. And they also know the reason why."

"Oh, I see. But you don't want to share what happened between you two?"

Ben returned but stopped with his plate in his hands. "Don't you like the things I picked for you?" He pointed with his thumb over his shoulder. "I can get something else if you'd like."

"No, it's not the food." I found it hard to look at him, being as mad as I was. This was supposed to be my chance for a new beginning and then Solomon was destroying everything, again.

Sitting down, Ben gave Salma a questioning look. "I thought you two were doing fine together. What happened?"

"It wasn't me." Salma's hands flew up in the air. "I didn't yell at her or anything."

I pushed the plate away and got up. "I'm sorry but I lost my appetite."

Both Ben and Salma were looking up at me, he in complete bewilderment and she with concern.

"What are you going to do?"

"I'm going to find Solo and tell him to leave right now."

"Maybe you should wait until you're not angry anymore. Words might slip out that you'll regret later," she warned.

"I don't care. If I don't confront him now, I'll be hiding in my room and *I refuse to do that.*"

Ben placed his hand on my elbow. "Sweet Willow, I'm not sure what this is about, but maybe it's better to meditate a little to clear your mind."

I exhaled harshly. "No. My fight trainer, Marco, once told me that anger can be a fuel and that attack is sometimes the best defense. I'm going to find Solo right now."

Salma and Ben exchanged a concerned look and then her eyes caught something behind me and she spoke low. "Looks like you don't have to look far. He's coming this way."

I spun around and all color left my face. The same old flight response was making my spine feel like a burning fuse.

There he was. Big and mighty, walking through the room like he owned it with his eyes fixed on me.
Toxic. Bad. Handsome. Dangerous. My thoughts were in a big jumble and I clenched my hands into painful fists along my sides in a desperate attempt to center myself before facing off with Solo one more time.

CHAPTER 10
The Threat

Solomon

"Hey." My face was stern as I waited for Willow to greet me back.

She didn't.

"Can I talk to you?"

Willow gave a stiff nod, so I gestured for her to go first and ignored the way the other Motlanders were staring at us.

As soon as we were outside in the foyer again, I led her around a corner and into an empty gym with a mat for fighting.

"What are you doing here?" Her words were harsh and direct.

I closed the door and turned to face her. "I didn't know you'd be one of the performers."

"You want me to believe that?"

My eyes narrowed. "Have I ever lied to you?"

"Pearl would have warned me." The way she took a step back as if I was a fucking threat to her made my throat burn. "Did you ask to come on the tour because you knew I'd be here?"

"No!" My voice rose a little from the overload of emotions raging inside me. "I wasn't given a fucking choice. Do you think I'd go looking for you after you told me that you hate me and wish me dead?"

Distrust was all over her face.

"Magni ordered me and Zas to join the security team. I'm doing my job, nothing else."

"Why? There's plenty of police. They don't need you here and *I don't want* you here."

My nostrils were flaring a little. It was surreal to face off with Willow like this and see her face twisted in resentment and anger. She was like an evil twin of the woman I'd once thought of as my mate and best friend. "My assignment isn't to protect *you*. I'm here to protect Salma Rose." It wasn't true, because although Salma Rose was my main focus, I had an obligation to protect all the Motlanders.

"Others can protect Salma Rose. It doesn't have to be you. You're not a policeman anyway."

I pushed out a huff of irritation. "Don't you think I wonder why I was ordered to be here? As far as I'm concerned Magni assigned me to this torturous mission as another fucking punishment and nothing else."

"Oh, so being around me is torture, is it?"

I groaned and dropped my head with exasperation. "Believe me, there are plenty of other things I'd rather be doing than fucking babysitting Momsies for a month."

"Don't call us Momsies, that's rude."

I was getting tired of her scolding me. "Welcome to the Northlands, we're fucking rude and obnoxious. You used to love that about us."

She leaned forward. "I used to love a lot of things that I now loathe. Some of us learn from our mistakes while others don't. I heard you made it your living to hurt and kill people, but I guess that was always what you did best, anyway."

Inside I was boiling with anger. Willow had no fucking clue what she was talking about. But years of training at suppressing my emotions paid off and I kept my face impassive. That only made her dig her knife deeper into my heart to get a reaction.

"How do you even sleep at night with what you've done?"

Every muscle in my body tensed up and my lips screwed together with my jaw so clenched that I couldn't answer her at first. When I finally spoke, my voice was hoarse and full of suppressed rage. "I protect women and their children from men who aren't worthy of them. I push large men against the wall and choke them so they can feel small for a change and see how they like it. I turn the abuse on the abuser."

Willow raised an eyebrow. "And if a man rapes his wife, then what? Do you rape him too?"

I growled low. "If a man rapes his wife, I kill him."

"So it's true? You've killed men?"

"Yes." I turned so she couldn't see me close my eyes. But there was no shutting out the imprint those eight men had left on me. Their faces flashed like projections on my eyelids, and I had to push dark memories back to the troubled corner of my soul where I kept them locked away.

"That makes you a murderer."

The judgment in her voice had me turn to stare at her. "No, Willow, it makes me a soldier, something you Motlanders will never understand." I hated to see the disapproval on her face. I wasn't some monster. Why couldn't she see that I was one of the good guys?

"You have to leave, Solo."

I didn't answer her.

"Surely, you can see that we can't both stay, and since I have a show to perform, you're the one who has to leave."

For Willow to judge me saddened me, but for her to think she was in a position to order me around provoked me. "I've never abandoned an assignment in my life. Until Commander Magni tells me to leave, I'm staying."

"Then call Magni up and tell him there's been a misunderstanding. Maybe he didn't know I was coming on the tour."

"I'm not calling Magni." My voice was firm. "You can go home or stay if you'd like. I don't care either way."

Willow scoffed. "You're such a bad liar."

My tone was flat as I turned back to the door. "You do you and I do me."

Willow made an outburst behind me. "Don't you see that the two of us being on this tour is a disaster?"

I shrugged and pretended not to care.

"There's no way we're both staying on this tour. Do you hear me? I'll find a way to get you reassigned." There was desperation in her tone.

I had my hand on the door handle but waited for her to finish.

"I'll tell Salma that I can't stay if you do. Being the star of the show, I'll bet she can have Magni remove you just like that." She snapped her fingers. "And until it happens you'd better stay away from me."

My hands gripped tighter around the door handle but I refused to look at her. "Why would I come near you? This might surprise you, Willow, but after seeing how much you've changed I'm no more interested in you than you are in me." A taste of acid spread in my mouth and my chest felt two sizes too small, as if my heart was banging against my rib cage protesting the lie.

Willow's voice lowered in a raw warning, "Just keep your distance or I'll tell the other Nmen that you touched me."

My pupils swelled and my breath stuttered when I turned my face and looked at her with disbelief. This was the woman who had once stepped in front of a gun for me, and now she was threatening to make false claims to have me killed.

She didn't waver but kept the hard expression on her face.

Feeling nauseated and shocked to my core, I went straight to the men's restroom. I needed a place to be alone for a second. To recover and think.

Willow truly hates me. Part of me had excused her harsh words from the reunion, telling myself that she had spoken in anger, but this time she had accused me of being a murderer and threatened to accuse me of touching her without permission. I pressed my head against the cool wall of the bathroom stall, assaulted by her words that she would set me up and her harsh statement from the reunion, which played in my mind again.

There is no pact. All there is left between us are painful memories and a deep feeling of hate. I will never forgive you for what you did...

My eyes were closed and I planted my hand next to my forehead, pushing out from the wall with a deep sigh. She had told me there were days when she wished the soldiers had killed me back then.

I knew how to fight large men with sharp weapons who wanted to hurt me. I had no clue how to defend myself against a woman who wished me dead. If she went ahead with telling the other men that I'd touched her, they would believe her. Especially with our history. Being alone with her had been a major mistake that I could never allow to happen again.

If there was a shred left of the Willow I'd once known, she'd regret it if her actions caused a man to be executed. Even if that man was me. My head felt heavy as I concluded that I had to protect Willow from herself. Maybe I should request Magni to reassign me but knowing the Commander, he would only double down on my punishment. The best I could hope for was that Willow would succeed in demanding me gone.

"Solo, are you in here?"

The sound of Zasquash's voice had me flush the toilet and yell out, "What is it?"

Men of the North #7 – THE DANCER

"You're on."

I opened the door to the stall and walked out to wash my hands. "I'll be right there."

"Good." Zasquash flexed his right biceps in the mirror with a small grin. "It takes fuel to keep this perfection going, you know? I gotta feed my beast."

He was referring to his always-hungry stomach and normally, I would have fired back at him. Today, I couldn't engage in the friendly banter that always ran between us. I was too rattled from Willow's threat.

"Hey, are you okay?"

"Yeah. I'm good. Go feed your beast and I'll babysit the songbird." It was a lame attempt to sound like myself but it got me out of the bathroom without him drilling deeper.

With my head heavy from dark thoughts, I stepped into the dining room and walked over to Leo. "I'm taking over for Zasquash."

He gave a small nod. "I know. I told him to find you."

The room was full of Motlanders eating, talking, and walking to and from the buffet of food. I took a moment to observe them in their strange fashions.

"They're very colorful."

Leo gave a low "Uh-huh."

"Do you think we look as strange to them as they do to us?"

Leo turned his head to me. "You more than me. I think they see you as a freak with your size and all."

I'd taken my limit of shit from people today and fired back at him. "It's not my fault they're all so freaking small. They look like children to me."

"Huh. Even that guy with the strange mustache? Or what about that guy who has hair down to his behind? Do they look like children to you?"

"They do," I insisted. "They need to pack on some weight and muscles. Even our teen boys have wider shoulders." My chin gestured to a man in an orange vest and tight shorts. "Some of them look so fragile I'd be afraid to whistle around them out of fear they would blow away."

Leo gave a vague smile. "I've been wondering though; maybe it's because these are all musicians and singers. I mean, Willow is the only dancer. I heard that a whole dance group bailed out at the last minute."

"What's your point?"

"My point is that these are musicians and they're probably not the most athletic of Motlanders. There must be other men who are muscular – I mean they have sport stars like us, right?"

"Only if you count soccer, tennis, drone races, dancing, ice-skating, and that sort of thing. They don't have any real contact sports like football, ice hockey, rugby, or basketball."

"Soccer *is* a contact sport."

I scoffed, giving him a dose of the irritation and frustration from my conversation with Willow. "Not their version. They aren't even allowed to head the ball or anything."

"Why the hell not?"

"Because they claim it can cause brain cells to die."

Leo laughed. "If that's true it explains a lot."

Salma, who had been sitting and talking with Ben, pushed her chair back and the movement made both Leo and me pay attention.

"She's returning to her room." Leo waited for Salma to get closer before he opened the door for her. She was just about to walk through when a fellow Motlander approached her.

"I love your songs. I'm a huge fan."

Salma gave the man a wide but rather stiff smile. "That's so kind of you to say."

"May peace follow you and may your songs continue to bring joy."

"Thank you." Salma waved at him but hurried out the door.

I kept in the back and let Leo lead the way to the lift, where a small group of performers were waiting.

"Salma Rose, can I have a picture with you?" a female performer asked and when Salma nodded, the woman signaled for her three friends to be part of it too.

"We're in the Floral Choral," the woman explained before posing for the picture.

Salma was polite. "That's wonderful. I can't wait to hear your choir sing on stage."

"Come on." Leo was holding the doors to the lift open.

After Ben and Salma got in, I took up as much space as I could. The lift was big enough to have included the singers from the choir, but I was there to protect Salma Rose and it didn't take a genius to figure out that she got nervous around people. The four singers would have to wait.

After the doors closed Ben asked me about Willow. "We waited for her, but she didn't come back after talking with you."

I kept my face toward the doors and spoke in a flat tone. "I'm guessing Willow returned to her room."

"Was she all right?" There was concern in Salma's voice.

"She was fine. I didn't hurt her if that's what you think."

"How was the buffet?" Leo saved me from further inquisition by making casual small talk with Ben and Salma about their favorite vegetarian dishes.

As we exited the lift and walked down the hallway to the suite, Ben yawned. "We have a long day tomorrow with rehearsals and our first show. Salma and I are going to enjoy a quiet night."

Leo kept going. "Whatever you like."

Salma stopped one door before the suite we were in and knocked on it. "I'm just going to check in on Willow before I go in."

Still reeling from Willow's threat, I hurried by and told Leo in passing, "I'll search the suite to make sure it's clear."

The last thing I heard before I walked into the suite was Willow's voice sounding friendly and soft. The way she had sounded when she spoke to me in the past. Back when we had been madly in love.

CHAPTER 11
Soft Words

Year 2440 – Seven years earlier
Solomon

"Willow." I stroked her shoulder and lifted a lock of her hair out of her face. She looked so peaceful in her sleep. "I brought you some berries to eat."

Lifting her hand, she rubbed her eyes before she opened them and gave me a small smile. "Did you say berries? I didn't hear you leave."

"I've only been gone for ten minutes."

Willow crawled out of the small improvised bivouac I had built to keep us dry from last night's rain. "How long did we sleep?"

"About five hours." I didn't tell her that I'd been awake most of the night, listening for dangers and making sure her body was covered from the rain.

"You're soaked." She lifted her hand and touched my hair.

"You should eat, Willow." I held out the berries to her.

She took a few. "Did you eat already?"

"Yes. These are for you."

"We can't live off berries, Solo." A line of worry formed between her eyebrows. "You've lost a lot of weight."

"It's just until we're sure they're no longer following us. Then we can light a fire and I can cook us something more filling. Rabbit stew tastes really good, you'll see."

Willow took some more berries and looked down. "I don't think I can eat rabbit, Solo. It's not right."

"But you ate meat that time at the Happy Cow, remember?"

"That was engineered meat. No cow had to die for us to eat it. How would you make rabbit stew without killing a rabbit?"

Raising my hand, I tucked another strand of her hair behind her ear and leaned in to kiss her lips. "Then I'll make you a green stew of some kind. You'll see, it will be all right."

Willow popped the three last berries in her mouth and caressed my cheek, giving me another of those loving looks that always melted everything inside of me.

"I love you." Her words were soft and sincere.

"I love you more."

We leaned our foreheads against each other and just sat like that for a few seconds.

"Willow, there's a river close by. We'll build a raft and go as far as the river will take us. It will be easier on you than hiking all day."

"Can we wash ourselves first?"

"Yes."

She pulled back. "Do we have time? Last night you said we should push through, and if we've slept for five hours they might be catching up to us.

"I know. But it'll take me a while to build the raft. You'll have time to fill our water bottles, wash yourself, and maybe wash some of our clothing too."

"I would like that."

I bit my lip. "Okay, but just stick to a few essentials. We'll have to hang them on our backpacks to dry."

Willow helped me carry the bivouac to the river, where I used parts of it to make a raft. We erased the most obvious traces of our night spent here. After eight days on the run she was becoming good at it.

The stream of water was cold but nice and refreshing. Our backpacks stood on the side and the morning sun was coming through the treetops creating that magical glow that I loved so much. When the basic raft was done I took a minute to wash myself too.

Willow stood in her panties and bra with water reaching her waist. The current was strong and I kept an eye on her, afraid she'd lose her footing. Her hands were busy washing some of our clothes and I admired the view of her toned body with the soft curves that I'd never get enough of. She had mosquito bites on her arms and thighs and last night they had been driving her insane. Now that she was distracted she seemed to have forgotten about them. Willow looked over and smiled. It felt like the sun came out, and I thought she was the most beautiful young woman the world had ever seen. Her long hair was wet from before when she'd dipped under the water and washed it. Joy erupted inside me knowing that from now on it would be me and Willow together. I just had to find a place for us to build our new life away from the adults that tried to control us.

"How sore are you?" I asked when I saw Willow place a hand on her back and stretch backward.

"I'm not used to running and walking this much." She smiled at me. "I'm not complaining, though. It's worth it to be here with you."

I had been squatting in the water, washing myself, but now I got up and walked over to touch her, my black briefs dripping with all the water they had soaked up. "Are you sure?"

Willow tilted her head back and looked up at me. "Yes, I'm sure." She wrapped her arms around my waist, the wet fabric in her hands falling down my backside.

"I want to give you the world," I whispered and kissed her.

Her smile widened. "We'll create our own world."

"That's right."

A bright sunbeam hit us as if someone in the sky had been searching for us and now shone a projector on us. It was nice and warmed our cold bodies.

Willow pressed up against me, kissing my collarbone. "I'm sorry about last night. I think I fell asleep while we were kissing, didn't I?"

"Don't worry about it."

"I'm sorry. I was just so tired. Maybe today it'll be different and we can try something new."

My arms wrapped around her back and I leaned my head on her hair. "It's okay. We have all the time in the world. There's no need to rush anything."

"But I like making out with you. Maybe we can try again?"

"Now?" My voice cracked. I hated when that happened. It was rare now that I was seventeen but Willow began to chuckle, her head still leaning against my chest.

"Wow, Solo, your heart just began hammering. I could literally hear it." She grabbed for my hand and brought it to the same spot her ear had been. "Do you feel it?"

"Yes."

"Feel my heart." Willow's mesmerizing green eyes blinked as she steered my hand to her chest.

"Yeah, your heart beats fast too."

She smiled and with her hand around my wrist she pulled my hand a bit to the right. I took her hint and cupped her breast. Eight days on the run had made it smaller, but Willow was a goddess in my eyes and my rock-hard erection, which began poking her belly, spoke volumes of my attraction to her.

"Are you sad that we won't have an official wedding ceremony?" Willow asked.

I drew in a deep breath. "Yes. I would have liked that. We may not be old enough or ever get the official ceremony that others have, but we're choosing each other and risking everything to be together. That should count for something."

She tilted her head. "We could make our own ceremony."

I laughed. "We're not old enough to marry yet."

With a smile she raised an eyebrow. "I'm almost sixteen and since we're not doing it the official way anyway, who says that we have to wait?" Willow took my hand and made her way through the water, looking over her shoulder. "Come on."

I helped her climb the rocks to get back to where we had left our backpacks. The place was full of wildflowers, ferns, and tall grass.

"Here." Willow led me ten steps to a large oak tree where the ground was covered by a soft layer of moss. "This spot is perfect."

I wasn't sure what she was planning to do, so I followed her lead. When she turned to me and lifted her hands, I took them.

"You start," she said with a serious expression on her face.

"Ehh... I'm not sure what to say."

"Something ceremonial."

"Okay." I thought for a second. "Willow, I have loved you from the first time I saw you. I would live anywhere in the world and survive on maggots and water if it meant I could be with you."

She wrinkled her nose up. "Eww, that's disgusting."

"Yeah. Let me try again." I looked down, biting my lip. "Okay, how about this? I'm strong enough to win any tournament I chose to participate in, but I'd give up a million dollars and a Northlander bride in the blink of an eye to be with you. Even if it means giving up everything else in my life too. Willow, a life without you is the most depressing thought. I love you so much it physically hurts sometimes."

She smiled and squeezed my hands. "I liked that one better. Now it's my turn." With a thoughtful expression, she turned her face against the sky for a second before looking deep into my eyes. "There are two Willows. The one that exists and the one that lives. The second only truly comes out around you, Solo. I know because when you left the school, I felt like a piece of me was missing. I could be surrounded by people and never feel truly happy. You are my soulmate."

I was touched and moved in to kiss her. "You're my soulmate too."

She laughed a little. "Of course I am, silly. You can't be soulmates with someone if they don't feel it too."

For a moment, we stood with our hands linked, big smiles on our faces, and eyes twinkling with endless love.

"Willow, will you marry me?"

She beamed a wide smile at me. "Yes, I will."

I walked a few steps and picked up a stalk of long grass. "Here, let this be a symbol of the commitment we're making to each other today. From now on, we'll be husband and wife." I wrapped the grass around her finger and tied a knot. Butterflies were flying a victory round in my stomach.

Willow held up her hand with the ring made of grass. "I love it, it's my favorite color."

I laughed with her. "Good, I picked it out just for you."

Hugging me tight, Willow whispered into my ear, "Husband."

Goose bumps spread down my arms and my head exploded with euphoria as I squeezed her body and said the magical word, "Wife."

"Remember what you told me?"

"About what?" I asked and kissed her along her jawline.

Men of the North #7 – THE DANCER

"About a marriage not being valid until it's been consummated." Willow pulled back and looked at me. "I want our marriage to be real."

My Adam's apple bobbed in my throat and I could hardly breathe. "You sure about that?"

She wasn't moving, just watching me with wide eyes as if expecting me to take the lead.

With fumbling fingers and my heart racing, I pushed her hair back and kneeled down in front of her, kissing her belly and waist while my hands rested on her hips.

Willow's fingers weaved through my hair and when I looked up to meet her eyes she gave me a smile. The idea that we were about to have sex for the first time filled me with nervous excitement.

My hand trailed up her waistline to the outline of her right breast and my mouth followed up to lick her skin. Pulling her top up over her head, I took a deep breath, enjoying the sight of Willow's naked chest. "You're so beautiful!"

"You think so?"

I swallowed hard, mesmerized by the two firm globes in front of my eyes, and especially the pink nipples that stood out straight like small light towers leading me home. "There's no one as gorgeous as you, Willow." My head leaned backward looking up at her. I guided her down on the moss underneath me. She followed my movements as I kissed just above the rim of her light blue panties.

When I hooked my fingers around both sides of her soft panties, Willow lifted her behind a little to make it easier for me. I literally felt my mouth watering as I slowly slid them off her. We had made out before and these last few days we had gone from my only touching her on the outside of her clothes to her allowing me to put my hands down her pants. Yet, seeing her bared in front of me with the sweetest triangle of hair was beyond exhilarating. I bowed down and pressed my nose against her pelvis area, breathing in the scent of Willow.

"I'm sorry about the hair."

I lifted my head. "What do you mean?"

"It's normal to have all your body hair permanently removed at the end of your teen years. I was just going to keep a tiny triangle like the women I know, but now that we're here I guess that'll be difficult."

"I'm happy you didn't have it removed. You already have a cute triangle." I planted a kiss on top of her sweet curls and pushed her legs open, continuing my kissing further down.

"Are you going to do that *thing*?"

I smiled at her. Willow and I had talked about sex for as long as I could remember. She had been curious and asked questions that I'd answered to the best of my knowledge, which in all fairness had been limited. After I turned fifteen and left for my current school, my access to sex-bots and porn had helped me get a better grasp on the nuances of sex. "You mean oral?"

"Yes."

I lowered my head and using my fingers to spread her folds, I answered her question with my tongue sliding against her soft skin.

Willow placed a hand across her eyes and made a sound of embarrassment.

"I told you already. It turns me on." I imitated what I'd seen in old porn movies and let my tongue tickle the little rose on top of her pretty pussy.

Willow jerked and lifted her head with her eyes wide open.

I did it again, enjoying the way her body arched up and she let out a moan every time my tongue drew her to a new level of pleasure.

"Do you like it?" I asked and kept licking her.

Her fingers had found my hair and she tightened her hold. "Yes. I didn't know it would feel this good. It sounded so gross when you talked about it."

I laughed low and gently bit her inner thighs, which made her squeal.

"I wouldn't use my teeth if I were you. I have strong leg muscles and your head is in a fragile place." She squeezed her legs around my head.

"Oh yeah?" My hands pushed on the inner side of her knees, opening up her legs again. I gave her a victorious grin. "You didn't think I was weak and defenseless, did you?"

"No." She reached for me, signaling for me to come higher. I moved up to be nose to nose with her. "I like that you're strong." Her hands slid across my shoulders and biceps.

We were smiling at each other and then our smiles morphed into more serious expressions, both of us knowing what the next step would be.

"You're really sure about this?" I asked her again.

Willow nodded, her breathing a bit shallow and fast when I quickly removed my briefs and she saw my cock.

Her hands clasped around my neck when I rolled on top of her. "I'll be careful," I assured her.

"Okay." She sucked in her lips and a line formed between her eyebrows.

"Open your legs wider," I instructed and she raised them up and planted her heels on my behind.

With my heart galloping in my chest, I pressed my cock against her opening and inside.

Willow whimpered under me.

"Relax, babe." I tried again, eager to be inside her but she was too narrow and it hurt her. Pulling back a little I tried making small rocking movements while supporting myself on my forearms and kissing her. "You have to relax."

"I'm trying but it hurts."

Nuzzling my nose against hers, I whispered, "Willow, I love you so much. You are my wife now and I will protect you with my life."

Her hands moved down to my shoulders and she returned my kisses with passion.

My small rocking movements became deeper, like I was working my way in. *Yes. Yes. Yes.* I chanted in my head. *It's happening. It's happening!*

"Are you in?"

"Almost. The tip is in."

"I don't think you'll fit. It already hurts."

"It's going to be okay. Just take a deep breath and focus on our kissing."

Willow and I were in the middle of a deep kiss when a sudden sound made us both stop and turn our heads.

She stiffened underneath me. "What was that?"

I rose up on my hands, still connected with her from my midsection and down. "I don't know."

Another rustling left no doubt that someone or something was in the area. I wanted it to be a deer passing by, but we couldn't take any chances.

"We have to go!"

Like me, Willow got up and worked fast to put on her clothes.

"Stay behind me," I warned her, my eyes constantly looking in the direction of the movements and sounds that we'd heard.

Within a minute we'd put on our clothes and were backing away from the direction the noise had come from. Moving silently down to the river, we placed our backpacks on the raft that I'd built and pushed it into the water.

"Come on," I whispered while holding back the raft in the strong current. Willow got up and the minute I jumped up to sit too, it took off carrying us down the river much faster than we could have run or walked on land.

"This will make it hard for them to find us. Water leaves no trace." It was my attempt at calming Willow down.

Clipping the backpacks to the raft, I was happy that I'd chosen waterproof ones to bring with me.

"Do you think it was an animal?" Willow was staring in the direction we'd come.

I had no doubt the people chasing us would eventually find out where we'd begun our rafting journey, but where we ended it would be more difficult. This was our chance to escape the adults following us once and for all.

"Yes. Tonight, we're eating a hot meal," I promised her with a smile. But then she gasped and I swung my head to see what she saw. In the place where we'd pushed the raft into the water three men were standing looking at us with mud-striped faces. Their uniforms were those of Huntsmen. I knew because for as long as I could remember I'd wanted to grow up and become one of them.

I pulled Willow closer to me. "They don't have a raft and it'll take them time to build one. They won't catch us, I promise."

She looked up at me just as the river took a curve and we were no longer visible to the Huntsmen. "Did you see the look on their faces? They'll kill you, Solo, I know they will."

"Then we'd better not get caught."

The two paddles I'd brought helped us stay in the middle of the river. Last night's heavy rain gave us the speed we needed to put distance between us and the three Huntsmen we'd seen. I kept looking up, expecting to see a drone any time now. They had our position and knew what direction we were going in. With the resources of the Huntsmen, it wouldn't take them long to get soldiers in place waiting to pick us up further down the river, and I feared Magni's large red drone would be hovering above our heads soon. Our only way to escape would be to get out of the water and find a place to hide until it was dark enough for us to not be seen from above. Traveling at night was dangerous. We would have to either run as quiet and fast as we could or get back on the raft and try making it past them. Both seemed to be risky options that I didn't like now that I was responsible for Willow's safety. If we did the night rafting, we'd have to hold on to the raft and stay in the water to be as invisible as possible when we snuck by their posts. It would be physically straining and cold as fuck. In my head I was going over ways to enclose Willow between my arms or maybe tie her to me. I would have to keep my knife in hand in case they spread out a net.

"Solo, do you hear that?"

I'd been deep in my own thoughts and tilted my head to hear better. "There's a waterfall coming."

We had only been in the water for around twenty-five minutes and even with the high speed, we couldn't be more than four miles from the place we'd spent the night.

"That way." I pointed with my chin in the direction where I wanted us to steer the raft. "We'll have to get back on land, carry the raft, and hide it."

"No, Solo, I can't carry it. It's too heavy."

"We'll do it together."

The current in the stream was powerful and although I paddled till my arms felt like falling off, we were getting closer and closer to the waterfall.

"I'm scared," Willow cried out.

"Paddle." I screamed to overpower the sound from the waterfall that grew in volume the closer we got.

Willow was crying but she kept paddling. The raft started spinning from the undercurrent and a large log crashed into us making her scream in fear.

Men of the North #7 – THE DANCER

"Come on, Willow, we got to jump and swim." We were only five feet from the brink of the river but the water was deep and with the way the raft was spinning, there was no way we could win against the strong current. "Get up," I shouted, unclipping my backpack and throwing it onto land.

Willow got up, unsteady on her feet as the raft spun and tipped in both directions, her arms swinging in the air to keep balance. "My backpack," she shouted over the noise from the waterfall.

"There's no time." I grabbed her hand and counted. "3. 2. 1. Jump." We propelled ourselves through the air and landed close to land. Still, the water was too deep for Willow to reach the bottom and the current was pulling her out.

"Solo," she cried with eyes full of fright, reaching out for me.

"I've got you!" Grabbing on to some roots sticking out from the brink of the river, I used the full force of my six-foot-seven body to battle the current and pull Willow to safety. My muscles cramped from the paddling and pulling and I was panting to get oxygen into my lungs faster. Willow was going under, swallowing water and sputtering when she got back up. We were so close to safety! Digging deep, I used my last push to get her high enough that she could reach a tree branch hanging over the water. Pale as snow and coughing up water, Willow turned her head and watched the raft and her backpack disappear over the edge of the waterfall.

"Are you okay?" I held on to a branch myself.

"Yes." She looked in to my eyes, her chest heaving for air as well. "That was scary."

"I know." I pushed her in front of me; we made it out of the water and lay down on the ground huffing and puffing to get our breath back.

"We lost my backpack."

I rolled to my side. "Maybe it'll wash up a little further down the river."

She turned her head and looked at me. "But they're going to search for us by the river. Don't you think we should head away from here to avoid them?"

"You're getting good at this." I smiled at her. "And we still have my backpack. That's where most of the tools are anyway."

Willow got up on her feet and looked down at her wet clothes. "I wish they'd just leave us alone. It should be my choice who I want to be with. Even if I'm not twenty-one yet."

I agreed but now wasn't the time to discuss how unfair our situation was. I got up too and walked upstream, searching for the backpack I'd thrown onshore with Willow right behind me.

When I saw it, I froze to the spot so suddenly that Willow collided with my backside, making an "umph" sound.

"Shhh," I warned but it was too late. We had found my backpack but so had a large black bear and her two cubs.

The cubs were investigating the green bag while the mother sniffed the air and turned toward us.

"Oh shit, oh shit." It was the first time I'd ever heard Willow curse.

With my arms spread out to hide Willow behind me and make myself large and intimidating, I backed up.

The bear rose to her hind legs making warning sounds to scare us off. Willow gave a short scream behind me when the bear made as if to attack but I kept my eyes on the mother bear.

"Don't be scared, we won't hurt your cubs. We just need that backpack."

Again, she rose up on her hind legs and I damned myself for leaving every weapon I'd brought in my backpack. I needed them to scare the bears off right now.

Willow was holding on to my wet t-shirt. "Come on, Solo, let's just back away."

"We won't survive out here without that backpack."

"We won't survive if she kills us."

With the way the bear was growling and roaring at us I was getting nervous too.

"Okay, let's back up."

We only took a few steps before the mother bear started at us again, this time only stopping three feet away, her mouth wide open displaying all her large sharp teeth and her claws out as she swept a paw through the air at us.

I pushed Willow backward.

"We can't back up more. The waterfall is right behind us," Willow cried and clung to my shirt.

In a quick movement I looked over my shoulder and saw that she was right. The waterfall wasn't as tall as I'd feared. At my last school we'd played around in a waterfall this size. "We'll jump then." Hopefully the river was deep at the bottom and we could jump to safety from the angry bear.

"Willow, do you trust me?" I asked, knowing that it would take a lot for her to make a twenty-foot jump like that. "There's only forward or backward."

She was crying with hysteria and couldn't answer me.

The large bear chose that moment to swing her head from side to side, warning us that she was going to attack again.

"Jump, Willow, jump." I turned around and for the second time today I took her hand and jumped for safety.

She screamed all the way down and then my head went underwater where only muffled sounds from the waterfall came through. As soon as I reemerged, I called for Willow, pushing away small twigs and larger branches floating in the water.

"Willooow."

Her body popped up close to a large log but she wasn't gasping for air like me. She was face down with only her head, shoulders, and backside visible. Her long hair was spread out like an eerie halo around her and I screamed her name in a panic as the current carried her away from me.

"Willooow." Swimming as fast as I could, I struggled to breathe and when I finally reached her and turned her around, her head dangled against my collarbone. She was unconscious and I knew instantly she had hit something that had knocked her out. "Willow," I called and shook her body. There was no reaction.

I used the rescue technique I'd learned in swimming classes years ago and got her out of the water. Placing her gently on the ground, I looked her over and saw a large cut on her neck that was bleeding hard.

"Fuck… Willow." The last thing we needed was to attract more wild animals with the smell of blood. Ripping off my t-shirt, I tied it around her wound to stop the bleeding.

"Willow… wake up, Willow, come on." My chest felt like I was still underwater, unable to breathe right. I was scared to death that she'd broken her neck and died.

Feeling for a pulse was hard with my own pulse racing out of control. "Willow." I kept shaking her and stroking her chin. "Wake up."

There was no reaction and with her lips turning blue, I lifted her eyelids, hating how dead her eyes looked.

"Willow, come on baby." I leaned down to listen to her mouth, but the sounds from the river made it impossible to hear her breath.

What if she's dead? With my hands shaking, I started CPR with frantic movements pushing down on her chest. "Willow, don't you fucking die on me."

Her unresponsive body was the scariest sight I'd ever seen and I could hardly focus on counting with the tears welling up in my eyes.

Nothing.

I blew into her nose and shook her shoulders, calling her name with raw desperation.

Again!

I pushed at her chest, counting out loud like Archer had taught me years ago. "Four, five, six, seven…"

The cough that erupted from Willow released a loud cry of relief from me. She rolled onto her side and threw up water in a violent burst of coughing.

"That's it babe, get it all out."

When the worst was over, I pulled her up and stroked her back. "Take deep breaths. That's right. Through your nose. Again. Yes, that's it." I kissed her forehead. "Are you okay?"

"No. Everything hurts and I'm seeing four of you."

Concussion.

I pulled her close to my chest. "I'm so sorry, Willow. I'm so sorry."

"Argh." She made a groan of pain. "My arm."

"What's wrong? Can you lift it?" I supported her arm when she tried to raise it, but it hurt too much and she had to give up. "I think it's broken."

With her large green eyes wet from tears, Willow looked up at me. "What do we do?"

"It's over. We can't run without gear. We won't make it and you need a doctor."

"No, I'm fine." She had only just said it when she threw up again.

I caressed her back and waited for her to get it all out.

"It's just because I swallowed water." She coughed and used the back of her hand to wipe her mouth.

"You have a concussion, and the last thing you need is to run. The Huntsmen will know how to get you to a medical facility fast." The awful feeling of being backed against a wall with nowhere to go made my voice thick with emotion. "They are trained paramedics. I'll make a fire and lead them here."

"No." Willow shook her head but that gave her more pain and she whimpered.

"Keep your head still." My nose itched from the tears that were pressing.

"They'll *kill* you, Solo. We have to keep running," Willow pleaded and held on to my arm.

I looked down, not wanting her to see how my eyes were tearing up again. "I'm sorry, Willow. I know I promised that everything would be fine, but..." My voice broke. "I'm not risking your life."

"But what about *your* life?"

She sniffled and I raised my head to look deep into her beautiful eyes, sending her a silent message that my mind was made up.

"No." Her eyes expanded and large drops of tears streamed down her cheeks. "No, Solo. We can't give up. They'll split us apart. I don't want to live without you. If they kill you, I'll kill myself."

My own tears were blinding me now, and I sniffled too. "I don't want to live without you either, baby, but you have to promise me that you'll live no matter what."

Willow was clinging to my shoulder. "No, Solo. Don't do it," she begged when I dried my nose and placed her back on the ground.

"I'll be right back."

I collected twigs and branches to create a fire and found two stones by the riverbank. Everything was wet and wouldn't burn, but I'd been trained for this and kept going until finally I got a spark. I was going for smoke rather than fire anyway and once the smoke rose up like a beacon telling the Huntsmen where to find us, I returned to sit close with Willow, thinking to myself that these would be my last minutes on earth.

"At least I'll die as your husband," I whispered into her ear. "What more could I ask for?"

Willow clung to me. "You're not going to die. I won't let them kill you."

We curled up close with her on my lap and cried together while whispering about memories from our past.

"Remember that time Archer sent me to bed without dinner because I had rolled my eyes at Kya?" I gave Willow a sad smile. "I was so angry at the world, and then there was a small tap on the window and you stood outside, giving me part of your dinner that you had smuggled out for me."

Willow's eyes were wet from crying. "Because I knew how hungry you had to be. You always ate enough for three normal people and you'd been out running for hours that day."

"I was starving!" I squeezed her closer. "You've always had my back when no one else did."

"You would have done the same for me."

I nodded. "Yeah, I would have."

We rocked back and forth, Willow crying with her head on my shoulder.

"We'll be together again when we're older." Her eyes were pleading. "Won't we?"

I didn't think I'd get older and it was hard to speak from the sobbing I was holding back. "I don't know."

"They're going to take me back to the Motherlands but as soon as I'm twenty-one and we can marry, I'll come back here to be with you."

I leaned my head against hers, crying over the unfairness of not having a free choice because of our young age. "You know they'll turn you against me. Motlanders don't like Nmen."

"I won't let them. I'll never let anyone come between us. Just promise me that you'll wait for me to turn twenty-one."

My answer was swallowed by the sobbing that I could no longer control.

Willow was squeezing my hands, her breathing shallow and her chest trembling from her own sobbing. "Promise me, Solo."

"I pro... promise..." I managed to get out.

"You can't marry anyone else. We're already married." She held up her hand but the ring of grass had fallen off her finger like a foreboding of the tragic ending to our attempt at a life together.

"There will only ever be you, Willow. You are my soulmate."

When we heard the first shouts from the Huntsmen, Willow called out to them, "If you kill Solo, I'll kill myself, do you hear me?"

One by one, the three solemn-looking men appeared on the other side of the river.

"Stay where you are," one of them shouted and pointed his gun straight at me.

"Willow is hurt. She needs medical assistance."

"We'll take care of that. You just step away from her."

"Don't you dare." Willow clung to me, her wet green eyes looking straight into mine. "Until they tear us apart, we stay together, do you hear me?"

"Yes."

"Promise me?" Her words were muffled from her crying.

"I promise."

"We called for a drone. It will be here in a few minutes. Just stay right where you are." One of the Huntsmen climbed a tree and shot a line across the river. It drilled deep into a large cottonwood tree close to us and after securing the line to the tree he was in, he ziplined across, followed by the two others.

When the last Huntsman arrived on our side of the river, the situation was heated, with Willow and me on our feet with two guns pointing at me.

"Lower your guns." Willow stepped in front of me, her face contorted with tears and anger at the men. "Solo didn't do anything wrong."

"Kidnapping a woman is cause for the death penalty."

"Solo didn't kidnap me! I wanted to be with him," Willow argued in a pleading voice. I was in awe of my woman standing up to the fiercest warriors in the world. They had to be scary to her with their dark green uniforms, painted faces, and weapons, but like a wounded lioness she faced them with raw indignation that they would threaten me.

I was scared of them too. They were here to kill me and I had no weapons to defend myself. Still, I couldn't risk Willow's getting caught between us and there was no way in hell I'd let her take a bullet for me. It should be the other way around. Although she protested, I pushed her behind me.

"Don't, Solo. They'll kill you."

I kept my eyes on the biggest of the warriors, who seemed to be the leader of the three.

Willow moved up close behind me and spoke, "If you shoot Solo, your bullet might go through him and kill me too."

The Huntsman tilted his head as if he couldn't believe a woman would be this protective of a male, but he adjusted his gun and pointed it at my head instead. With our difference in height, there was no chance of his shooting Willow if he put a bullet in my forehead.

Lifting both palms, I pleaded with him. "Willow is hurt. She has a large cut, a broken arm, and a concussion."

The men exchanged glances and made sounds of anger as if I had hurt her myself so I hurried to explain, "We ran into an angry bear and had to jump to safety."

"I've got this." One of the men kneeled down and pulled his backpack off. I knew that part of their skill set included medical training and when he fished out equipment to treat Willow, I sighed with relief.

"Willow, you have to let him treat you," I urged her, but she refused to leave my side.

"No. Not until they promise not to kill you."

In the end the three men each gave her a solemn promise that they wouldn't kill me, and I looked on as she was treated and her wound closed. Willow screamed in pain when the soldier applied blood blocker gel to close up her wound. I knew from experience that it burned. Her screams of pain tore at my heart. I had promised to protect her and here she was with broken bones and great pain.

"You lost a lot of blood, I'm going to give you some of mine," the Huntsman treating her said and brought out a small donor unit.

"No. I want Solo's blood."

"Yeah, well, we don't always get what we want." The large man grunted and pinned her arm down.

Willow was weak from her blood loss and her concussion but she screamed and bucked her body. It instantly made the two other Huntsmen step closer.

"What the fuck, don't hurt her!"

"She won't lie still," he defended himself.

"She will if you let me give her *my* blood," I argued, stepping closer too.

Still pointing a gun at me, the largest man made a decision. "You'll give her the blood and that's it. No talking, no touching. Do you understand?"

I nodded and sank to my knees beside Willow, our eyes locking and filling up with tears again. I didn't care that three soldiers were seeing me crying. This would most likely be the last time I ever saw her. The men would break their promise not to kill me as soon as she was gone. How could they not? I'd broken so many of our country's laws.

The Huntsman set up the donor unit between us. "Do you know your blood type?" he asked me. "Never mind, it doesn't matter. She only needs one unit and it can convert that from any blood type."

For a few minutes, I watched my blood run into the converter and then continue through a tube down to the needle in Willow's arm.

Willow reached for me and I wanted so badly to take her hand. One look at the large Huntsman, who shook his head, made me keep my hand in my lap. I leaned closer so she could touch me. "I'll always love you, Willow."

Willow looked tired, her eyes struggling to stay open. She lowered her hand and closed her eyes, her head falling to one side.

"Willow?" I called, but she didn't respond.

"She's out." The man treating her turned to the leader. "I estimate we have three hours before she wakes up."

"You drugged her?" My voice was accusatory but there was no regret in their eyes.

Without a word the leader of the Huntsmen walked over and kicked me to the ground. I tried to get up, but I was still hooked to the donor unit.

"Stay down," he hissed at me and the last thing I remember was his planting another boot in my face.

CHAPTER 12
The First Show

Year 2447
Willow

I looked on from the side of the stage as the Floral Choral entertained the hundreds of Nmen in the audience.

The ten women were dressed in flowery outfits and smiling brightly in between their songs about... well, I wasn't really sure what their songs were about because I hadn't been paying attention.

I had just warmed up and was now rolling my ankles while Salma distracted me with her nervous chatter that made it hard to concentrate.

Zasquash's eyes shone with curiosity and he followed the interactions around him, casting me and Salma smiles once in a while. Solo, on the other hand, stood brooding against the wall and didn't look at me once.

Maybe he wondered if I'd told Salma to get rid of him like I'd said I would.

I hadn't. After my horrible confrontation with Solo, I'd cooled down and realized that I didn't want to involve anyone in my messy affairs. Least of all Salma who was already pressed far out of her comfort zone.

I'd thought about taking back my threats but I was so ashamed of my behavior that I didn't know how to bring it up with him. My only consolation was that Solomon would know me well enough to understand that I hadn't meant it.

Loud applause was followed by the members of the choir coming off the scene with bursts of laughter and high energy. They had just sang their three a cappella

Men of the North #7 – THE DANCER

songs, but later they would go on stage again with the orchestra and do another song before Salma would join them and end the night as the highlight.

"You're on." Salma touched my shoulder and I nodded, took a deep breath, and waited for the sound of raindrops to start. The stage was pitch black and I got ready to make my entrance.

The sound and light show was designed to simulate a thunderstorm, dramatized by the specks of light simulating rain that quickly evolved into hail before thunder rolled in. I counted down from the rumbling sound of thunder. My entrance had to be timed to the second in order for me to be right in the spotlight when the flash hit the scene.

3. 2. 1. Go – I sprinted forward in the darkness, and jumped up high, making for a dramatic entrance with me leaping through the air doing a full split just as the lightning struck and lit up the stage.

The sounds of thunder died down, replaced by birds singing as the air cleared and the light came up a little.

A circle of light from a projector lit up the stage for the second time and found me lying on the floor, stretching and yawning, pretending it was a new dawn, and then I got up in one smooth rolling movement that only someone with my core muscles could muster. My outfit was tight with my arms bare. I danced across the scene, twirling, jumping, stretching my arms and legs in a melodic, beautifully choreographed dance, that showed off my agility and strength.

As always, the bright spotlights made it hard to see the faces of all the people watching me, but I knew they were there because I heard them gasping and commenting although their words escaped me.

When my dance ended, the audience of Nmen erupted in loud cheers and shouts. I bowed, waved, and walked offstage to the sound of their applause.

"Mother Nature, that was phenomenal." Salma was jumping up and down with excitement backstage and when she hugged me, I couldn't help a look in Solo's direction. Had he seen me dance?

His face was impassive and he showed no sign of having moved from his spot by the wall.

"I've never seen dancing like that." Zasquash grinned at me. "I didn't even know the human body could be that flexible. You're insane, woman."

I raised an eyebrow.

"I mean insanely good," he clarified.

Solo still kept his face straight, as if I wasn't even there. It was alarming to me that I cared what he thought of my dancing.

The orchestra was on stage now; their instruments had been in the back part of the stage from the beginning. The fine sound of a single harp began, soon followed by three violins. It sounded ethereal and Zasquash tilted his head to listen.

Soon the other instruments chimed in and all twelve members of the orchestra were playing beautiful music.

"Not bad." Zasquash walked over to stand in front of Solo. "What do you think?"

"It's fine."

"Fuck, you're in a strange mood today."

Solo's answer came out in a clipped fashion. "I'm not here to enjoy the concert. I have a job to do."

"I know, but Leo and his boys already got the audience taken care of. I think we'll be fine. Relax a little, will you?"

Solo shrugged. "You do you. I do me."

Ben came to join us and gave me a hug. "I was watching from the back of the theater. They *loved* your dancing."

"Thank you."

"So did I, by the way." He laughed. "You looked absolutely breathtaking on that stage. Have you ever considered acting? You're very expressive when you dance and there aren't many actresses your height. You could play a Northlander bride. Do you want me to put in a word for you with the film producer I was talking about?"

I nodded my head with eagerness. "That sounds fun."

Ben rubbed my arm and turned his attention to Salma. "You ready?"

She bit her lip and moved her feet. "I'm nervous."

"That's good. Now channel those nerves into greatness."

"But, Ben, what if they don't like my songs?"

A low laughter made us all turn our heads to Zasquash.

"What's so funny?"

He smiled at Salma and took a step closer. "It doesn't matter what you sing, honey. Seeing a woman as gorgeous as you will make them worship you. How could they not? You're the most talented and mouthwatering woman to ever visit the Northlands!"

She blinked her eyes and raised her eyebrows in a look of astonishment. "You think so?"

"Oh, for sure. Solo and I are already big fans. Right, Solo?"

Solo turned his face and to my surprise he gave Salma a soft smile. "That's right."

My belly twisted in irrational jealousy. Did Solo think Salma was prettier and more talented than me?

"Mouthwatering, as in they want to eat me?" Salma asked Zasquash, who flashed a wide grin.

"Sure, but not in a bad way."

Salma turned to me and whispered. "You said the rumors of cannibalism weren't true. How can eating someone be a good thing?" Her eyes were wide.

"When they say 'eat,' they mean... ehh... a type of kissing. The men are attracted to you for your beauty and they would all like to kiss you."

Salma turned back to Zasquash and looked up at him. "You'll make sure they don't, right?"

He puffed his large chest out. "You're damn right I will. Don't you worry. Solo and I are the biggest and meanest Nmen you can find. We've got you!"

I took a step back when it was time for Salma to go on stage. She brushed her hands down her long crimson-colored dress and walked in to join the band and choir.

Zasquash and Solo had heard her sound test, but they had never heard a full song like I had.

I watched them move closer to see better, exchanging a few looks of non-verbal understanding.

"She's good, isn't she?" I asked Zasquash while trying to ignore that Solo was close enough for me to touch if I reached out my hand.

"She's amazing." Even though we stood in the shadows on the side of the stage, I felt the energy that shone from Salma. It was no coincidence that she was among the biggest stars in the Motherlands; before I met her, I would have never suspected that the woman shining so brightly on stage suffered from anxiety.

"Look at her; she's breathtaking." Zasquash sighed and Ben grinned up at him.

"Yeah, she's *special*. I like her too." The words coming from Solo made me stiffen.

What was that supposed to mean?

The audience went crazy when Salma ended the concert. She called me in to take a bow with the rest of the performers and we were overwhelmed with the loudness of the men stamping their feet and howling, something we'd never experienced in the Motherlands.

As part of the program we had to do a short meet-and-greet with some selected audience members. Pictures were taken and interviews given to the press. By eleven that night we wrapped it up and returned to the hotel, tired and happy. Our first show had been a booming success, and all worries that the Nmen wouldn't like what we had to bring had proven wrong.

Salma was high on the stage adrenaline and talked more than usual. She insisted that I fly with her and Ben in the drone instead of going on the transport with the orchestra. I was honored by her interest in me and was quick to say yes, even though it meant being in a drone with Solo.

There were ten seats in the drone and Solo sat across from me, but not once did he acknowledge my existence by looking at me or commenting on anything I said.

I should have been happy about his lack of interest, but the more I saw him studying Salma Rose, the more I didn't like it.

While Leo and Zasquash were praising our show, Solo leaned back in his seat and placed both hands behind his head. "It's hot in here," he muttered.

Giving him a bright smile that lit up her pretty face, Salma leaned forward studying the tattoo on the underside of his bulging upper arm. "Solo, what is that green long line you have there?"

"It's a stalk of grass."

"Ahh... I thought so, but why would you get a tattoo of grass on your body?"

"It holds meaning to me."

"It's because he wants to be a cow in his next life," Zasquash joked.

Solo grinned at his friend. "A bull. Not a cow."

"Is that really why?" Salma joined in on the laughter and the two of them smiled at each other. It was the first time in seven years I'd seen Solo flash his teeth in a smile, and the transformation from his permanent grave expression to this charming smile made me suck in a breath. I had once lived for those smiles of his, and even now that I spoke of hating him, I still recognized the feeling that spread inside me, like someone was tickling my heart with a feather.

Don't you dare fall in love with him again. He's poison to you and you're not a naïve teen anymore.

"Salma." Zasquash claimed her attention by calling her name. "You know that hundreds of men will be dreaming of you tonight, right?" Zasquash leaned forward, his elbows on his thighs.

Salma made an "oh-please" gesture with her hand and pointed to me. "I'm sure most will be dreaming of Willow. She looked so graceful and beautiful with the way she danced."

Zasquash nodded his head. "I agree, you looked stunning, Willow. But who said that they can't be dreaming of you both? I know I will."

CHAPTER 13
Midnight Run

Solomon

"Shut up! You're going to freak them out," I reprimanded Zasquash, who had no experience with women and was like a fucking whale in a swimming pool. Too much!

"What? By saying that we men will be dreaming about them?" He looked puzzled. "I thought I was paying our guests a compliment."

Salma and Willow followed the exchange between us while I looked out the window of the drone. We were landing on the roof of the hotel. "Women don't like to hear that you dream of them. They think it's creepy."

To my surprise Willow spoke up. "That depends on who is saying it."

I lifted both palms signaling that I didn't want to argue.

Leo came to Zasquash's defense. "I'm sure it's not the first time you two ladies have been told men adore you." He pushed the button to open the door of the drone and got out first with Zasquash. After looking around they signaled to Ben that it was safe to follow. Ben held out a hand to support first Salma and then Willow out of the drone. I looked at how willingly they took Ben's hand and thought about the paradox that a simple touch like that could get an Nman like me killed.

"Thank you for taking such good care of me tonight," Salma said as I held the door to the lift open to her.

"You're welcome."

"Which of you three will take the night shift?" Ben asked when we were all inside the lift.

"Solo and Zas are splitting it. You don't have to worry about a thing. One of them will be awake in the living room all night."

Salma tilted her head back and looked up at me and Zasquash. "Is that really necessary? I feel bad about keeping you up at night. You must be as tired as the rest of us."

Leo answered for us. "The chance of anything happening is minimal but we don't take any chances. It's better to be safe than sorry."

I shrugged. "It's okay. Zas and I are used to working in shifts and skipping sleep. We're soldiers."

"I guess." A line formed between her eyebrows. "But even soldiers are human and we humans need to sleep."

The lift stopped and we exited, going down the hallway with Leo in front with Ben. Willow hurried after them as not to be stuck with me while Salma seemed to be in no rush and walked with me and Zasquash.

"It's nice of you to care." I shot Salma another warm smile. The woman had surprised me on so many levels. Not only was she truly talented and had an amazing voice, but she was kind too. And not in that sugary Motlander way where it's all about being pleasant and polite. Salma was genuine and vulnerable around us. She didn't boss us around but seemed grateful that we were there to protect her and ease her fears. It was so unexpected and refreshing after the disappointment of meeting Willow's hostile attitude.

"Good night." Willow was by the door to her room and turned to look at Salma. "I'll see you tomorrow."

Salma opened her arms and walked over to hug Willow. "You did amazingly well. I'm so glad that you're here. Sweet dreams, Willow."

I stood behind them and saw Willow's face when she hugged Salma and closed her eyes. "Same to you. I'm an even bigger fan now than I was before we met."

They laughed and pulled apart.

"Good night." Zasquash lifted his chin to Willow as she opened the door.

"Good night." She smiled at him and then for the briefest of moments her gaze landed on me. Like a mirror reflecting my own misery, Willow's smile vanished. My chest tightened, my mouth felt dry – and then she was gone.

Once inside the suite, Ben, Salma, and Leo disappeared into the three bedrooms.

"I'm taking the first shift." Zasquash planted himself on the sofa. "Solo, you should get some sleep."

"I don't think I can. I'm not tired. It's not even midnight yet."

"Yeah, same here, which is why I'm taking the first shift and you're replacing me at five."

"Fine." I got out my running gear and put on my shoes.

"I wish I could join you." Zasquash got up and walked to look out the window. "It's a perfect night for a run."

"See you in an hour. Hopefully, I'll be tired then."

He scoffed. "Ha! Only if you fucking sprint."

Walking out the door I passed Willow's room and stopped in my tracks. The sound of running water made me rub my face. She was showering and the images that popped into my head had me fucking losing my mind.

Move on.

Forget about her.

She hates you.

I would have given my left leg to be in that shower with her. To hear her talk about our future like we used to. To feel her lips on my lips. To touch that perfect body that hundreds of men had admired when she danced tonight.

I had seen her performance and she had been a vision out of this world with her fluid movements and sublime choreography. Every man watching her had been captivated by how beautiful she looked with her symmetrical features and large expressive eyes. Willow had spellbound them the same way she had me when she first appeared between the trees ten years ago. I had told her a million times that God had been inspired by an angel when he created her. Now I wondered if maybe the angel had really been an enchantress made to create havoc in men's lives.

Straightening up, I cast a last longing glance at her door and went outside to run the streets of Kingston like a madman trying to find someone he'd lost. In my case I knew where that someone was and I was trying to run away from my need to be close to her.

You lost her.

Accept it and move the fuck on.

Increasing my speed, my face was twisted in physical pain from the insane pace that served only to numb my emotional suffering from self-blame. If my actions had turned someone as pure, delightful, and kind as Willow had once been into a cold cynic, then I deserved to suffer.

It's only with you.

I hated that thought. We had been so close. How could a love as pure as ours have turned into hate?

She's still nice and kind to others.

I slowed down and stopped to orient myself. Where the hell was I?

Kingston was one of the larger cities on the East Coast, with around three hundred thousand people living here. Out of breath and with legs a bit shaky from the long sprint, I spun around but didn't recognize anything. My wristband told me I was around five miles from the hotel and I estimated that I'd already been running for more than half an hour.

I should have brought some water.

The sounds of laughter attracted my attention to a bar down the street. Three men were standing outside, one of them pissing against the wall.

With sweat dripping, I jogged over, and ignoring the men I entered the bar.

"Hey, handsome, my name is Laila, what would you like to drink?" The bar-bot was a newer model and cute with her long hair in a ponytail and an impressive cleavage.

"I just need a large glass of water."

"With or without ice?"

"No ice."

Using a happy singsong voice, she winked at me and purred, "Coming right up."

While the bar-bot got me my water I sat down and scanned a room that was pretty full for a Thursday night. Most of the men were chatting quietly but a group in the back were loud and rowdy.

"Bar-bot, get your tits over here, we need more beer," one of them shouted.

"I'll be right there," Laila called back to him, but he was drunk and when the bar-bot took time to bring me my water before serving the group, he threw a glass in her direction.

"Where's our fucking beer?"

"Hey." I turned in my chair to face them. "Quit it. You could have hit me with that glass."

"Shut the fuck up." The man flipped me a finger.

I wasn't used to being disrespected like that. Most men who saw me had the good sense to not mess with me but I wasn't in my uniform and I was sitting down.

"Just take it down a notch," I told him but that only drew the attention from the four other drunken fools at his table.

"Didn't you just tell him to shut the fuck up? So why is he still talking?" one of them said to the man who had thrown the glass.

I ignored them. It was late and I just wanted to drink my water and go back to the hotel. In one long slurp I emptied the glass and put it down on the counter. It would take me longer to get back since I had no intention of sprinting and I had to follow the GPS.

"I'll take the redhead in the choir any day. Did you see the size of her tits?"

That comment made me stay in my seat for a second longer, listening to the conversation among the rowdy group.

"You can have her. I'm taking the singer. I'll bet I can get her to scream really loud." His disgusting words were followed by a low rumbling laugh.

I didn't need to ask what choir or singer they were talking about. Their talk made me see red.

"Did you see how flexible the pretty dancer was? That tight body needs to be wrapped around mine. I'll bet she can squeeze around my dick and milk it really good."

I walked over in three long strides and pulled the man who had spoken about Willow out of his seat. My face flushed with rage.

"Don't you ever fucking talk about women that way."

His friends scrambled to their feet as I held the man dangling over the floor. He was suffocating from my grip in his collar, but I didn't care. "Show some god damn respect."

"Put him down." One of his friends picked up a chair to use as a weapon.

"Are you done being a dick?" I asked the dangling man, who now had a crimson-red face.

He couldn't talk but blinked his eyes to indicate a "yes."

I was just about to release him when his friend smashed the chair into my side. That enraged me further.

Dropping the first idiot, I went after the second.

He screamed when I got a hold on him. My knuckles touched his face with speed and force, making the man fall to the floor. I turned to the other three with anger. "Are all you fuckers done trash-talking women now?"

They all nodded their heads vehemently and then one of them gave me an instant's warning when his gaze slid behind me.

I turned fast and managed to block most of the impact from the bottle that crashed down on my shoulder, exploding with pieces of glass flying around.

My attacker was stabbing the air with the broken bottle, using it as a weapon, and got lucky enough to scratch my neck and jaw.

I hissed and ripped the bottle from him, throwing it across the room. By now the light in the bar was blinking: a signal that the police had been called.

I put my attacker to sleep with an elbow to his face and scowled at his friends, waiting to see if any of them were stupid enough to attack as well. They were sobering up fast and pulled back.

It was tempting to run instead of waiting for the police to arrive, but the bar-bots recorded everything. I wouldn't be able to hide so I might as well explain what happened.

It took me hours before I was done giving reports and making statements. The police worked slow and insisted on my coming to the station to clear things up. I was grateful that the other patrons in the bar backed me up, saying that the men had been drunk and throwing glasses at Laila. The fact that I was a member of the Doom Squad made a difference too, and by four in the morning, I finally walked through the hotel door to the suite.

Zasquash looked up at me. "Long run, huh?"

"Yeah."

"Hey, you're bleeding – what the hell, Solo?"

My hand flew to my face. "I'm bleeding?"

"Yes. Did you trip while running?"

"No."

"Then how did you get that cut?"

I walked over to a decorative mirror and leaned in to see the dried-up blood on my cheek and neck better. "Must have been a piece of the glass from the bottle."

"What bottle?"

"I stopped by a bar to get a sip of water." I gave him a quick look over my shoulder. "Some idiots were talking trash about the performers, so I asked them to stop."

Zasquash, who had been watching some nature show, got up and came closer. "Let me guess; they didn't stop?"

"Oh, they stopped. It just took a little persuasion." The corners of my mouth shot up.

Zasquash's large hand landed on my shoulder. "It's almost time for your shift to start. How about you do a quick power nap at least?"

"Nah, I think I'll take a shower instead."

"Now?"

"Yeah, I ran ten miles tonight. I need a shower."

"Okay, just no singing or whistling in the shower. People are sleeping."

I scoffed, since we both knew there was no fucking chance of my ever singing in the shower. That was something Zasquash would do, but not me.

Ten minutes later, I was back in the living room dressed in clean sweat pants and a tank top. My uniform could wait a few hours until the others woke up. I plunked down on the couch next to Zasquash. "Go cuddle up with Leo, I've got this."

"Thanks, man. There's only so much animal sex a man can take in one night anyway."

I looked at the wall, where a lion was on top of a lioness. "He's biting her, did you see that?"

Zasquash yawned. "I know, and they call us men brutal. I've seen at least fifteen different species have sex and it's horrifying. All I can say is that I'm happy I'm not a male bee. Did you know their penises explode while they're still inside the queen bee?"

"You're making that up."

"No, I'm not. It's the truth. Not only do the poor fuckers die, but it happens in the most gruesome way possible. Imagine your cock exploding while you're having sex."

I scrunched up my face and squirmed in my seat. "They die, right? I mean living on without your cock is pointless."

"Yeah. I just told you, didn't I? Animal sex is twisted and not in a good way. There's a lot of death and cannibalism involved."

"Then maybe we're the lucky ones for not having women in our lives."

"Maybe." Zasquash yawned. "But if nature can make a male spider or praying mantis try to hook up knowing that their females eat them during sex, then it's proof that we males are biologically programmed to risk anything to procreate. I see all these women on the tour and I swear to you every time one of them smiles at me I get a boner in my pants." Zasquash looked down at his crotch. "It's fucking pathetic, but I can't help it."

"It's because you're not used to being around women. The same thing happened to me and my friends at the school, but you get desensitized with time."

"So you don't react to them anymore?"

"No."

Zasquash looked skeptical. "Maybe your thing isn't working anymore. If you can tell me you watched tonight's show with all that beauty without getting a hard-on, then you're either a liar or you need to see a doctor."

"I don't need to see a doctor. Everything works just fine."

"You sure?"

"Yes. Thank you for your concern." I rolled my eyes.

"Good night then." Zasquash walked into the bedroom and left me alone with the nature show and my heavy thoughts. I spent ten minutes trying to find something less depressing to watch when I heard a bump from the other side of the wall.

I craned my neck and listened to locate the sound.

It's not Zasquash. He was behind the other wall and knowing him, he would have been asleep the second he hit the pillow.

A muffled voice sounded, and another bump that made me stiffen and pay attention. Willow's room was on that side of the wall.

Is she okay?

Another bump was followed by a moan and it made my protective instincts flare up.

I needed to know that she was okay.

CHAPTER 14
Checking Up

Willow

It was the sound of a running shower that woke me up.

Who takes a shower at four thirty in the morning?

For twenty minutes I lay awake unable to find sleep again. I rearranged my pillow, rested my head, and closed my eyes again. Still sleep wouldn't come.

Thoughts of Solomon's charming smile last night made me groan with misery. That man got under my skin like no one else, and now he had me tossing and turning thinking over every word exchanged between us.

With a deep sigh, I got up and went to use the rest room. I thought about Salma and wondered what she thought of the fact that everything was taller here than at home. The toilet, the vanity – it was all built for tall Nmen and since she was almost a head smaller than me, I imagined only her toes would reach the floor when she used the toilet.

After washing my hands, I walked back to the bed and massaged my thigh, which had been sore for a few days now. Maybe if I stretched thoroughly, it would help ease the tension. At first I did it on my bed, but the mattress was too soft and didn't offer the stability that I needed so I continued on the floor. Kicking the table and knocking over a lamp wasn't part of the plan and I scolded myself, hoping that I hadn't woken anyone up. Picking up the lamp from the floor, I bumped the back of my head against the edge of the desk.

"Really?" I moaned and rubbed the spot that had taken the impact.

Two minutes later, I was back on the floor doing long uncomfortable stretches, when there was a knock on the door.

"Who is it?" I asked in a low voice and got up from the floor, hoping that my noise hadn't caused complaints from neighbor rooms.

"Are you okay in there?"

I recognized the deep voice and opened the door. "What are you doing here?"

Leo yawned but craned his neck to look inside my room.

I turned to see what had him so interested, but there was nothing. "What is it, Leonardo?"

"Just Leo. We heard bumps and wanted to check up on you." His eyes slid down before he refocused on my face.

"Oh, I'm sorry, I just knocked over a lamp, that's all." I pulled down my oversized and washed-out soccer t-shirt that Hunter had given me. It was the shirt he'd played his first professional game in and I loved sleeping in it.

"So you're okay?"

"Yes. I'm sorry for waking you up. I was just trying to stretch out."

"At this hour?"

"My thigh has been giving me trouble." I rubbed it with an apologetic smile.

His eyes lowered to my hand on my thigh. "Do you need ice or a cooling spray?"

"No, but I would love to run a little – you know, to warm it up and see if I can stretch it out properly." I shrugged. "But obviously my room isn't big enough for that and I don't suppose running outside is an option?"

Leo rubbed his eyes again, looking tired. "There's an exercise room down by the lobby."

"That could work."

"Except..." He sighed. "I'm not letting you walk around the hotel alone at this hour."

"I'm not afraid."

"I didn't say you were afraid. I'm just saying that I'm not letting you."

"Could you take me then?"

He gave another long yawn. "Solo will take you down there. He has the night shift and he was the one who worried about the noise coming from your room in the first place."

Leo's words hit me square in my chest. "He was?"

"Yeah, he woke me up and made me come over here."

"Why didn't he come himself?" Even while saying it, I knew the answer to that question. After our confrontation yesterday, and my threat to say Solo had touched me, he would keep his distance.

Leo lifted his shoulders in a shrug. "I know you two have history and don't get along, but it's too early in the morning for me to give a fuck. If you want to run, Solo is going with you. I'll take his job of chilling on the sofa."

It was a no-brainer. I should have declined. But for some reason what came out of my mouth was, "He wouldn't do that."

"What? Go with you?"

"Yeah, as you said, we don't get along."

Leo snorted low. "Solo would go if I asked him to."

The idea of someone bossing Solomon around intrigued me. I knew he wouldn't like it. Especially not if Leo ordered him to be alone with *me*.

"Are you his boss?"

"No. Not directly. But the security of this tour falls under the police force, and since I'm the highest ranking here, I'm in charge. Zasquash and Solo have been lent to us for obvious reasons and while they are here, they both report to me."

I tilted my head. "Obvious reasons?"

Leo rested a shoulder against the wall and scratched his arm. "Yeah, their reputation and sheer size will keep men at a distance. You've noticed that they're bigger than the rest of us, right?"

I gave him a small smile. "It can't be much. I hadn't thought about it."

Leo's lip quirked upward and he straightened up. "Really? Well, I suppose to the eye of a Motlander we Nmen are all tall and muscular."

I gave a smile, enjoying his pride. "That's right."

"Okay, I'll tell Solo to meet you out here in a few minutes. You might wanna put on some pants."

This was the right time to say "No, I don't want to go with Solo." But my lips pressed firmly together, two treacherous autonomous parts of me that couldn't be trusted. My head too was in on the betrayal and sabotaged my decision to avoid Solomon by moving in a small nod.

As Leo walked away, I closed my door and leaned my forehead against it.

"Stupid, stupid, stupid," I mumbled to myself, unsure why I would behave in this irrational manner. I was supposed to avoid Solomon and now I had agreed to spend time with him alone in a hotel where almost everyone else was sleeping.

Nothing is going to happen. It'll be fine, I comforted myself while I cleaned my teeth and face before brushing my hair back in a ponytail. Throwing the soccer t-shirt on the bed, I grabbed my usual outfit to work out in consisting of tights, a sports bra, and a tank top.

Muffled sounds from the other side of the wall made me listen. I couldn't hear the words, but I guessed that it was Leo and Solomon arguing.

So what if Solomon didn't want to escort me to the gym at close to five in the morning... or any time for that matter?

I closed my eyes for a second, not liking the small-minded part of me that felt the need for him to see me instead of Salma Rose.

Besides, maybe it would give me a chance to explain that I hadn't been serious when I threatened him.

You owe him nothing! The psychologist's voice was in my head.

That's right. This tour was supposed to be my time to have fun and now Solomon is ruining everything. If I have to be miserable on this tour, why shouldn't he be miserable too?

It was like I was at war with myself. My vindictive thoughts made no sense and was against everything that I stood for. It wasn't tolerant, kind, or forgiving. It was petty, and by hurting Solomon I would only be hurting myself too. I *knew* that! Intellectually.

So why am I doing it?

I had no answer, except that being around Solo was like an itch I needed to scratch.

The sound of a door closing snapped me out of my confusing thoughts. With my hands shaking a little, I stepped out into the hallway.

Solomon stood there waiting for me with his face drawn tight and his eyes guarded. Like me he was wearing a tank top, but his pants were loose and his shoulder-length hair pulled back behind his ears.

I didn't speak to him because if I had, my voice would have revealed how nervous I was. Instead I began walking to the lift and heard him follow me.

After entering, we'd stayed in opposite corners without looking at each other, and when the lift stopped on the ground floor we exited without a word too.

Solomon took the lead and walked me to the gym, which was empty as expected. One of the walls was interactive, and I walked over to change the motif from a stadium full of people to a sunrise over a beach.

In another corner there was music but I couldn't figure out how to make it work.

"Solo?" I turned to see him sitting by the door, his back leaning against the wall, his elbows on his pulled-up knees, and his head hanging down as if he was resting.

"Solo," I repeated a little louder.

He lifted his head. "What?"

"Do you know how to control the music?"

"I guess."

"Would you help me then?"

He sighed but got up and walked over to stand a safe distance from me. "What do you want to hear?"

"Just something soothing. My thigh hurts; I have to warm it up and stretch it."

His gaze lowered to my tight pants before he quickly looked away. "Okay, I'll find something."

I waited but he didn't move.

He gave me a pointed stare. "I'm waiting for you to move."

"Oh." I took a step to the side.

Solomon raised a brow. "You got to move more than that. I'm not coming close to you."

"Look," I held up a hand. "I shouldn't have threatened you. Of course, I didn't tell anyone that you touched me. I would never put you in danger like that."

He looked unaffected by my admission of regret. "I figured," he said. "Otherwise, I wouldn't be alive, would I?"

There was no gratefulness or warm feelings in his words. As nice and charming as he had been to Salma last night, he was just as much cold and distant to me.

I moved to the corner and began running on a treadmill path in the floor. It was like the ones we had at home and adjusted to my pace. After putting on some music with a man playing a guitar and singing in a soft and melodic tone, Solo went back to sitting against the wall.

"I didn't think you Nmen had calming music."

He didn't answer me.

"Aren't you going to exercise?" I asked without looking at him.

When he didn't answer again I should have left him alone, but the itch got stronger and the fifteen-year old girl inside me craved his attention. Refusing to be ignored, I repeated my question louder. "Why aren't you exercising?" This time I turned my head and looked at him. "It's not like you to pass up the chance to be physical."

Solomon's eyebrows were drawn closely together. "Why are you talking to me?"

"That's what civilized people do."

That only made the line between his eyebrows deeper. "I'm not sure what your plan is but I'm fucking sure that it's not a good one, and I'm keeping my distance."

"Don't be so paranoid and rude."

He narrowed his eyes. "If you hate me so much, why not just leave me alone?"

I don't hate you. The words were right there on my tongue but I couldn't say them.

"Because you're here, aren't you? And so am I. Besides, from the dampness of your hair I have a feeling you're the one who woke me up by taking a shower in the middle of the night."

"Yeah. I did."

"That was rude and inconsiderate to the rest of us who were trying to sleep."

"At least I didn't use the dryer function. That's the noisy part."

"Still, I don't see why you shouldn't suffer with me now that you woke me up.

"Ahh…" Solomon's head fell forward before he looked up at me. "I see."

I kept jogging, my leg still bothering me and my breathing louder now.

"So forcing me to sit in a gym at five a.m. to watch you run is your version of revenge?"

"Let's just say that I take pleasure in the fact that you are inconvenienced. It's only fair."

Solomon ran his hands through his hair and it struck me how tired he looked. "Sorry to say it, Willow, but you might actually be doing me a favor."

I snorted in annoyance. "What are you talking about?" My leg hurt from the running and I was getting hot enough to stretch. Slowing down, I came to a halt and placed both hands on my knees, leaning forward and looking over at Solo.

His eyes widened at the view of my cleavage, but then his head turned to watch the artificial sunrise on the large wall. "When we got back from your performance I wasn't tired, so I ran ten miles. I had to spend time talking with the police because of a little misunderstanding as well."

"You ran ten miles?"

"Yeah."

"Does that mean you haven't slept at all?"

"Uh-huh."

No wonder he was looking so fatigued.

"Well, I'll take mercy on you soon. I just need my stupid thigh to ease up a bit."

"Did you ice it?"

"No. If I were home I would have gone to the pleasure parlor and had a massage. That helps."

"Isn't the pleasure parlors where you go to have sex?"

To hear him bring up sex made me even hotter but I kept my face straight. "Yes, but they are always located in physical centers that offer everything related to physical needs. Nails, hair, exercise, meditation, body massages, cuddling, and erotic massages, which can involve sex if one chooses. Some of them even offer tattooing and branding."

Men of the North #7 – THE DANCER

I kept stretching while using my hands to work on my thigh muscle. Being a dancer, I was flexible and the outfit I had on sat snug against my body. I lifted my heel behind me and used my hand to press it against my backside to stretch the quadriceps muscle on the front on my thigh. After that, I knelt down on the floor and did all the stretches I could think of to ease the pain.

"Is it helping?" Solomon asked, his eyes making my skin burn. My vanity stirred as I remembered him smiling at Salma so I kept my current stretch a little longer, knowing that my cleavage would be visible from his position.

Not so invisible now, am I?

"It helps a little." I turned around on my knees with my chest to the floor and my hands stretched out in front of me. It was no coincidence that I made sure to position myself with Solo directly behind me. He had always had a thing for my behind. Now he could see what he'd lost and blame himself for it.

A quick glimpse in the mirror confirmed that Solo's eyes were fixed on the back part of me. His forehead glinted with perspiration and he was rubbing his hands on his knees as if his palms were sweaty.

I used to love his strong hands and even though it made no sense, I craved for him to touch me at that moment.

"I need a massage," I repeated and still with my behind in the air, I craned my neck. "Solo."

He swallowed hard and gave a grunt to signal he'd heard me.

It was as if the sane part of me stood in shock next to an alternate version of myself who spoke with calmness. "Would you mind massaging my thigh? You're strong, I'll bet you could ease the pain."

At first Solomon looked as stunned as I felt beneath my calm and collected facade, but then his eyebrows lowered and anger washed in like a dark cloud forewarning of a thunderstorm. "I can't believe you'd be that cruel."

I turned around to sit on the floor. "How is that cruel?"

Solomon got up from the floor. "It's a fucking trap is what it is. The minute I touch you, I'm dead. You're trying to set me up." He took a step closer, his voice shaky. "You knew that you couldn't prove that I touched you the last time we were in here. The cameras would have proven I never laid a hand on you. That's why you lured me back in here and now you're trying to get me to come over and touch you in an inappropriate way. You're fucking trying to get me killed."

I got up from the floor too and stood in front of him. "Solo, that's not true. I would never do that."

When I took a step forward he moved back and hissed, "Don't you come closer."

"Solo." I hated the guarded expression on his face; it was like I was an animal with claws that might attack him at any point. He had to know I would never be a danger to him. "I'm not trying to get you killed."

His eyes were narrowed and he looked ready to run if I so much as leaned forward.

My embarrassment brought anger with it. I had almost died because of this man and now he had the audacity to make me look like the villain.

"This is ridiculous. We're trapped on this tour together and we should be able to be adults about it. How about we make a truce?"

He shook his head. "I don't think so. You're up to something."

"No, I'm not, Solo. I was just asking for your help massaging my leg." It had been a stupid idea and I was mad at myself for suggesting it. It felt especially humiliating with the way he rejected me by spewing angry accusations at me.

"Well, that's not fucking happening. How stupid do you think I am?" His nostrils were flaring and there was distrust in his eyes.

His harsh words only brought out the worst in me. "Fine." I walked towards the door. "If you don't want to help me, I'll find someone who does." Opening the door, I leaned out and called to the three policemen guarding the entrance to the hotel. "I need some help, please."

They all looked up and one of them came over.

"Hi, what's your name again?" I asked the man, who was in his early forties with long brown hair and a beard that was showing a few gray whiskers.

"I'm Cameron."

"Hey, Cameron, I'm having a problem with a sore muscle in my thigh and I need someone to massage it."

I was standing in the doorway with Solomon behind me inside the gym and Cameron right in front of me in the hallway.

"Maybe the hotel could make an appointment for massage later," Cameron suggested.

"Or maybe you could help me. Are you good at giving massages?"

Cameron blinked a few times, his eyes going down to my thighs and a smile growing on his lips. "Are you asking me to touch you?"

"Yes."

He looked back to his colleagues with a wide smile. "The dancer needs me to give her a massage."

"You can't touch her," one of them warned him.

"He can if I allow it," I called back. "You're the witnesses. I give my permission for Cameron to massage my right thigh."

They gaped at me and then looked at him like he'd just won a new drone.

"Willow." Solomon moved in from behind me.

I ignored him.

"Willow, look at me."

I turned. "What?"

"You're not serious."

"I am. Cameron will help me, won't you, Cameron?"

"It'll be my pleasure."

Solomon's foot was tapping, his hands were on his hips, and his jaws were pressed firmly together. "And you think Tristan will be okay with another man touching you?"

Oh, shoot, I'd forgotten that Solomon still believed that Tristan and I were together. I improvised. "Don't forget that Tristan for the most part grew up in the Motherlands like me. We're not possessive by nature like you are."

Solomon took another step closer. "I'm not letting anyone touch you."

Our eyes clashed and I lifted my chin. "You don't have a say."

Solomon's jaw was set in a stubborn expression and pointing at Cameron, he threatened, "Don't fucking touch her. I'm calling her fiancé."

Wrinkling my nose up, I spoke in an offended tone. "Don't you dare. I make my own decisions."

Solomon was already touching his wristband and I closed my eyes when a few seconds later, I heard Tristan's drowsy voice answering the call.

"Tristan, it's me, Solo."

"Solo, how did you get my number?" he asked.

"It's the same number you had when we were seventeen."

He yawned. "Why are you calling me at five in the morning?"

"I'm with Willow."

"You're what?" Tristan's voice grew high-pitched. "Are you two back together?"

"No." Solomon frowned. "I know she's with you now."

"That's right. Ehhm, so don't get any ideas."

I stood frozen. I should just tell Solo the truth. Earlier today, I had been rational and decided I wouldn't involve anyone in my messy affairs. But I couldn't bring myself to give up the buffer between us that Tristan offered.

"Willow is hurt. It's just something in her thigh that's giving her grief, but she's asking me to help her by massaging her."

"Hey, she was asking *me*," Cameron sputtered from outside the door but he was ignored by Solomon.

"Tristan, would you be okay with me touching Willow?"

"Fuck no! You keep your hands to yourself."

Solomon gave me a "told you so" look and scratched his neck. "When will you be here?"

"Ehh, I'm not sure. I've got a deadline but Willow and I are trying to figure it out."

It was a complete lie since I hadn't talked to Tristan since I left the reunion.

Solo looked straight past me to Cameron. "I'll make sure no one touches her in the meantime."

"Thank you. I appreciate that."

"Do you want to talk to Willow? She can hear you."

"Oh, okay. Hey gorgeous."

I played along. "Hey... babe. I'll call you later, okay?" Geez, that sounded so fake.

"Are you okay? What's wrong with your leg?"

"Oh, you know it's that stabbing pain I was telling you about." I only said it to make Solomon think Tristan and I spoke all the time.

"Right. Do you want me to come and massage it for you?"

"Would you? I really miss you a lot."

Tristan cleared his throat. "I miss you too. All the time. Just send me the address, all right?"

"Will do."

A vein on Solomon's neck popped out and he looked down when he disconnected the call and walked past me, stopping right in front of Cameron. There was a low growl in the back of Solomon's throat when he squared his shoulders. Cameron, who looked rough with large tattoos up his neck, took a small step back, gave me a last look, and then returned to his post by the entrance.

"So what am I supposed to do with this pain?" I asked Solomon with annoyance.

"Don't you have some painkillers?"

"No."

"Then use ice, a warm bath, or massage it yourself."

I inhaled deeply, not happy with his controlling things. "As always, you're being a domineering pest."

"Don't worry. I'm sure Tristan will make the pain go away once he gets here." Solomon's voice was gruff and I noticed there was a tic by his left eye.

Feeling pissed at him for calling Tristan in the first place, I raised an eyebrow. "Yeah, Tristan has nice strong hands."

Solomon stared at me, his neck growing redder by the second.

"What?" I asked and threw my hands in the air with an attitude worthy of a Northlander.

"Nothing!" He waved a hand at the lift. "Can we go back up now?"

With a pout, I moved in that direction. "I guess we might as well."

It was five thirty when we returned to the fifth floor. Solomon walked behind me and when I stopped by my door, he stopped too, still keeping his distance.

"What if I got hurt?" I asked.

Solomon exhaled noisily as if preparing for another round of my nonsense.

"I mean what if I had twisted an ankle at the gym. Would you have helped me to my feet? Carried me to my room?"

"You didn't!"

"No, I know." I tilted my head. "I just don't see how you can do your job if you're unwilling to touch me in case I get hurt."

"You won't get hurt with me around."

"Oh, but you said that I wasn't your responsibility, remember? You're only here for Salma."

Solomon looked down and rubbed his forehead. "Willow, what is this? What do you want from me?"

I want you to see me, a voice screamed from my insides but I didn't say that.

"I want you to respect that I make my own decisions. If I say Cameron can touch me, you don't get to call Tristan and overrule me."

"It was Tristan who overruled you. Not me."

"Who called Tristan? Huh? As if I'm unable to think for myself."

Solomon had been so controlled, but my last comment was like a trigger to him and he hissed, "Maybe you can't think for yourself. Maybe you were fucking brainwashed in that place of reflection that they took you to."

I jerked back, surprised by the intensity in his voice and the pain in his eyes. "What are you talking about?"

"Do you think you would have risked your life for me if what we had together was so bad? Do you really think I would ever try to hurt you intentionally?"

"I never said you did it intentionally."

His comeback came fast and harsh. "They fucking turned you against me. You swore no one would ever come between us, but you lied."

His words hit me hard, causing guilt to flare up and add to my confusing emotions. In self-defense, I lashed back at him. "Oh, don't you turn this on me. You're the one who is out of your mind," I hissed low at him, stabbing my finger through the air and taking a step closer. "You're the one who convinced a fifteen-year-old girl to run away with you. It was reckless and irresponsible, and you'd better admit that."

"I don't need to admit shit. I already apologized. You on the other hand have been fucking brainwashed and you don't even know it." Solomon had fire in his eyes and he stood his ground when my poking finger stabbed his chest.

"That's ridiculous. I'm a grown-up who has had plenty of time to reflect on what happened. I have every right to be furious with you." My head was leaning back and I looked into his eyes as my tongue whipped him. And then something changed. Solo's eyes widened and he sucked in a breath.

"What?" It took me a second to realize that the hand with my stabbing finger was now resting on his chest, but the moment I did, I jerked it back. "You know I'm kinesthetic. Touch is natural to me. It doesn't mean a thing."

I should move back.

He should move back.

And yet neither of us moved a muscle. We just stood opposite each other, his chest rising and falling fast, my head spinning.

"To you."

"Excuse me?" I blinked my eyes – unsure what he was referring to.

"Touch doesn't mean anything *to you*."

"I've touched you a million times. It was just a hand on your chest." I wanted my words to sound assertive and nonchalant, but I had to look away or he would see the conflicting emotions in my eyes.

"Willow, you should go inside your room now."

Why does his tone sound almost like a warning?

Looking down, I saw his hands formed into fists and his body rigid and tense.

"You can't wait to get rid of me, can you?"

He didn't answer but moved past me to the suite he shared with the others. "Go inside, Willow."

"Stop ordering me around," I answered, but by then he'd already closed the door behind him, making me feel like a big idiot.

CHAPTER 15
Tristan and Hunter

Solomon

The confrontation was inevitable.

The moment Tristan found out I was part of the security team, he told Hunter and by evening, the two of them showed up demanding that I be removed.

"I'm not letting my sister be part of this tour if he's here," Hunter threatened Ben, who called in Leo.

We had moved to the city of Whiteriver and were currently behind the stage that had been built for this event. No theater in town was big enough to host the amount of men interested in going. The solution had been to create an outdoor venue with the audience sitting on a sloping hill, while the stage was crafted below it.

"We have more than a thousand people waiting for the show to begin. Can't we deal with this later?" Ben asked in a diplomatic tone of voice.

Hunter looked over Ben's shoulder to Willow. She was standing some distance apart from us with Salma, who seemed scared of the raised voices. "You don't understand. Solo already kidnapped my sister once. I'm not fucking letting him near her again."

Ben's eyes expanded and he raised both hands to his chest, turning to me. "Is that true?"

I rolled my eyes. "Of course not."

"Liar." Hunter flew at me, shoving me back with two hands to my chest. It released an explosion of testosterone in my brain and I pushed back hard enough to make Hunter fall.

"Whoa, whoa," Leo stepped in front of me and Zasquash pulled Hunter back up.

"Your sister is under *my* protection." Zasquash placed a palm on Hunter's chest, using his body as a wall to stop Hunter from getting to me. "Look at me. That's right. My name is Zasquash and I'm here to protect Willow, Salma, and the others. You have my word that Solo won't mess with Willow."

"You don't know him!" Hunter hissed.

"Actually, I do. We're both on the Doom Squad; I'm his partner."

Hunter twisted his face.

"That's right. Not my choice either, but hey, we make it work."

I frowned. *What the hell* – Zas and I were best friends and now he was taking Hunter's side.

Ben raised his voice a little and for a Motlander he looked very upset. "Gentlemen, I'll have to ask you to lower your voices. You're scaring our performers and they have to go on stage in a few minutes. This is unacceptable."

We all looked over to Salma, who stood with her face on Willow's shoulder. Willow was sending me dirty looks, but I wasn't the one causing the trouble and she bloody well knew it.

"I'll calm her down," Tristan said and walked over to the women. I had no doubt he could do it. Tristan had always been charming and fun, with a natural gift of making people relax around him. With me it was the opposite and that was the fucking curse. My job was to fight for women in the Northlands and make them feel secure, but the one woman I wanted to protect most of all didn't feel safe with me. She wanted Tristan. My heart was still hammering from Hunter's attack, but I jerked away from Leo, who was still watching me.

Zasquash had managed to calm Hunter down a little. "How about we go over to watch the show from the other side? You'll be able to see it from a side angle. Your sister is phenomenal, but I'll bet you already know that."

Hunter licked his chapped lips and relaxed his stance a little. "Yeah, okay."

As on the night before, the choir were the first to enter the scene. They had kept far away from the backstage drama and had big smiles plastered on their faces. Members of the orchestra hung around on the other side of the stage from where I stood. Some of them moved to the side when Zasquash and Hunter joined them to see the show from that side wing.

"Hello." One of the females gave a nervous smile to Hunter and quickly looked down. It softened him a bit and he returned her greeting. Zasquash made some kind of joke that I had no way of hearing from my position on the other side of backstage, but I could tell that the pretty musician smiled.

Ben had gone to help Tristan calm down Salma Rose.

"So you kidnapped Willow, huh?" Leo gave me a sharp look.

"Don't be stupid. I wouldn't be alive if I had kidnapped her."

"Hunter seems to think that you did."

"We ran away together. Willow wanted it as much as me."

"Look, just answer me this: can you do your job or are you too distracted?"

I snorted, offended. "Have I ever not done my job?"

"No. But this situation is different and you know it."

"I'm following orders, that's all."

Leo gave me a long scrutinizing glance. "Tell me I have nothing to worry about."

"You have nothing to worry about." I fixed my eyes on the choir on the stage. "Tristan is here now. He'll take care of Willow. I'm going to focus on Salma."

"What's the deal with Willow and Tristan anyway? Are they married?"

"Not yet."

"Why the hell not?"

"I don't know."

Leo crossed his arms. "What kind of man doesn't seal the deal right away?"

"Tristan grew up in the Motherlands until he was fifteen."

"Ahh." Leo nodded. "That explains it."

"He's a... nice guy." I pushed the words out as if they were covered with thorns that made my throat bleed. It would be so easy to hate the man that had taken my place in Willow's life, and part of me did hate Tristan.

I looked away, putting on my stone face to hide the emotions that made everything hurt inside me.

Leo patted my shoulder. "For you to say that must be proof that you're over her."

"Uh-huh. It's been seven years and she's no longer the person I knew."

"Keep an eye on Salma, I'll check up on Willow's brother."

I looked over to see Tristan entertaining Salma now that Willow was getting ready to go on stage. The songbird no longer looked scared but was listening with her full attention, nodding and smiling at times. It pained me how easy it was for him to make people feel at ease.

I stepped back, making room for the choir to exit the stage and looked on as the darkness descended for Willow's entrance. As I did yesterday, I watched every part of Willow's dramatic dance. She was outstanding and seven years ago I would have told her so.

Again tonight, the audience went crazy, stamping their feet and whistling with excitement. Willow took a quick bow and ran to the side where Hunter stood with Zasquash. Hidden from the audience but visible to me, the three of them laughed together and Hunter picked her up in a fierce hug.

The dark-haired musician who had been chatting with Hunter and Zasquash gave them a warm smile before she walked on stage with the rest of her ensemble.

Hunter, Zasquash, and Willow stayed to watch, and Tristan and Salma joined them.

On my side of the stage, I stood alone in the shadows, my mood dark from the sight of my best friend, Zas, grinning with Hunter, who had once been like a brother to me. And Tristan, another former friend, hugging the woman I had once thought of as my mate. There were more than a thousand people in my near proximity, but I'd never felt as lonely as I did in that moment.

You don't need any of them. You're strong!

My face fell into the impassive mask I'd learned to put on to hide my true feelings. If anyone saw me they would think I was just having another day at the job. I was Solomon, named after one of the most powerful, wise, and wealthy kings the world had ever seen. I wouldn't be crushed by jealousy. So what if the people I loved all left me? I didn't need them anyway.

Leo came back and stood next to me. "Hunter is calm for now."

"Good."

"How are you holding up?"

"What do you mean?" Anger rose in me. The last thing I needed was his fucking pity.

"Aren't you tired? You didn't sleep last night."

I was fucking exhausted but I just shrugged.

Leo patted my shoulder. "Zas and I are taking the shift tonight. You need eight hours straight."

"Thanks."

"We're spread out in two different hunting cabins tonight. Salma, Willow, and the orchestra will be in our cabin. The choir and the technicians are going to a different cabin. It's twenty minutes outside of town but I'm told it has plenty of rooms so hopefully you can get your own bed."

"I don't care. I can sleep in the drone if I have to. It wouldn't be the first time."

"You're not sleeping in the fucking drone," Leo said and rolled his eyes.

Little did he know that two and a half hours later, I would be going to sleep in the drone. The seats could be adjusted to a lying position and even though it wasn't as comfortable as a bed, it was much better than sleeping inside the cabin where the after party was taking place.

The cabin was massive with twelve decent-sized rooms, some of them accommodating up to four beds.

Tristan and Hunter had joined the performers and no one seemed in a hurry to get to bed except me, since I couldn't wait for this nightmarish day to end.

Zasquash was in heaven with all the Motlander women and his idol, Hunter. He was entertaining them with stories and asking Hunter about all the other celebrity sports stars he knew.

Tristan was on fire and cracking jokes, and when I passed them with a pillow and blanket under my arm they were laughing and no one seemed to notice me except for Willow, who gave me a cold stare and turned to cuddle up on Tristan's lap.

They were a collective, I was a singularity.

Two of the people in the cabin hated me, and I was pretty sure Hunter was on board with his sister in wishing I was dead.

Inside the drone, I lay down and pulled a blanket over me. The night was cool and still someone had opened a few windows in the cabin, letting the sound of an acoustic guitar travel my way. A female began singing; I recognized Salma's clear voice. They were having a good time while I was out here, alone again. It brought back memories from my first year with the Huntsmen when they had treated me like a pariah. It had been the loneliest years of my life because not only had I lost Willow but I'd lost Hunter and my other friends too.

None of the soldiers had patience for a youngster in grief. They all believed I should have been executed for what I'd done and deep down I agreed. They despised me and there were times where death would have been the kinder option to the constant hazing that I suffered through. And yet, what had carried me through all the physical pain and loneliness were my memories of Willow's love for me. Our promises to each other that I'd repeated thousands of times in my mind. My hand slid up to the tattoo on my underarm. The strand of grass symbolized the day we spoke our wedding wows and I put a ring of grass on her finger. Willow might have forgotten all about it, but I never would.

For a few minutes my mind taunted me with images of how wonderful it would be if things were different if instead of being unwanted, I was part of the fun in that cabin. I imagined Willow cuddled up in my lap, her head resting against the crook of my neck and my arms wrapped around her with a big fat smile on my face. If Khan hadn't changed the age of brides from eighteen to twenty-one, maybe we wouldn't have run away. What then? How would our lives be different? Would Willow and I have been married now? Would Hunter and Tristan still be my friends? I allowed myself a few happy moments thinking about an alternate reality where things had gone my way, before my imaginary bubble of paradise burst and I was back to being alone in the drone. With a deep sadness in my chest, I tossed and turned trying to get comfortable. I wanted to fall asleep so badly and escape the questions in my mind. Like where would Tristan sleep tonight and did Willow love him more than she had loved me?

CHAPTER 16
Where Is Solomon?

Willow

"Good morning."

The sound of someone moving around in the room made me yawn and squeeze an eye open. "Good morning."

Tristan stood by the window looking out. "It's a beautiful day. We should go on a hike or something."

"Did you sleep well?" I asked him.

"Yeah, you?"

Stretching my arms, I sat up. "I had some weird dreams. You and Hunter were dancing with me on stage."

Tristan turned. "Were we any good?"

I laughed. "You were better than me, and I couldn't understand how that had happened."

"Hidden talents." Tristan grinned and walked over to sit on the foot of the bed. "Dancing is easy. Any child can do it."

I shoved at him and he grinned. "What? Did you think what you're doing on that stage is special?"

"Why don't you try it and let me know?"

"I'm a drone designer. We can do anything."

"Then how about you do a split, right here, right now?"

He smiled. "I would, but the room is too small and I care about my testicles a little too much."

Pointing my finger at him, I laughed. "Did you just admit that you can't do it?"

Tristan nodded. "I might have exaggerated my talent for dancing, but I meant what I said last night, you know."

I pulled my legs up in front of me and ran a hand through my unruly morning hair. "So did I. You're a wonderful friend, Tristan, but I'm not attracted to you that way."

"That sucks." He looked down.

"If you don't want to be my cover with Solomon, I understand."

Tristan shook his head and placed his hand on top of mine. "As long as you want me to, I'll proudly be your cover."

"Would you stick around a little longer then?"

"Sure."

"Great."

Crawling out of bed, I walked out of the door and looked down over the railing to the large common area on the ground floor. Six of the rooms were located up here on the second floor and most of the doors were still closed.

"Ah, it smells nice," I looked back at Tristan, who was still inside the room where we had slept. "There's a cook preparing breakfast for us."

"I know, I smell fresh bread." Tristan smiled.

"Did you already shower?"

"Uh-huh. There's a nice bathroom at the end of the hall. I'd hurry before the others wake up and there's a line."

"It's okay, my stomach is growling. I'm going to eat first."

Half an hour later I was full from feasting on fruit and warm bread. Hunter emerged with a drowsy yawn from a room downstairs with his hair all tangled.

"Shit you're ugly in the morning," Zasquash teased him and pointed to the nearest bathroom. "Go scrub up so you can look like the polished star we all know."

Hunter lifted his hand in a slow movement and flipped a finger at Zasquash.

"Is that a morning greeting?" Salma, who was sitting next to me, asked. Motlanders didn't flip fingers and I'd only learned its meaning when I moved here.

"Yup." Tristan smiled at her. "It's a quick way of saying I wish you a lovely day."

"Oh, that's nice." Salma sipped on her tea and spoke about how fun last night had been. "I like these cabins. I didn't think I'd enjoy being mixed in with so many new people, but I can't remember laughing so much, ever."

"Yeah, Tristan has that effect on people," I commented.

Zasquash raised his head, his mouth stuffed with bread and cheese. "Don't give him all the credit. I made Salma laugh too."

"You sure did," she agreed and turned in her chair when Ben came down to join us at breakfast.

"Ben, look at what I just learned." Salma lifted her middle finger with a warm smile. "It's a local way of wishing you a lovely day."

"Oh." Ben returned the finger and smiled. "Well, same to you, darling."

"What else can you teach us?" she asked Tristan, who kept his face a mask.

"Well, we Nmen can be a bit weird."

"But I thought you were from the Motherlands. Willow said you were born there."

"I am. It's just that I've lived in the Northlands for so long that I see myself as a Northlander. But I guess I'm both. Anyway, we kind of get all mushy inside when someone compliments our ears."

Salma blinked. "Your ears?"

"Yeah… we even have ear contests to determine who has the nicest ears. It's a huge thing here. Ears and noses too."

Salma and Ben exchanged a glance as he sat down at our table with a plate of food from the counter and a cup of coffee. "I never paid much attention to people's ears."

Tristan was messing with them and although it was innocent fun, I elbowed him in a warning that Tristan ignored.

"What do you say, Zasquash? Wouldn't you get all mushy inside if a woman told you that you have nice ears?"

Zasquash raised his coffee and swallowed a laugh. "For sure."

"But they are hard to see when your hair is down like that," Salma pointed out to Zasquash, who resolutely sat down his cup and pulled his hair back.

"What do you think?"

"They are *very* nice," Ben and Salma both agreed, being polite Motlanders.

"You have pretty ears too, Willow," Ben complimented me. "Especially when you have your hair up in a bun like that."

"Thank you."

Leo came in from the outside and approached Zasquash. "Have you seen Solo?"

My spine straightened because I'd been wondering where he was.

Zasquash frowned. "He's sleeping in one of the rooms, isn't he?"

"No. Everyone is up by now and I can't find him." Leo looked at his wristband. "It's close to eight. Solo wouldn't sleep nine hours."

I cleared my throat. "He walked outside last night with a blanket."

"What time?" Leo asked.

"Not long after we returned here. Maybe half an hour. We were hanging out down here and he left." I didn't tell them that I always knew when Solo was in the room or not. My senses were fine-tuned to pick up his energy, and yesterday I had been angry with my myself for feeling disappointed when Solo left. I could have asked him where he was going, but instead I focused on my charade and moved closer to Tristan in some infantile attempt to make Solo react, which of course he hadn't.

"Maybe he slept in the drone." Zasquash got up. "I'll go check."

"I already did. He's not there." Leo walked over to pour himself a cup of coffee. "I called him three times, but he's not picking up either."

"He wouldn't do anything stupid, would he?" Tristan asked.

"Like what?" Salma picked up a strawberry. "What do you mean?"

Tristan lowered his brows just as Hunter came out from one of the bathrooms with his bag in his hand.

"Hunter, have you seen Solomon?" Leo took another sip of his coffee.

"Yeah, we just took a shower together." Hunter said it in a *what do you think* tone of voice. "Why?"

"He's missing," Salma informed him.

"Should we worry?" Tristan's jovial humor was gone. "I mean it can't be easy for him thinking that Willow and I are a couple and all."

I pressed my lips together, understanding before Tristan did that he'd just blown our cover.

Salma tilted her head at me, but Leo and Zasquash didn't react so I figured they hadn't picked up on Tristan's mistake.

"Maybe he's out on a morning run," Zasquash suggested.

Leo frowned. "Then why isn't he picking up when I call him?"

"I don't know." Zasquash tore at his hair. "This isn't like Solo."

Walking into the kitchen, Hunter picked up a muffin and took a bite. When the pretty musician from yesterday came in with her empty plate he lifted a hand and waved at her. "Morning, Darlene."

"Did you see Solo?" Zasquash asked her.

Darlene stopped. "Who is Solo?"

"My partner." Zasquash rose up to his full height. "He's my size. Serious expression on his face. Dark blond hair, short beard, muscular."

"Ahh, yeah, I know who you're talking about but I haven't seen him since yesterday."

Hunter spoke with muffin in his mouth. "When you see him, do me a favor and keep your distance."

Darlene, who looked to be in her early thirties, widened her eyes. "Why?"

That made Zasquash groan and frown at Hunter. "Don't tell her shit like that. She's going to think Solo is dangerous or something."

"He *is*," Hunter insisted.

Zasquash shook his head. "You don't know what you're talking about. You might have known Solo when he was an impulsive teenager, but I know the man he's become and he would *never* hurt a female. Solo is my friend. I know him."

Hunter snorted. "I would have said the same about him when he was *my* friend. Until he *did* hurt a female. My *sister*."

"Hunter... don't." I tried signaling that now wasn't the right time.

"Either way, we need to find Solomon. I don't like that he's missing." Leo leaned his head back and downed the contents of his coffee cup, his dark bun of hair more messy than usual.

Tristan squirmed in his seat. "We should go search for him in the woods. I worry he might have hurt himself."

Guilt made me squeeze my glass of juice hard enough for my knuckles to turn white. I had said some horrible things to Solo. That I wished he was dead. That I hated him. That I would say he'd touched me. It was all spoken in anger, and now shame and regret filled me. My face flashed hot from my childish behavior the day before yesterday when I'd pushed him, provoked him, and involved Cameron in the power struggle between Solo and me. What if something had happened to Solo? My throat felt dry and swollen all of a sudden.

Zasquash snorted. "You people have no clue who Solomon is. To think he would hurt himself is just plain stupid. The man has been hated on more than anyone else in the Huntsmen unit. The mental and physical pressure he has withstood would break any normal man but not him."

"Then maybe this was his breaking point," Hunter muttered over the rim of his coffee cup. "Everyone has one."

Zasquash took a step closer to Hunter. "You might be a tough soccer player, but trust me, you have nothing on Solo. We Huntsmen don't mess around. I was twenty-four when I was selected to join the special forces and I was close to giving up many times. Solo was only seventeen when he was given over to the Huntsmen to keep an eye on him. A kid. But it still took a whole fucking unit of elite soldiers to keep him from going after Willow."

Salma gasped and widened her eyes at me. A spark of energy snapped through my gut and my pulse raced like I was already up and running to find Solo myself.

"That's right," Zasquash continued. "Do you realize how hard it is to be the rookie in any elite unit? And that's under normal circumstances. Solo spent his first week in the hospital because Commander Magni beat him close to death. We Huntsmen are proud men and when Solo pulled that stunt with Willow, he was fucking with the wrong crowd of men. Nobody humiliates a whole battalion of Huntsmen without paying a heavy price for his mistake. There are stories about the things he suffered through. I'm fucking proud to be his partner. Solo is young, but he's a seasoned Huntsman and a living legend among us."

Hunter looked unimpressed. "Your point is?"

"My point is that men don't come better than him, so don't you dare suggest that he would hurt himself."

"Nah, I think you're underestimating how much Solomon loves my sister. You never saw them together like we did. Seeing Willow with Tristan would have been harder than whatever drills in the forest he was put through seven years ago."

"Drills in the forest. Ha!" Zasquash snorted and shook his head. "You have no fucking idea and you're wrong about your sister. I talked to him about her. He says she's no longer the woman he used to love. Solo moved on and I think it's fucking time you people moved on too."

My eyes fixated on the crumbs on the table in front of me, my breath caught in my throat as an old scar from grief was ripped open in my heart. Solomon had told me the same thing, accusing me of being brainwashed. I played with my earlobe, not sure how to react.

"It's true," Leo chipped in. "He did move on. Solo even said he approves of Tristan. He called him a nice guy."

Tristan gave me a smile but I couldn't lift my lips and return it. Solomon had always been territorial when it came to me. It had been annoying at times, but I'd come to take it as a sign of his love. For him to tell his friends that Tristan was a nice guy and that he approved of us being together not only shocked me, it saddened me too. I never felt more adrift and lost in my life.

The others were still discussing Solo's disappearance until Leo cut through. "Can we do a little less talking and some more finding?"

"I'm on it." With hard steps Zasquash walked toward the door.

"Hang on, I'll send some of my men with you," Leo called out behind him.

On his way out the door Zasquash threw an answer over his shoulder. "Don't bother. I'm the best tracker in the Northlands. I don't need help to find him."

When he was gone, Salma moved in her seat and spoke with a worried tone of voice. "I hope Solo is unharmed. What if he was attacked by a bear or some other wild animal?"

Tristan began explaining how all Northlanders are raised to survive in the forest and that Salma had nothing to worry about. I zoned out, my heart and mind at war again. A week ago everything relating to Solo had been simple. I had hated him! That was all there was to it.

Now, it was getting harder to see things so black and white. Our talk by the lake at the reunion had made me remember things I'd forgotten about our time together. And having Solo ignore me and give Salma his attention had pushed at something inside me too. Now their talk about Solo being hurt made me want to cry. How could I hate him and care about him at the same time?

"Where are you going?" Hunter asked when I got up from my seat.

"I need some private time to meditate."

"Okay." He took my seat and as I walked away I heard him and Leo discussing technical specifications on the fancy drone Hunter owned.

My plan was to meditate and center myself. But I couldn't. Sitting on my bed with my back against the wall was hard when my legs still felt restless, like they wanted to get up and run out to find Solo myself, just to be sure he was safe.

I shouldn't care about him. He's the most selfish human being and... My thoughts were interrupted by memories of his carrying my backpack when I was tired and asking me to sit down and relax while he built a shelter for us.

That's doesn't mean a thing.

Another memory was of Solo volunteering to run back three miles when Mila couldn't find her sweater and thought she might have dropped it.

Okay, so maybe he's not selfish to the core, but he's bad for me. I almost died because of him. How many hundreds if not thousands of times had I told myself that? It had fueled my anger and worked as a safety blanket of familiarity. But my anchor of hatred wasn't working to delude myself any longer. I couldn't deny that I still cared about Solomon.

I gave up meditating and opened my eyes. A foggy memory of backing away from an angry bear was playing in my mind's eye. I rubbed my forehead as if I could somehow make the memory clearer.

The large bear in front of us was protecting her cubs. Her growling grew louder and the way she swung her head from side to side made me sure she was about to plant her teeth and a large claw in one of us.

"Jump, Willow, jump." Solo grabbed my hand and I screamed as we fell through the air.

I got off the bed and paced the floor. *Why didn't I ever feel gratitude that he saved me from the bear?* My programmed defense system spit out an answer. *Because we shouldn't have been in that forest to begin with. He should have known better.*

Opening the door, I stepped out to overhear more of the conversation going on downstairs.

"He was always very kind to me." It sounded like Salma was defending Solo to Tristan.

"Yeah, he has his good side, but Solo has a habit of messing things up for himself."

"I don't know about that. All I can say is that he has been nothing but kind and attentive. I really like Solo."

I frowned and grabbed my bag from my room. It was surprising how open-minded Salma was when it came to Nmen. They were attracted to her like ants to sugar but then she was Salma Rose, a superstar with a rare beauty and vulnerability that would speak to any Nman.

Solo and Zasquash had called themselves fans after the first show and complimented Salma for being the most beautiful and talented Motlander.

It wasn't that I disagreed with them, but it had still wounded my female pride that Solo, who used to tell me I was the most beautiful woman in the world, had changed his mind.

I walked to the bathroom, hoping that a shower would help clear my mind, but the obsessive thoughts wouldn't stop. As the water ran down my body I kept wondering: now that Solo thought I was with Tristan, would he go after another female entertainer? He had shown interest in Salma. Would he prefer her over me? Of course he would. With Salma there would be no bad history between them or hurtful comments to forgive. I closed my eyes and sighed.

Let it go, Willow. What ever happened between you and Solo is old history.

After pouring soap in my palms, I slid my hands across my body, feeling the weight of my breasts and for a split second imagining how Solo's large hands would feel on my skin.

Don't even go there! I scolded myself, but my body didn't care and my nipples grew hard as I thought about that early morning in the hallway outside my room when I'd had my hand on his strong chest and he'd been visibly affected by it. I remembered the longing in his eyes when he'd seen me stretch, and the desire I had suppressed for years grew bolder inside me. I imagined what he would have done if instead of jerking my hand back, I'd let it slide across his body, down his abs or across his chest to his shoulders and arms. Would Solo have let me?

This is stupid. Even if I wanted Solo back, it could never happen. Hunter wouldn't understand. No one would understand. I wouldn't understand.

I turned around and let the water fall on my face. It wasn't enough to wash away the confusion that had consumed me since Solomon had walked back into my life. One second I resented him, and the next I longed for his attention. Was this how having a split personality felt like?

Once, I'd been everything to him. Now he was guarded and reserved around me. His face no longer lit up when I came close and his smiles were reserved for others. Never me.

It's not like I'm smiling at him either. These crazy thoughts are all just my vanity talking.

Zasquash's comment from earlier that Solo had moved on and I should too, bothered me. I *had* moved on, seven years ago.

So why am I fantasizing about him in the shower? It's not normal to fantasize about someone you're supposed to hate.

I won't. It's going to stop right now!

My brain searched for someone else to think about but came up blank.

If only I could fall in love with Tristan. He was tall, handsome, and more than willing to be my partner. It would be so easy with him, but Tristan deserved someone who loved him as more than a friend.

My hands moved lower and I spread my legs to wash myself. Again forbidden thoughts of Solomon filled me. This time we were in the drone alone and he directed his charming smile at me. I allowed the guilty pleasure of a few strokes against my clit, and images in my head of Solo kissing my neck and holding me close.

This is wrong, the sensible part of me shouted again. *I shouldn't think about him in this way.*

But I did.

I thought about his tall, strong, muscular body, his dark blue eyes, and the way a scar cut into his upper lip. His face was like a map of my youth. The small bump on his nose from the time he broke it in a fight and I ran to get ice for him. The tattooed compass on his lower arm pointing toward SW that he surprised me with when he was seventeen. Everyone assumed that SW stood for southwest. Only we knew that SW was an acronym for Solo and Willow and the compass a symbol of home's being the two of us together. Then there were his lips. They had given me my first kiss and whispered promises and words of love at a time when I'd felt unwanted. Even his short beard brought memories of his youthful pride when the first stubble showed at the age of fifteen. It had left my skin red, revealing that we kissed at every chance we got. When I turned off the shower, my body was still humming with an unsatisfied sexual desire for a man I didn't want and could never be with.

I activated the dryer function and reached for the moisturizer that I'd brought into the shower with me. Rubbing my thigh muscle, another wave of sadness washed over me as I remembered Solo's refusal to massage me when I had asked for his help.

Would he have said no if it had been Salma asking?

I sighed, hating that inside me, there was still a young Willow who craved to be with the boy I had once loved and that the Northlander blood in me made me a little possessive of him. I was bigger than this. If Solo wanted Salma and she wanted him, I should be happy for them. Anything else would make me a small person.

Lifting my arm, I applied the last moisturizer to my back.

Maybe I could be happy for them if only I knew she was his second choice. But how would I find out? It wasn't like I could just ask him. Or could I?

CHAPTER 17
Danger

Solomon

The temperature was freezing but I dove deeper, using my muscles to push myself faster through the water. The pressure in my ears tightened, the darkness around me grew, and so did my need to breathe.

I forced my body to continue downward. It was my nature to push myself, and I had suffered through much worse pain than my lungs begging for air.

Four more long strokes and I reached the bottom of the lake. Planting my feet, I set off like a rocket with my arms reaching for the bright surface above me. My lips were pressed together and my eyes squinting in concentration.

Air – air – air, my lungs screamed in demand and as soon as I broke the surface, my mouth opened in a greedy gulp of fresh forest air.

"It was about time."

Gasping to fill my lungs again, I turned my head to find Zasquash standing by the edge of the water with his shirt in his right hand. "I was about to dive in and look for you. Thought the lake monster might have gotten you."

"How long was I down there?"

"I don't know. I've only been here for a few minutes. Did you break your record?"

"It felt that way. This lake is deep."

"Did you reach the bottom?"

Swimming toward him, I reached the part of the lake with shallow water and began walking up. "Yes, it was freezing cold down there."

He laughed and looked down my naked body. "It shows."

I wasn't amused nor was I offended. Every part of my body was large, and I was comfortable in my own skin.

"Leo worried because you weren't at the cabin and no one knew where you'd gone. Why didn't you tell me you were going for a swim? I would have joined you."

I snorted.

"What?"

"You were busy and I didn't want you to come."

Zasquash watched me put on my wristband, shorts, socks, and shoes. "Why not?"

I shrugged. "You do you. I do me."

"You always say that but I'm your partner. Your business is my business and vice versa."

"I don't think so."

Leaning his head back, Zasquash groaned out loud. "What the hell is wrong with you today?"

"Nothing."

"Do I have to beat you to make you talk to me?"

Even after the draining swim, I was still on edge and his talk about beating me up provoked me. "As if you could take me in a fight."

"Oh, I could throw you around and teach your arrogant ass a lesson for sure. You might be bigger than most. But you aren't bigger than me."

Most days we got along great, but after Zasquash's worshipping Hunter yesterday, I wasn't in the mood to take any shit from him. "Fuck off, Zas." I turned my back on him and began jogging back the way I'd come.

"Why don't you just tell me what your problem is?" he called out behind me.

"I don't have a problem."

"Then explain to me why you're grumpy as fuck." Zasquash jogged up next to me. "Is it because of Willow?"

I ignored him.

"Don't worry about her. She's not all that, anyway."

My brain shut down. All the sadness I carried inside me exploded in fury when I tackled him with my shoulder, making Zasquash lose his balance and fall to the ground. "Don't talk trash about her," I hissed. I hadn't allowed any boys to talk badly about Willow at the school and I wouldn't allow him to do it now.

He got up too, dusting off his pants and shirt and looking after me as I ran down the forest trail. "You're crazy," he shouted after me.

I turned around and jogged backward. "What? Did your new best pal Hunter tell you that or did you finally figure it out by yourself?"

Zasquash ran up to me, so I turned around to increase my speed.

"I've always known you're crazy, Solo. I didn't need anyone to tell me that."

I didn't respond.

"I didn't mean to trash-talk Willow. It's just that there's something fishy about her. I think she's playing you."

My scowl was all the answer he got.

"Yesterday she hardly touched Tristan and I didn't get a lover's vibe from them, and then this morning Tristan said something interesting."

"What?"

"He hinted that they wanted you to believe that he and Willow are a couple. I don't think they are, though."

My interest was instantly piqued. "What were his exact words?"

"Oh, I don't remember. But Tristan worried that you might have done something stupid to yourself because you thought he and Willow were a couple."

"Like what?"

"He was hinting at you possibly killing yourself."

Another snort escaped me. "He wishes."

"But don't you think it was weird he used the term *think*? Why didn't he say 'now that Willow and me *are* a couple instead of 'now that Solo thinks we're a couple'?"

"Maybe you heard him wrong."

"I heard him fine. I'm telling you they're faking it."

For fifteen minutes we ran side by side back to the cabin, my head analyzing everything relating to Willow and Tristan. She hadn't seemed overly excited about him coming and there had been annoyance on her face when I called him and told him about her thigh hurting. Because of all my thinking, I missed a turn and was mocked by Zasquash, who had to guide me in the right direction.

"It's a good fucking thing I came to find you or you would have been running in circles out here. Some Huntsman you are."

When we got back, Leo and some of the other police officers stood outside. "Ah, there you are. We were about to do a search and rescue."

I slowed down to a walk. "That's a joke, right?"

Zasquash moved past Leo and smacked his large palm down on his shoulder. "Told you I'd find him."

"Where were you?"

"Working on my diving skills. You said we wouldn't have to leave until eleven a.m." I looked down to check my wristband. "It's not even nine yet."

"Next time make sure you tell me where you go. Magni wouldn't be impressed if I lost one of his special forces."

I raised a brow. "I think he'd be more surprised than anything."

"Did you eat breakfast?" Zasquash waved me through the door to the cabin. Inside, the performers were hanging out but I didn't see Willow or Hunter. Heads turned as soon as I walked in.

"Finally!" Tristan threw his hands up. "What happened to you?"

I steered toward the leftover breakfast. "Nothing happened to me. I don't know what the fuss is about."

Salma's soft voice made me look up and see her smile at me. "We worried about you, Solo. I had all sorts of disturbing images in my head of what might have happened to you. I mean there are wild animals roaming these forests. It's not safe."

Tristan straightened up. "I told her not to worry and that these forests are where you're most comfortable. Isn't that right?"

"Yup," I agreed. "Nothing is going to happen to me." With my plate full, I walked past them. "I need a shower and a change of clothes before we leave."

"There's a nice tub upstairs. Maybe you can practice holding your breath some more," Zasquash joked behind me.

I had only taken a few more steps when Salma called my name. "Solo."

I stopped and turned. "Yeah?"

With the sweetest smile on her pretty face, Salma Rose sat with her right hand lifted in the air and flipped me a finger. "I hope you have a wonderful day."

I stiffened a little and narrowed my eyes. "Ehh, thanks. Same to you."

My eyes glided to Zasquash, whose eyes were dancing with suppressed laughter. Tristan raised up his finger too and flashed his teeth in a grin. I understood well enough that this was one of Tristan's pranks, and with a small shake of my head I picked up my bag of clean clothes and headed for the upstairs bathroom.

The door stuck so I pushed with my hip and entered. The room was full of hot moisture and the mirror was covered with steam. In the corner someone had forgotten a small bag.

I pushed the door closed behind me and dropped my backpack on the floor. Popping three grapes in my mouth from my plate, I sat it down on the sink close to the bathtub and locked the door before I turned on the water faucets to fill the tub. After making sure it had reached the right temperature, I pulled off my t-shirt, kicked off my shoes, and opened my pants.

"Are you sure you wanna do that?"

I jumped back at the sight of Willow looking at me from around the shower door.

"Fuck! Why the hell didn't you lock the door?" I blamed her in my defense.

"I thought I did."

I looked back at the door as if I could blame it too.

"It's okay, I'm done anyway. You can have the bathroom." She gave me a smile and it confused the hell out of me.

Bending over, I reached for my shoes on the floor. "I'll wait outside."

"Actually, there was something I wanted to ask you." Her head disappeared. The shower door wasn't see-through but just the thought that she might be naked on the other side of that thin separation had me sweating profusely.

"I shouldn't be here," I muttered and turned around.

"But now that you are here, could you hand me the white dress in the bag?"

My hand was on the door handle, my heart hammering in my chest. When I heard the shower door swing open behind me, I closed my eyes and focused on breathing and getting my brain to work again. The damage was already done. If I stormed out of the bathroom now and someone saw me, they would assume that something had happened between me and Willow. This was bad!

"Since you won't do it, I'll get the dress myself." Twenty seconds later she added, "There, now I'm dressed so you can turn around again."

My whole body was tensed up when I turned in a slow motion. Willow was wearing a white summer dress with thin shoulder straps, one that showed her arms, neck, and a nice cleavage, especially from my vantage point looking down at her. I averted my eyes to look at her elbow. "People will think I touched you."

She took a step closer. "Stop being so paranoid."

I gave her a hard stare. "Paranoid? Twice, I've gotten close to dying because I was found alone with you. The minute I walk out of here and someone sees me, I'm fucking dead and you know it."

She moved even closer and without thinking, I took another step away.

"Solo, relax, I'll tell them nothing happened."

"It won't matter. Tristan will have the right to..." I didn't finish the sentence because Willow had a look in her eyes that made my spine tingle. I'd seen it before and it wasn't one of hate or disgust. It was softer, and I swallowed hard.

"I can't imagine Tristan killing anyone. It's Hunter you have to worry about, but both of them think I'm meditating in my room."

"Good, then maybe we can get out without being seen together."

"Maybe." There it was again. The look of trouble in her eyes. "But I wonder." She turned around and stood with her back to me, the summer dress caressing her beautiful body as it slimmed in around her waist and fell loosely around her hips down to her mid-thighs. Looking straight into the wet bathroom mirror, her eyes met mine. The reflections of our faces on the steamy surface were a bit distorted, but she was still the most gorgeous woman in the world.

"If you truly think these are your final minutes on earth, how are you going to spend them?"

There was something less confrontational and more alluring in being behind her and not face to face. I was still suspicious of her motive for talking with me but allowed my eyes to take her in.

"Aren't you curious to know if we still have that special chemistry that we used to have?" She paused and looked down. "Despite my anger with you, I wonder about that."

"But you have Tristan."

She hesitated and Zasquash's words about her and Tristan faking it played in my mind. If I knew anything about Willow it was she loved with gusto. She might have started out loving Tristan, but whatever was going on between them now didn't excite her much. She wouldn't still be in this room if it did.

"Willow... what are you doing?" My voice was low and hoarse.

"So you don't wonder about it?"

I took a small step closer. A test to see if she would move. She stood perfectly still and then in a slow deliberate movement of her hand, Willow reached behind her head, pulling her hair to one side, baring her neck to me – something she had done so many times in the past as an invitation to kiss her and hold her. Instant tingles ran up and down my spine, but just below the excitement was that small voice whispering in warning that it might be a trap.

"I'm not going to touch you." My words seemed to be more for me than her.

"Is it because of Salma?"

"Salma? What does she have to do with anything?"

"You said you'd answer any question I had." Willow's voice was a soft caress.

"What do you wanna know?"

She looked back over her shoulder. "Are you in love with Salma?"

I scrunched up my face. "What kind of question is that?"

"It's all right if you are. I'm just curious." She turned back to meet my gaze in the mirror again.

"Why would you even care, Willow?"

"I wish I didn't but I've always been curious by nature."

My tone was flat. "So at least that part about you hasn't changed."

"No."

I moved a little closer, confused by her mixed signals. "I'm not in love with Salma."

"Do you think she's more beautiful than me?"

"Willow..." I sighed. "Why would you ask me that? Stop playing tricks with my mind."

She lowered her head and whispered low. "I'm just asking questions. If these are your last minutes on earth, don't you have questions as well?"

My head was exploding with questions and warnings at the same time. Looking around I searched for cameras, but this was a bathroom and there were none.

"If these are truly my last minutes on earth I would want to know one thing," I muttered low.

Willow gave a slight twist of her body and looked over her shoulder again, her green eyes calling to me like a cool lake in a lush forest. *Come play, come dive in.* In those eyes was a flashback to the young woman I'd known before the hate and the blame took over.

I could hardly breathe when I stepped close to her, my naked torso feeling the heat emanating from her delicious body. My t-shirt was on the floor, the top of my pants was open, and my hands were begging for me to touch her but our bodies were still a bit apart.

"What is that one thing?" she asked and while keeping eye contact with me in the mirror, she licked her lower lips in a way that made my pants tighten.

I managed to answer, "How it would feel to hold you in my arms again."

"Is that all? You just want a hug?"

Was that disappointment in her voice?

I closed the gap between us, my body now firmly pressed against her back, my hands still not touching, but my mouth breathing into her left ear. My nerves were on alert for any sign that she would call for help.

I closed my eyes when her hand touched mine. Our fingers merged together, squeezing each other as old friends saying "I missed you."

Fuck it!

Letting go of my fear and ignoring the warnings in my head, I placed my other hand across her belly, pulling her back against me and leaning my head against hers. Willow lifted her free hand to touch my hair and it made me insane with hunger for her. Turning her around I cupped her face and kissed her with a ferocious hunger, my whole body shaking with eagerness and desire for her. Our tongues were playing tag, like two children rediscovering games from the past.

"Fuck... Willow..." I moaned and picked her up while still kissing her. "What are you doing to me?"

She broke our kiss and looked into my eyes. "Don't think this means I've forgiven you."

With a deep groan, I turned our bodies to press her back up against the wall. Her legs were wrapped around my hips and her hands fisted deep in my hair. It hurt from the way she was pulling at it, but if she needed to punish me a little, I could take it. We kept kissing and I sucked in a breath when Willow rotated her hips. With my crotch against her soft core, I pressed harder against her, and she pushed back.

"Fuuck..." This brought back sweet memories from our week on the run. Our hips met in rhythmic movements imitating mating. I was so fucking turned on that I couldn't think straight. The tip of my cock escaped my briefs, making her white dress and panties all that separated her pussy from me.

As our bodies ground against each other and her heels bore into my back, Willow's hands moved downward over my naked shoulders and chest, leaving scratch marks from her nails.

I had one hand behind her neck, keeping her in place to kiss her, and the other slid up her body to feel those amazing breasts that had developed since I knew her.

Blood was pumping through every part of my body and I was breathing fast and heavy, enjoying the friction from rubbing my cock against her. We were having sex. Maybe not full intercourse but this was definitely in the category of sex and I was mind-blown that it was happening in a bathroom when both Hunter and Tristan were close.

The thought sobered me a bit, and I stopped grinding my hips and pulled back to look at her. "Why are you doing this?"

Again, her nails bored into my skin and I suddenly suspected it was all part of her plan. "You're going to tell them, aren't you?"

Willow opened her eyes and refocused from the haze she'd been in. "What did you say?"

I placed her back on the floor taking a step back and looking at my back in the mirror. "The scratch marks. You want them to think I raped you." She didn't need cameras when she had physical proof now. "Fuck! I fell right into your trap, didn't I?"

She tugged her long brown hair behind her ears and brushed her hands over it.

"Willow?" I stared at her in disbelief. "You planned this all along."

Finally, she lifted her gaze to look into my eyes. Every second before she spoke felt like a year. "I'm not going to tell them anything, so you can stop looking at me like I'm your enemy."

My shoulders were tensed up.

"I didn't plan anything." She looked down, straightened her dress, and cleared her throat, "This shouldn't have happened." She didn't meet my eyes. "I don't know what came over me but don't worry, it will never happen again."

I bent down to pick up my t-shirt. "Because of Tristan?"

"Yes. And Hunter. But mostly because of our history." She took three steps to the door and looked back at the bathtub, which was close to full. "Enjoy your bath."

I kept quiet when she cracked the door open and peeked out. Just when she was about to leave, I made a sound and her eyes asked a silent "What?"

Picking up her small bag from the floor, I handed it to her. When she took it, our fingers touched and I wanted to grab her and pull her back into my arms.

I didn't, though, and a second later the door closed without a sound behind her.

With heavy steps, I walked over and locked it.

She won't tell anyone.

I sighed and covered my face with my hands. *What did you do? She threatened you before and told you straight to your face that she hates you... still you jumped right in.*

Convinced that any minute now angry men would break through the door, I waited with my heart pounding, considering what I'd do. Should I fight for my life or let them kill me?

If I left now, I might have a chance of escaping into the woods and never be found again.

Except... Zasquash was here and he would be hard to trick. He knew me too well and would have a fresh trail to follow.

Would he let me go?

I ruminated on that while lowering my hands to my sides, my eyes on the bath in front of me. This wasn't the first time I'd flirted with death. As a Huntsman I'd fought men who'd done their best to kill me. I'd rappelled down steep mountainsides and climbed up in places where a single mistake would have killed me. That I'd made it to twenty-four was a miracle it itself.

"Fuck me," I mumbled. "A life lived in fear is no life at all."

That bath looked luxurious and inviting. It would be a good place to relive the exhilarating moments that had just taken place between Willow and me. If nothing else, I would die with the taste of her lips on my mouth.

CHAPTER 18
Freeman

Willow

We arrived at the capital of the Northlands around noon and were surprised to see a large group of people gathered in front of the hotel we were staying at.

Leo looked down from our drone to the sea of men. "Shit. I feared this would happen."

"Looks like you have a lot of fans here now." Ben smiled at Salma but after one glance, she pulled her legs up in front of her and wrapped her arms around them. Hiding her face against her knees she began rocking back and forth.

Tristan and Hunter were flying with us. Both of them gave me a worried glance, not understanding what was going on.

Ben talked in a calming voice to Salma and I regretted not taking the seat next to her. I wanted to take her hand and tell her everything would be all right.

Leo leaned closer to Zasquash. "Call up Solo and ask him to be ready to receive us." With Hunter and Tristan in the drone, Leo had agreed to let Solo fly with the orchestra. "I'll take the front and I want Zasquash and Solo on either side of Salma." Leo pointed to Ben. "You'll walk next to her and hold her hand. Make them think she belongs to you."

Zasquash scoffed and objected, "Ben is hardly going to scare any of them away. No offense, Ben, but they know Motlanders don't marry. It's public that's she single."

"How about Hunter holds her hand? He's used to the publicity anyway," I suggested, knowing that if anyone took Salma's hands the news media would be speculating that she was in a relationship with him.

"Or I could hold her hand." Zasquash pushed his chest out.

Leo gave him a sharp look. "No. You focus on protecting her and let someone else play the romantic part."

"Why? If Solo or I hold her hand, no one is going to fuck with her. How many men do you know who would go up against a Doomsman?"

"None. Which is why you'll be on either side of her.

"Salma won't be holding any man's hand," Ben cut in.

Leo gave him a hard stare. "We've never had a situation like this, but I guarantee you one thing. Those four or five hundred men down there all want to hold Salma's hand. If there's one thing that entices Nmen it's a single woman. The moment she's claimed by a man they back off. We can guard her with ten large men, but Salma's holding the hand of a large Nman will be the strongest protection she can get."

"How do you know they're here for Salma and not Willow or some of the other performers?" Hunter asked.

Zasquash frowned. "My guess is that they are here for both of you ladies."

"As I said," Leo said in a matter-of-fact tone, "I'll lead, Ben will hold Salma's hand to calm her down and hopefully send a signal to the Nmen that she's not single. Zasquash and Solo will..."

"But I thought she was going to hold Hunter's hand," I interrupted, knowing that none of the Nmen down there would take Ben seriously as her mate.

Leo threw up his hands with a sigh of exasperation. "I don't care who's holding her hand. I'm just trying to come up with a plan here."

I leaned toward Salma, speaking in a soft voice: "Salma dear. Whose hand do you want to hold? Ben's or Hunter's?"

She raised her head from her knees and surprised me by looking at Tristan. Although she quickly returned to hiding her face and didn't say that she'd prefer for it to be him, I got the hint. Tristan squared his shoulders and the expression on his face when he looked over at me said, *Did you see that?*

"We'll keep circling until Solo is in place." Leo was looking down at the area in front of the hotel where hundreds were standing hoping to get close to us performers. Right now, the large drone that had transported all the other Motlanders had parked and the other performers were exiting, waving to the waiting men.

"It's not different from back home in the Motherlands, just wave and smile at them." Ben used a soothing voice and stroked her back.

"Salma, if you want I can try and distract them," I suggested. "I'll draw their attention with a dance and you can slip in fast."

She didn't answer but kept rocking back and forth caught in a visible anxiety attack.

Tristan, who sat between me and Salma, leaned in and whispered something to her. Whatever Tristan had going on it seemed to work, because Salma leaned back in her seat and put one foot back on the floor.

Leo and Zasquash were talking to Solo, who was on the ground, and once the second large drone took off we began descending.

"You've got this," Tristan encouraged Salma, who was hyperventilating a little. "Remember what you told me. What is fear?"

"The body's alarm system." She closed her eyes and spoke in a fast rant. "It's just my amygdala that is making my heart beat faster so I can send more oxygen to my cells. I'm a brave person and brave people are still fearful but they manage their fear better. I'm brave and I can do this. I'm brave and I can do this."

"Woo-hoo..." Tristan gave a joyous laugh. "Now control that fear. Channel it into excitement."

Salma opened her eyes, her shoulders pulled high and her breathing fast. "I can do it. I can do it."

"You're damn right you can do it. Just smile and wave."

When the door opened, Solo was standing right outside. His eyes found mine and I felt an instant surge of my own excitement.

Leo got out. "Solo, how bad is it?"

"So far they're staying back. We've got a chain of police in place up front. I estimate there are around four hundred fans."

"Just do as you always do. Wave your hand, smile, and walk inside the hotel," Ben told Salma and followed Zasquash out of the drone, but Salma didn't follow. Biting her lips, she glanced at the large crowd and pulled back into the drone.

"Salma, look at me." Tristan stood in the opening and spoke directly to her. "A smile from you will be the highlight of their life; just sprinkle it like fairy dust and stay close to us. You're surrounded by protectors. No one will get close to you but us."

She moved forward and allowed him to help her out. The noise from the waiting Nmen rose up when they got a glimpse of Salma.

Leo's face tightened. "I don't like it. She should hold Hunter's hand."

Ben supported Salma out of the drone and shook his head at Leo. "I told you, she's not holding anyone's hand."

A roar sounded from the men as Salma raised her hand and waved while Tristan and Hunter jumped out of the drone. In a decisive movement Hunter reached up for me and set me down on the ground like I was nothing but a child. Solo watched us and turned to scowl at the large group of fans shouting for Salma. She waved at them with a stiff smile plastered on her face. Ben, Salma, and I were moving toward the hotel surrounded by Leo, Zasquash, Solo, Tristan, and Hunter when the crowd began shouting louder.

"Marry me, Salma."

"Dance for us, Willow."

"I'm your biggest fan."

"You're the prettiest woman in the world."

"I've got what you're looking for."

Shouts of all kinds came in a blurry white noise. I waved, smiled, and saw Nmen flashing t-shirts with my picture on them. These men were not all here for Salma. Many were screaming for me too.

"See you at the show tonight," I called back to them and did what I always did at home in the Motherlands, sending air kisses to the audience.

A roar of excitement erupted and Solo turned to see what I was doing to rile them up like that.

"Stop it!" he ordered and Hunter immediately barked back at him.

"You don't get to tell her what to do."

"I'm sorry." I lowered my hand just before one man broke through the chain of police officers and ran for me. "Willow, I love you," he shouted and received a fist straight to his face from Solo, who was closest. The police officers were distracted by the altercation and as they looked back more men broke through the human chain, running to get close to us.

Solo, Zasquash, and Leo reacted fast and in a unified motion they formed a wall in front of us, backing us to the entrance twenty feet behind us as they pulled their weapons. Salma screamed and hid behind Tristan while Hunter pushed me behind him.

"Get the fuck back!" Solo shouted at the eight or ten men who couldn't control their excitement. He lifted his weapon and fired a warning shot into the air.

That got the men's attention and they stopped or slowed down. But the sea of people were shouting and looking on as their fellow Nmen attempted to do what they all wished for: to get close to us women. The sea of Nmen pushed forward. We were still backing but not fast enough and that's when Solo turned his head and shouted to Tristan and Hunter. "Get them inside. NOW!"

This time Hunter didn't argue. With a tight grip around my wrist he pulled me to the hotel in a sprint. I looked over my shoulder, screaming for Salma. Ben was covering his head and ran for his life while Salma stood frozen in fear, hidden behind the wide shoulders of Leo, Zasquash, and Solo. Tristan tried screaming at her to run, but when she didn't, he picked her up in his arms and ran with her. He was almost at the door when a man pulled him back with a hand on his shoulder, shouting for Salma.

Tristan pushed forward, only a few feet away from the entrance now. "Take her," he screamed to Hunter, who stepped forward and pulled Salma into his arms, backing inside the hotel just as the attacker was flung to the ground by a wild-looking Solo. The barrier of police officers was overrun and I looked in horror at the mass of Nmen coming for us.

"Barricade the doors." Solo shouted the order before he turned to the attackers, taking the same fighting stance I'd seen him practice so many times as a young teen.

Hunter, Tristan, and some of the security officers inside the hotel pushed the wide double doors shut and locked them, leaving the sea of desperate men to pound at the windows.

"Get them upstairs. The windows are going to break," an officer shouted.

Men of the North #7 – THE DANCER

My eyes were on Solo fighting out there side by side with Leo and Zasquash, while Hunter dragged me back through the foyer toward the elevators.

All around us were fellow performers looking on in shock, but Tristan and Hunter kept their heads cool and ordered everyone inside the elevators and to the staircases.

"What about Solo and the others?" I cried out and craned my neck to see them through the sea of Nmen now blocking my view. Shots rang out and it made all the performers scream in fright.

"Leave your luggage here and get to your rooms," Hunter instructed and pushed two more into the elevator. "Go, go, go!"

We were in Freeman, the capital of the Northlands, and this hotel was larger than the one we'd been in a few nights ago. There were three elevators and two of them were already going up with frightened performers and technicians.

"Fill it up," Hunter ordered when everyone was trying to get into the last elevator to the stressful sound of pounding on the windows.

A crack was followed by a loud boom when the first wall-to-ceiling glass exploded. The sounds of the overheated shouting from the masses outside penetrated the foyer and my heart was racing so fast I thought I was going to faint.

"Women first," Tristan shouted and pulled out some male Motlanders to make room for me and Salma in the elevator. He pushed the button for the top floor and pointed his finger at me. "Willow, you're in charge, do you hear me? You're a Northlander. Tell them to hide." The doors were closing and the last thing I saw before they shut tight was Tristan looking at Salma before turning with a growl to face the mob behind him.

On the top floor, the large hallway was already full of confused and scared Motlanders.

"We need to hide. Who's gotten their room number?" Being taller than most I could see everyone.

Turned out that only a few people had been given access since it required facial recognition like in the other hotel. The registration desk had been busy scanning everyone when hell had broken loose.

"What is your room number?" I pointed at one of the men who'd raised his hand when I asked who had a number.

"Five hundred and ninety-two." He was pale as a ghost and looked unable to do anything.

"Everyone look around – who sees room five hundred and ninety-two?"

Far down the hall way a woman called out, "It's here."

"Everyone move up against the walls. You, run down and open the door."

Space opened for him to do as instructed and I called out for more room numbers.

"I have five-hundred-and seventy-four," A woman called out.

As soon as the first door opened, I ordered eight to enter with instructions to lock the door and be quiet.

Another door opened when a crying Motlander found her room number. Another eight hurried in and slammed the door shut. We worked together to find more room while my eyes kept going to the elevator, fearing any second now that it would open with Nmen high on the dream of getting close to us.

Too slowly the hallway emptied and I pulled Salma with me into the last room, taking a last look up and down the hallway to be sure it was cleared before I locked the door.

Men of the North #7 – THE DANCER

"You've got to stop crying, sweetie." I rushed her and two other women through the room and into the bathroom.

Click. I locked the door and turned to them.

"I know you're all scared, but you have to be quiet. Just sit down and take some deep breaths." I slid down next to Salma, who wouldn't stop crying.

"Listen to me." My tone grew firmer as I pulled a towel from the hanger on the wall and stuffed it under the door to block the sound of the three women crying. "I know that you've probably heard horrible things about the Nmen, but you've got to calm down. Nothing is going to happen. We'll be safe here. There are good men out there who will protect us with their lives and I promise you that none of those men in the crowd wanted to hurt us. They just got overly excited and lost their common sense for a second. Nmen aren't monsters like you've heard. Most of them are good men."

My words helped and the women's hysteria morphed into tense bodies and suppressed cries.

"I'm scared," the dark-haired woman said and hid her hands in her sleeves as if she was trying to crawl inside her sweater.

"Your name is Darlene, right?"

She nodded and sniffled.

"You spoke to my brother and Zasquash last night. They are both Nmen. Were you scared of them?"

"No. They were very nice to me."

"That's right, and right now they're standing guard to protect us."

"What if something happens to them?" Darlene's voice broke.

"Or Tristan," Salma added and it hit me that it would have been more natural for her to worry about Ben, who didn't know how to fight and protect himself.

"Tristan, Hunter, Zasquash, Leo, Solo, and all the other men you've come to know here are all superior fighters. They can take care of themselves." I spoke with as much authority as I could muster amidst my own fear for my friends and brother.

"But Tristan isn't a police officer or soldier like the others. He grew up in the Motherlands. I don't think he can fight." Salma's eyes were large with concern. "And Ben is caught down there as well. Oh, no, what about Ben?"

"Hunter and Tristan have been trained to fight and they'll protect any Motlander down there, but you have to understand no one is going to touch Ben or the other men. The Nmen aren't interested in them. I can't explain what happened out there except that it was like a mass psychosis of sorts. Trust me, when the fans realize that they've scared us they'll be ashamed of themselves."

More yelling and shouting was heard from outside, followed by shots that made us all jerk in fear.

"What's your name?" I asked the woman sitting next to Darlene, who was back to crying again. She was petite with a dark blond pixie haircut.

"Ava."

"That's a beautiful name." I was trying to distract them all by making normal small talk. "What instrument do you play?"

"The violin." She was curled up with her knees to her chin.

"I still don't understand why they would attack like that," Darlene sniffled.

I stretched my legs out in front of me trying to send a signal of calmness as I took Salma's hand. "I don't know. I've never seen anything like it."

Salma moved closer and leaned her head against my shoulder. "If Tristan hadn't been there I would have been dead."

"No, sweetie, no one would have killed you."

Men of the North #7 – THE DANCER

"He saved me." Her gray eyes were wet from all her crying.

My lips pursed upward in a sad smile. "Yeah, Tristan is a good guy."

"What did he mean when he said that you're a Northlander?" Darlene asked.

"What?"

"In the elevator. Tristan called you a Northlander and said that you were in charge."

"Oh, it's because my father was a Northlander. That's why I'm so tall."

"Did you know your father?"

"No. He was a donor. My mother was only supposed to have Hunter. I guess you could say I was the plus-one that no one expected… or wanted."

Darlene frowned, so I hurried to add, "Forget the last part, the family unit where I grew up was nice." There was no need to bring up how lonely I'd felt being the only child without a real parent.

Salma was still holding my hand, but her crying had died down. "I still can't believe your mother didn't want you. That's so odd."

I was twenty-two years old but thinking about it still hurt, and even more so that none of the adults in my family unit had adopted me as their own. Tristan and Hunter had speculated that it was because of the known fact that I was of Northlander blood. Too tall, too feisty. A wild card.

"But what did Tristan mean when he said that you were in charge?"

I brushed my free hand against my pants. It was clammy, and my mouth felt dry from all the angst we'd just gone through. "It's just that Northlanders see themselves as stronger leaders. To be honest, they think of us Motlanders as a bit fragile."

"Fragile?" Salma's voice was full of indignation and even though nothing should be funny at this moment, I hid a smile. With all her anxiety she would be perceived as fragile by Northlanders for sure.

Darlene lowered her brow. "I don't see us as fragile at all. I mean, we might not compare to them physically but I consider myself a strong woman."

"Me too." Salma brushed her hair back. "It took a lot to even come here to the Northlands. To get up on stage and conquer my fear night after night. A weak person couldn't do it."

I leaned my head back against the wall, a feeling of shame washing over me. Salma was right. Being one of the biggest stars of the world was more pressure than most people experienced in a lifetime. She carried it on her shoulders while battling her inner demons.

"You're right. A weak person couldn't do what you do," I admitted.

We squeezed each other's hands, a look of understanding between us.

"I don't hear any more gunshots." Ava tilted her head. "Listen."

We were all quiet and listening for sounds, but except for shouts outside there was nothing. "They ceased shooting. That's good, right?" Ava looked at me as if I had experience with this sort of thing.

"Uh-huh." I nodded. "That means the police have control." At least I hoped they did.

"What if someone got killed?" Darlene teared up again. "I can't stand the thought that our coming here might have resulted in someone dying."

"No one is dead." I used a firm voice. My brother, Tristan, and Solo were out there. The thought of any of them getting hurt had my stomach in a knot and I refused to even talk about it.

"Let's change the subject." Darlene looked at me. "When are you getting married?"

"Ehh... what do you mean?"

"Hunter told me you and Tristan are a couple."

"Right." I looked down. "But we don't plan on marrying any time soon." It was the best answer I could give without lying.

"Willow, I don't know how to say this but you don't seem to be in love with Tristan, and this morning he sounded like he wasn't in love with you either. Like it was something you did to make Solo think you were taken." Salma bit her lip.

I sighed. "Yeah, Tristan blew it this morning. I hope the others didn't pick up on it." I lifted my hands. "Please don't tell anyone about it."

"We'll keep your secret." Salma turned to look at Darlene and Ava. "Right?"

They both gave solemn nods.

"Tristan is a good friend and he's helping me by being a buffer between me and Solo."

"You mean the soldier who was missing this morning."

"Yes, that's Solo."

"I don't blame you for keeping him away. He's scary with his size, and he always looks so angry." Ava changed her position on the floor.

Salma was quick to defend Solo. "It's because you don't know him. Solo is a giant but very nice when you talk to him."

Darlene frowned. "Still, I'm impressed that Tristan is protecting you from him. I can't imagine many men would want to get in the way of someone like him."

Ava chimed in. "I heard he kidnapped a woman once. A priestess."

"No, that was Magni and it happened ten years ago," I corrected her. "Who told you that anyway?"

"Solo kidnapped Willow," Salma informed the two women. "Hence her need for a buffer between them."

"He kidnapped you?" Both Darlene and Ava made outbursts of shock.

"He didn't kidnap me. I've told Hunter to stop saying it a million times."

He didn't kidnap me... The sound of a young woman's scream inside my head made me sit up straight.

I could hear the three women's discussion in the background, but my mind had gone to a time seven years ago when I had defended Solo with everything I had.

CHAPTER 19
Reflections

Year 2440 – Seven years earlier

Willow

"You're not married to him."

"Yes, I am. We had a ceremony and I gave him my word."

The doctor shook her head. "He manipulated you, Willow. You didn't know what you were doing."

"It was *I* who wanted it."

"That's what he made you believe."

"NO!" I screamed at her.

"The marriage wasn't official and therefore invalid. You're *not* married and any promise you might have given him isn't binding. Sweetie, you might as well come to terms with the fact that you'll never see him again. It's for your own good."

"You don't understand. I *love* him," I cried.

"No, Willow, you only think you love him."

"Solo is my soulmate."

"Honey." The doctor came to sit next to me. "I know this is confusing to you and you're very young. We all want to help you and make you feel happy again."

"I'll never be happy until I'm with Solo again."

"You just need some time to see things in a clearer perspective. What kind of life would you have had in the forest? Huh?" Her stroking my hair made me turn my head away.

"How about a walk in the park? The ducks just had ducklings and they are so cute."

I kept my head turned away.

"At least eat something. I see you haven't touched your breakfast."

"I will if you let me see Solo."

"I'm afraid that's not in my power. I understand that he broke many of the laws in the Northlands and I've been guaranteed that he won't be allowed to travel here. You're safe from him."

"Then I'll go back."

"You can't. After what happened, you won't be allowed to travel back to the Northlands."

I lifted my head. "Ever?"

She gave me a sympathetic smile. "Not for a long time, Willow. Maybe when you're older and we trust that you'll make better decisions for yourself."

"But what about my brother? When will I see Hunter again?"

"Have you spoken to him?"

I shook my head. The shame of leaving my twin without a goodbye weighed heavily on me.

"Would you like to?"

My eyes closed and tears ran down my cheeks. "He's going to be so mad and disappointed with me."

"Can you blame him?"

My head drooped down, my shoulders high as if I could retract my body like a tortoise hiding from the world.

"Willow." Her hand was on my knee, her tone soft and patient. "We all love you and that includes your brother. If he's disappointed then that's okay. Think of the alternative."

"What do you mean?" My voice was hoarse from five days of screaming and crying.

"How would you feel if Hunter wasn't disappointed? If he didn't care?"

I dried my eyes and looked at her with confusion.

"If you had run away and no one had even noticed – how would that feel?"

Blinking my eyes, I thought about it.

"When you left, everyone panicked, and I heard that they sent out the army to fetch you back. Do you realize what that means?"

I didn't answer.

"It means that you truly matter, Willow. Your brother, the teachers, the Council, your friends, and family. Everyone was worried because they care about you. Don't you see that you're loved?"

I looked down, my bedcover twisted tight in my hands.

"We know that you were seduced to run away and no one is angry at you. Solomon was the older one and he lured you, didn't he?"

"No." I shook my head, confused from days of questions, lack of sleep, and hunger.

"Don't worry. You're safe now and all we ask is that you use that smart brain of yours to think for yourself. I'm sure you're intelligent enough to see that two kids couldn't have survived in the wild for long. It's too dangerous. Solomon isn't your friend, Willow. What he did was reckless and wrong. You were lucky to survive."

"You don't know him."

"You're right. I don't know him. I look only at his actions and what he did to you. He came close to killing you. I hope you understand that." She lifted my chin. "Look in the mirror and see what we see."

My eyes found my reflection in the mirror across the room. I looked malnourished, pale, and sad.

"When was the last time you showered? You have a broken arm, three infected wounds, you're underweight, and you'll have a scar from the cut to your neck. And that's not even mentioning the concussion you got from the fall. You could have broken your skull."

I looked away, not liking the sight of the sickly-looking girl in the mirror or the doctor's accusations against Solo.

"How about you take a shower and eat something? After that I would like you to come outside and get some fresh air. It'll make you feel better and stronger."

"No." I looked away.

"Willow." She said my name like it was an argument for me to do as I was told.

My face remained demonstratively turned away.

"All right. Maybe just get some sleep then." She got up and left the room with a last comment. "Think, Willow. Just think about it. You were saved by the soldiers. No one is punishing you. We're your friends."

I did think, but my loyalty to Solo was stronger and although some of what the doctors and caregivers kept telling me was starting to resonate, I still refused to eat or shower. It was my silent protest and my way of showing solidarity with Solo, whom I worried about.

On the ninth day, I was hospitalized and force-fed through tubes. They urged me to start living again, but how could I when I didn't know what had happened to Solomon?

Hunter came to see me. I was weak and tired but managed a small smile.

"Willow." He took my hand and sat down next to me; our green eyes met and I cried when I saw my strong brother tearing up. "Willow," he repeated as if he had no words. "What did he do to you?" His hands ran over my face and hair. "You're so thin."

"I'm sorry." I meant it, because out of all the people who had been to see me, Hunter meant the most.

"They say you've given up on life." He squeezed my right hand with both of his and placed his forehead against our hands.

I lifted my left hand and placed it on top of his head, my body weak and my broken heart falling further apart at the sound of Hunter crying.

Finally, he looked up at me with bloodshot eyes. "You're my only family, Willow. I love you. Don't I mean anything to you?" His voice broke as he breathed the last sentence.

"Of course you do." I sniffled. "I love you too. You're my twin brother."

"Then how can you choose Solo over me? He would have taken everything from you. Can't you see how selfish he is? Solo doesn't care about you. He only cares about himself."

I licked my lips and chewed on them, my eyebrows drawn together. "I never meant to hurt anyone. Least of all you. You know that, right?"

Hunter's head fell forward again. "I can't lose you."

Shame over hurting my brother filled me. "I'm sorry, Hunter."

"Why can't you see that running away with him was wrong?"

"I didn't mean to hurt anyone," I repeated.

"But you did, Willow. You hurt *me* and you hurt yourself. They told me you have post-traumatic stress disorder, did you know that?"

"No."

"That's why you're so confused about what happened. That and your feelings for Solo. You're not seeing him for what he is. No honorable Nman would put you in danger like that."

"Solo didn't mean to hurt me."

"Don't mention his name. I *hate* him and you should too. It's because of him you're here, in a hospital bed hooked up to feeding tubes." He pointed. "What happened to the happy gorgeous girl I used to know? I'll tell you what happened. *He* did!"

I sighed and closed my eyes.

"After what he did to you, he doesn't have a single friend left in the Northlands and I doubt he has much of a future. We don't tolerate men who kidnap women."

"Stop saying that he kidnapped me. And even if he did, Hunter, then what about Magni? You know he kidnapped Athena, don't you?"

"Yes."

"Then why wasn't he killed for it? As far as I know he still has plenty of friends left in the Northlands."

"That's different. Magni was trying to get Laura back."

"Are you saying that his desperate act of love can be forgiven, but Solo's can't?"

Hunter moved to the edge of his seat. "Magni never hurt a hair on Athena's head. He may have frightened her but he kept her safe. You came close to dying." He lowered his voice and pleaded, "Why won't you admit that he hurt you? Are you so traumatized that you have no grasp on reality? Look at you..." he pointed to my broken arm.

I knew he was right. "But he never meant to hurt me."

"I don't care. You're lucky to be alive. Admit it."

I gave a small nod that felt like a huge betrayal. "I know."

Hunter squeezed my hand more firmly, his worried gaze locked on me. "They told me you're not eating and I begged them to let me come and see you. I promised that I could get you to eat again. Please let me prove I'm right. If you do, they might let me stay longer."

"But you'll miss out on school."

Hunter's eyes were moist from all the crying. "I don't care about school. I want to be here with you and make sure you get back to being healthy and strong. You're my twin."

I whispered a soft "Thank you."

He wiped his face and took a steadying breath before picking his backpack up from the floor. "So, tell me, what

Men of the North #7 – THE DANCER

would you like to eat first?" Out of his bag came a box with chocolate cake and another with a sandwich.

"What's in the sandwich?"

"Not sure, but it's vegetarian."

I pointed to the chocolate cake. "Let me try some of that."

Hunter lit up and fumbled with eagerness to open the box. "Here you go."

I used my fingers to break off a piece and brought it to my mouth. "Mmm… it's good," I lied to make him happy. In reality it didn't taste like much, and I wasn't sure if it was the cake or because my taste buds had stopped working.

"Yeah? You like it?"

"Uh-huh." I took some more, wanting to make up for some of the pain I had caused Hunter. "Do you know what happened to Solo?"

He frowned and looked down at the sandwich. "I beat him up is what happened."

My hand stalled mid-air and a small gasp escaped me.

"He came to explain himself but I'm not listening to anything he has to say. If Magni and Boulder hadn't pulled us apart I would have killed him."

My eyes were wide with shock. "You tried to kill Solo?"

"Yes. I attacked the moment I saw him. I'm your protector, Willow."

"But you were best friends."

Hunter narrowed his eyes. "Solomon is dead to me and he'd better be dead to you too."

I turned my head away.

"Willow. I'm sorry if that's too harsh for you, but he deserves to die for what he did to you."

Turning my head back, I looked straight at my brother. "If you kill Solo, you're dead to me."

Hunter's head jerked back and for seconds he collected himself.

"I would tell Solo the same thing," I said. "If he killed you, I wouldn't speak to him ever again."

Looking down and clearing his throat, Hunter spoke low. "Fair enough. I know you don't like violence, but just so we're clear: if he comes near you, I'll do what I have to do to protect you from him, including killing him."

"What if I don't want to be protected from him?"

"Willow." A deep sigh escaped my brother. "What will it take to make you see that Solo isn't a good person? You've got to give him up. You already came close to dying when you were with him."

I couldn't deny that.

"Eat some more." Hunter pushed the chocolate cake higher up on the bed. "For me."

"Only if you promise that you won't go after Solo."

"I'll give you my word, but only if you start eating and living again."

"It's hard."

"I know. But the stronger you get the more you'll realize that you were lucky to get away from him. Solo never loved you or he wouldn't have put you in danger like that." He held up the chocolate cake to me and with a heavy sigh I broke off another piece.

"That's what everybody keeps saying."

"Because we're right and it's time for you to accept it, Willow. If Solo really loved you, he would have protected and cared for you. Not put you in a dangerous situation that almost killed you."

I swallowed hard, the chocolate cake feeling like a sandbox in my mouth.

"I love you, Willow, and I don't want anything bad happening to you."

"I love you too, Hunter."

He watched me chew every small bite.

I pointed to the sandwich in his hand. "Maybe you should eat that. You look thinner too."

"It's because I've been so worried about you. Do you have any idea how much it hurts to hear that your twin has given up on life?"

I closed my eyes, the pain of his words touching my soul. I'd been unwanted by our mother and until I came to the school, I'd been the only child I knew who wasn't living with her biological mom or with adopted parents. The psychologist here had speculated that it was the reason for my loyalty to Solo. According to her, it wasn't love between us but the fact that he'd been the first to make me feel a hundred percent wanted and accepted.

"Did you hear me? How would you feel if someone told you I didn't want to live anymore?"

The thought of losing Hunter made every part of my body hurt and I began crying again.

"I'm so sorry," I sniffled. For my twin to think that I didn't think he was worth living for made me ashamed of myself.

Hunter leaned in, using his thumb to brush tears from my cheeks. "I hate it when you cry."

I leaned my cheek against his hand. "I don't want to die." It was the truth.

"But you're not living either," he argued in a voice raw from emotions and with tears in his own eyes.

"I know." My head dipped forward, tears dripping on my hands.

Hunter got up on my bed to hug me. "Please live, sis. I *need* you to live."

I held on to him and we cried together. "I will... for you."

"No, Willow. It has to be for *you*," he pleaded.

I nodded and sniffled. "For me then."

"Yes." After planting a kiss on my forehead, Hunter got back in his chair and watched me. "I'll help you, sis. Let's start with you eating that cake and me eating this sandwich."

"It's vegetarian."

He opened the wrapping and sniffed at it. "I'll just pretend it's a roast beef sandwich."

"Then I'll pretend this is…" I tilted my head. "Chocolate cake."

It was a lame joke but Hunter gave me a small smile and kept his eyes on me as I forced myself to eat the cake.

He ate the sandwich in three bites and waited for me to finish. When I finally did, he gave me a smile of gratefulness and satisfaction.

CHAPTER 20
Cultural Breakdown

Year 2447
Solomon

"Do you need bone accelerator?" I looked at Zasquash, who was rubbing his wrist.

"Nah, I don't think it's broken. Just strained." He scowled and looked out the window, where a large group of men were being contained by the police and slowly led onto a transport. "Way to fucking ruin it for everyone. Morons!"

"At least all the Motlanders are safe." My tone was flat and didn't reveal the anger and worry still left in my body. I twisted my head from side to side and rolled my shoulders to work out the kinks and get rid of the tension.

Zasquash snorted. "The Momsies are fucking traumatized. It must have looked worse to them than it really was. How would they know the difference between angry Nmen and excited Nmen?"

Hunter stood a few feet from us, his head peeking in through the door to the room where all the Motlanders were gathered for a crisis meeting. He turned his head and spoke to Zasquash, "Of course they are traumatized. Some of those fuckers looked ready to kill to get close to the women."

Zasquash didn't respond. Like me his eyes had been drawn in by the interactive wall; it had been showing a tropical rain forest but we had switched it to the news that was covering the situation live.

"Leo is being interviewed." Zasquash folded his arms in front of him while Hunter moved closer to see as well.

"Inspector Leo da Vinci, can you tell us what is happening inside the hotel as we speak?" the interviewer asked.

Leo had a stern expression on his face. His uniform was ripped near the shoulder and his dark hair pulled back in a messy bun as always.

"Yes, well, ehh... right now the performers and crew are gathered to talk about what happened. I spoke with them ten minutes ago to assure them that nothing like what happened here today will occur in the future. When I left them, they were discussing among themselves whether to stay or go home."

The interviewer was a famous reporter called Zeus who had been on the news for as long as I could remember. His gray hair was thinning but he had a youthful curiosity about him and he was known to ask sharp questions. "How can you guarantee that it won't happen again?"

Leo answered fast. "Because we're doubling the security. I've already spoken to Commander Magni and more members of the Doom Squad are flying in as we speak."

Zeus nodded. "We've been told that there were no casualties today, but many got injured. Do you want to comment on that?"

Leo lifted one hand and scratched his neck. "To be honest, I'm pissed that some of my men got hurt just because some assholes can't control themselves."

"Do you think the rest of the tour will be canceled after this?"

Leo looked down and sighed. "It's very possible."

Zeus kept asking questions and looked into the camera as he spoke. "What do you think it will mean to the integration process between our nations that this unfortunate episode happened so close to the tragic death

Men of the North #7 – THE DANCER

of Josephine Martin, the Motlander bride who was killed by her husband only fifteen days ago?"

Leo groaned and rubbed his forehead as if the whole thing was giving him a migraine. "We can't know what the hell they'll do. I wouldn't blame the Council for building an even higher wall after all the stupidity we've seen from our countrymen lately. It's fucked up for sure."

"Do you have any last comment before you head back inside?"

Leo turned to the camera and narrowed his eyes. "Yeah, I have one message to all of you watching. If you think what happened here today was acceptable, then you're fucking dickheads. We're better than this. What happened to honor? And what happened to defending women? Right now we have a large room full of frightened females behind me. Women who came to enrich our lives with their art. I can't tell you how it broke my heart to find them hiding in hotel rooms, crying, shaking, and fearing for their lives. It made me fucking ashamed to be an Nman."

Zeus gave a deep sigh and shook his head. "I think many of us feel this way. You said you found the women hiding in their hotel rooms; can you elaborate on that?"

"No, I'm sure you get the picture and I have places to be."

"Thank you, Inspector, Leo Da Vinci." Zeus turned to the camera while Leo was already walking away.

Zasquash had his hands in his pants pockets and muttered, "He should have told them that we'll shoot to kill the next time someone tries to get close."

"Why didn't you?" Hunter asked.

"Because unlike what most people think, we Doomsmen don't enjoy killing people."

"I never said that you enjoy it. Just that some members of your squad like to *hurt* people."

Knowing full well that Hunter was referring to me, I moved away. Engaging in an argument to try and change his mind seemed like a lost cause at this point, so instead I walked in to the conference room and took up a position next to Tristan, who was leaning against the wall in the back.

"They are still discussing it," he whispered. "Everyone is being heard. The choir and the technical staff argued that they should all go home. The orchestra is split, and now it's Salma and Willow's time to speak as the last two."

"How is she doing?" I nodded to Salma, who stood up in front of the seated group. "I mean with her anxiety and all."

"She was petrified, but I'm surprised at how forgiving she is of the fans. She understands that the fans didn't intend to hurt them and she told me Willow was amazing at calming her down." Tristan smiled but kept looking straight ahead. "I'm so fucking proud of my woman."

My hands formed into fists at hearing him call Willow *his* woman. It was right there on my tongue: the truth about the things Willow and I had done this morning in the bathroom. I had always liked Tristan as a person, and under different circumstances touching his woman would tear me apart with guilt and shame. But this was Willow, and she was mine before she was his.

Salma cleared her voice and began speaking. "Thank you to everyone for expressing your points of view. I want to start out by saying that I understand those of you who want to go home. What happened today was awful and scary. I don't think I've ever been as terrified in my life." She looked down. "And that says a lot because I'm kind of an expert on fear. Ever since I was a teenager, I've suffered from anxiety and if there's anything I've learned about fear, it's that we can never bow down to it." She stopped talking and I was afraid she couldn't continue, but Salma stiffened her back and carried on. "Fear can be healthy

Men of the North #7 – THE DANCER

and keep us from walking into harmful situations. It's that feeling in your stomach when something doesn't feel right. But fear is greedy and dominant by nature. If we allow it too much power over us, fear will control us and rule our lives. It will terrorize us with worst-case scenarios in our minds, and I can tell you from experience that if you allow fear to become your master you'll soon find yourself living isolated and alone in the safety of your bedroom. Every day I battle my fear, and I don't wish it upon my worst enemy."

Willow placed a hand on Salma's shoulder and gave her an encouraging smile before Salma continued.

"On normal days my fear whispers about tripping onstage, making a fool out of myself, people hating me, or my performance being a complete failure. Today was much worse than that but I'm still here." She threw her hands in the air, and her chest lifted in a deep inhalation. "We were all frightened and let me repeat, that I don't blame any of you if you decide to go home. I just hope you're brave enough to overcome your fear and finish what we started." Her head turned to Willow. "Do you want to add something?"

The two women held hands as Willow stepped forward and spoke up. "If we go home now, there's a real possibility that no other performers will ever visit from the Motherlands. The political situation is heated. We can all see that." She paused. "But who better to build a bridge over troubled water than artists? We don't speak about political agendas or cast blame or shame on anyone. Our gift to the world is one of art, music, song, and dancing. It's a language that speaks to the soul. A strong man once told me that times of pressure offer us the chance to flex our muscles."

Tristan turned his head to me. "Sounds like something Archer would say."

"Uh-huh." I didn't tell him that Willow hadn't gotten that quote from Archer but me. I had told her that while we were on the run together.

"Northlanders think we Motlanders are weak and fragile. If we go home now no one will blame us, but we'll miss our chance to prove them wrong. If we stay we could serve as a colorful bridge of art that connects people in these times of strong division. What if we found the courage to stay and spread light in a dark time? What if our show gives hope to people who have none? Who better than us to show the world that there is beauty and joy on both sides of the border?"

"But it's dangerous," someone argued.

Willow nodded. "I'll be the first to admit that I was scared today. My biggest fear, however, is that our countries go back to how things used to be with no contact across the border. My brother is here in the Northlands and so are many of my friends. Not seeing them again scares me." It felt like Willow was looking at me, but then I turned my head and saw that Hunter had joined us together with Zasquash.

"Yes, some of the Nmen lost their minds today when they stormed the hotel, but this is all new to them and security has been doubled. Leo and his team say that they'll keep us safe. They have so far, and now they'll have more men available. I trust in them. And I guess what I'm trying to say is, *the show must go on*. Just like Salma Rose, I'm ready to finish what I came here to do."

Salma smiled at Willow and turned to the other performers. "Let's vote. Who's willing to stay with me and Willow?"

More than half of the other performers and crew members raised their hands.

"Who wants to go home?"

A few raised their hands, others looked torn.

Ben clapped and demanded attention. "With a majority of votes in favor of staying, we'll go through with the show tonight. If anyone wants to leave, come see me and I'll make the arrangements. For the rest of you, please get ready. We're leaving for the concert hall at three thirty. That's in thirty-seven minutes. And one last thing: please remember, security will be increased, so don't be alarmed by the extra number of police and military. They are here to keep us safe."

Salma and Willow were some of the last to leave the room.

"What a speech!" Tristan bowed his head to them. "You two should go into politics."

Salma smiled. "You liked it?"

"I loved it. Sounded like you were talking about me. I'm kinda like a bridge too, you know. I belong on both sides." Tristan gave Salma a charming grin, and the connection between them had me frowning. If I didn't know any better I would have thought he was coming on to her.

Again, Zasquash's suspicion that Willow and Tristan weren't together came back to me. It was the only explanation for this tactless behavior from him.

"Come on, ladies, you don't have long to get ready." Ben placed his hands on the smalls of Salma's and Willow's backs and hurried them along. It didn't escape me how Salma's head turned as if the connection between her and Tristan was hard to break.

He took a step to follow but before he could walk out the door, I closed it and pushed him back with a hand to his chest. "What the fuck is going on?"

Tristan looked surprised. "What do you mean?"

"You're undressing Salma with your eyes in front of Willow. Are you out of your mind?"

Tristan pushed my hand away from his chest. "You saw wrong."

"Oh yeah?" I moved closer. "I don't think so."

Tristan leaned back to create distance between us. "Willow is none of your concern. You know how she feels about you. It's long over between you and her."

It didn't feel over. Not when I could still feel the taste of her on my lips. I kept that part to myself.

Tristan lifted his right hand and patted my shoulder. "There'll be someone else for you. Don't worry."

I didn't answer but just looked after him as he moved out the door. If Willow were still mine and someone had accused me of being interested in another woman, I'd have reacted much more strongly than he did. Why hadn't he defended himself and convinced me how much he loved Willow?

My wristband vibrated and I took an incoming call from Leo.

"Where are you?"

I exited the conference room. "Right behind you. I'll be there in a minute."

"Speed up. I need you here *now*." He sounded annoyed.

"Did something happen?" I jogged down the hallway past Tristan, who automatically joined in, probably thinking something was wrong.

Leo groaned. "Just fucking get here."

I turned the corner and took the stairs two flights up with Tristan on my heels to see Leo standing outside room 281 tapping his foot. "There you are!"

Slowing down to a walk, I looked straight at him. "What do you need?"

"There's been a change. I just spoke to Commander Magni and he wants us to come straight to the West Coast. Khan is furious about what happened today, and he has decided that the remaining shows will be held at the Gray Manor. It's better for us since it's easier to guard the performers there."

"But what about all the tickets that have already been sold for shows in the different cities?"

"People will have to go to the West Coast if they want to see the show."

"Huh." I scratched my arm. "So, no show tonight then?"

"That's right." Leo turned to Tristan. "Hunter said he's coming with us to the West Coast. How about you?"

"Sure, I'll go."

"And you?" Leo pinned me with his eyes.

I raised both eyebrows. "I didn't know I had a choice."

"You don't. I just need to know that I won't have any problems with you and Hunter in the same drone. It's a three-hour flight."

I shoved my hands in my pockets. "I don't have a problem with Hunter. It's the other way around."

Leo rolled his eyes and released a deep breath. "I don't get paid enough to play the fucking mediator between you two." He opened the door to the hotel room and called, "Hunter, come out here for a second."

The large soccer player who had once been my best friend came out. As always, he ignored me.

"Hunter, I asked Magni about your request to have Solo removed from this assignment and he told me to tell you to go fuck yourself."

Hunter snorted but I doubted he was in any way surprised.

"I told you the Commander wouldn't like it." Leo tilted his head. "Right now I need both of you to give me your word that you can suck it up and get along. We have a bunch of traumatized Momsies and the last thing we need is you two getting in a fight on board the drone."

Hunter's eyes glided to me. They were frosty.

"I don't have time for your bad blood." Leo placed a hand on his right hip. "For the next three hours you'll be fucking civil. Do you understand?"

"I'm always civil." Hunter raised his chin up.

Leo narrowed his eyes, looking from Hunter to me and back again. At twenty-nine, Leo was older than Hunter and me. With his strong authoritarian no-bullshit attitude it was no wonder he was respected among his men.

Hunter's tongue pushed his cheek out and he looked torn.

Leo lowered his voice. "I mean it, Hunter. I won't tolerate any bullshit from you."

"Why don't you tell *him* that?" He lifted his chin in a nod toward me.

"Because Solo doesn't have a problem with you."

Hunter scoffed as if he didn't believe it.

"Are you two going to shake hands and make peace for the next three hours?"

The way Hunter tucked his hands under his armpits said it all.

Leo groaned. "Hunter, don't test me. Just fucking do as I tell you to."

I could have predicted Hunter's reaction. He was a strong alpha like me and didn't like to be told what to do.

"Sorry, Leo, but you're not the boss of me."

Leo mirrored Hunter's stubborn expression. "You're right, but I can make your life a living hell and so can Commander Magni. Don't forget where we're headed."

With a slick movement, Hunter brushed his hair back and gave a shrug. "How about I just fly my own drone? I can take Willow with me and you men can watch over Salma and the others."

"Take your own drone if you want, but Willow is under my protection and she's coming with us."

"Fine, I'll be close if something happens."

Half an hour later Hunter's drone had arrived and so had five more Doomsmen from our unit. Instead of flying in the large transport we were dividing the Motlanders into smaller groups.

"Zasquash, when you're done drooling over Hunter's drone could you get your ass over here?" Leo was looking more and more exhausted from dealing with the constant changes.

Zasquash turned to face us. "Hunter says he'll be flying – who wants to fly with me and him?"

Leo closed his eyes for a second, but to my surprise he didn't order Zasquash back to our drone or scold him for not sticking to the plan. Instead he waved four Motlanders toward Hunter and Zasquash. "You'll go with them."

"But I thought Darlene was coming with us," Salma complained.

The woman from the orchestra, whom I recognized as Darlene, stood torn in the middle of the two drones. Her three colleagues kept walking toward Hunter and Zasquash.

"Come on, gorgeous, we don't bite." Zasquash clapped the drone. "This is the fastest drone in all of the world. You don't want to miss this."

With a last apologetic glance back at Salma, Darlene continued.

"Everyone, get on board the drones." Leo made sure to spread out his police officers and us seven Doomsmen.

I took a seat and looked out the window at Hunter's drone. Zasquash was laughing with Hunter, who was showing off his drone with pride.

My drone was nothing like that. It was a plain model from 2435 that I'd bought from one of my colleagues. The twelve years of use showed, and it had several problems that I needed to get fixed as soon as I had time and money. My job gave me access to military drones and maybe that was why a new drone hadn't been on the top of my list. That, and the fact that all my free time and financial resources had gone toward building my large cabin in the woods. But to be honest, I would have loved to fly in Hunter's drone too.

The three-hour flight gave me plenty of time to study the dynamic between Willow and Tristan. He entertained all of us with stories that had everyone laughing and Willow touched him several times, but always like she would touch a friend. It was a hand to his back, a bump with her shoulder when he was teasing her, and at one point she tousled his hair and accused him of exaggerating.

Salma was on Tristan's other side and ate up every word he said. Her hands landed on his knee, arm, or thigh a few times, but then it might not mean much to her as Motlanders were used to touching each other excessively. From where I was sitting it looked like any attraction there might have been between Willow and Tristan had fizzled out. They seemed more like friends, while Salma and Tristan shared a spark of genuine interest. But maybe I was just biased and saw what I wanted to see. I decided to press the dynamics a little to test my theory. "By the way, Salma, did you think about the suggestion of holding hands with a Northlander to increase your level of security?"

Yes, there it was again. Her eyes flew to Tristan.

Salma tilted her head. "Do you think it's necessary now that we're going to be at the palace?"

"No. But it's a small thing that will make things easier. Like Zasquash said, choosing a Doomsman will be a sure way of keeping all others away. I'm happy to hold your hand if you want me to."

"Or you could choose Hunter," Willow added, and it almost made me smile. Maybe I was overinterpreting, but there was a real chance she didn't like the idea of me claiming Salma in public.

Tristan cleared his throat and squirmed in his seat. "You should pick the Nman you feel most comfortable with."

Silence filled the drone as we all looked at Salma.

"The Nman I feel most comfortable with would be you, Tristan," Salma said in a soft voice. "But maybe that's because you're half Motlander."

"That won't work," I declared. "He's marrying Willow soon. You're better off with me or Zasquash. We're single and that would make it more believable."

Leo nodded. "Or me. I'm single too."

It was so much fun to pretend to be unaware of all the tension emanating from Tristan and Willow. His lips were squeezed tight as if he was holding in the need to exclaim, "Pick me, I'm single."

"Thank you for the nice offer. Let me think about it." Salma turned her head and looked out over the area that we were flying over. It was gorgeous with rolling hills, valleys, and a river snaking its way through the wild landscape.

"The view is breathtaking," Salma whispered as if in awe.

"Yeah, you never get tired of all the lushness." I pointed ahead of us. "Do you see that large forest?"

"Yeah."

"It's called the Northwoods and it's the second largest forest in the Northlands."

Salma wrinkled her nose. "It seems endless. I would be afraid to go in there. I'm not a child of nature, that's for sure."

I smiled at her. "Then you wouldn't like living with me. My house is in a forest."

"You live in the wilderness?" Salma widened her eyes.

"Uh-huh."

Ben, who had been reading since we left the hotel, lifted his head from his book and wrinkled his nose. "Why?"

I shrugged. "Why not?"

He lowered his book. "But isn't it terribly isolated and lonely?"

"Isolated for sure," I agreed. "I built my cabin on a beautiful spot just by a river that holds a special meaning to me." When I said it, my eyes drifted to Willow, and her head leaned to the side and then her mouth opened in a silent *oh*.

Leo spoke up. "I've been there. It's gorgeous."

My lips quirked upward as I met his eyes. "Thank you. You should come by more often, then. The river is excellent for fishing this time of year."

Salma jerked in her seat. "Fishing is barbaric."

Leo didn't look fazed by her criticism at all. "I love fishing. Just say when and I'd love to come."

Salma shook her head. "I can't believe you'd be that heartless, Leo."

Chuckling, I shook my head. "You Motlanders crack me up. Do you think the fish worries about being heartless when it eats other fish? Or what about the bear that eats the fish? It's the food chain, Salma. It's been that way for millions of years."

"That doesn't make it right."

"Actually, it does. There's nothing better than a fresh-cooked fish roasted over the fire. You have no idea what you're missing out on."

"I don't fish," Tristan hurried to say. "And I'm a vegan too."

Willow raised her eyebrows and gave Tristan a pointed stare, calling him out on his lie. We'd both seen him eat meat several times.

"What?" he said with his shoulders popping up in a shrug. "You know I was raised in the Motherlands. I'm a vegan."

"Oh, for sure. Your blood type is basically chlorophyll." Willow's use of sarcasm went over the head of Ben and Salma, but the rest of us got it and my stomach filled up with butterflies. Fuck, I'd missed being around Willow when she was relaxed and not worried about our troubled past.

"Okay, so I may have strayed from the vegan path a little," Tristan admitted. "But I'm a vegan ninety-five percent of the time."

Willow and I exchanged a quick look of amusement.

"I hope you go back to being a full-time vegan again." Salma leaned in and placed a hand on his elbow and was rewarded with a warm smile from Tristan.

As expected, Willow didn't look bothered at all.

"Be careful with all that touching, Salma," I warned her. "Tristan is used to it because of his being half Motlander. He knows it doesn't mean anything to you, but other men would get the wrong idea."

Ben looked up. "That's a good point, darling. We don't want any more drama on this tour."

Salma folded her hands in her lap. "Thank you for reminding me, Solo. I'll be more aware and keep my hands to myself from now on."

The way Tristan tensed his jaw with suppressed irritation made me turn my head and look out the window to hide the smile on my face. There was no fucking way he and Willow were in love, and that meant I still had a chance.

CHAPTER 21
Taking Chances

Willow

I'd been to the Gray Manor a few times before, but it was still as impressive as the first time. Built to resemble something from the old world, the windows were large with black frames and the color of the façade a crème-colored beige.

Mila was there to welcome us, giving both me and Tristan big hugs and holding Ben's and Salma's hands in official Motlander greetings.

"I'd hug you too if you'd let me," she told Solo but he kept his distance.

"Thanks, but only a man with a death wish would hug Magni's daughter."

"You're silly. My dad isn't so bad."

The expression on Solo's face told me he disagreed.

"Raven is here somewhere. She and the kids are just helping some of your travel companions to their rooms. We're all so excited to fill the manor for once."

"You have room for all of us?" I asked.

"No, only the performers and technicians." Her eyes went to Solo and Leo. "The security will be sleeping in the greenhouse in the park. Don't worry, it's large and very nice. I helped set up beds and we even hung some adorable strings of light in there to make it cozy for you."

Solo smiled at her. "Mila, you're too kind, but I don't mind sleeping under the stars. It's summer."

"That's what Khan and my dad said, but I convinced them that you should at least have a tent or some kind of roof over your head. You know, in case it begins to rain."

"Who did your braid?" I asked. "It looks beautiful."

Mila's hands touched the braided circle of blonde hair on top of her head, her dimples popping out. "I did. I'm glad you like it. I wasn't sure if the flowers were a bit much."

"Not at all. It looks adorable."

The sound of running feet made us turn to the double entrance doors, where a group of children and Raven came out. One of the boys stopped right in front of Solo. He was a little taller than me with copper-colored hair and I recognized him from the reunion party as Magni's son, Mason.

Leaning his head back, the boy looked up at Solo. "I know who you are."

Solo wrinkled his brow. "So do I."

"Yeah, but do you know who I am?" the boy asked eagerly.

Solomon nodded. "I have a pretty good idea that you're Laura's and Magni's son, aren't you?"

"Could you tell from my size?" The boy straightened to his full height. "I'm tall for my age, just like my dad was."

"And strong too, it looks."

Mila stepped forward. "Mason just turned ten but he's very proud of his height."

"I'm going to be eight or nine feet tall at least," he bragged.

"Oh dear." Salma held a hand to her mouth.

Solo looked amused.

"My dad says that you're the best warrior he has ever trained and that when I can beat you, I can call myself the greatest warrior of my generation."

"Magni said that?" Solo looked surprised. "How good are you now?"

Mason threw a nod in Raven's direction. "I can take her."

Raven objected, "You took me by surprise, Mason. That was all."

Leo stepped closer and crossed his arms. "Have you ever fought a real fighter, though?"

Raven spun in his direction. "Hey, wait a minute. Are you saying that I'm not a *real* fighter? Who are you anyway?"

Solomon took a step forward. "Sorry, Raven, let me introduce my friend, Leo. He's a police officer."

"Police Inspector," Leo corrected him and squared his shoulders.

"Right. Sorry, I always forget about your promotion."

Raven lit up. "I plan to join the police force too."

Leo gave her an overbearing smile. "Women can't be in the police force here. It's too dangerous. Maybe if you go back to the Motherlands..."

Raven's hand landed on her hip, which she pushed out to the side. "The Motherlands don't have a police force. They have mediators and it's not the same thing. For the record I'm not going anywhere. This is my home and has been for ten years. Just because there are no women in the police force yet doesn't mean there never will be. Times are changing, or haven't you noticed?"

The grin on Leo's face grew. "You're a funny one, aren't you?" He shook his head and placed his hands in his pockets. "Female police officers, now that would be a sight."

Mason came to Raven's support. "She's a good fighter." He bit his lip. "But not as good as me."

"Is that right?" Solo bent down to eye level with Mason. "Tell you what: I'll let you fight me right now if you want. And to make it fair, I'll keep my hands on my back. If you can hit me, I'll let you fight me for real."

The interaction between them moved something inside me. Solomon might play tough with Mason, but I knew he adored children and wanted a family of his own.

Men of the North #7 – THE DANCER

After being stuck in the bathroom with Salma and the other two women, I'd thought about my time in the Motherlands more. Now, my hatred for Solomon that I'd nurtured for so long seemed out of proportion.

Mason's excitement was fun to watch as he moved away from the group of people and held his hands up in front of him. "Can I hit you as much as I'd like?"

Mila sighed. "Do you have to fight right this minute?"

Solo ignored her and focused on Mason. "Sure, you can hit me as much as you'd like."

"Can I kick you too?"

"For now, let's stick to you hitting me. Put as much force into it as you want, but I'm warning you, I won't make it easy for you." Solo walked over to stand in front of Mason, placed his hands behind his back, and waited for the boy to take his first shot at him. Mason was eager and moved forward with a right hook, but Solo was quick to move his head and Mason's hand swung through air.

"That was a nice one, keep going," Solo encouraged Mason, and moved his head and body every time the boy took a swing. They danced around each other, Mason full of energy and determination to get a blow in on the larger warrior, and Solo concentrating on using his instincts to move every time. For a man his size, Solo was fast and graceful in his movements. I shifted my balance, feeling the old familiar warmth in my belly from looking at him.

After a few minutes, Mason's arms got heavy and his head sunk with every hit he missed.

"Okay, let's stop." Solo placed a hand on the boy's shoulder. "You have good moves, Mason. If you want, I'll be happy to train with you later."

"Can I come too?" Three of the five children raised their hands and ran to Solo.

"Sure, we'll have a training session later. I'll bring my friend Zasquash, he loves kids. But just so you know, we're not the kind of grown-ups who let kids win just to be nice to them."

"I hate it when adults do that," Mason declared.

"I'll remember that." Raven reached up to tousle Mason's hair as he walked past her, but he was already much taller than her and quick to get away. "For now, show Willow and her friends to their rooms, will you?" she told him.

Mason's twin sister Aubri, whom I'd met at the reunion, picked up a bag.

"No, let me." Mason took it from her. "You know Dad and Khan would scold me if they saw you carrying stuff while I'm around."

The girl rolled her eyes. "It's so old-fashioned. Pearl says that men and women are equal."

"Whatever." Mason was already marching ahead with the bag and spoke over his shoulder. "Which room are we taking them to?"

"The Ghost Room."

Salma looked at me and then back at Mila. "Why is the room called the Ghost Room?"

Aubri answered in a tone that revealed she found it self-explanatory. "Because it's haunted of course."

Raven grinned. "It's all part of the charm of an old house. We think it's the old King who got killed in a rebellion. He's pretty harmless and he'll probably enjoy the company. It's rare that anyone sleeps in his part of the manor."

"Stop it, Raven, you're scaring her." I took Salma's hand, wanting to protect my new friend from Raven's wicked humor.

"Yeah, be nice, Raven," Tristan chimed in and I almost gaped at him. This was a man who loved pranks and loved to make fun of everyone.

When we got to the three rooms that were allocated for Ben, Salma, and me, the kids pointed to the right-hand door. "That's the Ghost Room."

"Willow and I can take that room. We don't believe in ghosts anyway." Tristan made it sound like he knew everything about me, but he didn't.

"Sure." I thanked the kids and walked inside. As soon as Tristan entered, I closed the door and whispered. "What are you doing?"

Tristan set down the bag he'd been carrying and walked over to sit on the bed. The whole room looked clean but outdated with a bright color scheme out of fashion.

"Can you stop drooling over Salma, please?"

Tristan looked away. "I'm sorry, it's just…" He rubbed his face.

"Just what? You're supposed to make it look like we're a couple and instead you might as well carry a sign that says I'm Salma Rose's biggest fan."

"You don't understand." He tucked his hands under his thighs and looked down.

I walked over and sat down next to him. "What don't I understand?"

Tristan lifted his head and looked into my eyes. "I've never felt this way before about *anyone*. I mean, I used to think I was in love with you, but…" He licked his lips. "With Salma it's a million times stronger and I get both nervous and euphoric around her. It's like I'm possessed, and I can't stop thinking about her."

I drew in a long inhalation. I knew what it was like and the sickness had been sneaking up on me too these last few days.

"It's bad, Willow." Tristan's large brown eyes stared at me with so many emotions that I had to close my eyes.

"I promised you and Hunter that I'd have your back and pretend to be yours, and I would never break my promise. I just wonder if there's a way we could tell Salma that it's a scam."

"She already knows, Tristan."

"She does?"

"Yes. I told her when we were hiding in the hotel."

"Why?"

"I'm not sure. The whole situation was so scary and coming up with a lie when she asked about us just seemed too much." I sighed and flicked my fingers through my long soft hair while looking down at the old-fashioned carpet on the floor. "I'm not going to stand in your way, Tristan. And if you're as in love as you say you are then I don't think anything can stop you anyway."

Tristan was quiet for a few seconds. "Be honest. Do you think I have a chance with Salma?"

"Maybe. It's hard to say if she'd be open to a romantic relationship. Few Motlanders are."

"I know, but the way she smiles at me. You've seen it, haven't you?"

Taking his hand, I thought about my words before I spoke. "Salma is amazing, sweet, and very pretty."

"But?" Tristan narrowed his eyes a little.

"But she's also delicate and comes with a lot of issues."

He nodded. "She told me about her anxiety."

"Right, there's that."

"I'm good at calming her down though; she says so herself."

"But think about it, Tristan. Salma Rose is a superstar and she travels a lot. She can't just give up on her career and come live with you here in the Northlands."

"So what? I can live in the Motherlands. Hell, I'd live on the moon if it meant being with the woman I love."

I lowered my head and rubbed my forehead. "It's not love, Tristan. What you have is an infatuation."

"How would you know?"

"Because that's what I had for Solo, and the psychologists who helped me get over him told me so."

"I see." Tristan rubbed the bridge of his nose. "Maybe love is different for everyone. I'm pretty sure I'm head over heels in love with Salma."

I stood up from the bed. "Yeah, could be. I just hope you don't get your heart broken like Hunter and I did."

"Hunter?"

"He doesn't talk about it."

Tristan was frowning. "Hunter had his heart broken? Why didn't he tell me?"

"It happened about three years ago. Alice was a friend of mine that he'd met a few times when visiting me in the Motherlands. When he asked her to marry him it came as a surprise to me. I never knew he was in love with her, but he must have been because he took her rejection hard."

"Why doesn't he talk about it? He should have told me."

"You know Hunter; he's proud."

Tristan stood up too. "It explains why he's always finding faults with every woman he meets. I figured he might not be into women at all."

"He got burned, and it could happen to you too if you're not careful."

Tristan looked thoughtful. "At least Hunter took his chance. I would regret it forever if I didn't take mine with Salma."

With a last sigh, I walked to the door and stopped when he asked, "What about Solo? You still want me to pretend that we're together, right?"

"Nah, with the way you're drooling over Salma it's pointless."

"Okay, but..."

I turned. "But what?"

"You'll tell him then, right? It's just that if he thinks I'm being unfaithful to you, he'll have my ass."

With a hand on the door handle, I paused.

"After your speech today, he pulled me aside, Willow."

"Solo did?"

"Yeah, he didn't like how I looked at Salma. He's still very protective of you."

A tingle ran up and down my spine but I didn't show my excitement. "Did you tell him anything?"

"No, of course not. I kept it cool and told him there would be another woman for him. He agreed."

My fingers squeezed the doorknob. "He agreed?"

"Yeah, that's a good thing, right? Hunter says Solo isn't over you, but you heard Zasquash and Leo. I don't think you need to worry about Solo anymore. I was thinking that maybe I could help set him up with one of the other performers; that way he would leave you alone. I'm pretty sure he'll be loyal to whomever he marries."

"Great. Yeah. That's good." Pressure built in my chest as I opened the door and walked out. It shouldn't bother me that Solo had agreed with Tristan about finding love with someone else, but the idea of Solo with any of the other performers made my heart hurt.

"Oh, by the way, Willow."

I was walking away from the room but turned around to see Tristan in the doorway.

"Can I still crash here with you tonight? I think every room is full."

"Sure." I hurried down the corridor feeling desperate for some fresh air and a bit of alone time. I should have known that getting alone time in a mansion full of people would be impossible, but I couldn't have known that I'd be dragged into a heated town hall meeting with Khan and Pearl five minutes later.

CHAPTER 22
Town Hall Meeting

Solomon

"Fucking hell, it's like an old-fashioned airport here." Khan shielded his eyes from the sun and looked up at the sky. "It's the seventh drone today. Did you hear that, Pearl? Seventh!"

Pearl sat on a garden chair with their daughter Freya in her lap. The girl was Mason's age and the way she leaned back on her mother told me the two of them were close. Both of them looked up as well and Pearl spoke: "That's what financial growth does to a country. More people own their own drones now and you have no laws restricting them from flying wherever they want to. This is why the drones in the Motherlands are restricted to flying certain routes."

"I don't care where they fly as long as they stay the fuck away from my home."

I sat down on a low brick wall. "Are you talking about the drones we arrived in with the performers?"

"No, I'm not counting those drones. These are different ones, and it's a security risk to have them fly over our heads. What if they shoot me or crash on my house?" Khan's dark eyes were full of fire as he stabbed a finger at the drone circling above us. "Do you see that fucker taking his time like he has every right to be there?"

"What he's doing isn't illegal," Pearl said in a flat tone.

"It bloody hell should be." Because he was looking up, Khan walked into a chair and kicked at it. "This day just keeps getting worse and worse." Khan turned to Magni, who was sitting next to Laura on a bench. "Did Pearl tell you about her suggestions on how to appease the Motherlands?"

"No." Magni raised an eyebrow. "Are you saying there might be a way to calm them down?"

Pearl whispered something in her daughter's ear and Freya left us adults to be alone. "According to Isobel, the Council agrees that the integration must continue. The problem is that people were already scared after the murder of Josephine, and now with the attack on the performers today, the country is in an uproar. We'll need to give the Council something to show how sorry we are. Something good."

"And what do you suggest?" Magni asked Pearl.

Her eyes wandered to Hunter, who was playing soccer with the other five Doomsmen and some of the police officers. With our being at the manor, the performers were under security by the regular guards and all we security guards were more relaxed.

Pearl leaned forward in her chair. "I suggest we call for a town hall meeting and discuss it in a forum."

Magni rolled his eyes and looked away.

"I know it's not your favorite thing, Magni." Pearl's tone was soft and patient. "But we might get some valuable input that we can use."

He pushed his jaw out. "Fine, but no children. There's no way I'm arguing with ten-year-olds again."

"I told you that discussion was for the benefit of the children. It's the only way to teach them the art of stating their case in a clear and precise manner."

Magni raised an eyebrow. "No children, Pearl, or I'm out."

"All right. No children today." Pearl gave a nod.

"I'm getting Boulder and Christina; they should be on their way anyway." Magni pointed to me and Leo, who sat next to me. "You two, go round up the soccer players and get some of the women to come down here too."

Fifteen minutes later around thirty-five people were gathered, including Willow, Salma, Ben, Hunter, Zasquash, and the other Doomsmen, who looked baffled by the whole thing.

"What the fuck is a town hall meeting?" Zasquash whispered to me.

"A Motlander thing. As kids we used to spy on the adults when they had them at the school. It's a lot of arguing back and forth."

He wrinkled his nose up. "Sounds like some of that democracy nonsense they believe in."

Salma, who sat on Zasquash's other side, leaned in and whispered, "Don't be so negative. Everyone deserves to be heard."

Zasquash pointed his thumb over his shoulder. "Yeah, but we were just playing ball. Why can't Khan just make a decision and get on with it?"

We didn't get a chance to answer because Khan stood up and spread out his arms. "Welcome to our home. I wish I could welcome you under better circumstances, but as you all know, today has been chaotic, and I want to personally express how sorry I am for what happened in Freeman. Here, you'll be safe, and our wonderful outdoor amphitheater nestled right here in our park will provide a secure location for the rest of your shows." He paused and scanned the crowd before his face fell into deep frown lines. "It is our hope that the Council in the Motherlands will see that what happened today will not be tolerated in the Northlands and that we're making your safety our highest priority. However, today's incident, in combination with the sad and untimely death of one of the Motlander brides only two weeks ago, leaves the integration process between our countries in grave danger." Khan looked to Pearl, who stood up to join him, her hand finding his in a discreet way and her shoulder rubbing against his arm.

It touched something inside me: the closeness between them and the looks of deep understanding. My head turned and I watched Willow, who was sitting one row in front of me and five seats to the right. Only her profile was visible to me and her gorgeous long hair that cascaded down her back. My chest swelled with the desire to be close to her, and then, as if she could feel me reaching out for her in my mind, Willow turned her head and looked at me. It was a few seconds only and there were no smiles between us, but it didn't matter. What mattered was that we shared a connection and if her heart was racing like mine, it had to mean something.

"You Motlanders will be familiar with town hall meetings and for the rest of you I should mention that it's a chance for you to express your free opinion."

Pearl spoke up, "As long as it's in a respectful and civil manner."

"Civil doesn't mean that we can't swear, does it?" Zasquash asked.

Pearl chuckled but it was Magni who answered. "Fuck no. By civil she means don't get physical and don't threaten to kill or beat up people who disagree with you."

"Got it." Zasquash leaned back. "Sounds easy enough."

Khan's deep voice was serious when he spoke again. "Today's agenda is how to get the integration back on track. We need suggestions on ways to calm down the Motlanders."

Ben raised his hand and when Khan told him to go ahead, he stood up. "I think what we have is a case of bad media and as an agent for famous people, I'd say it's one of my areas of expertise. The remedy is to apologize and spread another story to distract people. Like one time one of my sports clients was accused of improper communication and I admit it, she can be rude, but I made sure that the week after, she gave an interview in her house and talked about the puppy she'd just rescued. It worked like a charm."

Khan crossed his arms. "And how many puppies do you think we need to rescue to make them forget one of our men killed his bride and hundreds of crazy fans stormed your hotel this morning?"

Ben bit his lip. "Ehm... maybe you'll need something bigger than puppies for this one." He scratched the tip of his nose. "How about a movie that tells the romantic tale of how the integration process began in the first place. Something that would paint a positive picture of your culture and tell about how Christina first came here and fell in love."

Everyone looked to Christina, who sat next to her husband Alexander Boulder. The two exchanged a glance and then she shook her head. "It could backfire if everyone knew how I was forced to marry against my will."

Khan placed his arm around Pearl. "Not if the movie focuses on how well it turned out in the end. You and Boulder are happy together. I think a movie sounds like an excellent idea. Maybe they could make one about me and Pearl as well. Just make sure we have the right to approve the script."

Pearl inclined her head to Ben. "Thank you for your suggestion. I believe there is wisdom in the strategy of finding something positive for everyone to focus on. A movie is an option that we would be open to, but the downside is that it takes a long time to produce it. What we need is something immediate." Her eyes found Hunter, who was sitting next to Willow. "One of my suggestions is something that is guaranteed to excite Motlanders. I'm talking about sending one of our biggest athletes to play in the Motherlands."

Everyone turned to look at Hunter, who placed a hand on his chest. "You mean me?"

"Yes." Pearl smiled at him.

Hunter moved in his seat. "No, that wouldn't work."

"Why not?" Willow asked.

"Because I live here. The Motherlands is nice and all, but I couldn't fly my drone or play soccer the way I'm used to." He looked at Khan for support. "You know they don't even head the ball, right?"

Khan leaned his head to one side with a speculative glance. "It would be a big deal to them if our star player came to live and play with them. It would get a lot of media attention and you could adopt a puppy while you're there."

"I don't want a damn puppy." Hunter's brow was lowered and he had his hands tucked up under his armpits like a stubborn child refusing to eat his vegetables.

"What do you think?" Khan looked back at Magni, who walked forward and took a wide stance next to his brother.

"I think it's a great idea. Hunter, you'll do it!"

"You can't order me to go if I don't want to and I'm not fucking playing on a mixed team with a bunch of Motlanders. That's ridiculous."

Pearl spoke in a soft tone. "Hunter, sometimes the individual must sacrifice oneself for the greater good. I know you as a strong and kind person. I'm sure someone with your strong character is willing to do your part to secure peace and prosperity between our countries."

Hunter opened his mouth to speak but with everyone looking at him, only a low annoyed mutter came from him.

"It wouldn't be a permanent move." Magni rocked back on his feet. "Just a season or two. And think about all the women you'll be able to meet. Maybe find a bride while you're there."

Angelo, one of my colleagues in the Doom Squad, raised his hand. "If he won't go, I'm happy to do it. I'm a great soccer player."

"No, you're not. You just want to go because of the women," Zasquash teased him.

People laughed a little, but Pearl and Khan kept looking at Hunter, who was squirming in his chair.

"I don't see how my going will help anything."

"Let's ask the Motlanders here. Raise your hand if you think it would be a good idea to send Hunter, the biggest soccer star in the Northlands, to play in the Motherlands."

Fourteen hands including Willow's rose up high.

"That's a one hundred percent yes." Pearl clasped her hands together in front of her. "Hunter, can we count on your taking one for the team?"

"But who will I be playing for?"

Ben shot up from his chair again. "The Dolphins – they're the best team in the Motherlands and I represent their coach and top player. I can get you in there tomorrow. Just say the word."

Pearl clapped her hands again. "Wonderful, this is the strength of a town hall meeting. What other brilliant initiatives can we come up with?"

Raven raised her hand up high.

"Yes." Khan pointed to her and she got up to her full height, which wasn't so impressive.

"I think we should send a strong signal that the Northlands are serious about equality. Every time I'm in the Motherlands I always hear that women are limited here and that men don't respect us as equals."

"I'm listening." Khan had his arms crossed and was tapping his fingers on his arms.

"I volunteer to be the first woman to join the police force. That would be a positive story for sure."

"Yes. Raven, I love it!" Pearl lit up.

Not only did Khan and Magni protest but all we Nmen in the audience groaned, shook our heads, and muttered,

"No fucking way."

"It's too dangerous."

"Women aren't supposed to fight."

"What if something happens to her?"

"Women have no place in the police force."

Over all the voices rang a clear whistle and Laura stepped forward and held her hand high in the air to silence us.

"I challenge any man who dares say that women can't fight to go a few rounds with me." She banged a fist against her chest and looked mad as hell. "When the wall collapsed during the great earthquake of 2437 I went to bring back the criminal Nmen who had crossed the border illegally. Me. A woman!"

The intensity and outrage in her eyes made us quiet down. "You men might be bigger and stronger than us, but do not make the mistake of thinking we can't be anything we set our minds to." Stabbing her finger through the air like she was poking our very foreheads, Laura continued, "If Raven wants to be a pioneer and become the first policewoman in the Northlands then you'd all better support that and be fucking grateful that she's willing to do her part."

As to support his wife, Magni took a strong stance beside her.

"What do you say?" Khan turned to Raven's adoptive father Alexander Boulder, who sat on the side.

He sighed and stretched his long legs in front of him. "I don't think any father wishes his daughter to go into the police force. The thought that something might happen to her scares me."

"But Dad," Raven began before she was silenced by the palm that he held up as a stop sign.

Men of the North #7 – THE DANCER

"I do, however, agree with Laura and Raven that women can fight. I'm proud of the warrior my daughter has become, and she deserves the chance to follow her dreams like anyone else."

Khan was thinking hard with his head lowered and a finger rubbing the bridge of his nose. When he finally looked up, he shook his head in a slow movement. "I don't like it. Putting a woman in danger will only make us look worse with the Motlanders."

Pearl objected. "That's not how they think, Khan. Women in the Motherlands don't wish to be protected by men. They want equal opportunities and to be respected."

"But how is it respect to place a woman in danger when it's our very jobs as men to protect her from harm?" he argued.

"Yeah." Some of the men shouted. "What kind of man puts women in danger? That's just fucked up."

Pearl waited for everyone to be quiet before she spoke. "It's clear we have cultural differences and that's why a town hall meeting is good. Let's ask the Motlanders who are present what they think. In general, would Motlanders see it as a positive signal to have a female join the police force or would they see it as a negative? Raise your hand if you think it's positive."

Again, fourteen hands went up.

"But why?" Zasquash threw his hands up. "That's the most backward thinking I've ever heard. Why would we send a small woman like her to fight big-ass men like me? Are Motlanders suicidal by nature?"

"No, of course not," Salma whispered. "We are strong empowered women who can do anything that men can do."

"Bullshit." Zasquash stood up. "I'm sorry, ladies, but either you're blind or stupid because to claim that you can do anything we men can do is crazy. Look at my guns versus hers." Zasquash flexed his biceps that stood out like hills on his arms. "How the hell is she supposed to protect herself against someone my size?" He turned to Raven. "Tell you what, shorty, if you can take me in a fight you have my full support. You wanna give it a go right now?"

"Zasquash, sit your ass back down," Magni ordered. "No regular police officer can take a Doomsman like you in a fight. Not even the male ones, so you can shut it."

"Then let her fight Leo, he's only six feet two or something. I'll bet she can't even take a small guy like him."

"Yeah, let her fight Leo," others chimed in.

Leo looked back like he was annoyed to be dragged into this. "First of all, I'm not short. And second, I have no interest in fighting a girl."

"I'm almost twenty-two so don't you call me a girl," Raven exclaimed with indignation.

"Raven isn't fighting anyone today. I've seen her fight since she was a child. We've all helped train her." Magni pushed out his chest. "Just because you men get to have an opinion doesn't mean you get to make decisions." He turned his head to Khan, who still looked skeptical. "You're in charge."

After a long pause with Khan not saying anything, Pearl spoke up. "If you don't like the thought of a woman police officer, you could still send a signal of equality by changing the law that only sons can follow their father as rulers."

Khan's head snapped up. "I already agreed to making you my co-ruler when the Motherlands council has complete equality."

"I know, but that could take years and it may never happen. We have a bright daughter; why not make her your successor?"

Men of the North #7 – THE DANCER

Again, the crowd muttered and mumbled. The thought of a female ruler of the Northlands didn't sit well with us. We were the last free men not ruled by women.

"I'm not changing that law but Raven can join the police academy," Khan declared and was met by shouts of outrage from several men whom he had to quiet down. "She'll enroll in the training first and if she makes it through she can join the force."

"I think it's time to end this meeting. Thank you for all your input and ideas." It was hard to hear Pearl what with the Nmen's talk among themselves.

Zasquash had his face scrunched up in a grimace of *what the fuck just happened?*

"Wasn't it fun?" Salma smiled at him.

"Oh, it was fucking hilarious." He shook his head and mumbled. "Town hall meetings my ass." When he passed me he grunted, "Next time don't invite me. This was a big fucking waste of time – and to think we gave up playing soccer to be humiliated like that. Female police officers." He made a "tsk" sound and moved away.

Raven was glowing and hugging Willow and Mila as Pearl, Laura, Christina, and a bunch of Motlanders came to congratulate her as well.

"I wish you luck," I told her when Raven was no longer swamped by people. "It won't be easy but if you need someone to spar with to prepare for the fight test, I'm here."

Raven's eyes widened. "For real, Solo. You mean that?"

"Sure."

She tilted her head. "I thought you didn't like me."

"I like you fine when you're not scowling at me."

Raven was bubbling over with joy. "Ha, look who's talking. I think you came out of your mother's womb with a scowl on your face. You're always so damn serious, Solo,"

"Maybe you just don't know me that well."

"So, you're saying that you smile sometimes?" She grinned at me.

"I do, just not so much around Hunter and..." I looked away.

Raven said it for me. "Willow."

"Yeah."

There was an awkward silence and then she grinned again. "Anyway, I'm going to take you up on the sparring. I know I can learn a ton from working with you."

"All right, but I won't go easy on you."

"Didn't think you would. You never go easy on anyone, do you?"

As I walked away, Raven's words kept circling in my mind. No matter how I looked at it, I'd gone easy on Willow. For so many years I hadn't been able to get close to her because of the restraining order and then when I finally did, she'd turned cold and hateful.

I should have pushed her harder. Helped her remember how things used to be between us. Her charade with Tristan never should have held me back. Willow had loved me once and it was time I reminded her how it felt.

CHAPTER 23
Alpha to the Core

Willow

"Hunter, wait up," I called as he stormed off after the meeting.

When I caught up to him, he didn't look at me.

"Don't be angry. You heard what Magni said, it's just for a season."

"Or two... Magni said a season *or two*." Hunter corrected me and stopped to place his hands on his hips. "I don't want to live in the fucking Motherlands."

I jerked back. "But I live there. We could spend more time together."

"That's about the only positive I can find at this point."

"What about the fact that you're doing everyone a huge favor? Doesn't that mean something?"

He groaned and leaned his head back. "I guess. But I'm at the height of my career and it's not like I'll get challenged in the Motherlands. I'll be playing against girls."

I shoved at his shoulder. "How is that a bad thing? Girls are great at soccer. You'll get to experience equality and learn new things."

His downturned mouth didn't lift.

"Look, I get that you're upset, and it wasn't what you wanted, but it might bring something good with it. Magni had a point about finding love. Maybe you'll meet the woman of your dreams."

Hunter scoffed and turned away from me. "No thanks."

"Then maybe a guy?"

His eyebrows creased together. "I told you: I'm not gay."

"Then why aren't you flirting with some of the performers? I've seen several of them smile at you."

He kicked the gravel. "That doesn't mean anything."

"Of course it does. It means they like you."

"Motlanders smile at anyone, I learned long ago not to put anything into it."

"Hunter, come on, you're the most handsome Nman there is, and you know it."

"You're just saying that because you're my sister."

"No. I mean it. And you are such a warm and smart person too. Any woman would be lucky to have you."

"Thanks, but modern women don't want men in their lives. They don't need us."

"That might be true for many but not all of us. I want to marry and have children."

Hunter furrowed his brows. "Only because you've been influenced from your time living here in the Northlands."

"You could sign up for the Matching Program. I'll bet you'd be chosen in a second."

"For all the wrong reasons. I'm a celebrity and I'm rich. How would I know that wasn't the motivation to pick me?"

"Most Motlanders don't care about money."

Hunter snorted. "Until they come to the Northlands and realize how much more fun life is with money."

"I don't know how to make you see that not all women are out to hurt you. I'm sorry it didn't work out with Alice, but I could have told you she's not the kind of woman to marry. Alice is..."

"I don't care about Alice and I don't want to talk about this."

"All right." I stepped closer. "I won't mention her again. Just tell me if there's anything I can do to cheer you up."

We turned our heads when a male voice shouted, "Hey, Hunter." Leo was waving at us. "Come play soccer with us. We need help to beat the Doomsmen. It's time to show them that bigger isn't better."

Hunter's lip was tugged upward, and he lifted his right hand. "I'll be right there."

I smiled at him. "I should have known that the only thing to cheer you up would be soccer."

"You have no idea how much fun it is to play around with those huge guys. You'd think they would be slow with their size and all but they're surprisingly fast."

"Why would that surprise you? Solo was always athletic to the bone."

We were walking next to each other and he gave me a strange look. "You're not softening up around him, are you?"

"Of course not." The lie made my voice tremble a little. "But you can stop being so protective of me. I'm a grown woman and I make my own decisions."

"I know that!"

"Are you coming, Hunter?"

He squeezed my hand and nodded his head in a *see you later* gesture and ran to the improvised soccer game, while I walked to the large patio in front of the Gray Manor where people were gathered in the lounge area.

"Willow, dear, come get a glass of cider. This day is historic and we should celebrate." Christina hugged me. "I can't believe my Raven is joining the police. It's going to be hard not to worry about her."

"She'll be fine." Pearl smiled and was gesturing to me to come sit next to her when her daughter, Freya, came walking up with a piece of paper in her hands. "Hey, darling, what do you have there?"

"It's for Dad."

Khan stood in conversation with Alexander Boulder and Magni not far from us, and he looked up when Pearl called him over.

"What is it?" he asked and touched Pearl's shoulders when he was close.

"I made this for you." Freya handed him the paper and Khan's right eyebrow lifted as he read it.

"What is it, Freya?" Pearl asked.

"It's a decree. All it needs is Dad's signature and it will become law."

"What kind of decree?"

Khan read out loud, "From this day forth it shall be illegal to fly over the Gray Manor and other residences owned by the Ruler of the Northlands. Failure to comply with this decree shall result in confiscation of the drone in which the flying has occurred." Khan nodded his head. "I'm impressed, Freya, this is good work." He pointed to the left corner. "Although the drawing of the drone and the angry man below isn't strictly necessary."

"Can I see?" Pearl reached for the paper and smiled as she showed it to the rest of us.

I gave Freya a side hug. "I think the drawing is the best part."

"Thank you. If you want me to, I can show you how to draw drones. I'm good at it."

"Thank you, dear, maybe a little later."

I craned my neck. "Did any of you see Salma?"

Christina looked around and creased her eyebrows. "I thought I saw her a minute ago."

Laura emptied her glass. "Tristan offered to show her the park; they are walking together."

"Oh, okay."

"I'm sure they would have included you if you'd been here," Pearl added. "If you want to see the park, I'm happy to show it to you. We've added a fun area for the children since you were last here."

"Thank you, but to be honest I could really use some time by myself. It's been a crazy day."

Christina pulled me in for another hug. "We all feel awful for what happened at that hotel. Take all the time you need. Your first show isn't until tomorrow."

My thoughts were on the town hall meeting as I made my way up the stairs to my room on the second floor. It was located in the far corner and the hallways felt like a maze. Rounding the last corner, I came to a sudden halt when I saw Solomon leaning casually against my door.

"Hi, Willow."

"What are you doing here?"

"It's time to answer your questions." There was something different about Solo. Before, he'd been careful and guarded. Now he seemed confident and his voice had an edge of danger to it.

Every hair on my body vibrated, standing on end as an electric current sparked nerve endings. I looked over my shoulder, but the hallway was empty. "How did you know which room is mine?"

A smile tipped the corner of his mouth. "Mason volunteered that information. Aren't you going to invite me in?"

I walked closer at a slow pace, my heart in my throat. "What makes you think I'd invite you in?"

He took a step away from the doorway, waiting for me to get closer to him. "Because it's what we do, Willow. We sneak around and kiss when no one is watching. We did it ten years ago and we did it this morning."

All of a sudden the hallway felt like a tropical rainforest – way too hot and with butterflies swarming all around in my stomach. As a teenager, Solo's charming smile had made me fall in love with him, but the boy I'd once loved had nothing on the man in front of me. His blue eyes shone with desire and he had that confident, domineering glow in his eyes that had always melted me in the past. The heartbeat in my chest was hammering as I backed up a little. "I told you what happened this morning was a mistake."

"And yet we both still want more."

I froze to the spot when Solo moved forward, stopping right in front of me, his fingers stroking the backs of my hands and then continuing up my arms, while whispering in a husky voice, "If you don't want this you can walk away."

When I still didn't move, he wrapped an arm around my waist and pulled me against his body. "Thought so."

"Tristan and I..." I wanted him to know that it had been fake, but he covered my mouth with a finger.

"I don't want to hear about him now. Unlock the door, Willow."

I shook my head but it only made him hold out his hand. "Give me the key then."

"The room isn't locked," I whispered low as if my voice was trying to hide what I was doing from my brain, which was screaming out warnings.

"How convenient." Solo opened the door and waved his hand. "Ladies first."

"That's not a good idea, Solo. It's better if we aren't alone. Remember how nervous you were this morning that someone would find us together," I rambled on.

Solo gave me one of his alpha-to-the-core smiles and without warning he picked me up bridal style and walked into the room. When he sat me down it was only to close the door and lock it.

"All right. I don't mind talking and I would like answers to my questions, but just so we're clear there's not going to be any..."

He kissed me before I could finish my sentence and just like this morning in the bathroom, I felt my head explode in bright colors.

"Willow," he muttered into my mouth and on their own devices my hands found his hair and grabbed on to a fistful.

"Solo," I breathed and kissed him back with a primitive hunger for more. Why did the forbidden have to feel this good?

The room wasn't big and while kissing me, he backed me up against the bed. "I've been waiting years for this," he muttered into my mouth.

I closed my eyes, fighting the protests and objections in my mind. "Promise me that no one will know," I whispered in a raspy voice. "It'll be our secret."

He growled deep in his throat but didn't agree.

"Solo, promise me," I repeated while he placed his hands on my shoulders and pushed lightly, signaling for me to get on the bed.

Our bodies were working in synchronization, with me going backward until I was lying down on the bed and him following like an invisible string was attached between us.

He didn't speak when he pushed my shirt up and exposed my stomach, his hands grabbing onto my hips and his cheek pressing against my belly button with a deep sigh.

I smiled a little. "You've always had a thing for my stomach, haven't you?"

"Uh-huh. I've always known that one day our kid will grow in there."

"What?" I creased my brow. "No, Solo, we can't. That's not..."

He lifted his face. "You know it just as well as I do."

"Solo, you're not making sense." His words were both crazy and arousing. "You were going to give me answers. Making out wasn't the plan."

"Maybe not *your* plan, but definitely *my* plan." His hands opened my pants and, sliding a hand under the small of my back, he lifted my body like I weighed nothing.

Despite my raw desire for him, I held onto my pants. "What if someone comes?"

"Then you'll tell them to go away. Especially if it's Tristan or Hunter."

"Hunter would kill you."

"No, he wouldn't. Not when you tell him I'm your mate."

I pushed at Solo and looked in to his eyes. "You're *not* my mate."

He didn't answer but pulled off his shirt, revealing his body as the most ripped I'd ever seen. His scent of masculinity enticed me and activated parts of my brain that associated him with pleasure and trust. I inhaled and closed my eyes for a second, feeling emotional. This shouldn't feel so right.

"You okay?" His finger trailed down my thigh.

"Uh-huh." I opened my eyes and let my own fingers explore his body, touching the compass tattoo on his forearm, before I continued on to the scars on his torso. "Oh, Solo," I said in sympathy with all the pain he must have gone through. He didn't seem to be bothered and leaned down to kiss me again.

"We once tried to have sex, do you remember?" he asked and pushed my shirt and bra up higher. I freed myself from the fabric and lay only in my panties with Solo kissing and suckling my breasts like he'd been served his favorite meal in the world.

"We did have sex, didn't we?"

"Almost. We tried but the soldiers interrupted us."

"I don't remember that part," I whispered as a wonderful feeling spread throughout my body and memories of experiencing this with him before came back to me. "But I do remember kissing you."

Men of the North #7 – THE DANCER

"Oh yeah? Do you remember if you liked it?" He smiled and kissed me long and hard with our tongues dancing an intimate slow dance.

"Yes, I liked it," I breathed into his mouth.

"Did you miss it?" His eyes were blue points of desire and he swallowed hard, his Adam's apple moving in his throat.

"Yes," I breathed. "Did you?"

Solo opened his mouth to speak and then he closed it, instead placing tiny kisses from under my ear down to my neck.

"Is that a yes?" My arousal was making me a bit breathless.

"You know it is. Willow, I want to be with you."

I took it in a sexual meaning, ignoring that Solo was maybe referring to being with me forever. The ramifications of a relationship with him were too great to even consider. But I would take the satisfaction of his desire. This morning in the bathroom when he had ground against me, I had been so far gone in my desire for him that for a few stolen moments I hadn't questioned whether kissing him was a mistake. I'd let out a part of me that had been suppressed since I was fifteen. The Willow who didn't carry resentment in her heart had made me feel at peace for the first time in years. I wanted more of that.

"I want you too, Solo."

He stiffened and met my eyes. "Say that again."

"We might not get another chance to do this."

There was a slight narrowing of his eyes as if what I had just said displeased him, but then he rolled to my side and kicked off his pants.

I didn't get a good look at him because he was quick to roll back between my legs, his torso pressing down on mine as if he wanted to make sure I didn't go anywhere.

My hands nuzzled his nape. "It's just going to be this one time. You understand that, right?"

He growled and bit my jawline. It was gentle but so dominant in nature that my panties were getting soaked.

"We should hurry before someone interrupts us again."

My words made him pull back enough to tear my panties off. Instead of throwing the fabric to the ground, he brought it to his nose and sniffed with a sound of appreciation.

I wrinkled my nose. "Why would you do that?"

Solo gave me a crooked smile. "Because I love the smell of your arousal."

I reached out for him, but Solo stayed on my side, his fingers spreading my folds and circling my clitoris. "You're soaking wet." The satisfied smile on his lips before he kissed me went straight to my heart.

He used his strong hands to position me right where he wanted me. With my hips twisted, he pressed against me from behind, his shoulder next to mine, and his tempting lips opened in concentration.

I stiffened a little when I felt his large erection glide up and down my behind.

"Why is it wet?" I asked in confusion.

"It's just precum." His voice had a tremble to it and using his hand, he guided the head of him to rest between my folds. And then he pressed, slow and insistent, inside me. A loud moan escaped him as he breathed out. "Fuck, Willow!"

"Be quiet," I pleaded. "I don't want anyone to hear us." The only answer I got was another deep moan as he sunk deeper inside my slick wetness.

I closed my eyes, enjoying the feeling of our bodies connecting.

"You're so tight."

"I'm sorry."

Men of the North #7 – THE DANCER

Solo was on his side next to me, his right arm resting across my chest and holding on to my left upper arm while his head nuzzled against my hair. "Did you and Tristan ever…"

"Nooo." My answer came fast. "Never."

"So, this *is* your first time?"

"If you're sure that we really didn't do it, then yeah." Just as I finished my sentence, Solo pushed hard into me and it made me arch.

"Relax, baby."

Hearing him call me baby just like he had all those years ago made emotions swell in my chest. I closed my eyes, taking small fast breaths and feeling him rock back and forth inside me. I was having sex with Solo, my childhood crush whom I'd loved so deeply once. I opened my eyes to take in the unreal situation. My left hand resting on his large biceps, his arm across my stomach, holding me close against him as Solo's strong hips moved in a steady rhythm behind me. He was careful not to squeeze me as I lay completely engulfed in his arms, listening to the sounds of deep pleasure that were coming from both of us. I looked down to my belly, half expecting to see a bump on it every time he pushed deeper. He felt so large, and his rocking in and out of me had an erotic sound of its own. I moaned. It was impossible not to at the delicious feeling of being filled, taken, and devoured by Solo.

He growled. "Finally, we get to finish what we started."

"Uh-huh." I still didn't understand how I'd felt so sure that we'd had sex when he said we didn't.

"Is it like you imagined?" I breathed.

"Much better. Being inside you is heaven. It feels fucking amazing." Solo leaned back and looked down. "Seeing us connected like this… It's a dream come true to see my cock finally take possession of your tight pussy!"

His words got to me and made me even hornier.

"Did you fantasize about this?"

"All the fucking time." Solo bit my jawline again and fisted a hand into my hair.

More butterflies filled my stomach. I had longed for this, to hear Solomon declare how he still wanted me, and in my haze of lust, I didn't care that I was walking on fire.

He cupped my face and kept pushing in and out of me while kissing me, biting at my lips, sucking on my tongue, and making me feel like a molten pool of woman.

Pulling out of me, he turned me on my back. "Willow, lift your legs."

I had always been flexible and raised my legs. With his hands around my ankles, Solo pressed my knees back to my ears and got up on his knees. In this position he got in deeper and I squinted my eyes a little. "Careful."

Solo kissed my shin and pumped in and out at high speed. The bed was squeaking and I worried someone would hear us. At the same time, I never wanted it to end. The sensation of our merging in this position was taking my breath away. Placing my hands on his arms, I whispered, "I want you to go deep and stay there for a second."

Solo did as I'd asked, and it was the most peculiar feeling of a second heartbeat inside me.

"You like the feeling of me filling you up, don't you, babe?" His forehead was sweaty and he cupped one of my breasts like he owned it.

"I want to remember it," I admitted.

Solo moved a tiny bit, the friction creating delicious sensations that tickled at my core. I pushed myself against him, meeting his thrusts and moaning deeper the higher he pushed me, and Solo kept pushing me.

The fear of someone finding us kept poking up in the back of my head as he moved me around in different positions, each one showing me pleasure.

How long had we been at it? Our bodies were covered in a sheet of perspiration and Solo seemed like he could go on forever.

My inner walls were vibrating and when Solo intensified the pace, the sensation of them cramping made me hyperventilate. My body was spiraling out of my control.

"Solo, Solo, yes, yes," I closed my eyes, unable to form a full sentence. "More."

"That's right." He intertwined his right hand with mine, squeezing it while pumping in and out of me at high speed. "Let go, babe. Just let go."

At that moment I didn't worry about anyone finding us. I squeezed my eyes together, my body tensing up as I released a small scream. "Yeeess, Solo, yeess."

"Willow, fuck yes... take it." Solo was pounding into me and growling at the same time. "Mine, mine, mine."

I heard him through my orgasmic haze and held on to him as if someone would tear us apart again.

Solo bored his nose against my cheek, encapsulating me with his arms while pushing all the way inside me, and stiffening as he reached his own peak.

We were sweaty and out of breath as we collapsed in each other's arms.

After a minute, I pushed at him. "You're too heavy."

Solo rolled onto his side but kept a leg on top of my leg. "How do you feel?"

Still panting, I turned my head and smiled. "Good. And you?"

"Happy." He flashed his teeth in a wide smile.

When I tried to sit up Solo pulled me back down again. "Stay a little longer."

"It's better if we get dressed. Someone could come, and I don't want you to think there's more to it than sex."

"Willow, why would you deny yourself what felt so right?" Solo let his hand slide down my belly and placed it on top of my pelvis area. At the same time, he leaned in and kissed me like the kiss was a declaration of love in itself.

"It does feel right, doesn't it?" I whispered and immediately wished I hadn't said that.

"That's because we were always meant to be together. I've loved you from the first time I saw you."

The last pieces of resentment and hate that I'd held on to like a shield of ice around my heart these past seven years were melting fast, and my blood rushed through my veins like a powerful stream from a melted glacier.

"Solo, I can't." In a fit of perseverance, I pushed away from him and started dressing.

"Willow, don't deny what we have together."

"There's too much at stake and I'm not making the same mistake twice." My hands were shaking as I fumbled to close my pants. I couldn't look at him. "I told you it would just be this one time."

"Willow, listen to me." Solo held out his hand. "Do you remember what we were doing when the soldiers found us?"

"You said we were trying to have sex."

"No, Willow. We were trying to make love. Do you remember why?"

"What do you mean, why?"

"Do you remember the ring of grass?" Solo got up to stand in front of me. He didn't care that he was naked but reached out to touch me with determination. "We gave each other promises. I tied a ring of grass around your finger and…"

I gasped, my eyes unfocused as memories took me back to the river. I was fifteen again and holding up my hand and telling him the ring was my favorite color. "We made our own wedding ceremony," I breathed.

"Yes." He grabbed my hands and looked deep into my eyes. "You remember now, don't you? We were in the middle of consummating our marriage when we were interrupted."

My eyes blinked as more blocked memories returned. "That explains my memories of making love to you."

Solo gave me a soft smile. "We made the promises and now we made love. I would say the bond is tied."

Pulling away, I jerked my hands back. "No."

"Willow." Solo sighed. "We promised we would never let anyone come between us. Do you remember? I kept my promise and waited for you. I still love you."

"I'm sorry." I turned my back to him, overwhelmed with emotional memories from our time together.

"Don't you see that you never truly hated me? They made you think you did, but it was never real."

My head was exploding with painful confusion when I turned back to meet him face to face. "It felt very real."

Solo's arm fell down along his body and his chest fell in a deep sigh. "Willow, don't do this. Don't hide from me."

"You need to leave before someone sees you."

With harsh movements, Solo picked up his clothes and dressed. I stood watching him with my arms wrapped around me, and my brain splitting from conflicting emotions.

Before he left, he picked up my torn panties and walked close to me. "Maybe you're not ready to hear it yet, but you don't hate me, and I meant what I said." His eyes lowered to my abdomen. "One day our kid will grow in your belly and you'll call me your mate again."

Solo strode out of the room and when he closed the door behind him, I sank to the bed, releasing the breath I'd been holding with a loud "whoosh" sound. My body began to shake and tears welled up in my eyes. I didn't want Solo to complicate my life, but our time together on the run stood out clearly now and I remembered how sure I had felt that day by the river when I'd called him my soulmate. I'd promised him to be his forever and we'd been so in love. How could it be nothing more than an infatuation like the psychologists had claimed if, after all these years, being close to Solo still made me feel like coming home?

"He's not right for me," I whispered low. How could he be when being with Solo would be the ultimate betrayal against Hunter, who had vowed to protect me from him?

CHAPTER 24
Redemption

Solo

I'd taken a huge chance with Willow, but it had paid off. As far as I was concerned the lovemaking we'd shared was a consummation of the marriage between us that took place seven years ago.

Now, she'll remember what really happened between us, I told myself as I walked down the stairs in the Gray Manor.

But what if she's serious about this being a one-time thing?

My skin itched just from the thought of never being able to touch her again. Willow was mine! I'd just claimed her and with her knowledge of Northland culture she would know that.

I'd allowed her the silly comments about our lovemaking being a one-time thing because I sensed that she needed that piece of self-deceit in order to let go. Deep down Willow would have known that there was no turning back for either one of us. She was like me and wanted to marry and have children. Now, I needed her to acknowledge to the world that she wanted it with me.

My mind was deep in speculation as I walked out the large French doors leading to the park. If I found Hunter and somehow made peace with him it would help Willow make her decision, but if it backfired and his hate for me grew, it could make things worse.

"Solo."

I turned my head to see Pearl and Laura sitting in the same place as I'd last seen them. They were alone.

Pearl waved her hand, her blue eyes sparkling in the sunlight. "Come join us for a second."

"Ladies." I inclined my head and stopped in front of them.

"At ease, soldier, and come sit down." Laura patted the back of the chair next to her. There were ten chairs around the large table and I complied with her wish, looking over my shoulder not sure if this was a good idea or not.

"I'm pleased to see you looking so well, Solo." Pearl brushed her long blond hair back and smiled at me. "I was told you fought bravely this morning when the men stormed the hotel."

"It's what I'm trained to do."

"I know, and we're all thankful for the protection you offered our guests. Things could have been much worse if not for you and the rest of the security team."

"Just doing my job."

Pearl leaned forward. "Except in your case you're paying penance, aren't you?"

I lowered my brow. "I'm not sure what you mean."

"You didn't wonder why Magni chose you for this assignment? It must have been strange to both you and Willow to be forced upon each other after everyone has been so eager to keep you apart."

Leaning my elbows on the armrests, I intertwined my fingers and pressed my thumbs against each other. "We make it work."

"I knew you would, but I still think you're entitled to an explanation." Pearl looked at Laura with a small smile and then back at me. "I doubt Khan and Magni took time to explain to you why you were given this assignment and I don't want you to think it was a way to punish you. Heaven knows that you were punished enough as a teenager."

Laura moved in her seat. "I've told Pearl what the Huntsmen did to you, Solo. It wasn't right."

"I'm afraid it's partially our fault." Pearl used her nail to scratch the table a little. "You see, back when you and Willow went missing, you jeopardized the whole integration process. Those eight days none of us got much sleep, and Khan and Magni were ready to kill you for what you'd done. They didn't care about the promise the Huntsmen had given to Willow about sparing your life. I don't know if you realize how humiliated our husbands were that they couldn't find two teenagers."

Laura made a sound of agreement. "You made Magni look stupid, Solo, and you broke our most sacred laws. We had every right to be disappointed in you and the men's fury was justified."

I leaned back in the chair. "Do we have to talk about this? It happened years ago and Magni made his point clear. He beat me close to death, remember?"

Laura crossed her arms. "You may have spent a week in the hospital after that fight, but Magni was injured as well."

I failed to dial down the pride in my voice when I spoke: "Yes, I heard he's deaf in one ear because of it."

Laura raised an eyebrow but before she could speak, Pearl leaned in. "The point is that you were assigned to protect the Motlanders because I requested it."

That surprised me. "You did?"

Pearl nodded. "Yes."

"I thought Magni was behind it."

"Well, he gave the order, but I was the one suggesting putting you in charge of Willow's safety. I thought it would be an excellent way for you to do penance for putting her in danger all those years ago."

I frowned. "Why?"

Pearl tilted her head. "Because it was time, Solo. You're a different person than you were then and you both deserved a chance to set things straight."

I looked down, trying not to reveal my feelings about this.

"Life has a way of evening things out. In your case you hurt a woman and you now serve other women as a member of the domestic violence unit." Pearl gave me a sympathetic smile. "We all know how fierce a warrior you are, Solo. But none of us has the power to go back in time and correct your mistakes. All you can do is bring balance by doing penance."

"At first, I wanted Magni to assign you to guarding Willow. It seemed right to me that you do penance by watching over the woman you once kidnapped."

"I didn't kidnap her." I was still looking down but my words came out through gritted teeth.

Pearl sighed out loud and leaned forward with her hands on the table in front of her, as if she wanted to touch me. "Either way, Magni refused. He said it would be unfair to Willow so you were ordered to guard Salma Rose instead." She paused for my input. I gave none.

"Anyway, Solo, I just wanted you to know that we weren't trying to punish you further. We were giving you a chance to give back what you took."

"What I took?" This time I met Pearl's eyes.

"Yes, we all need to take responsibility for our mistakes, and you took Willow's sense of safety. She could have died. You both could have. That's why I wanted you to restore her sense of safety by protecting her."

To me it was twisted Motlander logic, but I was grateful that Pearl had made her suggestion. If she hadn't, Willow and I wouldn't have made love today and even though things hadn't ended as I'd hoped, I was more hopeful than ever.

"We know things haven't been easy for you," Pearl continued. "I fear that you'll end up bitter and cynical if you go through life without a chance to talk about what happened. We humans heal through dialogue."

"Maybe." I scratched my head, seeing an opportunity. "It's not just Willow, though. It's Hunter too. I think he hates me more than she does."

Laura and Pearl exchanged glances.

"He has every right to hate you," Laura said, her bright red hair glinting in the sun.

"Ahh, I see. And here I thought you were all about healing people through dialogue. But maybe that privilege is reserved for people other than Hunter?"

Pearl lifted her mouth in a speculative smile. "I see what you did there." She leaned back. "You want us to help you make peace with Hunter."

"I doubt you can. The hate he feels for me runs deep."

Laura tilted her head. "Maybe he'll listen if you sit down and apologize to his face. Just tell him that you're older now and can see how wrong it was to take Willow away. And give him your solemn promise that you'll never come on to her again."

I bit down on my lip and frowned. There was no way I could make a promise like that. I had every intention of being with Willow, whether or not Hunter agreed. I thought about how to respond without revealing too much, but Pearl's quiet laughter revealed she had seen right through me.

"Wow, Solo, your level of determination and loyalty is admirable. You're never going to give up on Willow, are you?" Her eyes were full of life and curiosity.

"Would Khan give up on you?" I turned and looked at Laura. "And what about Magni? He never gave up on you either, did he?"

"That was different. Magni and I were married, and I loved him. If Willow doesn't love you, there's no point in waiting for her." Laura swung her hand. "There are beautiful women in the choir and orchestra; why not seduce one of them?"

My brow lowered, and I pulled back in my chair letting my dismissive body language answer for me.

Pearl tapped her lip. "I don't mind talking to Hunter, but maybe it's better if Laura does it. He might hold a grudge against me for coming up with the suggestion of having him play soccer in the Motherlands."

Laura was just about to answer when her head snapped up at the sound of loud voices shouting in anger.

"Where's Mason?" She flew up with her eyes wide in worry. "If that boy got himself into another fight, I swear I'll…"

"Stay here," I instructed, but she didn't listen. Laura got around the table and ran down from the patio before sprinting toward the sound. I set after her and with my longer legs I caught up fast. "It's not Mason." The voices were those of men.

That didn't slow Laura, who ran like Mason was being beaten to death and she needed to rescue him.

"This way," she called out and took a left turn leading us to the large lawn in front of the greenhouse where the security staff had set camp.

I slowed down, taking in the sight of at least two handfuls of police officers and Doomsmen fighting. Five or six of them were pounding on each other in a big pile and Laura must have feared that her son might be on the bottom, because she shouted for them to stop and pulled at the first person she reached. I recognized Zasquash from the back and saw him jerking his elbow backward with a growl to shake her off him. His elbow hit Laura right in the face and she fell back with both hands covering her nose and an ear-shattering scream of pain. It was as if someone pushed a pause button and the fighting men stopped to locate the female outcry. All of them turned their heads in her direction including Zasquash, who paled when he realized what he'd done.

"Laura?" I squatted down in front of her. "Let me see."

When she lowered her hands, they were full of blood and her lip was large and puffy. Loud angry outbursts echoed all around me as the men understood the magnitude of what had just happened.

"Who did that?" I recognized Leo's voice but kept looking at Laura.

"I think it was me, but I didn't mean to. I was on top of that fucker." Zasquash pointed to Cameron, the police officer whom Willow had asked to massage her thigh.

Laura's face was dripping with blood, so I pulled off my uniform shirt and offered it to her. "Do you have all your teeth?"

Her tongue raked over her front teeth but the second she opened her mouth it was evident that one of her lower front teeth was missing.

"That one." I pointed to my own front tooth to show her.

"Don't tell Magni," she muttered. "He'll shit a sheet and he's already stressed out enough as it is."

"He's going to find out." I had only just said the words when Magni, Boulder, and Khan arrived on three of the large white hover bikes I'd seen guards use when patrolling the park.

"What the fuck is going on?" Khan thundered and jumped off the machine. "We heard your fighting all the way from inside my office. The Motlanders are traumatized enough after today! Has every man in my country lost his fucking mind?"

My body was shielding Laura but as soon as I stood up and turned to face the three men, they saw her sitting on the grass with her hands and face smeared in blood. Khan and Boulder stopped cold while Magni hurried to Laura's side. He didn't shout as expected. He just tensed up and kept his eyes locked with hers as he kneeled down in front of her. "Tell me who did this to you." His hands lifted her face as he looked over her cracked lip and missing tooth while his own lips were pressed into fine lines.

Laura shook her head. "It was no one's fault. I tried to stop a fight and got hit. It happens."

"You tried to stop a fight? Why?"

"I thought Mason was involved."

Magni's eyes narrowed and then he rose up to his full height, offering Laura a hand to pull her up, and stepped in front of all us men speaking in a tone dripping with cyanide. "Who. Hurt. My. Wife?"

There were around fourteen Nmen present and every man was looking down, including Hunter, who stood in the back.

"Who hurt…" Magni had only begun to repeat his question when Zasquash stepped forward.

"I did. By accident," my brave friend said and kept his gaze to the ground.

I closed my eyes and wished there was something I could do for him. But our laws were black and white, and my hands were tied.

Next to me, Laura moved forward while drying off the blood on her face with my shirt. "Can I say something?" She was looking at Khan, not Magni.

He too was stiff with anger on his face, but he nodded.

"I know our laws and I know it looks bad, but can we just think about this for a second. Zasquash never meant to hurt me, and a broken lip isn't the worst I've suffered during sparring with you men." She used her chin to point at Boulder and Magni.

"I'm a warrior and I was the one who threw myself into a fight. You can't punish Zasquash for something that was an accident."

Laura's words were met by silence and she moved over to whisper something to Magni. The two of them seemed to have a private argument while Khan shifted his balance and addressed the men with a deep frown on his face. "Why were you men fighting in the first place?"

A few mutters were heard.

"Zasquash, speak up," Khan ordered.

Zasquash placed his hands on his back and stood straight like the soldier he was. "Some people made comments about the women that we Doomsmen didn't appreciate."

"What kind of comments?" Khan pointed to Leo. "Did you hear it?"

Leo scratched his shoulder and looked to the side. It was clear he didn't want to answer.

"What comments?" Khan's tone became deeper and he took a threatening step forward.

Leo wet his dry lips. "Many of us were upset about a woman joining the police force, and there might have been some inappropriate jokes."

"About Raven?" Boulder's gaze narrowed into daggers and he looked ready to attack any man who had been disrespectful of his daughter.

"No. It was more general and then one or two names were mentioned."

"Who?"

Leo looked down. "I didn't hear it, but it set off Zasquash. When he and Cameron began fighting it escalated to include the rest of us pretty fast. I was trying to break things up but when you get punched at, you punch back, you know."

Khan zoomed in on Zasquash. "What names did you hear?"

This time Zasquash lifted his head to look straight at Khan. "Salma Rose, Willow Darlington, and Darlene Long."

"I see. And what was said about these women?"

Zasquash squared his chest. "It was comments about their looks. They were crude and don't deserve to be repeated."

I looked back to see that a crowd had gathered. Pearl stood a few steps behind Khan now and further back were Mila, Raven, Christina, some of the children, and a handful of Motlander performers. I didn't see Willow or Salma, but Darlene was there, looking on with her eyes wide open.

"All right, you can tell me later." Khan pointed to Zasquash and Cameron. "Sounds like you two initiated the fight. You'll come with me. The rest of you will talk to Boulder and explain what you saw. He'll give me details."

Zasquash and I exchanged a long look as he walked past me, our hands landing on each other's shoulders, squeezing tight. I wanted to plead his case or challenge Khan and Magni to a fight for Zasquash's life. I think he saw it in my eyes – the silent question if he wanted my help – because Zasquash mumbled a low, "Don't do anything stupid."

Laura and Pearl walked after Khan, Magni, Cameron, and Zasquash, but I doubted there was much they could do to stop the inevitable.

Standing stiff as a stone gargoyle, I watched their backs until I couldn't see them anymore.

"Solo, please, I don't understand what happened." A female voice penetrated my dark thoughts and I looked down to see Darlene, the woman from the orchestra who had been kind to Zasquash on several occasions.

"Ehhm…" I tried to gather my thoughts. "Laura was hit in the face by Zasquash."

"But it was an accident."

"Yes."

"Will they punish him for it?"

"Yes."

Darlene looked in the direction he'd left. "Can't he just apologize?"

"No. I know it's hard to understand for Motlanders but we have harsh punishments for touching women, and to hurt them is a sure death sentence."

Darlene gave a small shriek and grabbed my arm. "NO!"

I stepped back, wanting to break the physical contact with her, and looked around fearful that someone might mistake her outburst for something I'd done to her. "Let go." I shook my hand.

"Are you saying even this can get you in trouble?"

"Yes." I used my other hand to loosen her grip and moved back. "It's better if you don't touch me."

"There is no way we're letting Zasquash get killed for that accident." Darlene had a look of defiance and determination on her face. "I'm going to fight this."

"Fight?" I looked at her small frame with confusion. "You can't fight Khan or Magni. You're not strong enough."

Darlene lifted her chin. "You just watch me!" Turning around, Darlene marched toward her friends and like a swarm of bees their group was buzzing with outrage. I looked in awe as Darlene sent the five women out in different directions. They were running and aiming straight for other Motlanders, talking, nodding, gesturing their arms.

Darlene came back to me. "Where's Salma?"

"I'm not sure."

"We need to find her."

Leo was close and I asked him if he knew where Salma was.

"She's with Tristan and Ben. They went to row a boat down by the pond. I think some of the children went with them too."

When we found Salma she was braiding Aubri's hair and smiled at us. Darlene sat down next to Salma and spoke fast and with great passion about Zasquash's situation. The more she spoke the more Salma looked like crying.

"That's horrible. How can I help?"

"We started a petition and we need you to use your influence and help us have as many sign it as possible. We need to work fast. It's life or death."

Salma got up from the grass and brushed off her dress. "I'm on it. I'll spread it to all my fans, and Ben and I will call every celebrity we know and enroll them too. Trust me, this petition will have millions of signatures in no time."

"Good, we're meeting at the scene; I'll see you there." Darlene couldn't be more than five foot three, but for a pacifistic Motlander, she worked like a general – ordering her troops around and setting up headquarters by the amphitheater where all the Motlanders gathered. When Willow arrived and heard what had happened, she immediately joined in and took it a step further.

"You there." Willow pointed to a group of police officers and Doomsmen who were watching with amazement how the Motlanders were buzzing around.

One of the men pointed to his chest. "Who, me?"

"Yes, and the rest of you too. We need your signatures."

"What for?"

"Because it's time to modify the outdated laws you have. Do you think Zasquash should die for what he did?"

"It's the law."

Darlene and some of her friends protested. "You can't have laws that make women afraid of getting good men killed by accident. You have thousands of women here now, not just a few."

"But those laws are our way of protecting women from harm."

Willow addressed all the men. "Don't you see how wrong it is for your ruler to execute a good man because of an outdated law? Especially on the same day your country has taken a great step toward equality by allowing Raven to join the police. She won't be able to do her job if every time a man touches her he's committing a crime. With this new opportunity for women comes the need to change your strict laws."

"But what if a man hurts a woman on purpose?"

"Then he should be dealt with the same way as if a woman hurts a man."

Mutters broke out among the men. "Are you saying we should kill women too?"

"No." Willow planted her hands on her hips. "I'm saying you shouldn't kill anyone."

"She's trying to make the Northlands into the Motherlands." One of my colleagues wrinkled his nose up.

Willow stared at him. "That would be impossible. Use your brains. What happened to Zasquash could have happened to any of you."

"I agree on modifying the laws," I said and stepped forward. "Where do I sign?"

"Of course you would say that," Hunter, who had been silent until now, called out loud. "But those laws are in place for a reason."

"I'll sign too." Leo stood up and raised his hands. "This law is too rigid. I don't think Zasquash deserves to die."

"Hunter, we need your help." Willow walked down from the stage and toward her brother, who sat up high in the back of the theater. "Zasquash isn't a bad person and you know it."

"I never said he was."

"You have millions of fans. If you ask them to sign the petition we can gather even more signatures."

He looked down.

"Please, Hunter. Nmen signatures are going to matter more to Khan than Motlander signatures. Your fans will listen to you."

When Hunter didn't answer Willow, she pressed him. "Imagine if it was you."

"I'm all for saving Zasquash's life, but we need strict laws or no woman can be safe here. If men are allowed to touch women it'll be like the mob who attacked you at the hotel the other day."

Willow pleaded with him. "We didn't say they should be allowed to touch us, just that the default reaction shouldn't be to kill the man. Maybe it was an accident like today, maybe the woman and man were in love and wanted to be together without permission from her protector. Every woman should have a right to choose for herself and to be heard when it comes to the fate of the man who touched her."

Hunter sat up straight and his glance traveled from Willow to me and back again. I moved closer.

"What the fuck are you talking about? Willow, are you doing this for *him*?" He pointed to me.

I was close enough to hear Hunter, but the other Nmen had gone down to the stage where they were being sweet-talked into signing the petition by the female performers.

"If I hadn't intervened back then, Solo would have been killed," Willow argued and kept her eyes on Hunter. "That would have been wrong."

Hunter stood up, his body seething and his green eyes darker than usual. "You'll stay away from him."

I straightened up too. "This isn't about me and Willow. It's about Zasquash, who's been nothing but nice to you. You haven't known him as long as I have, but he's the most loyal friend you can have. That man would take a bullet for any woman, and hurting Laura was the last thing on his mind. If you have any decency, you'll help him avoid getting executed for an accident he had no control over."

Hunter got up and walked a few steps down to stand in front of me. "I'll sign the petition and I'll encourage all my millions of fans to do the same, if…"

My eyebrow rose up as he stared at me.

"You'll give me your word that after this tour, you'll stay away from my sister *forever*."

I swallowed hard. "You can't ask me to do that."

"Yes, I can!"

He was asking me to choose between the love of my life and my best friend, who was like family to me. Both Zasquash and Willow had saved my life in the past and I loved them both.

Giving up Willow was like giving up breathing. I just couldn't!

But Zasquash's life was on the line and Hunter had the power to help save it. My eyes found Willow's, my heart breaking as I was torn between loyalty for my best friend and the deep love I felt for her. Willow didn't believe in the death penalty. Would she forgive me if I chose her and Zasquash was executed? Would I forgive myself?

"So, what is it going to be?" Hunter asked impatiently.

My hand rubbed my chest as if I could hold together my heart to keep it from breaking in two, and with deep sadness I opened my mouth to answer.

CHAPTER 25
The Verdict

Willow

"I'll sign the petition and encourage all my millions of fans to do the same, if…" Hunter's words made my spine stiffen and I kept my eyes fixed on him as he looked straight at Solomon and finished his sentence: "You'll give me your word that after this tour, you'll stay away from my sister forever."

I closed my eyes, a scream of frustration forming in my throat.

"You can't ask me to do that." Solo sounded outraged.

"Yes, I can!"

I knew Hunter was trying to protect me, but he didn't understand how things had changed for me. The thought of never seeing Solomon again made hysteria bubble up like burning acid in my stomach. My feet felt like ants were crawling up my ankles, and my head was hurting from reliving the trauma from my past. Ever since Solo and I first met ten years ago, laws, rules, and worried people had tried to keep us apart and for the last seven years they had succeeded.

Solomon and I exchanged a look and it was as if he was asking for my forgiveness. He was going to choose Zasquash, and how could he not? What kind of man would let his best friend die if he could prevent it?

Hunter crossed his arms. "So, what is it going to be?"

I was done letting others make decisions for me. The anger from all those years ago flared up like a heaven-sent fuel for me to choose my own destiny. Stepping forward, I spoke up. "Solo can't promise you that."

"Sis, stay out of this," Hunter warned me and groaned.

But I couldn't stay out of it. I couldn't bear to hear Solo promise never to see me again when being with him today had been the happiest I'd been in these past seven years. With my face serious and my shoulders tensed up, I stood my ground against Hunter.

His ultimatum to Solomon had been turned on me. *I* had to make the choice between my brother and Solo, and it tore me apart.

"Hunter, please don't hate me, because I love you so much," I whispered.

Solo took a small step toward me, but I signaled for him to stay back.

"Willow, what are you saying?" Hunter's face had lowered and so had his voice, and when I didn't answer, he closed his eyes almost like a shield against whatever horrible thing I was trying to tell him.

"Solo can't promise you to stay away from me because I won't stay away from him."

"But you hate him."

I shook my head. "No, Hunter. I don't hate him."

Hunter's face scrunched up. "Yes, you do. You're just confused."

"No, Hunter. It's the other way around. I'm remembering things clearly again and my feelings have come back." Tears were forming in my eyes. "Solo and I made promises to each other. We had a ceremony."

"What are you talking about?"

I inhaled and spoke on my exhalation, "Solo is my husband."

"The fuck he is," Hunter hissed low. "I would know if he was." His hands flew through the air and landed in his hair. "It's not true, Willow. You hate Solo!"

I reached for my brother in an attempt to calm him down. "That's what I thought too, but Solo and I…" my voice broke and I looked up to meet Solomon's eyes, which were beaming with raw emotion.

"We loved each other all those years ago. It wasn't just a fleeting infatuation and I can't stop those feelings from coming back again."

"But he hurt you," Hunter pleaded with me and got my attention back. "Willow, don't you remember? I promised to protect you from him. You almost died."

Solomon moved closer to me. "I won't hurt her again."

His words were met with vivid distrust on Hunter's face as he narrowed his eyes and pointed a threatening finger at Solo. "I'm going to Khan and Magni. They'll have you reassigned to some god-forsaken place in Alaska if you don't stay away from her."

"Hunter." I was still holding out my hand, touching his wrist for connection. "No one could ask for a better or more loving brother than you." My eyes teared up. "But remember what I said to you earlier. I make my own decisions. Being with Solo feels right to me. We're no longer teenagers, and that means Magni and Khan can't decide for us any longer and neither can you."

"Willow, why are you doing this? What did he tell you?"

"It's not like that, Hunter. When Solo and I ran away together, we…"

"You never ran away with him. He kidnapped you."

I shook my head and with sadness in my heart, I made my tone insistent. "When Solo and I ran away together it was because we couldn't wait six years to get married and live together. We made our own ceremony and made promises. It was my idea to get married, not his."

"Willow, don't." Hunter's face was drawn in pain and he lifted his hands to my shoulders and shook me. "That marriage wasn't real. It wasn't official, and it was never consummated. He's *not* your husband."

I wet my lips. "It *was* consummated." My gaze fell to my feet as I whispered the rest: "A few hours ago."

Hunter stepped back and jerked his hand away from my touch. He was looking straight at me, but it was like he didn't recognize me anymore. The confusion and disbelief on his face made my whole body hurt.

"Hunter." Solo stepped forward with sympathy written all over his face. "It's going to be all right."

Hunter just shook his head and kept backing away from us.

"I'm so sorry. We never wanted to hurt you, but Willow is the love of my life."

My brother's mouth opened and closed, and his moist eyes blinked, but no words came. He was in shock and there wasn't anything Solo or I could say.

"He needs time to digest it." Solo pulled me against his chest as we watched Hunter jog away.

I cried, "You don't understand. I'm all the family he has and the only one he trusts. He felt so betrayed when we first ran away together. You were his best friend and he never forgave you. And then there was Alice, who broke his heart. I was the only one he trusted and now I just betrayed him again."

"Hunter is a strong man, he'll be all right."

My voice dripped with sadness. "I don't think he'll ever forgive me."

"He will. Just give him time." Solo pulled me close and let me cry against his shoulder while he stroked my hair.

We stood like that for a long time, until I heard Leo's voice behind me. "Is Willow crying because of Zasquash? You should tell her that there are already millions of signatures and that all the performers are threatening to leave if Zasquash is harmed."

"She's crying because Hunter got upset when she told him we're together now."

I lifted my head and gave Solomon a blameful look. "Don't tell Leo that!"

Solo raised a brow. "Why not?"

"I never said that we're back together, just that I don't hate you anymore."

Solo tilted his head. "You told Hunter we were married."

"Because he made you choose between Zasquash and me. I couldn't let you make a promise of never seeing me again."

Drying away one of my tears, Solo gave me a small smile. "I would have never given a promise like that. We *are* together, Willow. I'm never letting you go again, so you'd better get used to it." Lifting my chin, he kissed my lips, and right in that chaotic moment of not knowing if Hunter would ever forgive me and Zasquash would survive, I felt calm. At least my feelings for Solo were no longer confusing to me. As I accepted his words that we were together, my body relaxed against him.

"That's great news." Leo's eyes softened. "Who would have known that a beautiful woman like you could fall for a mutant like him?"

"Hey, watch it, Leo." Solo used a warning tone and kept me in his arms.

"No offense, Solo, but you're fucking huge and you know it. Most Motlanders would be terrified of you. It's a miracle that Willow isn't intimidated by your size."

"It's because I've known him since we were children."

"Hmm, it's a shame there were no mixed schools when I was a teen. Maybe someone would have fancied me then," Leo pondered out loud before leaving us.

I considered myself a strong woman but hiding away in Solo's arms for a minute felt amazing.

"When all of this is over, I'm taking you home to the house I built for us," he whispered and kissed me on the top of my head.

"Did you really build it by the lake where we married?"

"Yes, I did."

"I wish we could go right now and pretend everything is fine."

Solo sat down on the stone seat and pulled me down on his lap. "Me too, but I'm not leaving Zas behind."

"You were going to pick him, weren't you?"

Solo leaned his head against mine. "He would never forgive me if I had let myself be blackmailed from being with my mate. I know Zas looks big and frightening to some, but he's a romantic at heart and he's…"

My fingers kneaded Solo's shoulders as I waited for him to continue.

"Zas is loyal and funny. He's the best friend a man can get and the closest thing to family I have besides you. I never had to worry about being afraid when we got in trouble because I knew he was there. I swear, if you knew him better you'd understand why it's so easy to love him."

"Maybe Khan will show him mercy."

Solo's voice was hoarse from emotions. "I don't see how. I mean not only is Laura a woman and practically royal, but she's the commander's wife. And Zas didn't just touch her, did he? He cracked her lip and punched out her tooth."

"Yeah, I know. It's bad."

We sat close, not speaking for a few minutes until chanting made us turn our heads and look down to the stage. "What the fuck are they doing now?" Solo muttered.

Darlene, Salma, and all the other Motlanders were creating banners from white clothing with different messages written on them and attaching them to wooden sticks.

"Now let's protest outside Khan's office and make sure he hears us," Darlene shouted and waved her hand for everyone to follow her.

Solo and I got up as the large group of around thirty people walked off, repeating the same chant in singsong voices.

"We should be up front." I pulled at Solo's hand and we snaked our way through the Nmen who were following the parade of Motlanders with baffled expressions on their faces.

"No more killing. No more killing." I joined in on the chant while reading the messages on the improvised banners that the Motlanders were holding up.

*Why hurt people
who hurt people
to show that hurting is wrong?*

*Women against murder.
Don't kill for us!*

An eye for an eye makes everyone blind.

You kill – We leave!

Pacifists have more fun.

We were making a spectacle as we chanted the same words over and over while marching to the manor.

"No more killing. No more killing."

"Why aren't you shouting the words?" I asked Solo.

He looked torn as if he'd never considered there would be a real alternative to the death penalty. "Sometimes a death penalty is the right choice."

I frowned. "But not today."

"No, not today," he agreed.

"Then chant for Zasquash."

Solo's deep baritone voice started low but grew in volume as we kept chanting together with all the others.

Men of the North #7 – THE DANCER

Mila and Raven pointed to the right-hand side of the building and led the way. "Khan's office is on this side."

The children were running around us, energized by the chanting. The security team were following the events but didn't participate.

After fifteen minutes of our protesting outside Khan's office, Khan and Magni came out with Cameron and Zasquash between them. Pearl and Laura stood by their husbands' sides, and I wondered if they'd been allowed in Khan's office all this time.

"Pearl tells me this isn't a rebellion but a peaceful protest," Khan began and looked like five flies had just landed on his dinner. "I have noted that you're not in favor of the death penalty, and you're free to go about your own business now." He gave a dismissive wave of his hand but we protesters weren't done.

"If you don't release the men we'll pack our things and leave at once," Darlene threatened.

Khan arched an eyebrow and raised his chin. "Who are you?"

"My name is Darlene Long and I play the bass."

"Well, Darlene Long, you should know that blackmail is a serious offense in the Northlands. You might want to reconsider your words."

"I'm not blackmailing anyone. I'm simply stating an ultimatum."

Magni moved a step forward, his face red as chili. "No one gives the ruler of the Northlands ultimatums. We don't tell you how to fucking run your country. This is anarchy."

Every man in the country would have been intimidated by Magni's anger, but Darlene didn't waver. Only her shoulders dropped a little. But then Mila walked over to stand beside Darlene, close enough for their arms to touch. She didn't speak, but the signal was clear. She was siding with Darlene against her father.

"Mila." Magni's frown grew as I walked over to stand on Darlene's other side. Salma followed, and then Raven, and every other Motlander. Together we formed a wall, standing shoulder to shoulder in silent protest with the banners speaking for us.

The smile on Pearl's face said it all and she covered her mouth when Khan scowled at her.

"For fuck's sake," Khan hissed and tore his hands through his hair. "I'm not going to let Motlanders dictate our laws."

There was a tension-laden atmosphere with everyone waiting for Khan to speak again but his eyes widened at something happening behind me. I turned to see Solo walking over to take a stand right behind my back. At first, he stood alone but then Leo followed and soon eleven Nmen formed their own line, backing us up.

Magni had his hands on his hips and was shaking his head. "This is what happens when you do fucking town hall meetings. People think their opinion matters. I told you it was a mistake."

Khan held up his hands and spoke to us. "You're wasting your time since my decision has already been made."

A gasp went through us and we collectively held our breaths.

Zasquash was looking straight at Darlene when Khan continued talking.

"Laura and Pearl have made persuasive arguments that Raven will face situations similar to what happened today. As a result, I've decided that female warriors will be exempt from the law of no physical contact while they participate in fights." He held up his hand. "That is as far as I'll stretch at this point. As a result of this new law and Laura's insistence that it was an accident, Zasquash and Cameron may return to their work." Pivoting around, Khan strode a few steps before he turned again and faced everyone with a grumpy expression. "And the same goes for everyone else. Get back to work!"

Zasquash walked like he was in shock and when happy Motlanders swarmed him with congratulations he stiffened and stuck his hands straight up in the air as if to avoid anyone blaming him for touching a woman.

Most people patted him on the shoulders and back but Darlene hugged him and didn't seem to care that Zasquash didn't hug her back. When she released him, Darlene turned to Solo. "Told you I'd fight the injustice, didn't I?"

Solo gave her a nod of respect. "I've never seen anything like it. Thank you."

"You're lucky that Khan gave in," Darlene told Zasquash. "You wouldn't have liked my plan B."

Zasquash had lowered his arms now that he was no longer swarmed. "What was your plan B?"

"I was going to smuggle you out of here in my bass case and take you home with me. But with your size it would have been a tight squeeze and I don't know how well you'd breathe in there."

"What do you mean – home with you? To the Motherlands?" Zasquash pulled at his lip.

"Yes. I figured you'd rather live without meat and alcohol than not live at all."

Zasquash's Adam's apple bobbed in his throat. "You would take me home with you?"

"Yes." Darlene said it like it was a no-brainer.

"You know they only give residency to Nmen who are married, right?"

Darlene had her head leaned back to look up at Zasquash. "I'm not scared of you if that's what you're asking."

Zasquash blinked his eyes. "No, I guess you wouldn't be if you're willing to marry me."

"Well, now we don't have to marry since you're free."

A small smile tugged at Zasquash's mouth. "Would you consider marrying me anyway?"

Darlene chuckled. "You don't mean that."

"Oh, I've never been more fucking serious in my life." Zasquash moved closer to her. "To see a woman stand up to Khan and Magni to save my sorry ass is about the craziest thing I've ever seen. I don't know where you came from but you're one badass woman."

Darlene looked a little offended. "So my behind is a little bigger than most. But to call it bad to my face is rude."

I laughed. "No, Darlene, you misunderstand. Zasquash isn't referring to your actual backside. Badass is his way of saying that you're strong and amazing."

"Oh." She relaxed a little, but Zasquash was still high on his unexpected pardon and with a mischievous glance in his eyes, he joked:

"I don't know. Why don't you turn around so I can get a better look at your ass? Bigger than most sounds good to me." He winked at her. "I'm a greedy man and like something to hold onto."

"Ha." Darlene scrunched up her face. "That's coming from the man who was afraid to give me an innocent hug two minutes ago. I didn't feel you hold on to anything."

My large friend stared at her with bewilderment and then his eyes turned to me. "Is she for real?"

"I think so."

He wet his lips and looked straight at Darlene. "Do I have your permission to hug you?"

"Why would you ask me that after I already hugged you?"

As soon as she finished her sentence, Darlene was dangling in Zasquash's arms as he squeezed her in a bear hug. "You are the most spectacular woman in the world."

I took Solo's hand and we smiled at each other. Minutes ago we'd been scared for Zasquash's life; now he was flirting with Darlene and seemed untroubled.

"Set me down," she insisted but her arms were around his muscular shoulders. "I'm too heavy."

Zasquash leaned his head back and laughed. "How about we test how far I can carry you? I'll bet we could make it behind some bushes so I could kiss you."

They were laughing together when we left them.

CHAPTER 26
Crowded Bedroom

Willow

Solo and I spent all evening together, talking, holding hands, and walking around the park. When we reached a quiet corner with no one in sight, he pulled me behind a tree and seduced me into having sex with him in the outdoors.

Not that I was hard to convince. After accepting that I still loved Solo, my desire for him was out of control. There was still that forbidden feel about it although I assumed that by now rumors would have reached almost everyone, since many had seen us sitting together in the outdoor theatre.

My thoughts went to Hunter but knowing him, he would need time to lick his wounds before he was ready to talk.

We skipped dinner in favor of more time together alone. Food didn't seem important when we could be spending time talking, kissing, and making love in secret places. Once we got back to the manor it was close to eleven at night. I stopped when we passed a mirror and lifted a hand to my face. "Oh, no."

Solo stopped too. "What's wrong?"

"My face. Look at my face." My cheeks were flaming red. "It's your beard. Remember how the same thing happened when we were younger?"

He gave me a forlorn smile. "I'm sorry, babe. I didn't want to say anything. I was afraid you'd stop kissing me."

Turning one side of my face to the mirror and then the other, I made sounds of horror. "I look like I had an allergic reaction."

"As long as you don't tell people that you're allergic to me."

I widened my eyes. "What if I am?"

Solo scrunched up his face. "That's not even funny."

When we heard voices approaching, we hurried up the stairs. This wasn't the right time to bump into Khan or Magni and explain what was going on. We'd already decided that we would face them together tomorrow.

Snickering like children, we made it to my room, where we found Tristan.

"So, it's true then?" He sat on the bed with his feet stretched in front of him and his hands behind his head. "Salma told me she saw you two holding hands. Does that mean you're back together?"

"We are." Solo intertwined his hand with mine. "And this time we're not letting anyone come between us."

"What about Hunter?"

I sighed. "He's not happy about it, but he'll accept it, eventually."

"Let's hope so." Tristan yawned and looked at Solo. "You do know that Leo is pissed at you, right? You're still on duty and no one knew where you were. Zasquash went missing too but he turned up with Darlene about an hour ago."

"I was with Willow." Solo squeezed my hand. "I should get back and talk to Leo. It's probably better if I sleep down there to avoid drama."

"Okay." I reached up on my toes and kissed him.

"Are you coming?" Solo gave Tristan an impatient stare.

"Coming where?"

"You're not staying here with Willow."

"Ehh... yeah, I am." Tristan tilted his head. "She said I could sleep here."

"In your dreams." Solo raised his voice a little.

Tristan frowned. "Come on. You know I won't touch her, and every other room is full."

"Then sleep on the lawn for all I care." Solo squared his shoulders. "No one sleeps with Willow but me."

"Why not? We've already slept together and nothing happened. Didn't she tell you that?"

"Yes, she told me but to be honest I already suspected that much. Her acting didn't convince me she was in love with you."

I scoffed. "That's rude, Solo. Ben says I have a talent for acting."

But Solo didn't pay attention to me. He was waving his hand for Tristan to come with him. "Come on, Tristan. You must be high if you think I'm letting another man sleep in the same bed as *my* woman."

Tristan rolled his eyes. "Okay. Then I'll sleep on the floor."

"No! You two aren't sleeping alone in here."

It annoyed me that the two men were talking over my head and that neither of them asked me what *I* wanted. With a sigh of irritation, I walked over and picked up my bag. "You two can share the room! I'm not sticking around to hear you make decisions on my behalf."

Solo followed me down the hallway. "Where are you going?"

"To Mila's room. I'll see you in the morning."

"Do you even know where her room is?"

"Yes, she told me."

"At least let me escort you there."

To my surprise it was Raven who opened the door to Mila's room. "Willow. What's wrong?" She narrowed her eyes at Solo. "What did you do this time?"

Solo held up both palms in a sign of peace. "Nothing."

"Can I sleep here? Tristan is in my room."

Mila came running to the door with a puppy in her arms. "Of course you can. Come on in." Her large blue eyes were wide with excitement. "This is just like old times."

"Bye, Solo." Raven waved at him and when he walked away, she called out, "Are we still doing that fight session tomorrow morning?"

He didn't turn but lifted his hand. "Seven a.m. on the lawn."

"How about eight a.m.?" Raven asked.

"Six a.m. it is." Solo turned a corner with a chuckle and left Raven to look at me with her head tilted.

"Is he serious?"

I smiled. "I think so."

Closing the door, Raven walked into Mila's spacious room with me next to her looking around in wonder.

"Wow, this room is gorgeous." The sounds of excited puppies drew me to a fenced-in area where three golden-brown puppies were on their hind legs with their heads reaching over the barrier. Their tails were wagging, and I just had to pick one up. "Look at you, aren't you the cutest?"

"His name is Trailblazer and he's one big bunch of high energy." Mila smiled. "Don't get him unless you plan to let him get out and run a lot."

"I wasn't planning on getting a puppy. He's just so cute."

"They all are." Raven picked up one of the other two and kissed its little paw. In return it licked her chin.

Looking around again, I took in the large bed, the en-suite bathroom, and the lounge area. My room at home was about a fourth the size of this place and my bathroom was tiny. I could have opted for something bigger, but it would have meant having a roommate and I didn't have the best experience with roommates. "This is a different room from when you were younger, isn't it?" I asked Mila.

"Yes. This suite used to be Finn's, but he agreed to swap with me. He says he and Athena don't need much space when they come to visit. They are always out and about anyway."

"Do you see them often? Finn and Athena."

"Yes, they are my parents' best friends. I love Finn and Athena." Mila put down the puppy she'd been holding and Raven followed her example. I exchanged Trailblazer for a darker-colored puppy that had been yapping for attention. "That's Samba, she swings her hips when she walks and it makes it look like she's dancing."

"Oh, a fellow dancer, that's so nice." I kissed her and looked into the cutest brown eyes, melting a little. "Mila, do you know if Finn and Athena are coming to see one of our performances?"

Mila shook her head. "We invited them, but they couldn't. That's why we let some of the performers stay in their room. Athena is at the yearly priestess meeting. Finn said she'll get another tattoo this year." Mila pointed to the spot right above her eyebrow by the edge of her temple.

"Do you think it would be wrong if I got a tattoo there as well?" Raven asked and threw herself on Mila's bed. "It looks so mysterious."

"You can't. Only priestesses can have tattoos on their foreheads. You know they earn them when they master something important. Athena's last one symbolizes her profound knowledge of some ancient religion or language."

"I know that, but I wouldn't get any of hers. I would get something related to my own personal journey."

"Like what?" I curled up in a comfortable chair close to the bed with Samba cuddled against my chest. She was a much calmer dog than Trailblazer and closed her eyes when I stroked down her back. Mila sat down on the armrest next to me and brushed her hands through my hair. "Why is your hair so tangled? Do you want me to comb it?"

I didn't tell her that it was tangled because Solo loved to fist his hands through my hair when he kissed me. Or that I'd been on my back in the soft grass with Solo on top of me more than once today. I just smiled at Mila and said, "Sure, that would be nice."

Mila got a comb and some silk oil to brush out my thick locks while I asked Raven again, "What tattoo would you get?"

"Maybe a P for police or a raven because of my name."

"Don't you want to complete the training and become a real police officer before you tattoo your body?"

Raven lifted her head from the bed and raised an eyebrow at me. "You don't think I can do it."

I leaned forward in the chair, giving Mila more room to brush my hair. "I believe in you, but I don't trust the men. We all know they want you to fail. If you complete the training they'll have to let you work as a police officer, and there's no way they'll ever let you do that."

Raven sat up. "You think Khan is setting me up to fail?"

"Yes."

"What do you think, Mila?" Raven asked.

Mila drew a deep inhalation. "They're not trying to be mean, it's just that things are going a little fast for some of them."

"So, you think I'll fail as well?"

"Yes. Unless you align yourself with someone who'll keep an eye on things and make sure you're being treated fairly. Someone with power and influence."

"Laura!" Raven pushed up from the bed. "Laura is a warrior like me. She'll want me to succeed."

"I was thinking about Pearl. But if you can get both of them on your team then your chances are higher," Mila pointed out.

I cleared my throat. "What about your dad? Boulder has influence and power." Samba had fallen asleep on my chest and was making the cutest snoring sounds. "If your father turns up once in a while that wouldn't hurt either."

Pacing the room, Raven swung her arms. "I'm not letting anyone stop me. No matter how hard they make things for me, I'm going to show them that we women are tough and that I can be the best police officer they've ever seen."

"Good for you." I ducked my head. "Argh, careful, Mila."

"I swear your hair is worse than my siblings after they've been swimming all day. What did you do?"

"It was windy tonight and I was out walking."

Raven stopped and walked over to stand in front of me and Mila. "Okay, can we stop pretending that nothing weird is going on. What is happening with you and Solo?"

Just the mentioning of his name made me smile.

"Wow." Raven's brow rose up high.

Mila, who was behind me, couldn't see my face but Raven repeated a loud "Wow."

"Wow what?" Mila said while her fingers braided my hair.

"She's in love with him." Raven pointed at me.

Mila pulled at my hair to make me turn and face her. "Are you?"

"Yes."

Mila made a happy sound and hugged me so tight it woke up Samba, who gave a yawn. "That's so romantic. I always hoped that you two would end up back together."

"No, you didn't." Raven planted her hands on her hips. "I never heard you say that. Not once."

"That doesn't mean I didn't think it." Mila kept braiding my hair. "All that matters is that Willow is happy."

"I *am* both happy and sad." I bit my lip. "Hunter didn't take it well."

"Sorry." Mila's voice was sympathetic. "He'll come around. Give him time."

"Maybe. But I'm also worried about telling Khan and Magni."

"Why?" Mila finished the braid and took my hand instead. "Why would you be afraid to tell Magni?"

"Because Magni never liked Solo to begin with. The two of them have always been at odds, and I fear Solo and me being together will remind Magni about the humiliation of not being able to find us when we ran away together. I don't want Magni to take it out on Solo. He is his commander after all, and he holds enormous power."

Mila sank to the floor next to the chair and kept my hands in hers. "My father isn't the cruel man people think he is. I've heard him praise Solo many times. He calls him the greatest warrior of his generation."

"Then why did he make life so hard on Solo? You wouldn't believe what the Huntsmen put him through when he was younger."

"You mean after he ran away with you."

"Yes."

"Ahh…" Raven plunked down on the floor too. "I know why. I've heard the men talk about it."

"Did you know they left him to survive in the cold for days without food and tools?" I felt emotional as I recounted a few of the examples that Solo had told me about today. "And why would they cut his skin open and tell him to treat the wound with only what he could find in the forest? He almost bled to death."

Raven arranged herself in a yoga position and spoke in a low voice. "Because they wanted him to understand what it means to live in the forest with no safety net. That's what he was planning to do with you, and they needed him to see that he was just a kid with no idea what it would have been like once it got freezing cold. They were trying to burst his bubble of immortality and shock him. The problem was that Solo was tougher and more stubborn than anyone could have imagined. It all spiraled out of control. At least that's what they say."

I looked away. "Solo admitted that it was a mistake for us to run away together. I just wish people would see that the way things were handled by the adults was wrong too. We were in love and no one seemed to understand that."

Raven sighed, and Mila looked down. It wasn't fair to take it out on them.

"Anyway, it's water under the bridge now," I breathed. "This time we're over twenty-one and we can make our own decisions."

"So, what is your decision? Is he willing to move to the Motherlands with you?"

"I don't think that would be a good idea. It's easier for me to be here. I've lived here before and visited often. Solo has a cabin in the forest and with the drone it's only ten minutes from the nearest city."

Raven pulled her knees up in front of her and scrunched up her face. "Are you out of your mind, Willow? You can't give up dancing just to be with a man."

I grinned. "You've never been in love, have you Raven?"

"No." She lifted her chin. "Nor do I want to be. It makes people give up on their dreams and that's not happening to me."

"I'm not giving up on my dreams." I kissed Samba again and smiled. "In fact, Solo encouraged me to start my own dance studio. He was saving up for a newer drone, but he offered me the use of the money he has to find a location in town. It would be the first dance studio in the Northlands, as far as I know."

Mila lit up. "That's so exciting. Will you be teaching children? I'll bet my younger sisters would love to go. I could help you decorate the place and we could make a fun opening night and have Khan, Pearl, and my parents go. That way you'll get a lot of publicity, which is good for business. Hunter should be there too." Mila was already planning ahead but her mention of Hunter brought back the feelings of letting him down.

"I would love your help with planning everything." I smiled at Mila and turned to Raven. "And yours too, of course."

Raven tilted her head. "I'll help but I might not have much time, you know, being away at the police academy and all."

"I understand."

Raven got up from the floor and placed her hand on my shoulder. "But I'm happy to hear that you're not giving up on your career or your dreams. That would have been sad."

I smiled up at Raven. "We're going to show the Northlanders what women are made of. Business owners, police officers, and…" I looked at Mila. "What is it you want to do for a career?"

Mila's dimples came out. "I'm not sure. For now, I'm running a small rescue center here at the mansion for dogs. I'm thinking about becoming a veterinarian but I'm not good with blood, so it might not be the best way to go."

I got up with Samba still in my arms. "Whatever you set your mind to, you have our full support."

"Group hug." Mila spread out her arms and little Samba got squeezed in the middle as Raven, Mila, and I hugged.

"It's late, I should get some sleep if I'm sparring with Solo at six a.m." Raven walked to the door.

"You're welcome to sleep here," Mila offered.

"Nah, your bedroom is getting a little cramped with all the puppies and you two. I promised I'd sleep with Samara anyway."

"How old is your sister now?"

"Seven." A soft smile spread on Raven's face. "She's the princess in the family. The boys and I are all into fighting and doing crazy stunts outside, but Samara is a mini Christina and we're all smitten with her."

"Well, good night then."

Raven looked back at me. "Good night, Willow. Get some rest before your big show tomorrow, I hear every seat is sold out."

"I will."

"Night, Mila."

Mila blew Raven a kiss before the door closed and she turned to me. "Are you nervous about the show?"

"A little."

Mila squeezed my hand. "Don't worry, everything is going to be fine. I'm sure of it."

CHAPTER 27
Breakdown

Solo

The outdoor theater next to the Gray Manor had room for twelve hundred people. It was built on a hillside with a natural slope and over the hundreds of years that it had been in use, the twenty-two wide rows of stone seats had been polished by rain, snow, and the backsides of countless men watching a variety of shows.

The Gray Manor hadn't been added until sixty years ago when a self-obsessed narcissist named Augustus had ruled the Northlands for seven miserable years. The man had gone down in history as a tyrant who loved to tower above his people from the balcony that faced the theater. It was rumored that he had built the large mansion for that purpose alone.

Maybe he wouldn't have if he'd known that only two years after he completed the house, he would die on that very same balcony – shot by one of his own guards in the spring rebellion of the year 2389.

Our country had been through so many wars, revolutions, and changes in rulers, kings, and presidents that it had become part of our identity.

Many were sighing about Khan's progressive ways of running the country, but between his father and him, we'd been at peace for forty years, which was historic in itself. Then there was the integration between our nation and the Motherlands, something no one in the old generations had thought possible. Sanctions had been lifted against us, new hospitals and schools had been built, and over all we were experiencing a growth in employment and living standards. I was sure that Khan Aurelius would go down in history as one of the greatest rulers the Northlands had ever seen.

Today, he was sitting on the balcony flanked by family and friends as they watched the first show ever performed by Motlanders on this stage. The choir had smiled and sung their way through their first part; Willow had danced and received a standing ovation. Security was a breeze at this facility compared to the others, but we were still on alert in case some idiot tried to get too close.

Like the other times, Leo, Zasquash, and I were positioned backstage. Salma had been nervous all day, crying several times and having long conversations with Tristan. The last hour before she went on stage, she'd been with Ben, who didn't seem to have the calming effect on her that he used to.

All three of us, Zasquash, Leo, and I, had assured Salma that no one was going to storm the stage or try to get close to her, but it hadn't helped much.

Now that she was on stage performing her first song, Salma's voice sounded like a weak imitation of the first time I'd heard her. At the other two concerts, she had used her whole body, gesturing with her arms, and singing with her mouth opened up wide. Now her arms were folded in front of her and she didn't look at the audience.

"She looks so uncomfortable," Willow whispered next to me. "Should I go in and dance next to her, do you think that would help her relax?"

"No, I think it would distract her and maybe confuse her."

Ben was rubbing his earlobe with a troubled look on his face when more than once Salma looked to her right where Zasquash and Leo stood hidden by the curtains, and to her left where Willow, Tristan, Ben, and I stood and watched.

Willow was moving her feet and wringing her hands. "We need to do something. She's terrified."

We didn't have time to do anything before all of a sudden, Salma stumbled back on the stage, her face pale and withdrawn in fear.

Concerned mutterings broke out among the audience members as she began crying and ran to our side, straight into the arms of Willow and Tristan.

"I've got you." Tristan hugged Salma tight. "You're okay."

"There... there was a man," she stammered. "He stood up and I thought..."

I looked out over the audience and saw a man walking toward the exit. "He's heading for the bathroom, Salma. No one is going to hurt you."

"Salma, look at me." Tristan spoke in a soft but insistent tone and waited for her to raise her head. "Remember what you said yesterday in your speech to the other performers?"

She was blinking her large gray eyes, which were wet from tears. "No."

"You said that fear will paralyze you and make you his bitch if you let him."

"That's not what she said," Willow protested. "Salma would never use a word like that."

Tristan kept his gaze locked with Salma. "You have battled your nemesis for years. You can't let fear make you give up now. I won't let you."

"But what if..." She sniffled and shook her head. "What if..."

"You're scared someone is going to attack you, is that it?" Tristan asked and seemed to be in no hurry despite the white noise from the audience that overpowered the instruments from the orchestra, who were still playing on.

"Let me go with you. I'll hold your hand and I guarantee that it'll make every man in that audience back off."

"That's right," I added. "They'll think you're allowing Tristan to claim you for his own."

Salma looked back to the stage and drew in a deep breath to calm herself.

"I've got you," Tristan repeated. "You don't have to do this alone."

Salma formed her lips into a round O and exhaled forcefully, her shoulders falling a bit, and then she filled her lungs again.

"Except the singing." Tristan gave a small smile. "If I start singing with you, the men will attack me for hurting their ears."

Salma's eyes softened but she didn't smile. Taking the hand Tristan held out to her, she turned to Willow. "Is my make-up all right?"

Willow used her thumbs to correct a few spots before giving a nod of approval.

Salma took a last deep breath before she walked back on stage with Tristan right next to her.

The orchestra stopped playing, the confused mumbling from the audience died down, and the few who had been standing up hurried back to their seats.

Salma was the star of the show and now that she was back, all eyes were on her.

Holding Tristan's hand in a tight squeeze, she looked back at the orchestra and collected herself before facing the audience. Instead of singing, she spoke to them.

"As you all know, yesterday was a hard day for us performers. I walked out here on stage today with fear in my body. Fear that one or more of you would storm the stage and hurt me."

No one said a word, but I think every one of us Nmen felt a heaviness in our chest.

"These past days, I've learned a lot about your culture. I am told you men of the north have a high level of honor."

The audience gave approving nods and comments.

"I've also been told that you respect women and take pride in protecting us." Salma's hand was still entwined with Tristan's when she raised it a little. "I'm sure there are many amazing men in this country and I know that I've only met a few. But one man stood out to me from the first moment he made me smile. Meeting Tristan was like finding a loved one from a previous life. Not only is he the kindest, dearest, and sweetest of men, but he makes me want to challenge myself." Salma smiled up at Tristan. "So, to you, Men of the North, hear me when I declare that I, Salma Rose, claim Tristan for my own."

The audience members were dead silent for a second before they exploded in a mix of laughter and applause.

My shoulders were jerking up and down, my chest rumbling with laughter. I met Leo's and Zasquash's eyes across the stage. They were bent over from laughing.

"What's so funny?" Ben asked me.

I didn't know how to explain how bizarre it was to us Nmen to see a woman claim a man and emasculate him at the same time by calling him sweet and pretty in front of a large audience. The fact that Tristan took it with a big smile and stood next to her like she had just nailed it made it even funnier.

Looking up, Khan was drying away tears of laughter from his eyes and everyone with him on the balcony was standing up and applauding too.

The waves of joy and positive energy lifted Salma and made her relax. She signaled for everyone to quiet down. "I owe a lot of my knowledge of your culture to Tristan, so before I do my next song for you, I just want to say that Tristan has the nicest ears I've ever seen."

Tristan grinned and showed off his ears by pulling his hair back.

The audience was still laughing, and Salma's voice was full of amusement. "See, he's making you laugh too. It's just a gift he has." With the widest smile, she tilted her head. "I think I can take it from here, Tristan."

Tristan leaned in and gave Salma a kiss square on her lips. For a second, he looked into her eyes and with a sweet smile she lifted her right hand and caressed his cheek in an intimate gesture.

"Say goodbye to Tristan, everyone. I was going to send him off the stage with eternal bliss in our traditional Motlander style, but instead let's all wish Tristan a lovely day with one of your local greetings that has become a favorite of mine." Lifting her hand, she raised her middle finger and pointed it at Tristan while smiling wide.

A new wave of laughter sounded from the audience as they joined in on the orchestra and Salma's flipping fingers at Tristan.

"Oh, how could I ever be scared of you. You're such an amazing audience," Salma said and inclined her head to all the Nmen in front of her. "My next song is called 'Energy of Life' and it goes like this." With a swing of her hand the orchestra began to play.

Tristan came walking offstage with a proud bounce in his steps.

"What the hell happened?" I grinned and patted his shoulder. "You were supposed to claim her, not the other way around."

Tristan didn't look bothered but was grinning from ear to ear. "In the spirit of equality, I just went with the flow."

Ben smiled up at Tristan. "You did marvelous. Look at how relaxed she is now." He pointed to Salma onstage; she was singing her heart out. "If I'd know a little fake publicity would make her this good I would have agreed sooner."

Tristan's smile stiffened as if the word fake bothered him.

"You know it was just for show," I reminded him. "To keep her safe."

"Maybe not."

"What's with that secretive smile?" I teased him, squeezing his shoulder.

"Let's just say some things happened between us this morning that make me very optimistic."

Willow's eyes dilated with excitement and she whispered, "Details, I want details."

Tristan grinned and shook his head.

"Did you tell Salma how you feel about her?"

He nodded.

"And what did she say?" Willow asked eagerly.

Tristan smiled. "She said she felt the same way about me. Don't look so surprised. Just because you didn't like me that way doesn't mean others can't."

"No, I didn't mean it like that. I'm sorry, Tristan." Willow tilted her head with an apologetic expression. "It was just that Solo was always in my heart. There was nothing wrong with you. We just weren't right for each other."

"I know." Tristan's eyes were fixed on Salma and he sighed a little.

"Oh, Tristan, I'm so happy for you." Willow gave him a spontaneous kiss on his cheek.

"Did you ask Salma to marry you?" I pressed him.

"We don't need to be married to be a couple. I think we'll find our own way."

I frowned. "No. That's the Motlander in you speaking. Make sure she marries you."

Tristan patted my chest. "Solo, relax. I'm not as possessive as you are. If I were, I couldn't share my woman with the rest of the world. Salma is a star and she lights up people's lives. I'm just pinching myself that she feels as in love with me as I feel about her." Tristan gave us a distracted smile as he turned back to watching Salma, who was moving on to the second song. "Isn't she amazing?" he breathed.

We all nodded in agreement.

When the show was over, we security members made sure only the selected few were allowed to stay for a meet-and-greet in the banquet hall inside the Gray Manor.

Salma held hands with Tristan all the way through, while talking with Nmen who declared she had a voice like an angel. Tristan looked proud and not bothered by their sugary words to his woman. I on the other hand scowled at every male who spoke with Willow. And when a handsome tall man made her laugh, I walked over and stood next to her.

Provoked by my glaring at him and unwilling to move along, he kept chatting with Willow. "Is it true that your brother is Hunter Hercules?"

"Yes."

"I'm happy to hear that. Many of us were disappointed to see you hold his hand. For a minute there, we thought you might not be single after all."

Willow gave him a serene look while I wanted to yell at him that she was no longer single.

"Any chance you'd be open to a relationship with an Nman?" the large man asked with a hopeful smile.

"Uh-huh." Willow gave me a sideways glance. She was amused. "I like big strong men."

"You do?" The man lit up and squared his chest.

"Yes, I like them slightly possessive and dominant too."

I wasn't sure if Willow was playing with him, me, or both of us, but I gave a low growl in warning.

"I'm dominant and possessive by nature," the man claimed and moved a tiny bit closer, his voice lower now and his eyes fixed on Willow like she was prey ready to take down.

"Move along," I ordered him, but he ignored me. "The lady isn't single."

"She just said she was."

"No. She confirmed Hunter was her brother."

"I've read every article and seen every interview. She's single," the man defended himself, and puffed himself up like a goddamn gorilla in a territorial dispute.

My body pumped out testosterone in a high dose and another low growl came from my throat. My size and muscles should be intimidating enough for any rational man to move along, but this fucker had his eyes on Willow and I couldn't blame him, because she was gorgeous and worth fighting for.

"I said, move the fuck along," I repeated. "Willow Darlington is *taken*."

Raising his chin, he hissed, "By whom?"

"By me!" I placed my arm around her waist and pulled her close to me. "Willow is *my* wife."

His eyes narrowed in suspicion. "Fuck you. You're lying."

I looked down at Willow and saw freaking amusement in her eyes. Leaning in, I planted a solid kiss on her lips. The loud gasp from the man in front of us made others turn to watch.

"Mine!" I mumbled and looked into her eyes, which crinkled with soft lines when she broke into a sweet smile.

"Took you long enough."

We both ignored the man, who finally had the wits to move along.

"You wanted me to claim you sooner?"

"Yeah, I did." Willow lifted her hand and cupped my face. "I was talking to Mila last night and she asked me an interesting question that gave me a bit of an epiphany."

"Oh, yeah?"

"We talked about all the hate and anger I'd felt for you for years, and you know what she said?"

"No."

"She asked me if maybe the root of my anger wasn't what happened to me when we ran away together, but that you didn't come for me after they separated us.'"

I swallowed hard. "Willow, I tried but they kept you in the Motherlands, and I was being kept under supervision by a whole fucking squad of elite soldiers."

Her gaze lowered. "And when I turned twenty-one – why didn't you find me then?"

I pulled Willow to the side to get us away from curious looks from others. "Because of the restraining order. Getting close to you would have cost me my life and I knew I had to stay alive for the day I would get my second chance. Willow, trust me, I prayed every day that I'd be free to pursue you again or that you'd come and find me. When Khan finally lifted the restraining order, I showed up at the reunion to see you, remember?"

"I know." Willow sighed. "It's just that Mila helped me see things that I hadn't been aware of. Like, isn't it weird that I blocked so much of the experience from my memory? But then, I was only three when Hunter was taken from me and being torn from your twin would be traumatic for any child. When they tore us apart it was the second time I was powerless and lost someone I loved. Blocking things from my memory must have been a way for me to cope."

"I'm sorry, Willow." I caressed her hair.

"You know at the reunion when I said I had nightmares about being with you?"

"Uh-huh."

"It's not true." Willow bit her lip. "I had these bizarre dreams about you coming for me and claiming me for your own." Frown lines deepened on her forehead. "When you're convinced that you hate someone, having erotic dreams about them makes you feel dirty and wrong. I used to think I was losing my mind."

I leaned my forehead against hers. "If it helps I had plenty of sexual fantasies about you too."

Willow relaxed a little and smiled at me. "About claiming me?"

A grin grew on my face. "Now you're just begging for it." With a quick movement, I bent down and picked Willow up on my shoulder, carrying her toward the other end of the room where a whole wall opened up to the empty balcony. Zasquash, Leo, and some of the other men on the security team moved closer and everyone turned to see what was going on when I stepped out on the balcony that overlooked the now almost empty theater.

The view was beautiful and like I was an emperor, I spread out one hand and shouted to the world, "I, Solomon Samson, hereby claim Willow Darlington as my mate and partner."

Willow was laughing and wriggling on my shoulder, so I set her down. Looking flustered with a bright red color in her cheeks, Willow brushed her long brown hair back.

"Willow, are you okay?" Leo asked, and we turned to face the crowd that had gathered behind us. The Motlanders looked confused and the Nmen exchanged glances as if not sure whether to intervene or not.

"Yes." She had a giddy grin on her face. "It's just Solo who is messing around."

"I'm not messing around. I'm dead serious. I want all of you to know that I'm claiming Willow for my wife."

"Can he do that?" Darlene asked Zasquash, who stood close to her.

Zasquash shrugged. "I think he just did."

"No." Darlene shook her head and looked to Willow. "You need to be okay with this. Just because he's big and strong doesn't mean he gets to swing you over his shoulder and claim you for his own. Tell him you're not some kind of property."

"Hang on." I laughed. "Before you start a petition to free Willow, she can tell you she wants this too."

"Do you?" Darlene stepped closer. The other Motlanders followed her example like a damn swarm of bees ready to attack if given the order.

"Actually…" Willow's face fell, and she suddenly looked sad and unhappy.

My heart stopped beating. No! It couldn't be a trap. She had spoken of love and we were together again. This was what she wanted too, but then why was she looking like she was about to break down?

"Willow?" With panic in my chest, I touched her and when she shook her head and teared up, I jerked my hand away as if I'd been burned. My throat suddenly felt too small to breathe. My eyes darted around as inside my head a voice screamed, "Why? Why?"

I saw the pity on Zasquash's and Leo's faces and turned to Willow again. This couldn't be happening.

All the air whooshed from my lungs when she lit up in a wide smile and pointed to me. "Psyched!"

There was a gasp of relief from the others and I bent over with one hand on my thigh and the other to my heart. "Fuck, Willow, you scared the shit out of me."

"And you said I couldn't act. Now do you see I'm a great actor?" Everyone joined in on her laughter, except me. I was still shaking from the shock.

"Willow, that wasn't nice. You almost killed Solo," Salma pointed out with concern in her voice.

I kept my hand on my heart, kneeled down, and scrunched up my face in pain.

"Solo?" Willow squatted down. "What's going on?"

"Pain…" I pushed out the word.

"Oh, Mother Nature, he's having a heart attack," someone cried out.

"No." Willow paled. "Solo, I'm sorry. It was just a prank. I didn't mean to scare you like that. I'm so sorry." This time her eyes teared up for real.

Zasquash moved in. All we Huntsmen had undergone medical training. My head was low, my chest heaving up and down, but my arm lifted and with it outstretched, I kept him at a distance before looking up. My smile grew as I locked eyes with my best friend. "Just teaching my mate a lesson."

Zasquash, who was on his knees in front of me, leaned back on his haunches and crossed his arms. "You two are fucking nutheads."

I chuckled and turned to Willow, who was wide-eyed with worry. "You're not the only one who can act, baby."

"So you're okay?" Willow breathed.

When I nodded she threw herself around my neck and squeezed me tight to her.

"What a performance." Ben stepped forward, clapping his hands together. "That was magnificent. You had my pulse racing. What a spectacular performance." He kept clapping and soon the Motlanders joined in on the applause. "We must discuss representation. I could see you two in movie roles. You'll be stars! I'm telling you I can make you into movie stars."

Rising up to our full heights, Willow and I hugged and kissed. "Don't ever pull shit like that on me again, do you hear me?" I whispered into her ear. "It wasn't funny."

"I'm sorry." She pulled back and met my eyes. "Maybe in a year you'll think it was funny."

I gave a small smile. "Maybe."

Ben was still talking about contracts and movie roles when someone tapped me on my shoulder.

Turning my head, I saw Leo with a stern expression on his face. "Khan and Magni wish to see you both, right now."

We held hands as we walked behind two soldiers from the Ruler's guard.

The time had come to face the two most powerful men in the country.

I was expecting to be met by questions and to be pressured, but we were led into a large dining room where Magni and Khan were surrounded by their families.

"We heard the good news." Laura was the first one to come and hug us.

"Wait a minute, Laura." Khan held up a hand and waved us over to the table. "The kids wanted a late-night dessert. Do you want some too?" He gestured to the selection of cake and ice cream.

"No, thank you."

"We were just informed that you two have made it official that you're a couple." Khan didn't smile. "Not that it surprised us. Mila already let the good news slip."

I looked at Mila, who gave a small apologetic smile. "Sorry, it was too good to keep to myself."

"You're not angry?" I asked Khan.

"Angry? Why would I be angry?"

I blinked my eyes, a bit confused by his reaction, and turned my attention on Magni, who was spinning a spoon between his fingers. "And how about you?"

"Are you asking what *I* think?" Magni scoffed. "Since when do you give a fuck about what anyone thinks?" Magni smiled a little. "I think it's a fucking miracle that Willow wants you. She must be oblivious to how stubborn and annoying you are."

"I love Solo." My fierce mate stood up for me, and my chest burst with pride.

"Well, that's your prerogative, and I can't dispute that Solo is a fine warrior."

I inclined my head to him. "Thank you, sir."

Magni leaned over the table. "Let's put it this way: if you'd fought for my daughter and won her in a tournament, I'd have been a happy man. You're a fine Nman and I approve of Willow's choice to marry you."

"You do?" After Magni had made my life hell for years by keeping me away from Willow, I was surprised to hear his words of praise.

Khan slammed his palm on the table and grinned. "I approve of your marriage too. So how about we set up the ritual and make it official?"

Willow and I squeezed each other's hands, and then she spoke, "We would like that, but we have one wish. Could we have the wedding at the cabin that Solo built? There's a place by the river that has a special meaning to us."

CHAPTER 28
Last Chapter

Four weeks later

Willow

Laying on the grass, I let the warm sunbeams play across my naked body. My hands combed through my hair, which was still cold and wet from my swim in the river.

Reaching for my pants, I took out the pocket-sized screen and unfolded it, my fingers navigating the device and pulling up news stories.

"Is your wristband still not working?"

I rolled onto my belly and looked up at Solo, who'd come from the cabin, carrying two bowls in his hands.

"I brought snacks." He plunked himself down and placed the bowls in front of me.

"You're going to get me fat with all the chocolate you have me eating."

"Then there's more of you to love."

I shook my head but still reached for the chocolate. "Is it the kind that is slimming?"

Solo, wearing only shorts, rolled onto his stomach too. "I didn't know that was a thing."

"It's not. Can you believe it?" I sighed. "We're in 2447 and still no one has found a way to make fine chocolate as healthy as vegetables. Talk about an error in priorities."

"You should complain to Shelly. I'll bet she could come up with some way to make chocolate slimming."

"I heard she's busy revolutionizing the way we grow our crops, and according to Mila, Shelly is on a beach somewhere down south with Marco."

"Good for them." Solo folded his arms under his head and used them as a pillow. "You'll just have to close your eyes and pretend the river is a warm ocean."

I leaned over and kissed his shoulder. "I wouldn't want to be anywhere but right here with you. Where else can I be naked and not have to worry about a thing?"

Solo smiled at me. "So, you don't worry about tempting me?" He gave me a lazy grin and lifted up to swat my behind. "I'm trying to restrain myself. You said you were too sore."

"I am, and that hurt."

"Here, let me kiss it and make it better."

Craning my neck to see Solo kissing my backside, I defended myself. "It's no wonder I'm sore when you're on me night and day."

He tilted his head at me. "You try being married to the most gorgeous woman on the planet and see how horny you'd be all the time."

I laughed. "You didn't think that one through, did you? I'm not into women so I wouldn't be horny at all."

With both hands he squeezed my firm cheeks and stroked down over the back of my thighs. "You know what I mean, and you can't blame me for being insatiable when it comes to you."

"I'm not blaming you, but my body isn't a machine like yours. It needs time to recover, and more than four hours of uninterrupted sleep would help. How many times did you wake me up last night?"

"Only two." Solo stopped kissing me and propped himself up on an elbow next to me with a sheepish smile. "I'm gonna stop. I promise. It's just that the first time, I woke from a nightmare thinking you'd been taken from me again. Then I found you next to me and I got emotional and relieved. I had to touch you to shake off the nightmare and one thing led to another."

I raised an eyebrow. "And the second time?"

"You can't blame me for that one. You were the one who spooned up against me and pulled my hand around you. That was a clear invitation."

"I was sleeping."

He chuckled. "Then you were talking in your sleep, Darlington, because you whispered that you wanted me."

"Probably because I was having an erotic dream about you."

"Yeah?" Solo leaned in, his lips almost touching mine. "Wanna tell me about that dream?"

"No, because it'll only turn you on again and there's something serious I need to discuss with you."

He pulled back and waited for me to continue.

"Do you think we should cancel the wedding?" My tone turned serious.

Solo sighed. "Hunter still hasn't answered?"

"No." I turned on my side to face him. "He's not responding to any of my calls or messages." My chest was tightening just from speaking about Hunter.

Solo brushed his fingers down my arm. "He'll come around."

"You always say that." My nose was twitching and I was trying to hold back tears. "But what if he doesn't? What if I've lost my brother forever?"

"You can't ever give up hope. Hunter is a proud man. He worries about you and he'll need time to see that we're happy together. Just keep reaching out to him. Sooner or later, he'll respond."

"I worry about him, Solo. And I feel so bad for telling him we could spend more time together if he came to the Motherlands and now that he's there, I'm here. He must feel so betrayed by me. I think he hates me now."

Solo reached for my hand. "Hunter doesn't hate you."

"You don't know that. He looks troubled in every picture I see of him."

Solo wrinkled his forehead. "I've seen him on the news several times. He looked serious, but I wouldn't say he looked troubled. Maybe you're overinterpreting."

"I'm not. You haven't seen the interview from this morning, but let me show you and you'll see for yourself." Sliding my fingers around, I found the latest interview with Hunter, which I'd already seen twice today.

"Who's she?" Solo asked and pointed to a woman standing next to Hunter.

"That's Emanuela. She's one of the biggest soccer stars in the Motherlands. Ben has her as a client, remember?"

Solo widened his eyes. "Is she the one who had to buy a puppy?"

"Yes." The woman was wearing sporty clothes with her hair up in a ponytail. I could tell that she was shorter than me because she only came to Hunter's shoulder, but confidence oozed from her. "She's a celebrity in the Motherlands and she's the captain on Hunter's new team."

"Fuck me. Did Hunter know that when he agreed to go?"

"What do you mean? Why would that matter."

Solo chuckled. "Oh, trust me. It matters."

I started the video clip and shushed Solo when he wouldn't stop chuckling.

"Emanuela, it's been two weeks since Hunter joined your team and you're only a few weeks away from the new season starting. Are you happy with what he's bringing to the team so far?"

The woman hesitated a little before she spoke. "Hunter's way of approaching the sport is different from what we've seen before and we're still adjusting."

"Is it true that several of your players have complained that his style is too physical and aggressive?"

She lowered her brow. "As I said, we're still adjusting, and it might take a while to teach Hunter how to play a more sophisticated style of soccer."

Hunter shifted his weight from one foot to the other and looked down at her with a displeased frown.

"See how troubled he looks?" I pointed to the screen.

"Babe, that has nothing to do with our wedding. Didn't you hear how she just insulted him? He's pissed at his captain," Solo argued.

"No, but just listen."

We both focused on the screen, where the interviewer was now looking at Hunter.

"How do you like living and working in the Motherlands? Have your teammates been welcoming to you?"

"Uh-huh. The players have been great." Hunter looked away. "Most of them anyway."

"And how is it for you to have a female coach and play for a mixed team? I assume that's a new experience for you."

"Yup. Very new."

"But a positive one?"

"As Esmeralda said, we're all adjusting." Hunter raised his chin in a greeting to someone passing them outside of camera range.

I sighed and looked at Solo. "See, he looks like he can't be bothered with the interview. That's not like him at all. Where is the charming athlete that we know? It's a façade, and I know he's hurting underneath."

"Shit, you missed that. Go back."

"What's is it?"

"The thing she just said about names." Solo pointed to the screen. "Damn, she might look small, but that woman is not to be messed with. She's one fierce Motlander."

I went back in the clip to hear her response to Hunter's last comment again.

"As Esmeralda said, we're all adjusting."

The small woman raised her eyebrow and crossed her arms before looking straight at the camera. "True; for example, Hunter isn't used to being surrounded by women and it's hard for him to learn our names. For some reason Emanuela sounds like Esmeralda to him."

Hunter shrugged. "They both start with an E and end with an A."

Emanuela rocked forward on her toes, making her look a little taller. "The good thing is that he can spell. Now we just have to teach him to play proper soccer."

Hunter put his hands down his pockets. "There's nothing wrong with how I play soccer. If anything, I can teach *you* a lot."

"Did she just roll her eyes at him?" Solo gaped at the screen. "There, shit, she did it again."

I played the part again. "Oh wow, I've seen this interview already, but I never noticed that she rolled her eyes. Wow, she should be careful or someone might report her for improper communication again. Rolling your eyes at someone is rude."

Solo snorted. "Oh, come on, if anyone reports her they should go fuck themselves. Who is that lady anyway?" A grin grew on Solo's face. "Motlanders are supposed to be sweet by nature, but she's not taking any crap from him, is she?"

"No." I furrowed my brows. "I can see why she got in trouble before."

"I like her style." Solo smiled.

"I don't. She doesn't seem very nice to Hunter. I mean if she's this rude to him in front of the camera, then how is she when they're alone? He looks sad, Solo, and I worry about him." I sighed. "We might have to postpone the ceremony. It means the world to me to have Hunter be part of it, and if he doesn't answer soon I'm going down there to see him."

"He'll answer." Solo's voice was serious. "Hunter loves you, Willow. We both do. And now that he's stuck with that badass Motlander woman who's giving him shit about his soccer style, he'll need moral support. Just keep calling him and one day soon, he'll pick up, I promise you."

"I hope you're right, but I don't want him to be with people who don't treat him with kindness."

Solo picked a blade of grass and tickled my nose with it. "You don't really think any Motlander can truly offend Hunter, do you? He's a Northlander and an athlete. He's used to taking huge piles of shit from coaches, other players, and fans. Trust me, her worst will be pure entertainment to him."

I squinted my eyes. "You think so?"

"Guaranteed. I worry about her more."

"Why?"

Solo brushed his own nose with the straw as if he wanted to feel how it tickled. "Because Hunter is an angry mess and she clearly has no clue whom she's dealing with. If she keeps poking him like that, she's going to regret it. He's not a sweet Motlander man."

"Don't say that. Hunter is a good person. He would never hurt a woman."

"Of course not. But think about it, Willow. There's nothing Hunter wants more than to be sent back to the Northlands. No one can blame him if playing in the Motherlands doesn't work out. We all know that Motlanders are weird."

"We're not weird."

"No, not all of you." Solo pointed to the screen. "That lady is different. I think she might be my favorite Motlander."

"Heeey." I pushed at his shoulder. "What about me?"

"You don't count." Solo moved closer and when we were shoulder to shoulder, he leaned in and kissed me. "You're a Northlander like me."

"Nice try, soldier, but just because I lived here for three years and my father was a Northlander doesn't mean I'm not a Motlander. But apparently I'm not your favorite one." I sulked.

Solo opened his mouth to protest but then a smile grew on his face. "Wait a minute. Are you jealous of *her*?"

"No. I just don't appreciate you calling her your favorite when I'm right here. How would you like it I called Zasquash my favorite Northlander?"

Solo wouldn't stop smiling. "That is so cute. I love that you're jealous."

"Answer my question. How would you like it if I called another man my favorite Northlander? I could pick Leo or Zasquash, you know."

"But you wouldn't." Solo was enjoying himself and bit my neck in a playful manner. "Zasquash is already way too cocky after Darlene said yes to marrying him. The last thing I need is for you to pump his ego further." He picked at some grass and gave me another smile that melted me a bit. "Besides, there's no comparison, if you ask me. You're in your own category."

I gave him a skeptical pout.

"You are!" Solo made his voice boom out loud. "Willow Darlington, you're my all-time favorite person on the whole planet and I love you."

"Aww. Do you love me enough to consider the offer from Ben?"

Solo groaned. "I'm not an actor."

"Neither am I, but doesn't it sound exciting with a show about how it all started? Pearl says it could help the integration process. I really want to do it, Solo. We would get to work together and help create something that would make an impact on other people."

Solo rubbed his beard. "I don't know, Willow. I think it's weird, and I have no desire to become a celebrity."

"As long as we have our hideaway here in the forest we would be fine."

"Yeah, maybe. I mean the idea of traveling and the money they are offering appeals to me."

"Think about it this way. If I take the job and I play Christina or Laura on the show, they'll have to find another actor to play the man I fall in love with. There might even be a scene where I have to kiss him. Would you want it to be you or someone else?"

Solo tilted his head. "You're not playing fair right now."

"Just think about it."

"I'm not playing Boulder; he was more than ten years older than me when he met Christina. And I don't think anyone can play Magni to his satisfaction."

"Probably not. But no one can do it better than you. You could be his younger brother in looks and you're both fierce warriors."

Solo looked thoughtful. "But if we did the acting job, I couldn't be on the Doom Squad anymore."

"Would that be so bad?"

He brushed a bug from his arm. "There are parts of the job that I would miss for sure."

"Like Zasquash and Leo?"

"Yeah."

"You could still see them outside of work. We could invite Zas and Darlene to come hang out here some time."

Solo kissed my shoulder. "That's a good idea."

"Is it?" I gave a playful grin. "We couldn't be naked if they were around."

"On second thought, let's not invite them. I like you naked." Solo rolled on top of me and planted little kisses on my shoulder blades and neck. "Hmm, you're so delicious."

Arching my body, I pushed against his crotch, enjoying the old game of bump and grind.

"Tell me again, how sore are you?" he muttered in a low sexy growl.

"Pretty sore." I followed his rhythmic movement, pushing back and forth.

"You're playing with fire, woman." Solo pressed his large hand into my hair and turned my head. "I don't want to hurt you but you have me fired up now."

"Then how about we cool you down?" I wriggled away from him, got up, and ran for the river with a joyful scream while Solo chased me.

The weather had been dry for weeks and the water only reached to my navel when I stood close to the side of the riverbank. Solo, grinning, pulled off his shorts before he jumped in with me.

"If you want to be physical with me you can take me for a swim." I turned him around and jumped up on his back. Solo was quick to hook his arms under my knees and walked with me through the water to the middle where it was deeper.

"This isn't swimming."

He got down and when he began to swim I released my legs around his waist. With my hands still holding on to his shoulders we glided through the water together.

"It's crazy how strong you are." I smiled at him when he turned around to face me.

"Come here." Solo stood up in the water and pulled me up to sit astride him, his hands planted firmly under my cheeks.

"What happened to the swimming?"

"It's not cooling me down enough. I still want you." With us both being naked, it was easy for him to reach down and spread my folds to position his hard erection just right.

"Solo." There was a warning in the way I said his name.

"Can't we at least try?" There was a mix of lust and concern on his face.

It didn't hurt when he pushed in a little. Maybe the cool water served to numb my sore skin. "If I can't walk later it's because of you."

"Good thing you've got a strong mate who can carry you around, then."

We looked at each other, love radiating from the both of us. "Go slow," I whispered.

Solo nodded and as he lowered me down on top of him, I felt every erogenous zone inside me come to life. Closing my eyes, I moaned and loved the sound of his deep sigh of pleasure.

"Fuck, Willow. You're my everything, do you know that?" Solo wasn't as rough as normal, and he kept looking into my eyes. Our breathing came faster as we made love in the water. His arm and shoulder muscles were flexed from the way he bounced my body up and down in front of him at a slow pace. It had to take immense strength for him to keep us balanced in the water.

When he increased the pace and almost lost his footing on the slippery stones in the river, Solo moved us to the riverbank where he lay me down in the wildflowers and moss. He was ready to go again, but I placed a hand across my eyes. "I'm sorry, but can we just cuddle this time? You've used me up."

Solo rearranged himself and with his head resting on my stomach, our bodies formed the letter T. "I'm sorry, I should be more careful with you."

"It's just that every part of my body is sore and I'm tired." I weaved my hands into his thick blond hair and tugged at it.

"Argh, why do you always have to pull at my hair?"

We lay quiet for a while, listening to the tranquil sounds of birds singing in the distance and the ripple of the river next to us.

"Can I ask you a question, Solo?"

"Sure."

Butterflies lifted and took flight in my stomach as I asked, "Did my breasts feel heavier to you?"

Solo moved his head. "They felt perfect, why?"

I bit my lip. "What if I'm sore and tired because I'm pregnant?"

Solo turned his head with wide eyes. "Do you think you are?"

I lifted up on my elbows to see him better. "Could be. I'm craving chocolate."

"Yeah, but you've always had a sweet tooth."

"But my nipples are sensitive."

"Right, but maybe it's because I play with them all the time."

I gave a small pout. "So, you don't think I'm pregnant?"

Solo came to lie face to face with me. "Do you want to be?"

"I just thought you'd be more excited that I might be pregnant."

"Willow, there's nothing I want more than to start a family with you. You know that. We've talked about it since we were teenagers. I just don't want to get my hopes up yet. If you're truly pregnant it would be the greatest thing that ever happened to me."

"Really? And here I thought that us getting back together was the highlight for you."

"Of course it is." He scratched his nose. "But can you imagine holding a baby and knowing that it grew from us? That we made a human together? The thought blows my mind."

"Me too." I stretched my hands and soaked up warmth from the sun. "I just worry about you. How are you going to last without sex during a pregnancy?"

Solo tilted his head. "What are you talking about?"

"We don't want to hurt the baby, do we?"

"Will sex hurt the baby?" Solo looked horrified. His hand lifted to his hair. "I never thought about it. Does that mean we can't have sex for nine months?"

"I think so." I kept my face straight for as long as I could until I began to laugh.

He narrowed his eyes. "Are you messing with me again?"

"Maybe."

He was on me in a second, tickling me for revenge. "But wait, hang on. You can't take on a role in that series if you're pregnant."

"Yes, I can. If I play Laura."

"Are you sure?"

"I think so. They'll start the series from the beginning when Christina first came to the Northlands. Laura left shortly after Christina arrived and she was gone for more than a year. Do you see how perfect that is?"

"Ehh... so maybe it could work – but what happened to your plans about starting a dance studio?"

"That was before Ben began talking about acting. I never thought I'd have an opportunity like that. Acting would be my biggest dream ever. Not to mention that if you play Magni you'll be shooting some scenes in the Motherlands, and that means the Council will have to lift your ban on going there. We could visit Hunter."

Solo looked down. "Don't get your hopes up, babe. I doubt Hunter wants to see me."

I rubbed my forehead and sighed. "True."

Solo moved over to kiss me softly on my lips. "Cross your fingers that Hunter will fall in love soon. If he does, he'll understand."

I lit up. "Yes. That's it!"

"What is?"

I got up on my knees with a sound of glee. "Solo, I just thought of the most brilliant idea. You're going to shave a sheep with excitement when you hear it."

"Shave a sheep?" He laughed. "You always mix up our sayings. It's shit a sheep, and that's not something you do out of excitement."

"Okay, but listen, I know how to get Hunter to talk to me again. It's like you said: he needs to fall in love. People in love are happier and more forgiving."

"But you can't control that."

"No, but I can help. We need to talk to Ben. I'll bet he can convince his clients to introduce some wonderful women to my brother. Don't you see – it's the perfect plan?"

"What clients?"

"Emanuela and the head coach. Ben knows both of them."

"You want *her* to play matchmaker?"

"If by her, you mean Emanuela, then yes. I'll bet she and the coach want him to stay. We're basically helping them. I can give them pointers on the type of woman he'd be interested in."

"How would you know?"

I tilted my head. "Give me a little credit. Hunter is my twin. I would know."

Solo raised both hands. "All right, but I'm warning you: I have a bad feeling about this."

"Don't be so negative. I'm a dancer, we're creative people."

"Yeah, but I'm a Doomsman. We deal with realities." Solo got up and offered me a hand to pull me up. "Sounds to me like your brain is fried and you need to get out of the sun." He swung me over his shoulder and began walking with me.

"For real? Is this how you're going to carry me? Like I'm a big sack of coffee beans?"

He swung me down in his arms. "Is this better?"

"That was a nice move. You'll make a good dance partner."

Solo squeezed me tighter. "Honey, you don't want to dance with me. I might step on your toes or something."

"No, you won't. I'll teach you how to dance, just like I'll teach our children how to dance."

"Deal. Then I'll teach them how to fight. That way our girls can protect themselves if their dance partners don't behave themselves."

We had reached the cabin and Solomon carried me to our bedroom.

"Take a nap and rest a little."

"Only if you come lie with me for a second," I tempted him, and when he gave in and threw himself on the bed with me, I cuddled up against his naked body and entwined our fingers.

For minutes neither of us spoke, and I was just about to doze off when he mumbled, "What if someone makes a film about us one day? Wouldn't that be weird?"

"Uh-huh." I spoke with my eyes still closed. "They'd better not."

"Why not? Who doesn't like a story about young love and never giving up?"

Squeezing one eye open, I sighed. "But I *did* give up, and I'm embarrassed to think about the awful things I said to you at the reunion. People would judge me for it."

Solo kissed my forehead. "Who cares what other people think? I'm just grateful you gave me a second chance. That's all that matters to me."

I thought about it. "If they tell our story, I want it to be honest and not some polished comedy version. Our story wasn't fun or cute. It was painful and dark."

"I know." Solo yawned. "But from now on it's going to be bright and sunny."

"It will be once Hunter forgives me."

Solo closed his eyes and pulled me closer. "Let's just hope Hunter isn't as stubborn as you were. I waited seven years to be forgiven."

"Sorry."

"It's okay, you were well worth the wait."

I kissed his cheek. "This time we'll stick to the plan and grow old together." My last words were muffled by a yawn. "I just need a nap first if that's okay."

Solo kissed me again and whispered, "Sleep, my beautiful dancer, we have all the time in the world."

This concludes Men of the North #7 – The Dancer

Thank you so much for reading Willow and Solomon's story. We're not quite done with them and I promise they will appear in the next book in this series. Before I tell you more about that, I wanna ask you to do me a favor and take a second to review the story you just read

What's next?

I think you know.
Of course, we have to follow Hunter to the Motherlands and get his story.

The Athlete – Men of the North #8

How do you win a soccer game when you're not just playing against the other team, but your captain too?

When Hunter Hercules, the biggest soccer star in the Northlands, is transferred to play in the Motherlands, he's mad as hell. Not only is their style of soccer different, but they have mixed teams and his female captain, Emanuela, calls him unsophisticated and claims that she's a better player than him. What a fucking joke!

The whole thing is ridiculous and infuriating to Hunter. That's why when the soccer club sends all the players on a team-building trip, Hunter shows up determined to put the little woman in her place. It should have been easy, but Emanuela isn't a normal sweet Motlander he can push around. She's competitive to the bone, and when Hunter plays dirty she's fast to adapt and hit him back tenfold. Someone should have warned her not to mess with an Nman.

The Athlete is book #8 in Elin Peer's highly praised series *Men of the North*. Readers call these books "unputdownable" because of the sharp dialogue, fast pace, and depths of the characters.

If you like strong women, alpha males, and a roller-coaster ride of emotions, then this romantic sci-fi is a safe pick for you.

For a full overview of my growing list of books, please visit www.elinpeer.com

About the Author

With a back ground in life coaching, Elin is easy to talk to and her fans rave about her unique writing style that has subtle elements of coaching mixed into fictional love stories with happy endings.

Elin is curious by nature. She likes to explore and can tell you about riding elephants through the Asian jungle, watching the sunset in the Sahara Desert from the back of a camel, sailing down the Nile in Egypt, kayaking in Alaska, river rafting in Indonesia, and flying over Greenland in a helicopter.

After traveling the world and living in different countries, Elin is currently residing outside Seattle in the US with her husband, daughters, and her black Labrador, Lucky, who follows her everywhere.

Want to connect with Elin? Great – she loves to hear from her readers.

Find her on Facebook: facebook.com/AuthorElinPeer
Or look her up on Goodreads, Amazon, Bookbub or simply go to elinpeer.com

Made in the USA
Monee, IL
20 January 2021